"I'm

She started for her car when she heard something—footsteps, a twig crack. Someone was out there. Breath held, she stared into the thick brush, her gaze shifting from tree to tree.

She pulled out her gun.

"FBI," she called. "Come out!" The wind seemed to carry her words away. "I said, come out! Now!"

Only the rattling of the dry leaves clinging to the trees echoed back.

She started toward the tree line. Only a few feet inside the thicket and it suddenly felt like the dead of night. It took a few seconds for her eyes to adjust and when they did, she saw what looked like a person running behind a tree.

She bolted after the shadowy figure.

# PRAISE FOR CHRISTIE CRAIG

## *DON'T BREATHE A WORD*

"*Don't Breathe a Word* is a roller-coaster ride with riveting suspense, relentless emotion, and characters that will steal your heart."
—*New York Times* bestselling author Darynda Jones

"Leaves you wanting more and holding your breath until the very end."
—The Reading Cafe

"Christie Craig is an auto-buy author for me and I loved *Don't Breathe a Word*. It was twisty and gritty and real and made time fly!"
—Award-winning author Joss Wood

## *DON'T CLOSE YOUR EYES*

"Craig delivers pulse-pounding suspense."
—Lori Wilde, *New York Times* bestselling author

"Romantic suspense fans will mark this as a series to watch."
—*Publishers Weekly*

# ALSO BY CHRISTIE CRAIG

# DON'T LOOK
# BACK

*A Texas Justice Novel*

## CHRISTIE CRAIG

FOREVER
New York   Boston

Copyright © 2020 by Christie Craig

Cover design and art by Jerry Todd
Cover copyright © 2020 by Hachette Book Group, Inc.

Forever
Hachette Book Group
1290 Avenue of the Americas, New York, NY 10104
read-forever.com
twitter.com/readforeverpub

First Edition: December 2020

Forever is an imprint of Grand Central Publishing. The Forever name and logo are trademarks of Hachette Book Group, Inc.

The publisher is not responsible for websites (or their content) that are not owned by the publisher.

The Hachette Speakers Bureau provides a wide range of authors for speaking events. To find out more, go to www.hachettespeakersbureau.com or call (866) 376-6591.

ISBN: 978-1-5387-1167-5 (mass market), 978-1-5387-1165-1 (ebook)

Printed in the United States of America

OPM

10  9  8  7  6  5  4  3  2  1

*To my dad, Cary Neal (Pete) Hunt. It's hard being a daddy's girl with you gone, but if you taught me anything it was to keep going, to find something to laugh about, to find a reason to be thankful. And I'm thankful I had you as a father. You taught me to work hard, to laugh hard. I always knew I was loved. I will forever carry that love in my heart. The paths I choose, the books I write, my crazy sense of humor, my whole paradigm, it is in part because of you.*

# Acknowledgments

I need to tip my hat to a lot of people. To my editor Junessa Viloria for helping me make this book even better. To Kim Lionetti, my agent, for giving me feedback and endless support. To my husband, Steve Craig, for doing my laundry, for the late-night laughter, for finding the right shows to binge-watch, and for being a great quarantine and pancake buddy. To my daughter, Nina Makepeace, for being who she is, kind, understanding, artistically brilliant, and the greatest mom I've ever known to my granddaughter, Lily. To my son-in-law, Jason, who is a man of true character. I couldn't find a more deserving man to be a part of my daughter's and granddaughter's lives. To my son and his wife, Steve and Sarah Craig, thank you for the grocery store runs, the gifts of chocolate and wine, and the social-distanced-front-porch visits during the coronavirus time. You two, together, make me happy. To friend and confidant Susan Muller, who, even though six feet away, listens to me whine, shares wine, and laughter. Thank you for the walks and talks that get me through the good and bad times.

I would also like to give a nod to two other friends I lost this year. William Simon, a man so robust, so full of life, a writer who had so much to say that I was sure he would never leave us. And Nita Craft, your zest and the way you embraced life, it inspired me. I miss you. The world misses you both. Thank you for being a part of my life.

And last but not least, my dog, Lady, who, through serious barking and herding techniques, forces me to leave the keyboard for our much-needed afternoon walks where we spot the deer and rabbits who share our neighborhood.

# PROLOGUE

W hy do I not like this?" Detective Connor Pierce, with the Anniston Police Department's Drug and Gang Unit, put his hand close to his weapon as he and his partner eased down the alley. Darkness and danger hung heavy. The only streetlight, about twenty-five yards down, cast a bluish hue on a parked car as they approached.

A breeze carrying the scent of garbage from the dumpsters lining the graveled path flowed past. That smell was welcome compared to the foul smell of human urine. A few murmured voices echoed in the distance like background noise. His ears automatically tuned in to listen.

Detective Donald Adkins froze. "Is that him?" His voice lacked the concern Connor felt.

"Can't tell." Connor stared at the two figures standing at the back door of what he thought was the liquor store, wishing they were not still too far away to see clearly.

Rumor had it that Carter Thompson, a small-time drug dealer, did business behind that liquor store.

They weren't even after Carter. They were after his cousin, a guy known as Dirt. He was a more serious and harder-to-find dealer. Dirt was suspected of selling counterfeit oxy containing fentanyl.

There had been fifteen overdose victims and a total of eight deaths. Three of those fatalities had been teenagers. Adkins, who was ten years older than Connor, had a teenage son who went to school with one of the victims. For him, this case was personal.

After seeing a comatose sixteen-year-old girl on a respirator yesterday, it felt pretty damn personal to Connor, too. They had to catch this guy before more people died.

"I don't think that's him," Connor said as they drew closer.

"Too tall," Adkins confirmed, just as they were spotted.

"Cops!" someone screamed, and loud popping noises followed.

"Shit!" Connor and Adkins dove behind a dumpster. Both hit hard on the gravel. Connor pulled his weapon and peered around to locate the shooter. "Two of them, behind the car."

When Adkins didn't respond, Connor looked over his shoulder. His partner for the last year lay on the ground, a pool of blood collecting around his head.

Before Connor's knees even hit the ground, he saw white matter mixed with Adkins's spilled blood. Then he saw his partner's eyes.

Open.

Empty.

Dead.

"No!" Another bullet whizzed past. He grabbed his phone, hit dial, and yelled out, "Shots fired. Officer down." The words physically hurt to say. No one could save Adkins. "Two one three Fourth Street. Alley behind Lone Star Liquor Store."

A car's engine roared to life, and it started backing out. Panic pumping through his veins, he peered around the heavy metal container and saw movement behind a pile of boxes.

"Anniston PD, drop your weapon!" He darted out and ran to the next dumpster. "Throw down your weapon!" He'd give the bastard one chance. Then all bets were off.

Another bullet *clanked* against the metal. The car sped out.

Connor shot off three times. He heard a grunt, saw a figure fall. Racing forward, heart hammering in his chest, gun held out and ready, he cut behind the boxes. There on the gravel, bleeding from his chest, lay his shooter.

"Shit!" Connor yelled out in both fury and horror when he saw the young shooter desperately trying to breathe. He was just a pimply-faced kid. A weapon lay beside the boy's hand. Connor kicked it away. "Fuck! Why did you do this?"

"Tell my mama..." Blood trickled from his lips as he took a raspy breath.

"I'm scared," he whimpered.

Emotions raged in Connor's chest as the image of his dead partner flashed through his mind. Somehow Connor found it in himself to reach for the boy's hand. "Help's coming."

The boy's head slumped to the side and his young dark eyes went as empty as Adkins's.

# CHAPTER ONE

*Three and a half years later.*

*H*ow had she lost him? Brie Ryan white-knuckled the steering wheel and slammed her foot on the gas pedal so hard, so fast, the Mustang's rear end fishtailed.

"Fudge bars!" She could lay down some trash talk that would make concrete blush, because sometimes you had to keep up with the guys to earn respect. But when really mad, she deferred to the creative cursing of the one true parental influence in her life, her manny.

Sucking air through her teeth, she kept looking. One minute the Porsche was there then it wasn't. She hit redial on her phone, hoping to reach Carlos Olvera, the only person who knew what she'd been up to for the last four months. The call went straight to voice mail. Again. It didn't make sense. He never turned off his phone.

Had something happened? No, she refused to believe that. His part in this hadn't come with risks.

She took the exit ramp off the freeway, hugging the wheel and praying she'd see the Porsche's taillights.

She didn't see shit.

Not even the cop car waiting on the side of the road. Well, not until she zoomed past it.

"Nooo." Foot off the gas, she watched her side mirror. It was after midnight. Maybe the cop was sleeping. Holding hope and her breath, she followed the road around the curve. Right before the patrol car disappeared from her sightline, blue lights filled the night behind her.

"Mother Cracker!"

*Decision time.* Drive like the devil or pull over and become a sweet-talking angel. She looked up. Four cars waited at a red light about fifty yards up the street. None of them, however, was Dillon Armand's red Porsche.

She. Had. Lost. Him.

And she had a cop on her ass.

Rationalizing that she was better at sweet-talking than outrunning and outmaneuvering a cop, she pulled to the side of the road.

She prayed this decision didn't get her arrested. There was a slight chance the car's owner had left the club early, discovered his car missing, and reported it stolen. It wasn't. She'd just borrowed it.

Putting the car in park, knowing she had a few minutes while the officer ran her license plate, she reached across the seat into the glove compartment. Relief came as she pulled out the car's registration and insurance card. She might have even smiled when she spotted a credit card with the name TAYLOR DUNN on it. Probably good ol' Charlie's wife.

She tossed the registration and insurance card back

into the glove compartment. Checking to make sure the cop was still occupied, she yanked open her purse and snatched her driver's license and credit card from her wallet. Not that these had her real name on them either. Those had come from a job last year.

Eyes on the rearview mirror, she stuffed the two fake cards between the seats.

Next to her Glock.

Then she slid Dunn's credit card into her wallet.

Leaning back, she outlined the story she'd pitch. Frankly, she was a better storyteller than driver.

Her job demanded it. More times than not, her life depended on it.

Three minutes later, the officer exited his car. She checked her mirror to make sure the red wig hadn't slipped. In leaving the Black Diamond club, she'd snagged the wig off another girl's station, just in case Dillon Armand spotted her following him and recognized her as one of the waitresses.

Eyes locked on the rearview mirror, she watched the uniform officer move cautiously toward the Mustang, his right hand at his hip in case he needed his weapon.

She waited for the big sandy-haired cop to stop at the driver's door before she rolled down the window.

"Ma'am." His on-guard expression faded when he saw her. "Can you cut off your engine?"

She turned the key and offered him her softest smile as she read his name embroidered on his shirt. "Sorry, Officer Johnston." She let the Alabama accent she'd spent most of her life hiding roll off her tongue. "Was I speeding? This is the first time I've driven my mom's Mustang and it has more power than my Smart Car."

"I imagine it does." A straight pair of white teeth showed behind his lips.

"But I know that's not an excuse, so if you have to ticket me, I'll understand. Thankfully, I got a new job and I can afford it."

"Where's your job?"

"Teaching at Jones Elementary off Oakwood. I love it." Eliot, her manny-slash-bodyguard-slash-only-one-who-gave-a-damn-about-her, always said her best weapon was her ability to talk someone to death.

"What grade?" His smile widened.

"Kindergarten. They like to hug at that age. I was lucky Mrs. Brown is having triplets and they needed someone to finish out her year."

He nodded. "Can I see proof of insurance and your license?"

"I hope Mom put her card in here. Dad's always fussing about it." She started to lean over then stopped. "It's in my glove compartment. I watch police shows and they say I need to ask before reaching."

"Go ahead, and thanks for being conscientious. You haven't been drinking have you?"

"Just a glass of champagne with dinner. My best friend got engaged." She reached over the seat and pulled out the car's registration and insurance card. "Thank you, Daddy." She passed him the paperwork.

He gave them both a look. "And your license?"

"Oh, sure." She grabbed her purse. This was where the real acting began. Opening the wallet, she let out a big oh-my-gosh sigh. "Where...? No, no, no. I bet the bartender who waited on us at the restaurant didn't give it back to me." She flipped through her wallet. "And he has my credit card." She reached for her phone in the console. "Can I call and make sure he has them?"

"Do you have anything else with your name on it?"

"I have another credit card. I'm Taylor Dunn."

She pulled out the borrowed Visa. "Do you mind if I call the restaurant?"

He confirmed the name on the card then handed everything back. "Why don't I just let you go, and you can drive there—slowly." He smiled.

"You're a lifesaver." The words had barely left her lips when a red Porsche eased past, as if rubbernecking. Her heart raced, screaming for her to give chase. Thankfully, the light at the end of the street turned yellow, and with a cop nearby, the car stopped. *How the hell did he get behind me?*

"How long have you been in town?"

Now he got chatty? *Fracking Hades!* She needed an exit strategy and fast.

Suddenly Officer Johnston's lapel mic went off. She couldn't hear what was said, but his gaze shot up and she knew her exit strategy would have to involve more than sweet-talking.

"Out of the car!" He pulled his weapon.

Decision time. Her mind flashed images of her sister's body: beaten and bloody. For four months, she'd lived with the guilt of knowing she could have saved her and hadn't. Armand would do it again if someone didn't stop him. Mind made up, she stepped out of her car.

"What's wrong?" She kept up the innocent façade.

"Turn around," he said, then spoke into his mic, which usually meant he was requesting backup.

She half-turned as Eliot's instructions played in her

head. *One: Knee to the groin. Two: Right hand goes for the gun. Three: Left palm hits the throat.* Not everyone had an ex-Special Forces officer for a manny. He'd taught her this move before she wore a bra.

At the *wisp* of the officer's gun slipping back into his holster, and the *clink* of his handcuffs releasing, she swung into action.

He groaned as her knee hit the mark. And again when she hit his throat.

He reached for his gun. But too late. His frown deepened when he saw the muzzle of his Glock an inch from his nose. She snatched his handcuffs away and yanked his mic off.

Now she needed to find... she spotted the light pole. Perfect.

"This way." She cut her eyes down the street, relieved the Porsche still sat at the red light.

The cop half stood while measuring her up. "Don't think about it. I'm feistier than I look."

His expression gave way more to fury than fear. "You don't want to shoot—"

"Do as I say, and you won't get hurt. Go to the light post. Now!"

With his arms around the pole, she cuffed his hands. No time to waste, she raced back to the Mustang, dug in her purse, and pulled out the business card—her get-out-of-jail-free card—she'd been hanging on to in case of an emergency. Detective Pierce, actually the Cold Case Unit, owed her after she'd helped them out on a case a few months ago. Of course, they hadn't known her real identity, but...

She hotfooted it back and stuffed the card in the

officer's shirt pocket. "Do me a favor. Find Detective Pierce. Tell him to look into the Ronan case."

"You know Connor?" he asked.

She tossed his gun in the bushes. "Ronan case. Got it?"

He nodded.

Minding her manners, she added, "Sorry about this." Sirens rang in the distance. Before she got to the car, the light turned green and the Porsche took off.

"Mother Heifer." She burned rubber trying to catch up.

* * *

Detective Connor Pierce walked into the all-night diner, with a headache throbbing in his right temple. Two waitresses worked the night shift to keep the drunk patrons under control. With three bars located within a block, the diner was a good place to grab some coffee and food, and sober up.

Connor showed up at least four times a month—sometimes more. Not to sober up. It was the nightmares and guilt that brought him here.

He paused at the door. When he saw Flora open a pad to take someone's order, he moved to a table on her side of the restaurant. He always sat in her section. Her tired brown eyes cut to him and she offered him her normal generic nod. Never too friendly. Never hostile. At least fifty, twenty years his senior, her face was a road map of the hardships she'd encountered in her life.

She moved behind the bar, punched in the order, then grabbed a mug and the coffeepot, and came to his booth. Setting the cup down, she filled it, leaving room for the four creams she pulled from her apron and set beside his cup.

"The usual?" Her voice carried a slight accent.

"Yup," he said.

She walked away. Talking wasn't her thing. And that was okay; in fact, it was probably best. Opening the newspaper he'd brought with him, he started reading.

Ten minutes later, she walked up and set the two-egg special, with hash browns and pancakes, down in front of him. He pulled his finger away from his temple where he was attempting to rub the thumping pain away.

Her gaze met his. "Maybe you should stay home and sleep. When was the last time you slept eight hours straight?"

*Probably the same as you.* "A long time ago."

She walked away.

He'd only downed four or five bites when his phone rang.

Who the hell was calling at this hour? He snatched his phone out of his pocket. Billy Johnston's name appeared on the screen. Connor worked with the Cold Case Unit, and Billy was a friend and patrol cop with the Anniston PD. "What's up?"

"A friend of yours pissed me off."

"Who?"

"That's what we're trying to figure out. Just get your ass here to the station and identify the woman on my bodycam. I want that bitch caught."

"What?" The line clicked silent.

He ate two more bites, pulled three twenties out of his wallet, and set them on the table. Flora walked up to refill his cup.

"That's okay. I gotta run."

She spotted the money and frowned. "You always... that is too much." When she looked up, he could swear for a second—maybe two—he saw something flash in her eyes. Had she figured out who he was? Hell, had she known all along?

"Never known a waitress who complained about a large tip." He waited for her reply, willing to take anything she dished out—wasn't that part of why he came— but she just walked away.

\* \* \*

Brie had caught up with Armand's red Porsche. Unfortunately, it hadn't been worth the hornet's nest she'd stirred up with the Anniston PD. But if she'd learned who Armand was working with—who helped him do his dirty work—even jail time would have been worth it.

But the man just went back to his hotel.

Parked at the Omni, she waited thirty minutes before feeling assured that Armand was retiring for the night. She tried to reach Carlos. Again. And got nothing. Again.

Disappointed, she drove to a grocery store parking lot, returned the credit card to the glove box. She stuffed her red wig into her purse, prepared to return it to its rightful owner, and left a twenty on the seat for gas. Stepping outside the car, she slipped her arms into the leather jacket that served to hide the Glock tucked inside her jeans. With a don't-mess-with-Brie gait, she walked a block to a bar and called Uber.

The downtown area of Anniston was, by far, the most happening place in this medium-sized college town. Under other circumstances, she might have even enjoyed living here. Well, except for the god-awful Texas summer heat.

Thankfully, that part of the year had given way to fall. As if to prove her point, a cool late-October breeze stirred her blond hair into her face.

A couple of men leaving the bar offered her a ride to anywhere she wanted to go—to heaven, the tall cowboy offered—but she turned them down. She excelled at sending men packing. Even before she'd started waitressing at the strip club, saying no came easy. She could thank her ex for that.

While she waited, she tried Carlos again. This time, she left a message. "Carlos, it's me. I'm officially worried now. I'm going to drive by your hotel." They'd spoken briefly when he'd arrived in from their hometown of Baton Rouge, but hadn't connected since.

Her Uber, a white Equinox, pulled up, and Brie crawled in. "The Black Diamond, on Rayford."

The driver gave her the once-over at the mention of the strip club. He tried making chitchat. She grunted undistinguishable answers until he got the message. Giving him a tip, for not being completely obnoxious, she hurried to her car. She hadn't turned the key in the ignition when her phone rang.

Carlos's number flashed on her screen and she smiled. "Where have you been?"

"Ma'am," the voice said, one that wasn't Carlos's.

"Who is this?" Concern lodged in her throat.

"I'm Officer Heyes. Does this phone belong to a friend of yours?"

"What happened?" Brie demanded.

"Can you tell me his name?"

"Where is he? Let me speak to him."

"He can't talk now. He's been brought into Westside Hospital emergency room. Can you tell me his name?"

Panic-fueled adrenaline coursed through her body. "Can't talk because he's busy or because he's unconscious?"

His nonanswer told her what she needed to know. "How bad is it?"

"If you'd just tell me—"

"How bad?" she bit out.

"Critical. He's in surgery."

Brie moaned. "Look, his name is Carlos Olvera and he's FBI. Make sure he gets the best care. I'm on my way!"

"FBI?" The officer's tone deepened. "Was he working—"

She hung up and drove like hell was chasing her. Because it was. This was on her. She had brought Carlos into this.

How much guilt could one person take before it ate their soul away?

# CHAPTER TWO

Brie parked and sprinted into the ER. Upon being told Carlos was in surgery, she rushed up to the surgical waiting room. When she walked in, she spotted two other families, prayers in their eyes. Then there was the cop walking toward her.

"You here for Carlos?"

After one nod, he wasted no time slamming her with questions. Some were easy. Some not.

"Who is Olvera's closest family member?"

The thought of having to call Carlos's new husband brought tears to her eyes and more guilt to her gut. Hell, she'd been the best woman at their wedding last year. "His husband is Tory Vale. I'll call him."

The man nodded. "Was the victim working a case? Is that why he was in Anniston?"

She hesitated. Carlos had told her his trip to Anniston had been approved, but the possibility of him doing it without permission was just as likely. He'd been pissed when the agency had refused to help her.

"He was looking into opening a case," she offered.

"You FBI?"

She hesitated. "Yes, but I'm on leave."

"You got ID?"

She opened her purse, unzipped the hidden pocket, and handed him her real identification.

"So you aren't working the case?"

*I'm not supposed to be.* "I just gave him the lead."

"What kind of case is it?"

"Human trafficking."

"Here? In Anniston?" he asked.

"Possibly," she answered in her vague FBI-trained tone. But she was certain of it. How else would her half sister's body have ended up in Guatemala chained to a bed in a massage parlor? Then Dillon Armand's name popped up on a Guatemalan police report as being seen man-handling her sister. He'd been their only possible suspect. Or was, until that witness recanted the statement. But that didn't sway Brie, because Armand just happened to be a part of the largest organized crime family in South America. Guns. Drugs. Humans. If they could profit from it, they had a stake in it.

That stake had been driven through her heart twice before. Pablo. Then her sister. Now Carlos.

"Olvera family," a doctor called out.

Brie rushed across the room. When she saw the doctor's expression, it felt like that stake got pushed deeper. She didn't say anything, just waited, waited for the guilt to consume her.

"He's alive," the doctor said. "But it's bad."

Sighing with relief, she grasped hold of the tiny thread of hope. With both hands.

"We got the bullet out of his chest, with few issues, but the head injury is causing brain swelling. He's comatose. We're running tests to see how extensive the damage is. The next twenty-four hours are critical. You may want to prepare—"

"He'll make it." She pushed the words through the choking emotion. "He's not a quitter."

The doctor met her gaze head-on. "Good, because he's got a fight on his hands. A nurse will let you know when you can see him."

The doctor had barely walked away when her phone rang. She frowned when the name TORY VALE came on her screen. Had someone already contacted him?

Heart ready to break, she took the call. "Tory."

"Brie?" Panic sounded in his voice. "Carlos didn't call me last night. He always calls me. I've tried him, but he's not answering. Something's wrong, isn't it?"

She breathed in through her nose. Her sinuses stung. "He just got out of surgery."

"Surgery? Why didn't you call me?"

"I just found out and got here as fast as I could. I'm sorry."

"How bad is it?"

She swallowed to keep her voice from trembling. "He's alive."

"What happened? Was he…shot?"

"Yes, and he sustained a head injury. But I just got to the hospital, so I don't know much."

"Damn it! I'll get on the next plane to Texas. Anniston, right?"

"Right." Her grip on the phone tightened to the

point her hand ached. Glancing around the room, her attention was temporarily sidetracked by Officer Heyes, who was on his phone. And considering the way his gaze was riveted on her, she'd bet her bottom dollar she was the topic of conversation. Was she already suspected of stealing the car?

Tory's next question eked through the silence. "Who did this, Brie?"

"I don't know...yet. It wasn't supposed to be dangerous. He was just confirming my lead. But you know I won't stop until I find out. I'm about to call Agent Calvin."

"No! Didn't he tell you?"

His tone sent chills down her spine.

"Tell me what?" When Tory remained silent, Brie said, "Tory."

"I've never seen Carlos like this. He said if it was what he thought, then they might want to shut him up. Permanently. He even—"

"Slow down. What are you talking about?"

"I know he's not supposed to tell me this stuff, but he did. He's been digging into an old case. The Sala case."

"I know. Did he find something else?"

"He thinks there was a leak. A mole."

Tory wasn't telling her anything she didn't already know. They'd suspected a leak the day the case went terribly wrong. And again when her informant, Pablo, was found dead.

"He was scared, Brie."

She dropped into a chair. "Did someone from the Bureau of Alcohol, Tobacco, Firearms, and Explosives contact him?"

"I don't know. Why?"

"That's where the leak's from."

"No. He thinks it's internal."

"You mean...? Not someone from the Baton Rouge bureau?"

"That's exactly what he meant."

"Who?"

"He didn't say," Tory answered. "I'm not sure he knew for certain."

Chills ran up her spine. "Tory, could you have misunderstood?"

"No. He told me if anyone from his work contacted me, not to answer. He made me come to my sister's in San Francisco. And now this. I'm telling you, someone with the agency did this."

"I don't..." The need to argue rose up inside her. She trusted everyone at her bureau. But the person she trusted the most was Carlos. Did she really know Agents Bara and Miles? They'd both only been working there for a little over a year.

Her mind spun. The Sala gun trafficking case had been considered a slam-dunk. But when they went to make their big bust, there hadn't been a gun in sight. The next day Brie found her informant, Pablo Ybarra, dead in his RV and his live-in girlfriend, Rosaria Altura, missing.

She'd spent a month searching for Rosaria, fearing she'd been killed alongside Pablo, but Brie could find nothing. She also continued looking for the leak, which had to have come from the ATF, who had assisted with the case. She'd come up with zilch on both counts. Agent Calvin had insisted she let it go. Carlos, who'd been in her corner on this, had finally agreed with him. "*We win some. We lose some.*"

Losing the case had stung. Losing Pablo had cost her emotionally. She'd worked with him several times and trusted him. More than that, she'd made the mistake of getting to know him, of caring.

A month after accepting there'd be no justice for Pablo, her sister went missing. Five weeks later when her body was found in a foreign country, the State Department saw Brie, an FBI agent, had listed her as missing, and contacted her. When she read the Guatemalan police report, a name stuck out. A name she recognized from the Sala case: Dillon Armand. A cousin to the Sala family. She then discovered he was part owner of the Black Diamond, the strip club where her sister had worked for a month before she went missing—and where Brie now worked unofficially undercover.

Coincidental? No. Coincidences were like the tooth fairy. They didn't exist.

Tory spoke up again, "Carlos didn't want to believe it either."

"Okay, but not Agent Calvin, right?" When he didn't answer, she started to question it. She'd worked under Calvin her entire FBI career, five years. Had met his family. He had met Eliot, *her* family. Okay, she might not have known him well enough to confess what she'd been doing these past few months—or maybe it was that she knew him too well. He'd have a conniption if he knew she'd been doing her own investigation. "Did Carlos take this to Agent Calvin?"

"I don't think so." Through the phone, she could hear Tory banging away on his keyboard. Probably looking for a flight.

"What hospital are you in?" Tory asked.

"Westside." Brie's mind raced at the same pace as the banging computer keys echoing on the line. "Do you know if Carlos got the official okay to come here?"

"Yes. But that was two days before all this other shit came up." Tory paused. "There's a flight leaving at six a.m. I need to buy a ticket. Brie…?"

"Yeah."

"Will you be at the hospital? I mean, if the FBI shows up, and they're the ones who did this—"

She looked at Officer Heyes, still on the phone, still eyeballing her with a shitload of distrust.

"I won't leave." *Not without kicking and screaming.* They hung up.

Officer Heyes walked over, as if he'd been waiting for her to end the call. He held out his cell. "An Agent Calvin wants to talk to you."

*Great.* Decision time. Trust Calvin? Or don't.

\* \* \*

"You left me half, right?" Juan Acosta asked.

Connor looked up from his computer screen as his two partners, Juan and Mark Sutton, walked into the office. Was it already eight? The last time he'd checked the time it was five a.m. He'd left Billy super pissed when he couldn't identify the woman on his bodycam and went in search of the Ronan case file, hoping it'd help him figure out who the redhead could be.

Connor's sleep-deprived mind replayed Juan's senseless words. "Half of what?"

"The early worm. I'm always here first."

Connor didn't have it in him to make jokes. He frowned down at the open file. "Did you hear about Billy?"

"What?" Juan's smile vanished.

"Is he okay?" Mark came to a dead stop. Mark and Billy had known each other for years. In fact, it was through Mark's poker games that Connor had met the guy.

"He's fine. But his pride took a huge-ass blow."

"What happened?" Juan dropped in his desk chair.

"He pulled a car over for speeding. The driver was a pretty redhead. Right before he let her go, the car got reported as stolen. Before he could contain her, she busted his balls, grabbed his gun, cuffed him to a light pole, and left him there for his backup unit to find him."

Juan chuckled. "Do you know how much shit he gave me when Vicki got the upper hand on me?"

Connor managed a small grin. "Yeah, I remember, she beat you up before you convinced her to fall in love with you. But I wouldn't go at Billy yet. He's pissed. So am I. The woman claimed to know me, even gave him my card."

"So who is she?" Mark dropped into his chair.

"Don't know. Billy thinks it might be connected to a gang of Houston car thieves. They take high-end cars. But I don't know any car thieves."

"How many pretty redheads have you given your card to?" Juan asked. "You pass them out to chicks at bars, right?"

"My cards are on my desk," Connor added. "Anyone could've picked one up." But Juan was right. He had given them out to women he met at bars. Of course, that would've been over two months ago. He'd been skipping the bar scene lately. "Besides, I know it's work related. She called me Detective Pierce."

"Not 'Baby' or 'Hot Stuff'?" Mark joked.

Connor sent them both a scowl. "Billy also said she asked me to look into a case."

"One of our cases?" Mark pulled his gun from his shoulder holster and put it in his drawer.

"No. It's not a cold case, but it might as well be. It's gone untouched for months. It's a missing person." Connor turned the page of the file. "I just opened it. I've been studying Billy's bodycam."

"And you don't recognize her?"

"I might if the quality was better. Even the sound is fuzzy." Connor clicked on the video to watch it again. "They're sending it off to see if they can clean it up."

Juan and Mark moved behind Connor's chair to watch it. "It *is* bad," Mark chimed in.

Connor exhaled. "We never get a good shot of her face."

"Email it to me." Juan moved back to his chair. "I have a program that might clean it up."

"Do you have anything on the stolen car?" Mark asked. "Where was it taken from?"

"Billy's supposed to talk to the owner." Connor rotated his sore shoulders. "He'd reported it stolen from the Waffle House. Then the guy came in an hour later, and said it was Denny's. Poor guy can't keep his lie straight."

"So, maybe he was at his girlfriend's house," Juan said in his speculating tone. "Doesn't want his wife to know."

They all looked back at the screen while it processed the video. "What you want to bet you dated her?" Juan tapped a pencil on his desk.

"Even slept with her." Mark chuckled.

Connor suddenly felt mocked by both his partners' grins. "Since you two got into relationships, you act like my dating life is a joke." As soon as those words had left his lips, he wanted them back. Why?

It couldn't be that he was jealous or wanted anything different. That dream had gone down in flames at the same time as his career. He could still hear his wife's words as he'd signed the divorce papers. *You suck at being a husband.*

Ever since she'd had her second miscarriage, he'd been fighting for their marriage, for a love he thought would last forever. Then he lost his partner, shot a kid, and he didn't have any more fight in him.

"You mean it isn't a joke?" Juan asked. "Don't you remember calling me when you were hiding in a bush, half-naked?"

Connor's frown deepened. "That's enough!"

The seriousness in his tone sucked all the levity from the room. Giving each other hell was status quo, but damn, Connor was just tired.

"Sorry. Didn't sleep last night."

Juan's screen flickered as he started playing a cleaner version of the video.

The image hadn't really improved, but the audio had. "Turn it up and play that again," Connor said when it stopped. "I know that voice."

"I was thinking the same thing." Juan hit replay.

"This has to be someone from an old case." Connor stared at the screen even though it was mostly a blur.

"And recent," Mark muttered. "I don't think we'd all recognize it if it wasn't."

They went silent. "*I'm sorry about this.*"

"She's a polite car thief." Mark chuckled.

"What case involved a redhead?" Juan asked.

"It doesn't have to be a redhead," Connor said. "Women dye their hair willy-nilly."

"True," Juan said. "Her accent doesn't sound Texan."

"Yeah, she's got a drawl," Connor said. "Mississippi, maybe."

"I swear I remember hearing that voice," Juan added.

"Shit!" Connor said. "I know who it is."

# CHAPTER THREE

Who?" Mark straightened.

"The waitress at the Black Diamond. Her name was Star...something. We interviewed her and she gave us information concerning the Noel case. Blond with pink streaks, too young."

"Star Colton?" Juan asked.

"Her?" Doubt surrounded Mark's one word. "The accent might be right, but she's not much over five feet and can't weigh more than a hundred pounds. How could she take out Billy?"

"Look at Vicki. She got the best of me," Juan said.

"But Vicki trained for a triathlon. Star's a waitress," Mark said.

Mark's argument played in Connor's mind. He mentally measured up the woman in his mind. "But I remember her looking...fit."

"You mean hot?" Juan grinned.

"That too." Connor grinned.

"But she didn't come across as a car thief." Juan looked back at Connor. "Wait. She took my card, not yours."

"I gave her mine when I went there and questioned a few of the Black Diamond employees. She even said something about wanting to have a friend in the department."

Juan gave the pencil another *tap, tap.* "She said that to me, too."

"Yeah, but I'm sure she really meant it with me," Connor joked.

"So you slept with her?" Mark asked Connor.

"No!" Connor said. "I don't sleep with women who might still believe in Santa Claus."

Laughter filled the small office.

"Seriously," Connor added, "the younger they are, the clingier they are. I don't do clingy. I don't do—"

"Women with kids or women who might actually want a second date," Mark added. "I'm shocked you ever get a first."

"I get very few complaints." Connor grinned.

Juan cut off the video. "Well, you screwed the pooch on this one. When I met her, I didn't think she was old enough to serve drinks, so I checked. Her license put her at twenty-nine."

"Damn," Connor said with sarcasm. "Then again, I don't do car thieves either." He looked back at Juan. "But you're right. I didn't peg her as that type."

"So why is she wanting you to look into the Ronan case?" Mark walked back to his desk, dropped into his chair, then turned to face them. "We need to find her."

"Yeah." Connor glanced at Juan. "I remember she called you. Do you still have her number?"

Juan scrubbed his palm over his chin. "I think I jotted her number down in the file."

* * *

"What's wrong, Brie?" Eliot asked, his voice coming in extra loud over the line.

All she'd said was *hey*, but obviously he'd heard the emotion in her voice. Seeing Carlos had been hell. His face had been beaten beyond recognition, and there was a tube down his throat forcing air into his lungs.

"Brie?" Eliot repeated. Since she was eight, Eliot had been there for her. Scraped knees, broken hearts, attempted kidnappings. The whole shebang. As the stepdaughter of one of the most popular international political writers, she'd lived in countries some Americans wouldn't visit.

Eliot had kept her safe. Oh, for the first few months after he'd been hired as her bodyguard, he'd tried to keep his heart out of the job, playing tough. But with her parents too busy to care, she'd needed him. And even as young and oblivious as she'd been, she knew he'd needed her.

A knot formed in her throat. "Carlos has been shot."

"What happened?"

She told him the high points, which included coming clean about what she'd been doing these last four months.

"I should've known you weren't just taking a break," he growled. "I told you a thousand times that your sister's death wasn't your fault."

And a thousand times she hadn't believed him. "If I'd just called her back—"

"You barely knew her."

Only partially true.

"She didn't even say why she was calling. For all you knew, she wanted to borrow money."

Logically, Brie knew he was right. Emotionally, it didn't matter. "My father said he'd told her to call me because she was worried about something bad going down."

"And if you'd known that, you'd have called her back."

Would she have? Or was her grudge more important? She swallowed. "I still wish..."

"Wish all you want. Just don't blame yourself." Taking a deep breath, he asked, "So, your father called you again?"

"No. I called him when I heard that her body had been found. He had a right to know." Before this, Brie hadn't spoken to her father since she was seven. That was when he'd left her and her mother to go live with his second family, whom he'd kept a secret. And when she'd learned he had another daughter her age, it made the abandonment worse. He hadn't just left her—he'd chosen someone over her.

"How did it go?" Eliot asked.

"How do you expect?"

"So no apology for walking out of your life?"

"He blamed Mom." She looked at the door leading into the ICU, keeping tabs on anyone going in or out.

"I should've killed him when I had the chance," Eliot snapped.

"He wasn't worth it."

The line went silent. Eliot spoke first. "So, Carlos was helping you? Why didn't you call me? You know I would've been there."

"Carlos came only to collect Armand's prints. Otherwise, I was handling it."

"Obviously, things weren't being handled if Carlos got shot. You can't do this alone."

"I know... that's why I'm calling." She told him what Tory had said about the Sala case.

"Fudge!" His creative cursing came out. "You told me you blamed the ATF." He paused. "Do you believe this?"

She hesitated, collecting her thoughts. "I want to say no. But Carlos isn't one to toss out something like that if he didn't have some proof."

"Do you think Tory could have gotten it wrong?"

"No." Brie nipped at her lip with worry. "He was sure."

"Have you talked with anyone from the FBI?"

"Yeah, with Agent Calvin a little while ago."

"Did you tell him?"

"About what Tory said, yes."

"What did he say about the leak being internal?"

"He said he'd look into it, but he thinks Tory misunderstood. He doesn't believe it's possible."

Eliot got quiet. "You don't think it might be Agent Calvin?"

"I don't know," she said. "You've met him. You went to his house for that barbeque. He's a good guy."

"Good people sometimes do bad things, Brie."

"I know that."

"Who else worked the case?"

"Agents Bara and Miles."

"You trust them?"

"If you'd asked me that yesterday, I would have said, yes. But honestly, I don't know them that well. Problem is that's who Calvin is sending to look into Carlos's attack. And if Carlos was right and one of them is behind this?

I need someone at the hospital, so I can work the case. Is there any way you could come here? Just until I know who I can trust."

"You know I can. Why don't I see if Sam can come, too? We can take shifts."

Sam had served in the Special Forces with Eliot. And since Sam lost his wife last year, they'd spent a lot of time together. "That'd be great."

"I'll be on the next plane, Brie."

Her phone beeped with an incoming call. She frowned when she saw it was from the Anniston Police Department.

*Dang it.* The officer she'd cuffed to the light post must have gotten word to Connor Pierce. Earlier, she'd been prepared to face the music. But that was when she'd assumed Carlos would take her lead back to Calvin and open a case. That would've gone a long way in getting any charges dismissed.

She remembered Eliot was still on the line. "Call me when you have a flight."

"I will. Brie, be careful. Whoever did this to Carlos could—"

"You know I can take care of myself."

"So could Carlos," Eliot said.

They hung up. Her phone beeped with a voice mail.

She hit play to see just how much trouble she was in.

"Ms. Colton. This is Detective Pierce." Yeah, she recognized his voice. Deep, kind of sultry. An image of him flashed in her mind. Tall, blond, broad shoulders. A bad-boy smile, with maybe a hint of bad-boy attitude.

She'd met all three of the cold case detectives. Dubbed by the press as the Three Musketeers, they were touted as officers who played by their own rules. But from everything she'd read about them, their rules came with a moral code and it got scum off the streets. Brie respected that.

"We met a few months ago," Detective Pierce continued. "You helped APD out on a cold case. We need to talk. Can you please call me back?" He ran off his cell number. "It's imperative we speak."

"Yeah, I get that," she muttered to herself. "But you're going to have to wait."

* * *

Connor wasn't going to sit by and do nothing while waiting for Star to return his call. He called the Black Diamond, but no one answered. So he called Star three more times. When she didn't answer the fourth time, he ran her through the database. No priors. No warrants. No tickets.

No shit!

She'd gotten a California license a year ago, then applied for a Texas license four months ago. The fact that there was no record of her identity before that made him skeptical. The fact that she had no priors and now had stolen a car made him suspicious.

He copied her address down. He knew the complex from some busts when he'd worked the Drug and Gang Unit. The place seemed to have cleaned up its act but was still a bit dodgy.

Finding her apartment, he pounded on the door, but got nothing. Almost ready to walk, he saw the front curtain flutter. He knocked harder. "I'm not going away!"

A gray longhaired tabby cat jumped up into the window, but when the cat saw him, it bolted.

"Stop. For God's sake, she's not home." A woman stuck her head out from next door.

He flashed his badge and she disappeared as quickly as the cat.

After searching the parking lot, and not finding her silver Chevy Cruze, he headed to the office. A woman in her late fifties, who looked like someone's grandmother, sat behind a desk.

"Hi," she offered with a looking-for-a-sucker smile. "Hope you're in the market for an apartment. I have three freshly painted units that are move-in ready."

"Sorry." He showed his badge and asked about Star Colton.

The apartment manager's smile diminished. "I don't know what to say. She pays her rent on time—which is a rarity around here—keeps to herself, and never causes trouble."

Connor handed the woman his card. "Keep an eye out and when you see she's home, call me."

The woman's mouth thinned. "Has she done something wrong? Is she dangerous?"

Billy might think so, but Connor couldn't say *dangerous* fit. Then he remembered her in her short-shorts and low-cut tank top when she was serving drinks, and well, yeah, *dangerous* fit. "We just need to talk to her."

Heading to his car, he decided to leave his card under Star's door. Maybe if she realized he knew where she lived, it would convince her to return his call.

When he was only a few feet from her door, he noticed it stood slightly ajar. Another step and he saw the wood splinters on the concrete by a green welcome mat.

Had someone just broken in?

Reaching inside his shirt, he pulled his Glock from his shoulder holster. His heart bounced around his chest as he pressed himself against the outside wall. Counting to three, he leaned over until he could see inside. The living room appeared empty, but an oversized sofa was large enough to hide behind.

Grip firm on his weapon, he eased open the door a bit and cut his eyes to the small kitchen area. Empty. He quickly moved inside and positioned himself against a wall, so he could see behind the sofa and the hallway. Was the perp gone or hiding in the back of the apartment?

"Police," he called out. "Come out with your hands up."

He heard a noise, as if someone had knocked something over.

"I said come out!"

He inched down the hall, his gun tight in his palm. His finger pressed against the side of his weapon, while a memory pressed against his conscience. For a fraction of a second, he was no longer in the apartment, but in that dark alley where he'd lost his partner. He shook it off.

He heard another clatter. The bedroom door inched open. His finger eased onto the trigger, then the gray feline hauled ass down the hall.

His heart slammed against his sternum as he tore through the door.

The window over the bed was open and the drapes hung half off the curtain rod. He bolted to the window. The alley was empty.

Why had someone broken into Star Colton's apartment?

His gaze caught on the bed, or rather the white comforter, with dirty shoe prints on it. Large shoe prints. Definitely male.

Before he left, he took pictures of the prints, and because the front door didn't close all the way, he put the cat and its litter box in the bathroom. He ended up getting a damn six-inch scratch up his arm for his trouble. He and cats never got along. Maybe he'd add that to his list of deal breakers. Never date a woman with cats.

He called in the break-in, and when a black-and-white arrived, he used the I'm-just-a-cold-case-detective card and managed to hand it over. He was too exhausted to deal with paperwork, but he did warn the guy that the demon cat was locked in the bathroom.

Before leaving, he knocked on the neighbor's door to see if she'd seen the perp.

"I thought it was you again. I ignored the noise."

Frustrated, he went back to his office. Mark and Juan were still thumbing through old files, looking for their next case.

Juan stretched back in his chair. "Find her?"

"No. But I found out I'm not the only one looking for her." Connor's sleep deprivation sounded in his voice.

"What?" Mark looked up.

"Her apartment was broken into."

"No shit?" Mark said.

"Did you call it in?" Juan sat back up.

"Yeah." He gave them the facts and dropped in his chair. The dang thing squealed as if protesting. Running a hand over his tired eyes, he actually considered going home for a nap, but he spotted the file in front of him. There had to be a reason why Star mentioned the case.

He went and snagged a cup of coffee, opened the file, and vowed to stay awake to read it.

After only five minutes, he hadn't found an answer, but

he had confirmation that Star was the car thief. "It has to be her," Connor announced.

Mark stretched his hands over his head. "What did you find?"

"Guess where Alma Ronan worked a month before she went missing? The Black Diamond," he answered. "And look at this." He held up a picture of the missing woman. "She's blond with blue eyes. Looks a little like Star, doesn't she?"

"You think they're sisters?" Juan asked.

"That's what I thought, but according to this file, Alma didn't have any siblings. Maybe a cousin?"

"Does it say where she was from?" Mark asked.

"Dallas."

"Didn't Star say she was from Alabama?" Juan asked.

"But the resemblance is so close. It's suspicious."

"What's suspicious?" Sergeant Brown walked into their closet of an office. They looked at him then at one another with the same unspoken question. *Who'd done it this time?* Nine times out of ten, when Brown showed up, he was here to call one of them out for some infraction. And yeah, they bent the rules a little, but they'd also solved more cold cases in the last two years than had been solved in the previous fifteen.

"Just a case." Connor grew an inch in height. Brown always had his spine tightening as if he were back on the football field playing defense.

"What's up?" Mark asked, probably wanting to get the reaming over with.

"Can you push those cases to the back burner? I'd like you three to help out with something else."

"Define 'something else.'" Connor picked up a pen and

tapped it on his desk. Chances were Brown was trying to stick them with some grungy, unsolvable case no one else wanted. Connor was allergic to grunge.

Brown tugged at his belt. Between the man's gut and stained tie, he wasn't what you'd call a good face for the department. But his seniority kept him on the job, or at least at a desk. Connor really hoped he wasn't looking at himself in thirty years.

"An FBI agent, Carlos Olvera, was attacked and shot this morning. He's alive but in bad shape."

"Was he on the job?" Mark asked.

"I hear he was confirming a lead in a case," Brown said.

"What kind of case?"

"Human trafficking was brought up, but we don't have anything official yet. The agent was found under the bridge at Fifth Street and Chestnut. We aren't sure if the assault happened there, or if he was moved. We have the crime scene preserved and guarded. Someone needs to get over there."

Connor rolled the pen in his hands. "Won't the FBI be working this, considering it's one of their own?"

"They're sending someone, but they've asked for assistance."

"Isn't that odd?" Connor asked.

Brown frowned. "Not when you consider they'll kick us off the case and take the credit after we solve it."

"And if the Feds are going to make the department look bad, you figure to let the shit fall on us three. Is that what this is?" Connor asked.

Before Brown answered, Mark added, "If the guy's in bad shape, why not give it to Homicide?"

"Homicide got four new cases last month. And haven't closed one." Brown looked at Connor. "I'm not looking for a fall guy, or fall guys, on this case. If we could solve this before they even show up, or do it so they couldn't take credit, it'd be a feather in the department's cap. I need someone on this who isn't afraid to stand up to them or piss them off if need be."

"Well, we're really good at pissing people off," Connor said, "but I don't know if—"

"You want it or not?" Brown spit out. "I'm not begging."

Connor knew he was pushing it, but after the department had hung him out to dry, he deserved to push. "Really—"

"We'll do it," Mark said.

Brown strolled over to Mark's desk and dropped a Post-it note. "Here's the crime scene address. The vic is at Westside Hospital. I was told there's an on-leave FBI agent there looking into the case as well. Someone needs to shake him up and see what we can get before his cronies get here. And let me know what you need to get this one done. The quicker the better."

No one spoke until Brown was out of earshot.

"You could have let him beg a little," Connor said to Mark.

"I agree." Juan laughed.

Mark picked up the Post-it note. "That was already as close as he gets to begging. Two of us should take the scene and one go to the hospital." He motioned to the file on Connor's desk. "I know you wanted to dig into that, but let's get this started first."

"Yeah." Connor stood. "I'll go to the hospital. I'm in a bad enough mood that interrogating an arrogant, know-it-all FBI agent sounds fun."

* * *

On the drive, Connor got a text from Billy reporting that the Mustang had been found, and he wanted to know why Connor hadn't figured out who the woman was who'd humiliated him.

Connor called Star...again. It went to voice mail... again.

He left another message. "Call me. I'm not going to drop this." He hung up and got out of his car.

Crossing the parking lot to the hospital, his mind pulled up an image of the car thief. Blond, blue eyes, and hot. Thankfully, her young appearance had saved him. If he'd slept with her that would've made this awkward.

Getting to the front desk, he learned Carlos Olvera was in the ICU. On the elevator ride up, his phone dinged with a text. He recognized the number. Star.

He swiped his screen to read what the little ballbuster had to say.

Sorry. On vacation in Florida. Will call when I get back.

"Fuck." He hit her number again. She didn't answer. "Look, Ms. Colton, you're in trouble. I know you stole the Mustang. Don't make it worse for yourself! Call me."

The elevator doors opened. Properly pissed to face down a high-and-mighty FBI agent, he walked to the family waiting room. Five people waited in the somber, church-like atmosphere. While he wasn't a churchgoer himself, his mom had been. She'd dragged his sinful soul to church every chance she'd had, but the quiet reverence of the room reminded him of the last time he'd sat in a pew. His mom's funeral six years ago.

He continued to look around. No one fit his mental profile of a black-suited FBI agent with a rod up his ass. Then he saw the patrol officer sleeping in a chair.

He walked over and read the name on the uniform. "Officer Heyes, I'm Detective Pierce."

The man's chin lifted quickly, no doubt embarrassed for sleeping on the job. Connor couldn't blame him. He fell asleep in church every dang time he went and got elbowed for doing so. Then again, if Heyes had let the FBI agent slip away...

"Sorry," he said. "I work a second job and I'm already into overtime on this shift."

"Where's the FBI agent?"

He looked around, then glanced at the clock on the wall. "I think she's in with the victim."

"She?" Had Sergeant Brown just assumed the agent's gender?

"Yeah. Agent Ryan. Brie Ryan."

"You verify her identity?"

"Yes. She showed me her driver's license and I spoke with her boss at the FBI. He identified her."

"Okay," he said, already tamping down his attitude. Oh, he believed in gender equality, but his upbringing by his southern churchgoing mom assured he'd go in soft, until she earned his indignation.

"Were you the first one on the scene when the victim was found?"

"No, that'd be Officer Monroe. He stayed at the scene and asked me to follow the ambulance here and locate next of kin. I contacted Ryan through the victim's phone. Ryan's boss said other agents are on their way."

"Fine, you can head out. I'll take it from here."

He handed Connor a hospital bag. "The victim's things."

Connor glanced at the bag. "Wallet?"

"No. It's missing. Only thing the guy had on him was his phone. But there's a nice ring and a gold necklace in there. So it doesn't look like a robbery."

Connor took the bag and headed to the ICU. As soon as he pushed through the double doors, he was met with a chorus of heart monitors keeping pace. He'd left the church atmosphere only to enter one that was cold and morgue-like. He approached the nurses' station. "Carlos Olvera's room?" he asked in a hushed tone.

"Room three." She motioned to the left. "You family?"

He pulled out his badge.

She nodded. "He's unconscious, but his wife is there."

*Wife?* This wasn't adding up. He moved toward room three.

# CHAPTER FOUR

Brie forced herself to touch Carlos's swollen hand. He'd obviously put up one heck of a fight. The knot in her chest doubled, knowing that if Carlos could talk, she'd bet he'd say something like "*You ought to see the other guy.*" And she wished she could see him. The need to find the son-of-a-beach who did this bit hard.

"Carlos." Swallowing, she contemplated her words. The nurse had told her that sometimes comatose patients said they had heard people talking to them while they'd been unconscious. If so, Carlos deserved to know he wasn't alone.

Brie had met Carlos the day she started at the FBI. He'd been one of the few who hadn't gotten pissy because she'd been brought into the agency in an unorthodox way. Hadn't judged her for her size and gender.

"I'm here. I got your back. And Eliot and Sam are coming." Her throat tightened. "And Tory should be here soon. Don't you want to wake up?" A few hot tears fell to her cheek. "I'm going to find who did this. I swear."

She heard the door swish open behind her. She batted away her tears before turning around.

"How's the weather in Florida?"

Standing six foot plus, wearing a frown, a pair of dark gray khakis, and a sage button-down, Detective Pierce loomed in the doorway. Inanely, she noticed the shirt brought out the green in his eyes.

Eyes filled with a crapload of suspicion.

"I can explain," she said.

"Really? This is going to be good."

She started out of the room. But he blocked the door. She half expected him to start Mirandizing her.

"Do I need to handcuff you, or are you going to be civil?"

"I'm not going to run." Her chest tightened.

"But not be civil?" His voice deepened.

"I'm not in a civil mood." Honesty came out, while she held close to the vulnerability quaking inside her.

He stared down at her, as if cuffing her was still an option.

"Get your head out of your ass." She forced her chin up. "If I'd planned on running, would I have given the officer your card?"

"But you lied about who you were two months ago, and there's the text about Florida. So we haven't built up a good foundation of trust, now have we?"

Yeah, there was that. "I needed a little time."

"For what?" he asked.

She glanced at Carlos. "Let's talk somewhere else." She spoke as if she owned this conversation.

His disgruntled expression said she didn't own crap.

She breathed in through her nose, fighting the sting in her eyes. "They say he might be able to hear." She waved the detective aside.

He stepped away from the door, even let her lead the way. But she didn't fool herself, his heavy footsteps told her he was less than an arm's reach away.

She pushed open the double doors, exiting the ICU unit, and saw the small seating area in the hall was now empty. Dropping down in one of the chairs, she debated over where to start. He claimed the seat beside her. His knee bumped against hers; the human contact sparked an ache, and she jerked away.

He noticed her quick movement and frowned. "Start explaining."

"I'm with the FBI."

"But on leave, right? Officer Heyes said—"

"Yes, I took a leave of absence to investigate my sister's murder."

His brow arched. "Alma Ronan?"

She nodded.

He held up a couple of fingers and wiggled them. "Two problems." His dead-serious tone seemed to come from deep in his chest. And considering the size of his chest, there was a lot of depth there. "First, from what I read, Alma doesn't have a sister. Second, we don't know she's dead."

"Her body was found in Guatemala five months ago. I didn't want to report it to the local police until I had a chance to look into it. But her parents have been notified."

"You can prove that?"

She nodded. "I have the report."

"On you?" he asked.

"I can get it on my phone if you think it's necessary."

"I do."

Frowning, she pulled her phone out and went to her email where she'd forwarded a copy. She passed him her phone.

He skimmed the email, then glanced up.

"I'll need you to forward that to me. Now, back to the other issue. The records state that Alma didn't have any siblings. And you just said 'her parents,' not 'our parents.'"

"We're half sisters. Our father was married to two women at the same time. I haven't seen her since I was six. *Dad's a bigamist* isn't something you put on your paperwork. And I don't consider him my parent."

He studied her as if he'd heard the emotion behind that truth. "How did Agent Olvera get involved?"

"I contacted him."

"About?"

"The manager at the Black Diamond started talking about a foreign investor, Dillon Armand, being in the States. He was listed as a person of interest in my sister's murder by Guatemalan police. I called Carlos. When he looked into this, Homeland Security didn't show he was here. Oddly enough his cousin Marcus was listed as entering the States. Part of the reason the FBI didn't feel the need to investigate Armand was because he wasn't listed as being in the States when my sister went missing. We did some checking and found they look enough alike to be twins. That made us suspicious that Dillon Armand may have traveled here using his cousin's passport."

"And you think he was who shot your agent?" When

she didn't answer, he continued, "Or do you think this was random? A robbery?"

Her mind raced. Could she, should she—confide in him about the possible mole? Every inch of her FBI training said no, to leave it to Agent Calvin to look into this internally. But he hadn't believed her, so how hard would he investigate? And one of the two agents coming here could be the leak Carlos had found. The real question: Could she risk *not* telling him? Her loyalty was with Carlos. Not the FBI.

"Maybe not random," she said. "It's possible that the person responsible for shooting Agent Olvera is connected to the FBI."

Detective Pierce's eyes rounded.

"I've just been informed that Carlos, Agent Olvera, suspected there was a dirty agent."

"Informed by who?"

"Tory Vale."

"Another agent?" he asked.

"No, he's Agent Olvera's husband. I trust Tory, and I trust Carlos even more. Have you ever heard of the Sala family?"

"Just that they have a connection to the cartel out of Mexico."

"They are a Guatemalan crime family as big, if not bigger, than the cartel. Nine months ago, the FBI, along with the ATF, worked a gun trafficking case. It went awry. We were certain then that someone with ATF had leaked something, but we couldn't prove it."

He held up a hand. "I'm confused. What does a gun trafficking case have to do with your sister's murder and Agent Olvera getting shot?"

"You really aren't very patient, are you?"

He frowned. She continued, "According to Tory, before he left, Carlos was going through the Sala case and came across something that made him believe the leak from that case was internal."

"So you think someone from your agency shot Agent Olvera? That would mean his attack is connected to an old gunrunning case and not your sister's murder."

"Except Dillon Armand is a cousin to the Sala family and he just happens to be part owner of the Black Diamond where my sister worked."

"Then maybe Armand did shoot Olvera?"

"No, I had him in my sights most of the night."

Silence fell, as if he was gathering his questions. "Something was mentioned about human trafficking. Is that what you think happened with your sister?"

Guilt resettled in her chest. "Yes. It's rumored the Sala family are also into human trafficking, but we have no proof."

"What I don't understand is if Armand's name is connected with the police report and the club, why didn't the FBI or the Guatemalan police investigate it?"

"The Sala family has deep pockets and practically owns the authorities down there." She sighed. "Armand denied knowing my sister, and the witness who put him with her recanted his story. And because Armand hadn't been to the States in several years, there was nothing to tie him to her."

"So are the FBI opening an investigation now?"

"Not yet. Carlos was here to get his prints. If we could prove he's been entering the country all this time as his cousin, then it might be enough to open the investigation."

He nodded. "And stealing the Mustang?"

"I didn't steal it. I borrowed it. It's in a grocery store parking lot on—"

"It's been found," he said. "Why did you... borrow it?"

"Armand came into the club. I heard him on the phone setting up a meeting. I decided to follow him, hoping he might lead me to the bastards he's doing business with. But when I went to the parking lot, I realized he'd parked beside my car. Afraid he'd recognize it, I ran back into the club and snagged a customer's, Mr. Dunn's, keys. He's careless with them. Leaves them on the table so they're not in his pocket, in case he gets a lap dance. And since he's sleeping with one of the dancers, he always closes the place down. I thought I'd have time to follow Armand and bring the car back without him knowing."

Pierce sat there, staring at her as if her answer wasn't good enough.

And it wasn't. Taking the car hadn't been her brightest move. But she couldn't turn down the chance to find out who Armand was working with. "Look, I didn't hurt anyone."

"Obviously you've never been kneed in the balls." He lifted one brow.

She held up a hand. "You're right. I did do that. The police officer was about to arrest me when Armand's Porsche drove by. All I could think about was the picture of my sister—dead, naked, and chained to that filthy bed in some Guatemalan whorehouse. Tell me you wouldn't have done the same thing!"

When he didn't answer, she said, "See."

"I'm going to have to take you in." He started to stand up.

"Not yet. I have backup coming to watch over Carlos.

As soon as they arrive you can take me in. And once I solve my sister's case and find out who did this to Carlos, you can toss my ass in jail."

His green eyes narrowed. Their color darkened. "You don't get to call the shots, Agent Ryan."

She knew her only out was to reason with this guy, but was he reasonable? "They should be arriving in a couple of hours—"

He shook his head. "I'll have an officer—"

"The officer on duty has slept more than half the time he's been here!"

"Officer Heyes left. I'll get someone different." He reached for his phone.

"I can't accept that." She frowned.

"Look, this whole thing sounds..."

"Crazy. I know. But I'm not willing to bet the life of my friend on it. I'm the one who pulled Carlos into this, so this is on me." She inhaled and hoped her air of authority would at least earn her some respect. "All I'm asking for is time. Let my backup get here, then as soon as I catch who did this, you can lock me up for all I care."

She watched the debate happening in his eyes.

When he didn't seem happy, she added, "Didn't I go to y'all when someone came in looking for your witness at the club a couple of months ago? I gave a description of him. I didn't have to do that."

He stared at her. "Do you think this Armand guy is on to you?"

"No."

"Well someone is." He pulled up his sleeve and showed her what looked like claw marks up his arm. "Your attack cat did this to me."

"You were in my apartment?"

"Only after someone broke in."

"Broke in?"

"You haven't been notified?"

She remembered she'd missed a call earlier. "I got a message but haven't listened to it." She struggled to wrap her head around what he was saying. "Is my cat, Psycho, okay?"

"Fitting name," he said. "I locked him in the bathroom with his litter box and food."

"Thank you." She realized what he was insinuating. "I don't think my cover's blown. Other than Carlos, no one knew I was here, until now, and the FBI still don't know I'm working at the club."

"Maybe Agent Olvera told—"

"He'd never do that."

"Then it's one hell of a coincidence. The agent you brought in to confirm your lead is shot, then your place is broken into."

"Wait!" She grabbed her phone. "I have a nanny cam."

She pulled up the app and hit rewind. He leaned in so close, his shoulder brushed against hers.

The fast-moving film showed someone walking into her place. She paused it and went back. The gun-toting guy on the screen was big, blond, and sitting next to her.

"It happened right before that." His deep voice came right at her ear with a warm breath.

She started playing it again. The film showed her front door being kicked in.

"There," he said.

She hit rewind. The guy moving into her living room was equally big and had red hair, and his back was toward the camera. He finally faced the camera. He looked familiar, but...her mind played connect the dots trying to identify him. "Fudge."

"You recognize him?"

"Yeah. It's one of Mr. Dunn's construction guys."

"Who?"

"Dunn. The owner of the Mustang. He runs a construction company and brings his workers in sometimes. Someone might have noticed me take his keys. Or I guess he could have figured it out, since my car was still at the club. He must've sent this guy to my house." She looked at Detective Pierce. "Did you release my name to the cops about the car?"

"No. But how would this Dunn character know where you live?"

"Grimes, the club owner. Dunn probably accused me of stealing his car and Grimes gave him my address. They're friends."

"Excuse me." A doctor walked up. "Are you Mrs. Olvera?"

Brie glanced at Detective Pierce, hoping he'd stay silent. "Yes. Is everything okay?"

The doctor eyed Connor.

"It's okay," Brie said. "Just tell me!"

# CHAPTER FIVE

Connor listened. The doctor's update wasn't good. He said things like "blood pressure dropping," "prepare yourself," and "call other family members."

"Can I see him?" Her voice shook.

"Perhaps in a few minutes. They're working to get his blood pressure up."

When the doctor walked away, she sat stoically. No tears. No words. No outward emotion. But he felt it. He recalled in detail the gnawing grief that losing Adkins had brought on. "I'm sorry."

Anger filled her blue eyes. "He's not going to die. The doctor doesn't know Carlos. He won't give up." Her intake of air sounded like pain.

Knowing there were no words to offer, he let the silence take over.

It was Brie who spoke next. "Where did they find Carlos? Do you have any leads? Why aren't you out there looking for whoever did this?" The edge to her voice said she was close to losing it.

"Just take some breaths." He understood exactly what she felt. The anger. The need for justice. He'd been there when he lost Adkins. For Connor, however, that justice had been swift and bittersweet. It hadn't helped that the kid's bullet wasn't the one that took Adkins's life. Fortunately, the lowlife drug dealer was caught two weeks later and now sat on death row.

Officially, what happened that night had been deemed a good shoot. The media, however, crucified Connor. He became a stain on the department. They didn't like stains.

He pushed back the past and focused on her questions. "He was found under the bridge at Fifth Street and Chestnut. My partners are at the crime scene now."

"Brie?"

Agent Ryan shot up. Two men, one black and one white, both in their late fifties, came striding in. While one of them walked with a slight limp, both of them were big men, who carried themselves with authority. Agent Ryan literally fell into the arms of the black man.

Connor tried to assess the relationship but couldn't label it, though with the age difference it didn't appear intimate.

"How is he?" the man holding her asked, as his dark eyes found Connor.

Head still on the man's chest, Agent Ryan answered, "His blood pressure's dropping, but he's not going to die. He can't!" Her tone was brittle. Forced. She looked extra small in the man's arms. Almost fragile.

The embrace ended and in seconds Brie Ryan's spine stiffened.

"You okay, kid?" the other man asked.

"Fine." Her light blue eyes met his, and the brief seconds of vulnerability were gone. She looked back at the African American man. "How did you get here so fast?"

"I know someone who knows someone who has a plane."

"You always know someone." She half-smiled. "Thanks." She focused on Connor. "Detective Pierce, this is Eliot Franklyn"—she motioned to the man she'd hugged—"and this is Sam Keith."

Connor and Sam shook hands. Then Connor extended his hand to Eliot.

"A detective?" Eliot asked in lieu of shaking Connor's hand.

Connor nodded, dropped his hand, then looked back at Brie. "Is this your backup?"

"Yes."

"Then we should go."

"Slow down, bucko." Eliot held up his hand

"That's Mr. Bucko to you," Connor countered.

The man's jaw clenched. "Go where?"

"To the precinct. We have some matters to discuss."

Brie looked prepared to argue, then stopped herself.

"What matters?" Eliot barked.

"It's okay," Brie offered. "I confiscated a car. I just—"

"Did you return it?" Eliot directed the question to her, but his dark gaze never shifted from Connor.

"Of course." Brie brushed a strand of hair off her cheek.

"Was it wrecked? Damaged?" A frown tightened Eliot's lips.

"No," she answered.

"Then what's the problem?" The man's tone deepened.

"She assaulted an officer," Connor answered.

Eliot's shoulders widened. The man was as tall and almost as thick as Connor. Not that Connor flinched. He had the guy by twenty years, but his gut said the man wouldn't go down easy.

"I'm sure she had a good reason," Eliot said.

Connor countered. "I think the department's policy is that there is never a good reason for stealing a car."

"It's okay." Brie put her hand on the man's arm.

She looked back at the ICU doors. "Don't let anyone see him alone. No one."

"I got it," Eliot said. "Sam, go with Brie."

"No, I'm fine," she said as Connor motioned for her to start walking.

Before she moved, Eliot spoke up again. "Detective." The man looked him dead in the eyes. "Treat her with kid gloves." His tone was more threat than suggestion.

Connor nodded curtly before he and Brie headed out.

When they got in the elevator, she asked, "Could we stop at the crime scene? I need—"

"We're going to the station."

"Time's wasting," she insisted. "First let me figure out who did this, then—"

"Sorry." Neither of them said another word as they made their way to his car.

When they climbed into his Malibu, his phone rang. He hit the locks before grabbing his phone. Mark's name flashed across the screen. Connor answered the call. "You at the office?" Connor cut Brie a look. She looked both pissed and exhausted.

"We just got back," Mark said. "You get anything?"

"Yeah."

"What?" Mark asked.

"I'll tell you when I get there. I'm on my way." Connor hung up, started the car, and looked at her. "So Eliot's your stepfather?"

"No."

"You seem close," he said.

She stared at him. "He raised me."

"I could tell."

"How?" she asked.

He half-smiled. "I've seen that look on every father of every girl I've ever dated."

"We're dating? How did I miss that?"

"Let's just say I know that touch-my-daughter-and-I'll-kill-you look."

She lifted her chin. "Thing is, Eliot means it."

He grinned and backed out of the parking lot. "Are he and Sam ex-FBI?"

"No. Military. Special Forces."

"I'm impressed."

She watched him drive. "This is a waste of time. We should be trying to catch who did this to Carlos."

"But first, we need to get the facts."

* * *

Connor, with the evidence bag from the hospital in his hand and Agent Ryan at his side, walked into the police station and up to the front desk. Mildred, the receptionist, looked up and smiled. Her ready smile was something he looked forward to every day.

But then her gaze landed on Brie and that daily ray of sunshine faded. He remembered the two of them meeting when Ryan, aka Star, had stopped by the office. Brie hadn't followed Mildred's wait-here orders, and it hadn't sat well with Mildred.

"You changed your hair," Mildred said.

"I did," Ryan said, her frustration visible. He reminded himself not to judge, since her partner's life was still on the line.

"Good, you two know each other," Connor said.

"I don't think we were properly introduced," Mildred said.

"Then let me fix that. Mildred Lincoln, this is Brie Ryan."

"I thought it was Star something."

"We all kind of thought that." Connor saw Ryan's lips thin. "Can she visit with you a minute?"

"Sure." Mildred waved to the chair across from her desk.

Connor pulled the chair around and motioned for Ryan to sit. She frowned but sat. He reached back and pulled his handcuffs off his belt.

Mildred's eyes widened.

"It'll be fine," Connor said.

"How is this fine?" Agent Ryan's frown deepened. "Seriously? This is not necessary."

"How's the weather in Florida?" he asked.

"Florida?" Mildred pondered aloud.

Agent Ryan's eyes tightened to slits, and all he could see was a sliver of angry blue. "And I thought I liked you."

"He has that effect on a lot of women." Mildred chuckled.

Connor motioned for Brie to hold out her hand. "Only for a few minutes."

When she didn't follow his request, he caught her hand and cuffed one of her wrists and then connected the other cuff to a drawer pull. "I need..." He paused. "I'll be right back."

She looked at Mildred. "Is he always a hard-ass?"

Mildred lifted a brow. "Only when provoked. Did you provoke him?"

"Yes." Connor stared down at the blonde with a mix of emotions. He empathized with her for being worried about her fellow agent and felt equally bad about her half sister, but he needed to play this right. Which meant he needed to run everything by his partners first.

"Only to protect someone." Brie glared up at him.

"Interesting," Mildred said.

"What's interesting?" Connor asked.

"Nothing." Mildred looked at Agent Ryan. "Are you good at crossword puzzles?" She picked up the newspaper from her desk.

"Uncuff me," Brie ordered him. "I'm not going anywhere."

"Be right back." He left the two women to work puzzles while his own mind puzzled over his growing respect and maybe even admiration for the little spitfire.

* * *

Mark and Juan looked up when Connor walked into the office. "What you got?" Mark pulled a pencil from behind his ear.

"I found Billy's ballbuster."

"What?" Mark asked. "You were supposed to be at the hospital."

"I was. That's where I found her."

"I don't understand," Juan said.

"Get this. She's FBI," Connor said. "Her real name is Brie Ryan."

"No shit!" Juan said.

"No shit." Connor dropped the bag that contained Agent Olvera's clothing and phone. "She's been looking into the Ronan case. Alma Ronan is...was her half sister. She's dead."

"Why didn't she tell us this when we met her?" Juan asked.

He shrugged. "She's got a little issue with telling the truth. But in her defense, she probably didn't have anything to tell then. She just got her first lead recently and that's why Agent Olvera was here."

"So Agent Olvera's shooting is related to the Ronan case?"

"That's where it gets confusing and interesting," Connor said. He gave them the whole spiel. The two cases, Dillon Armand being the connection between the cases, and Brie's suspicion that one of the FBI agents was behind Olvera's attack.

"Damn." Mark's tone sounded amused. "So, not only are we going to be butting into the FBI's case, we're also going to be looking at one of them as possibly being dirty. We're really going to chap some special agent asses."

"Probably." Connor rotated his shoulders.

"At least this explains how she was able to take down Billy." Juan looked back at the door. "Where is she?"

"Cuffed to Mildred's desk."

Mark chuckled. "You cuffed an FBI agent to Mildred's desk?"

"She might be a little annoyed at me right now."

"Did she really steal the Mustang?" Mark asked.

"Confiscated it." Connor wiped a hand over his smile. "She was following the suspect in her sister's case."

"How's Olvera holding up?" Juan asked.

"Doctors aren't hopeful. And if we are going to get to the bottom of this, we'll need Brie Ryan's help." He ran a hand over his unshaven chin. "Did either of you tell Billy I'd identified the car thief?"

"No," they both answered.

"What do you say we hold off on that and work with her on figuring out who shot Agent Olvera?"

Mark seemed to consider it. "You trust her?"

"She thinks someone with the FBI is responsible for her partner's shooting. So I think she'll work with us."

"Okay," Mark said. "But if Billy finds out, he's your problem."

* * *

Mildred tapped her pencil on her desk. "Hoover's area. Three letters."

Brie looked at the older red-haired woman and wondered about the irony. "FBI."

"And here I was thinking about a vacuum cleaner." Mildred wrote in the answer. "So what did Connor bring you in for?"

"It's a mistake." Brie tried to formulate a plan, one that included catching Carlos's shooter and still keeping tabs on Armand, but her brain felt fried from no sleep.

"Yours or his?" The woman's brows arched.

Brie started to lay the blame all on him, but the truth leaked out. "Both. But mostly his." Yeah, she shouldn't have stolen the car or hit the officer, but at the cost of losing a lead on her sister's murder, she'd do it again. Cuffing her to a damn desk when the person who attacked Carlos was running free was too much.

"You're honest. I like that. I say if you can't learn from your mistakes what's the use in making them." Mildred paused. "Did you learn anything?"

Brie met the woman's gaze. "What I did wrong, was for the right reason. You ever do that?"

"Maybe, but it didn't land me in handcuffs." She grinned. "Except that one time in the sixties."

Brie almost smiled. "Don't feel you have to share."

"Oh, I wouldn't." Mildred laughed.

Brie decided under different circumstances, she might have liked this woman.

Right then, Brie's phone rang. She reached for it in her purse, forgetting she was cuffed. The metal jingled, then she went for it with her left hand.

"I don't know if you should answer." Mildred put her hand on Brie's purse.

"Please?" Emotion leaked into her voice. "My friend's in the hospital. This could be about him." When she hesitated, Brie added, "Would Detective Pierce have let me keep my purse if he didn't want me to answer my phone?"

Mildred hesitated, then nodded. "Since you said please."

"Thank you." Brie pulled her phone from her bag and saw it was Eliot. Her stomach knotted, and fearing the worst, she sent up a little prayer.

"Everything okay?" Her voice rang a little too high-pitched.

"Yes," Eliot said. "Tory just arrived, they let him go back to see Carlos. Right before he showed up, the doctor came out. He said Carlos's blood pressure has risen. He's stable."

Brie's shoulders slumped and her eyes stung with relief. "Thank God."

"And I just hung up with the assistant to the governor."

"About me?" she seethed.

"About them possibly arresting you. I also spoke with a buddy of mine who has connections to—"

"How many times have I told you not to interfere with my job?" Brie's jaw clenched.

"It isn't your job. You're on leave. And I'm not going to stand by and see you arrested for trying to find your sister's killer."

"I haven't been arrested." *Yet.*

"Another buddy is putting a call into the Anniston mayor and—"

"You have to stop," she snapped. "I'm an adult."

"I could tell that detective was going to be a problem," Eliot said.

Her phone dinged with a text. "Call me if anything changes."

"I will." He hung up.

The text was from Agent Calvin saying that he and Agents Bara and Miles had just landed. Earlier he'd said he wouldn't be coming. Did this mean he was taking the possibility of the leak seriously?

"Everything okay?" a deep voice asked.

Targeting her frustration on the owner of that voice, she looked up. And up. The man was so tall and big he made her feel . . . small and something else she refused to put a name to.

"Just dandy." She rattled her cuffs.

He pulled the key from his pocket. Leaning over, his face came within inches of hers, and she couldn't help but stare at his five o'clock shadow, those long lashes that shouldn't be on a man, and the emerald of his eyes.

Then she realized that she wasn't the only one looking. Gazes locked, she shifted to reclaim her personal space.

"Let's go talk to my partners." He glanced at Mildred. "Thank you."

"Anytime." Mildred smiled at her, then said to Connor, "Play nice."

"I always do," he said.

"Please." Rubbing her wrist, Brie moved from behind the desk.

He glanced at her hands. "I only did it because—"

"Because you're a small-minded, presumptuous ass." She followed him into the cramped office, which held three desks littered with dirty coffee cups, one filing cabinet, two other tough-looking detectives, and enough testosterone to blow the building.

"I think you all know each other..." Connor did a quick introduction then pulled a chair from against the wall and centered it in front of the empty desk in the room. "Have a seat."

Brie remained standing because his order annoyed her. His attitude annoyed her. His good looks annoyed her. She nodded at the two other men, then focused on Connor. "Can I offer you a piece of advice?"

His bright green eyes grew suspicious. "Offer away."

"Before you cuff someone, check to see if they're carrying!" She looked at the other men. "If you'll allow me." She reached into the waist of her jeans and pulled out her gun, keeping it pointed downward, then placed it on the desk.

She heard disguised chuckles from the two other detectives. Detective Pierce didn't laugh. Much to her disappointment, he didn't appear pissed off, either. She'd just have to try harder. Because yeah, right now she wanted to be a pain in his ass, like he was hers.

"Frankly, I wasn't worried about you shooting anyone, just leaving." He said it with such straightforwardness she almost believed him. "Now sit down so we can figure out how we can help each other."

"You can help by letting me go."

"And that's our plan," Detective Mark Sutton said, pulling her attention to him.

Had she heard that right? "I'm not being detained?"

"No," the detective said, "but before you go, you need to fill us in on a few things."

She looked back at Pierce. "See, he's reasonable."

Now Connor appeared pissed. "Just sit down." He dropped down behind the desk.

"Maybe I want to stand."

"Why would you want to stand?" he snapped back.

"Because I've been stuck in a chair, fracking cuffed to a desk!"

"Fracking?" He smiled, but it was the kind of smile meant to dig in someone's crawl.

And consider her crawl dug into. "Excuse me. Fucking cuffed to a desk."

He stood. "Well, maybe I would've trusted you if you hadn't lied to me about being in Florida!"

"Please, I'm sure this wasn't the first time someone lied to you."

"You're right. What was I thinking? I should've expected it from an FBI agent."

Detective Sutton cleared his throat. Both Brie and Pierce looked at him. "How about you two schedule this little party for later. We should concentrate on the case."

# CHAPTER SIX

Sorry," Brie said to Detective Sutton. She dropped into the chair, unsure and slightly embarrassed that she'd let herself get distracted.

Detective Sutton took over the conversation. "Connor has given us some details but we'd like to hear it from you."

"First, I heard you went to the crime scene. Did you find anything?" Brie slipped into full FBI mode.

"It appears the shooting took place elsewhere and he was dumped there."

"Any witnesses?" she asked.

"Not that we found, but there's evidence that some of the homeless hang out there," Sutton offered.

"You should be looking for witnesses instead of sitting here—"

"We need some facts, Agent Ryan." Sutton's tone was firm, but not insulting. "Then I guarantee you we'll be looking into all of this. Tell us, exactly, what brought

Agent Olvera to town? We were told it's about your sister's murder."

Brie pushed back her impatience. "Yes." She started by giving them the bare facts. The date Alma had gone missing and when she'd learned of her sister's death.

"Are there records of your sister leaving the U.S.?" Sutton asked.

"No. We checked. She didn't even have a passport."

"We heard Agent Olvera was looking into a sex trafficking case. Is this tied?" Sutton asked again.

"Yes. Most victims are taken to the Middle East, but some end up in countries like Guatemala and Venezuela."

"When your sister was found, did they come across any others, dead or alive?" Detective Juan Acosta asked.

"No, but her body was found where prostitution was ongoing."

"How was she killed?" Sutton asked.

The question yanked at Brie's heartstrings. "She'd been beaten and stabbed. There was also a large dose of heroin in her system."

"Is it possible your sister got into drugs and left the country willingly?"

Brie reached into her purse and pulled out a charm bracelet. "My father admitted she'd had a drug problem in the past, but he thought she'd gotten clean. I think he was right. The only thing I got back with her body was this bracelet. One of the charms on it is an AA ornament celebrating one year sober."

"Do you know where she attended meetings?" Sutton asked.

"No. I've checked the local AA groups, and no one recognized her. But she could've gotten this earlier." She looked at the bracelet, the half-heart charm caught the light and glittered up at her, bringing a spark of pain to her chest.

When she was six years old, she and Alma had become best friends when they'd both visited their paternal grandmother for two weeks. At the time, they'd been told they were second cousins. The bracelet and charm had been a gift from their grandmother. Brie had been given the other side of that heart on an identical bracelet, but when she was seven, after her father had left and she'd learned the truth of Alma's identity, she'd thrown it away. Hating her grandmother for lying. Hating Alma because their father loved her best.

Pulling herself out of the past, she dropped the bracelet back into her purse and looked up. "Before my sister went missing she called to talk to me about something she was worried about."

"What was it?" Detective Acosta asked.

Guilt twisted Brie's stomach like a wet rag. "I don't know exactly. I never called her back."

Her answer was met with a pregnant pause until Detective Acosta spoke up again, "Why not?"

"I wasn't in my sister's life. I only met her once when I was a kid." She paused.

Sutton rubbed his chin with two fingers. "Then why would she have called you?"

"She told me my father suggested it. He'd heard I was with the FBI."

"Did she tell your father what she wanted with you?"

"He said she alluded to the fact that someone was missing. He got the feeling it was someone from her work."

"Wait." Pierce jumped in. "Was she working at the Black Diamond at the time?"

"No." Now she was getting into some of the reasons why the FBI wouldn't take the case. Would these detectives feel the same? "She'd quit a month before, and there's no record of her being employed after that."

She went on to explain about Armand and how Carlos found out that Armand wasn't even supposed to be in the States.

Detective Sutton picked up a pencil and turned it. "If he's traveling under a fake passport and visa, why don't we have someone pick him up? We could question him about your sister then."

"We don't have his prints in the U.S. Carlos was planning on requesting a copy of them from Guatemala. And unless you can find a reason to hold him while you wait on his prints, he could leave the country and we'd lose any chance of catching him."

"Do you have any proof to back up your human trafficking theory?" Sutton asked.

"There have been three other women who worked at the Black Diamond and fell off the face of the earth."

"What?" Disbelief echoed in Acosta's tone. "We investigated the Black Diamond when working another missing person case and we never learned of any other missing women."

"They quit their jobs before going missing. Linda Kramer was the most recent. She was my sister's roommate and was interviewed in my sister's case. She's disappeared now. The other two, Kathy Logan and Tammy Alberts, worked there two years before. I've spent the last three months searching for them and found nothing."

Officer Sutton spoke up. "Is it possible they just moved?"

"I think I would've found something on them. Just

like my sister, they worked at the Black Diamond, quit, then turned up missing. Don't you think that's too coincidental?"

"It's suspicious." Sutton adjusted his chair.

"And this wasn't enough to convince the FBI to open an investigation? Why?" Pierce asked.

She hesitated. The answer weakened her case and was the reason even Carlos hadn't felt it was enough to take to Agent Calvin. "I originally went to Carlos with the names of eight girls I couldn't locate. He found five of them and discovered they were using aliases and fake Social Security cards to hide from warrants."

"So chances are these three aren't really missing, just living under different identities." Acosta put it out there.

Brie's shoulders tightened. "We don't know that. And I still think it's too coincidental."

"I agree with her." Pierce came to her defense.

She met Pierce's green eyes. In spite of their earlier butting of heads, he seemed willing to help her. She regretted her earlier attitude. A little.

She refocused on Acosta. "As soon as I get home, I'll send you everything I have on the missing women."

Sutton nodded. "Back to Agent Olvera. If the FBI hadn't officially opened a case, why was he here?"

"Armand has eaten dinner at the same place every night since he arrived. Carlos drove into town yesterday and was going to the restaurant to get Armand's prints and prove his identity, so we could show he's been coming to the States under his cousin's name."

Sutton sat up straighter. "Why didn't you just get the prints?"

"I'm not supposed to be here, remember? And with my

family ties to the case, and being on leave, it might make a judge question the evidence."

Sutton nodded. "So Agent Calvin knew Agent Olvera was here?"

"Yes. Carlos told Calvin he wanted to check and see if there was any merit to my theory of what happened to my sister. But Agent Calvin thinks I only arrived here since Carlos was shot." She swallowed her emotions as images of her partner in the hospital bed filled her mind.

"Why didn't you tell Calvin?" Acosta asked.

She exhaled. "He wouldn't approve. I was reprimanded for not dropping the case when I was on the payroll. If he knows I've been here this whole time and Carlos was helping me, it wouldn't just be my job on the line. And..."

"And what?" Sutton asked.

"He would've ordered me to stand down. I won't do that. Armand's here. My job at the club is the best chance of getting him."

The three guys looked at each other. "Okay, so what happened in the Sala case that made you suspect a leak?" Sutton asked.

"It was an easy bust that went bad. Guns were being moved out of Baton Rouge in an eighteen-wheeler heading to Mexico. The informant was someone we'd used before. Someone good. We contacted the ATF, and it became a joint investigation. Three weeks later, when the guns went on the move, we pulled the truck over. It was filled with butterfly valves for an oil factory. We suspected someone from ATF had leaked it, but weren't able to prove it."

Brie hesitated. "The next day my informant was murdered."

"Did you find out who did it?"

"No."

They sat there, digesting the information. Sutton spoke up again, "And Agent Olvera never told you his suspicions about the internal leak?"

"I'm guessing he planned on telling me when we saw each other. It's not something you'd talk about on the phone."

"We have Olvera's phone, but not his wallet," Pierce said, pointing to the bag he'd brought in.

"This wasn't a robbery," Brie spoke up.

Sutton frowned. "We have to look at every angle."

Brie nodded.

Sutton placed his palms flat on the desk's surface. "I'll get the clothes over to the lab and see if there's any blood on them besides Olvera's."

"Let's go to Olvera's hotel first." Pierce was looking at her. "Maybe he brought something with him that will shed light on his suspicions of a mole."

"What does he drive?" Sutton asked.

"A black Honda," Brie answered.

"If it's not at the hotel," Pierce said, "we'll get a BOLO out on it."

She sat up straighter. "Fine. I don't work at the club until eight. If Armand comes in tonight, and I can get his prints, will you run them?"

"You think going in to work is a good idea?" Acosta asked. "I mean, if there's a chance your cover is blown, whoever went after Agent Olvera might come after you."

"It's not blown. I told you, no one at the FBI knows I'm working at the Black Diamond. I'm *this* close to getting this guy. I'm not backing off."

Sutton brought up the fact that her apartment was broken into. Detective Pierce explained about the nanny cam and her recognizing the man.

Sutton ran a hand over his face. "What do we do about this guy?"

"Nothing," Brie said. "Let him by with it. Now that Dunn has his car, he'll probably drop it."

Sutton frowned. "And if he doesn't?"

Pierce spoke up. "Why don't we talk to Dunn and just mention to him about the gang stealing cars out of Houston. Let Dunn make some assumptions that she didn't take the car."

"Yeah." Sutton's gaze shifted back to her. "If we get the least little hint that your cover is blown, you quit."

She nodded.

The office door swung open and slammed against the wall. Brie looked back. She half expected it to be Agent Calvin. Instead, an older, heavy man, stood there in a dark suit that looked a little snug. A red tie rode the mountain of his gut. His gaze shot to Brie then to the detectives.

"Can I have a word with you?" He motioned to Detective Sutton. "And you?" he pointed to Detective Pierce.

Pierce leaned his elbows on his desk. "What is it now?"

"Out here." He stormed off.

Brie saw the two detectives look at each other skeptically. Then they walked out, shutting the door behind them.

She looked at Detective Acosta. "What's that about?"

"Beats me." He smiled. "I'm just glad I'm not included." He went over and collected the bag that held Carlos's things. He pulled out the phone and went back to his desk. "You could have confided in us two months ago."

"There wasn't a lot to tell then."

He looked at the phone, then glanced up and stared at her, as if deciding to say something or not.

"What?" she asked.

"Connor might have overstepped by cuffing you to Mildred's desk, but he did it so he could come in here and go to bat for you. He's the one who suggested we overlook the car incident and work with you. Remember that when you two go back into the ring for another round."

* * *

Connor stared at Sergeant Brown's bulldog face. The man was raging. "I went to piss. To piss. Granted it takes me a little longer these days, but it wasn't *that* long. And when I got back, I had five messages. Five!"

He held up his hand. "One from the chief. One from the mayor. One from the governor. And one from an old army buddy of mine."

*An old army buddy?* Was Eliot Franklyn behind this? Connor's gut said yes. He looked at Brown's fingers wiggling in the air. "That's four," Connor said, obviously not too tired to count.

Brown jerked his hand down. "Hell, by the time I get to my office I'll bet the pope's called." He pointed a finger at Connor. "I do not know what you did to stir up this shitstorm, but it was your name that was brought up. Please tell me you haven't arrested her."

"No," Connor and Mark said at the same time. Then Connor continued, "We hadn't planned on arresting her."

"Good," Brown said.

"But I don't understand," Connor added. "Didn't you assign this case to us because we wouldn't take any shit?"

"I don't want you to take any shit. But I don't want shit raining down on me either. Solve the case. But don't start World War Three. Oh, hell! Maybe I should get someone else to take care of this."

"We got it." Connor and Mark spoke at the same time.

"Make sure you do." Brown started to walk off, then turned back around. "What did she do anyway?"

The two of them looked at each other.

Brown's frown deepened. "I know that look. You're saying I don't want to know, right?"

They still didn't say anything.

"Oh, hell." He groaned. "Do we at least have any leads on the shooting?"

"A few," Mark said.

"Okay. But put this to bed ASAP before more shit flies." He stormed off.

Connor reached for the door, but Mark stopped him. "Look, you're going to have to play nice."

"You're the second person to say that to me today. I always play nice."

"Then play nicer..." He pointed to the door. "And I mean with her. We need her help."

"I'm not the one taking potshots. Did you see how smug she was when she pulled her gun out? Do they train their agents to do that?"

"You cuffed her to a desk."

"So she wouldn't run off."

Mark shook his head. "I swear, I give it a week. If

you two haven't killed each other, you'll be screwing like rabbits."

Connor let out a sound, that was half laugh, half disbelief. "She's not my type."

"Right," Mark said then, "you want me to work with her instead? I'll go with her to the hotel."

"No."

Mark chuckled. "That's what I thought."

# CHAPTER SEVEN

$B$rie liked how Pierce and his partners worked. Breaking down the investigation. Debating the case without anyone pushing back. The camaraderie among them reminded her of how she and Carlos worked. And since these guys functioned as a team, she needed to be a team player.

"Look, Detective Pierce. About what happened with the gun," she said as she followed him to his car.

"It's Connor. And if you're apologizing, I accept."

*Apologizing?* Could this guy *not* be annoying? She weighed her words carefully. "I wasn't going to apologize exactly. I still think you were wrong to—"

"And I think you were wrong to lie to me. Nevertheless, if you're wanting to sweep it all under the rug, I'm willing." They got in his car.

"Fine." She pushed the word out. "Consider it swept."

He drove off. "So how did you end up working for the FBI?"

She focused on the passing buildings outside the passenger window. "That's a long story."

"I like long stories."

"What made you want to be a cop?" She threw out the diversion question, not caring if he realized her intention or not.

"Okay. I'll go first," he said. "I learned in college that I was good at stopping big guys."

"Stopping big guys from doing what?"

"Getting a football."

She lifted a brow. "You played college ball?"

"Uh-huh."

"You didn't try for the NFL?" The question slipped out before she realized it might hit a nerve.

"No. I was injured my second year of college. Tore my ACL and Achilles tendon. I saw several other guys with similar injuries return to the game, but they couldn't live up to their own standards. Several even reinjured themselves trying. They hated the sport after that. I decided if I couldn't chase the football, I'd chase criminals, and changed my major to criminal justice."

"How's the injury now?"

He shifted his leg up and down under the wheel. "Don't even notice it. But I'm not getting hit on the field."

"You regret giving it up?"

"It's not my biggest regret."

*And what is?* The question sat on the tip of her tongue. She swallowed it. Questions like that either got you locked out, or invited in. She wasn't sure either was a good thing. They needed to get along, not to be able to finish each other's sentences.

He refocused on the road. She thought the conversation

was over, but his deep voice filled the car again. "Actually, when I look at the guys who made it and played, I'm sure I did the right thing. One of them has a brain injury and can barely feed himself, and several of the others can hardly walk without pain pills. I kind of like feeding myself and moving on my own two feet."

"Brawn and brains, huh?" she said without realizing it sounded like a compliment.

His lips twitched, as if he'd almost smiled. He stopped at a red light and glanced at her. "Your turn."

Was he implying she needed to answer his earlier question? The silence in the car thickened. She decided to play, to a point. "I turned someone in to the FBI. They needed help getting evidence, so I assisted. When it was over, they asked me to work for them."

"You must have done a bang-up job."

"They didn't complain."

"You still had to go through training. I mean, Billy, the cop from last night, isn't an easy mark."

"Is he a friend of yours?"

"Yeah."

She realized the complications in that. "Is he upset that I'm getting a pass?"

"He will be. I'm hoping his boys quit hurting before I have to tell him."

A touch of guilt hit. "I did what I thought I had to do."

"I'll make sure to tell him that." Silence hit again. "How long did you train?"

"I took a few classes, but I was taught to defend myself before the FBI."

He stared at her, as if she was a puzzle he was working on solving. "Eliot?"

"Yeah."

"You said he raised you. Are we talking foster care?"

After a couple beats of silence, she gave in. And why not? A Google search by someone with mediocre intelligence would give him the same info. Her attempted kidnapping when she was fourteen had been all over the news. "He was my bodyguard."

His head swerved.

"Ever heard of James Ryan?"

"The big-time reporter?"

She exhaled. "He was my stepdad. He traveled the world, and Mom and I traveled with him."

He let that soak in. "That must have been an adventure."

"Yup."

He glanced at her as if he heard everything she didn't say. "Didn't he pass away several years back? I remember seeing some documentary about his stories."

"Yeah."

"Sorry."

She gazed out the window. She could only talk about her past for so long before it tried to suck her back in. And she had no time for the past.

Right then two police cars with lights and sirens blaring flew past them.

"That's odd," Connor said.

"What?" When she looked up, she saw the two cop cars pulling into the Marriott where they were heading. "Coincidence?" She looked at him.

"Maybe." He took the first parking spot, and they hurried into the lobby.

Connor pulled his badge as he met the first officer. "What happened?"

The officer eyed his credentials. "A maid was attacked."

"Is she okay?" Brie asked.

"Paramedics have been called. But the manager just told us the victim was having problems with her husband." The officer was waved over by another patrolman.

"So most likely a coincidence," Connor said. Brie wasn't completely convinced.

Connor flashed his badge to the tall, suited woman working behind the registration desk. "I'm going to need the key to Carlos Olvera's room."

"Is this about the incident?" the hotel employee asked, as her regulation customer smile faded.

"We don't think so," Connor said.

Brie spoke up. "What floor is Carlos Olvera's room on?"

The woman tapped on her computer keys. "Third."

"And what floor did the incident with the maid occur?"

The woman's eyes widened. "Third."

"How long ago did this happen?" Brie asked.

"It just happened."

"Have they caught him?"

"Not yet," the woman said.

Brie looked at Connor. "He could still be here."

"Give me the key," Connor insisted.

"What's the room number?" Brie asked.

"Three twenty-two."

Brie took off while Connor waited for the key. She saw the elevator door close. "Where are the stairs?" she asked a bellman pushing a luggage cart.

He pointed, and she ran in that direction.

She'd only gone up a few steps when a slamming door echoed above her. Footfalls with the same intensity as hers pounded down the stairs toward her. Could it be the maid's attacker?

Stopping, she leaned in and looked up. Between the stair's spindles, she made out what looked like a pair of jeans. The heavy footfalls continued downward.

She pulled out her Glock. A man, medium height, with light brown hair came around the turn and stopped when he spotted her—or when he spotted her gun. Brie noticed his bruised face. Too colorful to have just happened. She'd bet her best bra that Carlos had caused that damage.

"FBI," she announced as she lifted her gun.

The man tore back up the stairs. Brie raced after him. She heard a door bang open and she pushed herself faster. Heart thundering in her chest, she grabbed the door and shot into the hall on the second floor.

She looked left, then right, following the patterned carpet, which could make a person dizzy. She saw no one. Then clattering noises came from a restaurant to her right. She bolted through the door. "Where did he go?" she asked a hostess.

She pointed to the balcony. Brie darted between the tables, calling *excuse me* every time she bumped into a customer.

When she got out on the second-floor deck, people were standing up and looking over the railing. Another restaurant was below, and several patrons were standing around a table that had been upended. Plates and scattered food littered the patio floor. Then she saw her perp running for the street.

This was the piece of kangaroo crap that put Carlos in a coma. She glanced at the seven-foot drop and made an assessment. Risk was low. Odds of catching the bastard high. Without thinking, she went over. Her feet slammed against the hard tile floor. Jarred, but injury free, she called out, "FBI."

She ran for the street, but stepped in a puddle of refried beans and went down, landing boobs first in a plate of enchiladas.

Bouncing up and swiping off a blob of guacamole, she took off. When she got to the street, she saw the guy turning the corner. Pulling a pound of oxygen into her lungs, she ran faster.

* * *

Twenty minutes later, Brie was still jogging down the Anniston streets, looking for the man. The cool October breeze whisked past. While it was probably only sixty degrees, sweat poured down her back.

People strolled the sidewalks, window-shopping. She passed coffee shops, ice cream parlors, salons. A car pulled beside her and the window lowered.

"Get in." The deep, familiar voice reached her ears.

She cut her eyes at the burgundy Malibu—Connor's car. Bending her knees, she rested her palms on her legs and drew in air. Her heart thumped in her chest and she looked across the street. "He could still be around."

"We have officers combing the area."

"They don't have a description," she blurted out. Rising up, she looked through the glass front of a sandwich shop to confirm her perp wasn't there.

"Yeah, they do. Several restaurant patrons took pictures of him. Get in."

Yanking the door open, she crawled in with an

overwhelming sense of defeat. The air felt too thin. Her chest walls too thick. "How did you find me?"

A smirk appeared on his lips. "You kidding? We had at least five reports of an angry white woman covered in"—he looked at her and inhaled—"chicken enchiladas, running through the streets." He grinned. "Now I'm starving."

God only knows why laughter escaped from her. But two seconds later, her throat tightened, and her eyes stung. She'd let the piece of crap get away.

"It was him. He had bruises on his face and Carlos had bruises on his knuckles. That no-good piece of slime is the reason my best friend is barely hanging on to life." Her voice cracked and something in her chest followed suit.

The humor faded and something soft filled his green eyes. That look felt like her kryptonite. Her eyes stung harder, her heart beat faster.

"We'll get him," he said softly.

"Don't," she snapped.

"Don't what?" He looked puzzled.

"You know damn well what! Pretend you care."

His expression tightened. "If you just need someone to be angry at right now, I'll take a hit for you. But for the record, I'm not faking jack shit! I lost a partner three years ago."

She looked away from the indignation darkening his eyes. "You're right. I'm—"

"Forget it." His words didn't sound like they came from anger, but from honesty.

"No. I was wrong. I'm sorry. I'm exhausted and I know it's not an excuse but...I'm not normally a bitch."

Their gazes met—and held. He blinked. "Forget about it."

Two, three seconds had passed when she asked, "Did he get into Carlos's room?"

"Yeah. We have someone dusting for prints. Did this perp have anything with him as he ran?"

"Not that he couldn't fit in a pocket," she answered. "The maid okay?"

"She's beat up, but paramedics said she'd be okay. Juan's going to the hospital to confirm the guy you chased is the same one who attacked her."

She nodded, then dropped her head back and closed her eyes. Fatigue threatened to unravel her sanity. "I can't believe I let him get away."

"I'd say you gave it more than a college try. You jumped off that balcony." He stopped at the red light and cut her a look. "Which was stupid, but kind of badass." He offered her a smile.

It was soft. Gentle. A moment of humor meant to heal, to lighten the mood, and make this somehow more tolerable. It almost worked. But she couldn't help but wonder if she'd lost her one chance at catching this guy.

She looked out the window. Like a computer with a spinning cursor, her mind was in some kind of a buffering mode. She continued to stare at the street, seeing—but not really seeing—the businesses as she passed. Clothing shops, bookstores, a bank, and...

*A bank.* She turned to Connor. "Cameras?"

"What?"

"There have to be cameras outside the hotel. We just passed a bank and they'll have cameras, too. We might get footage of what he's driving. A car is easier to find than a person."

"You're right. I'll make some calls and get someone to start checking into that."

She nodded. "We also need to see if Carlos's car is at the hotel."

"Mark's checking on that."

Connor's phone rang. He grabbed it and checked the number. "It's Mark."

He took the call. "Yeah. I found her." Pause. "What time? No. I will." He hung up.

"What?"

"Olvera's car wasn't at the hotel. Mark's putting out a BOLO. And Agent Calvin wants to talk to us. You too. He's coming to the office at three."

"That gives us time to hit the crime scene and then the hospital." She needed to visit Tory.

Connor's gaze lowered to the front of her blouse. "You have part of an enchilada stuck to your... I have some shirts in the backseat that I was dropping... They aren't clean, but they're cleaner than what you're wearing. And they'll swallow you, but you're welcome to one."

# CHAPTER EIGHT

Connor watched Brie snag a shirt from the backseat. Before he knew what she was doing, she'd yanked off her leather jacket and shirt. He quickly looked away, but not before the image of her in a soft lacy bra had tattooed itself on his brain. And not before she caught him looking.

"It's a bra. I'm sure you've seen one before."

"Maybe one or two," he said. *But not in a while.* The anniversary of his partner's death had thrown him off his game, and into a funk.

Two minutes later, he pulled up to the crime scene and called Mark to get an update. Brie got out of the car and Connor watched her roll up the sleeves of his white shirt and knot the ends in the front. She made his shirt look almost like suitable attire and had him wondering how many times she'd borrowed a man's shirt.

An image of her wearing nothing but his shirt flashed.

He quickly pushed it out of his brain and got out of his car. Moving closer to her, he noted the purple shadows under her eyes. She looked exhausted, but determined. He figured any suggestion that she go home and get some rest would be met with attitude.

She glanced back. "What did you learn?"

"Olvera was found on the right side of the street, a few feet under the bridge."

They crossed the road. She stopped and took it all in. When she spotted blood on the gravel, agony flickered in her bloodshot eyes. Seeing her pain opened up the doorway to his own. He remembered Don's blood. Don's empty, open eyes. Then he saw the kid's.

"Why here?" Her question pulled him back. "Why drop him here?"

"It's dark, looks abandoned. Mark said there was a . . ." He moved down farther. "There. Behind the trees. There's a tent. But at night you probably wouldn't see it."

Brie walked behind the trees, knelt down, and stuck her head inside the one-man tent. Connor's gaze shifted to her ass and he recalled Mark's rabbit comment. *Not happening*, he told himself, but for the first time in months he felt a little blood move south.

"It's empty." She pulled her head out and stood up. "There are thin wheel tracks. Whoever sleeps here probably pushes a grocery cart." She followed the marks to the side of the road then stopped.

"How did they find Carlos?"

"A truck driver spotted him and called it in."

She paused again, and he could almost see her mind spinning. Looking for clues. Wanting answers. Needing justice. He wondered if she thought by solving this, the hurt would go away. It wouldn't. He knew. Then again, Olvera wasn't dead. And she hadn't killed a kid.

She pulled her phone from her back pocket and checked the time. "Drive me to Pecan and Logan Street. Then you can drop me off at the hospital."

"What's at Pecan and Logan Street?"

"The shelter. They serve lunch on Fridays. We might find someone with a cart, or I might find Betty."

"Betty?"

"A homeless lady I know."

"You've been here four months, how do you know...?"

"I volunteer at one of the shelters. Betty might know whose tent that is. My gut says whoever sleeps there saw something or they wouldn't have cleared out of here."

He considered her theory. "If he really cleared out of here, wouldn't he have taken the tent?"

"Not if he was scared."

Ten minutes later, Connor drove up to the shelter. "There she is," Brie said.

Connor parked and watched as Brie pulled some cash from her purse and tucked it into her pocket before exiting the car. He followed her over to the group of homeless people sitting against a brick building.

"Star!" an elderly woman called out. Connor noted her long wild-looking gray hair, faded jeans, and her black jacket two sizes too big. "You serving lunch today?"

Connor had continued the family tradition of dishing up Thanksgiving and Christmas dinners to the homeless since his mom passed. So why was he surprised Brie volunteered? Maybe he shouldn't be so fast to judge.

Brie walked over. "Not today. How are you?"

"Fine, thanks to you. The antibiotics worked like a charm."

"Can we chat a minute?" Brie stepped away from the group and waved for the woman to follow.

Betty's evil eye had Connor pulling back a few steps. "Why are you hanging with cops?"

"Someone I care about was hurt. They're helping me find the person responsible."

"Sorry. Is your friend okay?"

"Still in the hospital. Look, he was found shot under the bridge at Fifth Street and Chestnut. Someone lives there in a tent. Do you know who that is?"

"You think a homeless person did this?"

"No, I think this person might have seen something."

Betty gave Connor another look that said back off, but he held his ground. "Fifth and Chestnut, huh?"

Brie nodded.

Betty leaned in. "I never told you anything, right?"

"My lips are sealed," Brie promised.

She cut her eyes to Connor before continuing, "That's Tomas's domain. Big guy. Almost as big as your cop. He has a ponytail. Other than his size, he looks like that country singer who likes pot. The one who can't sing, but people love anyway."

"Willie Nelson?" Connor guessed, though he'd love to argue about the can't sing comment. His mother had been a country and western fan, and he'd grown up listening to Willie and the boys.

"Yeah. Looks like a big Willie Nelson. Even wears a bandanna."

Connor moved in. "Does Tomas have a last name?"

"I never heard one. But I gotta tell you, I'm not sure

it'll do you any good. Even if he saw something... he's not friendly. Doesn't like cops. Doesn't much like anyone." She looked at Connor. "He refuses to let anyone else camp there. A couple of new guys tried. One of them ended up in the hospital, lost his right eye. Tomas has a mean streak in him. I heard he's got issues from Vietnam."

"Is he here?" Brie asked.

Betty glanced around, concern etched on her face. "Haven't seen him, but I haven't been looking either."

Brie tucked a strand of hair behind her ear, and Connor noticed again how tired she looked. "Could you call me if you see him around?"

"Yeah."

"Thanks!" Brie reached into her jeans pocket and handed the woman some cash.

Betty held up her hand, her fingers gnarled with age. "No money. Thanks to you, I'm no longer pissing blood."

"Take it." Brie slipped it into the women's hand. "It's a gift."

"You are good folk, Star Colton." Betty closed her fist around the bills and stuffed them into her bra.

Brie studied her. "Are you staying at the shelter at night like you said you would?"

"Most of the time. Some nights are too pretty to sleep inside."

"Streets aren't always safe." Brie frowned.

"I'm tougher than I look." Betty gave Connor a head-to-toe glance then whispered something in Brie's ear.

"No," Brie said, and he could swear her cheeks pinkened.

"Well, maybe you should." The woman smiled back at him. "Looks like he could keep you warm at night."

Brie and Betty said goodbye, but before walking off, Betty met his gaze. The humor had faded from her blue eyes. "Don't let her go see Tomas alone. He's dangerous."

* * *

Brie ran into Tory as she stepped off the elevator, and one glance at his worried face brought tears to her eyes.

"He looks so bad." Tory's voice cracked and Brie felt his pain in her own chest.

"I know, but he's alive." She hugged him. Tory held on longer and tighter than any time she'd known the man, who in his own words was "a serial hugger."

When they pulled apart she asked, "Have you spoken to the doctor?"

"Yeah. He...he's not very positive."

"He doesn't know Carlos," Brie insisted.

"That's what I keep telling myself. They are doing some brain scans to make sure the swelling in his brain isn't increasing." Tory scrubbed a few tears from his eyes, and Brie's throat tightened to the point where swallowing hurt. "Oh, you have no idea how good it made me feel seeing Eliot and Sam here. Eliot said that Agents Calvin, Bara, and Miles came by when I was with Carlos. Eliot made them leave. I'm so glad. I'm afraid I'd—"

"It's okay." Brie hugged him, but couldn't help worrying how the meeting went. She knew Eliot would have tried to do it diplomatically, but when pushed he could grow a third head and spew fire.

Tory continued, "If one of them did this, I—"

"Don't go there yet," Brie said. "Where are Eliot and Sam?"

"Sam left to get some rest. They're taking shifts."

"Where?" She could kick herself for not offering them a key to her place earlier.

"There's a hotel connected to the hospital. Eliot's camped out in that little seating alcove in front of the ICU." He waved down the hall as his gaze lifted over her shoulder. Brie turned and saw Connor.

Brie introduced them and they shook hands.

"I was hoping to ask you a few questions," Connor said.

"Sure." Tory grabbed Brie's hand, silently asking her to stay with him.

Connor waved Tory into the waiting room and started off confirming all the facts Brie had already shared. When Tory got emotional, Connor was patient.

"Did Carlos have anything with him that would be worth breaking into his hotel room for? Maybe evidence?"

"Someone broke into his room?" Tory asked.

Brie nodded.

"He had a computer, but that's about it." Tory looked at Brie. "Did he show you anything?"

"I hadn't seen him yet. He didn't get in until late last night."

Tory's brow pinched. "He left Tuesday morning. It's less than a five-hour drive. He dropped me off at the airport, then left to come here. He had his suitcase with him."

Brie shook her head. "He told me he wasn't arriving until Wednesday."

"Was he going anywhere else?" Connor asked.

"No," Tory answered.

Connor looked at Brie. "I'll check with the hotel and see when he got in."

"Hey." A voice came from the door.

Eliot stood there, so she went to him. He frowned at Connor then focused on her. "Get anything?"

"A few leads, but nothing's panned out yet. I heard Agent Calvin and the others came by." She saw the way Eliot studied her face and knew what was coming. The man was worse than a grandmother.

"You got purple moons under your eyes, Brie. You need some rest or you'll have strep within—"

"Quit mothering me."

"Then start taking care of yourself and I won't have to."

"If I didn't know how to take care of myself, I'd've shriveled up and died by now." She frowned. "How did it go with Agent Calvin?"

"Just how you expected it to go."

Brie closed her eyes. "How bad did it get?"

"No one threw a punch. He told me I could leave. That his agents would stand guard. I told him I preferred they left. We debated and I won, but he wasn't happy."

She'd bet that was an understatement. "Look, I have an extra key to my apartment. You guys don't need to stay at a hotel."

"Actually, staying at the hotel is better. We're closer. And Agent Calvin just called me three minutes ago. He's trying to reach you."

Brie pulled out her phone. "I need to charge it." She looked up. "What else did he say?"

"Not much, but he did ask if I'd gotten to spend a lot of time with you since you've been on leave."

She bit down on her lip. "Does he suspect I've been here in Anniston the whole time?"

"It didn't sound like he was fishing. Just making conversation to cover up the awkwardness."

She nodded. "Wait. How did he get your number?"

"We exchanged numbers last year when we went to his barbeque."

She frowned. "So you could keep tabs on me?"

"No."

"Can I use your phone to call him?"

"Sure." He looked back at Connor. "Is the pissant cop behaving?"

"He's not . . . they're helping me."

"They?" He handed her his phone.

"The Cold Case Unit. For some reason, they've been assigned to Carlos's case. I helped them solve a case before. They have a good reputation."

Eliot frowned. "I don't like that one's attitude."

"Well, he's helping me." She found Agent Calvin's recent call and hit redial. "So don't shoot him or anything."

"Too bad," Eliot said. "I needed some target practice."

# CHAPTER NINE

The phone conversation with Agent Calvin had gone bad, and now the face-to-face was going down the same road. "How could you have told them about that?" Agent Calvin, who looked like a healthier Alec Baldwin only with less hair, ranted at her as soon as she showed up at the precinct meeting room. "I told you I would handle this. Do you know how this makes us look?"

"I'm more concerned about Carlos's safety than how it makes the agency look."

"Tell me something, Agent Ryan. Are you the one who encouraged Agent Olvera to come here? Is it because of you that Tory Vale came up with this conspiracy theory? First there was a leak at the ATF, and now there's a leak in our own agency."

"I never spoke with Tory Vale about the case. But it's not a conspiracy theory. Someone leaked information about the Sala case. Someone killed Pablo Ybarra. And if Carlos said he found evidence—"

"We don't know what Agent Olvera found."

"No, but—"

"You never answered my question. Are you the one behind Agent Olvera coming here?"

Her silence was all the answer he needed. "Goddamn it! Have you been working this case all along? I gave you a direct order to let it go. And now you tell our dirty secrets . . . This could end your career!" His face turned an angry red color that almost matched his burgundy tie.

"Someone shot Carlos. There has to be—"

"Carlos was probably shot because he was asking questions about your sister's case, which has no connection to the Sala case."

"Dillon Armand's name was in the Sala report and then in my sister's—"

"And we looked into that! We couldn't prove shit. Even if you're right and Armand's connected, airing our dirty laundry to the cops is wrong. And so is calling Eliot to sit guard."

"I don't know Agents Miles and Bara that well."

"So *I* could have looked into it! Now, look at the mess you've created." With that parting shot, Agent Calvin stormed out of the conference room.

Brie took a few seconds to mourn the probable loss of her career, one she'd been proud of. Then again, Calvin hadn't asked for her badge yet. Still, tears threatened to fall. She'd gotten ten steps into the hallway when she saw Detective Pierce standing inside the open bathroom door.

Had he been eavesdropping? *Probably.*

"Sorry," he said. So he'd definitely heard her conversation.

She refused to look at him. "Do you always butt into other people's business?"

"Do you always need to kick a dog when you're upset?"

She swallowed a knot of frustration. "Just do your job."

"I didn't purposely eavesdrop." His tone lost its edge. "I was in the bathroom and as I came out...well, Agent Calvin's voice carries. That said, you did the right thing. Trusting us."

She looked up. His bright green eyes were slightly bloodshot. His shirt wrinkled. His chest a mile wide. For one second, she wondered what it would feel like to lean against that solid torso. To feel his arms around her. To...she slammed the door on that thought. What the Hades was wrong with her?

"Prove it by finding out who did this to Carlos." She continued walking, wanting to leave him and the crazy temptation behind.

But wanting something didn't make it so. His heavy footsteps echoed with hers. "Olvera didn't check into the hotel until Wednesday evening."

She stopped. "So he went somewhere else first. To do what?"

"Could he have...someone on the side?"

"No. He just married Tory. And anyway Carlos's not like that."

Connor nodded. "When you talk to Tory again, ask him about Carlos's credit cards. Maybe he can see if he used them anywhere."

"I'll ask him. Call me if you get anything else." She met his eyes. "And sorry for reacting like I did."

"No problem."

She started to leave, but he caught up with her again. "Where are you going?"

"Back to the hospital and then to work." She kept moving.

He caught her arm, not a tight hold, but one that was almost tender. His touch sent a warm tingle traveling through her body, reminding her what it felt like to be a woman—not just an FBI agent.

She shifted her arm, and he released her.

He slipped his hand in his pocket and took a fraction of a second to respond, almost as if he'd felt the same spark she had. "What if you're wrong about your cover not being compromised?"

"I'm not."

"But Agent Calvin knows you are the reason Agent Olvera was here."

"He thinks I talked Carlos into looking into the case. He doesn't know I work at the club."

"You'd stake your life on it?" He sounded aggravated again.

"Yeah. I would."

\* \* \*

*Stubborn. Smug. Sexy.*

Damn! Connor hadn't been able to burn away the image of her in that lacy bra. Nor could he stop staring at her perky jean-covered butt power walking away from him. He released a hot breath. He again envisioned his shirt hanging midthigh with nothing beneath it. A shot of something sweet headed south.

Could this mean he was ready to get back out there? Hell, he had quite a few willing women and phone numbers. But he knew that not just anyone would do. Great. Now his libido was getting picky.

Rubbing the back of his neck, he started down the

hall to meet up with the three FBI agents. After what he'd overheard of Brie and Agent Calvin's conversation, his gut said this meeting could get intense. It also said he needed to keep his temper in check.

When he walked into the room, Mark and Juan hadn't arrived yet, and Special Agent Calvin stood speaking with his two underlings. All dressed in black suits and varying colored ties, the thought that hit him was...*birds of a feather flock together*. Only there was a distinct possibility that one of those birds was guilty of hiring a hit man to take out one of their own.

"Hello," he said. "I'm Detective Pierce." He held out his hand to the oldest man in the room.

It went unshaken. "I spoke with Detective Sutton," Agent Calvin said, as if Connor didn't make the cut. The muscles in his abdomen tightened. He already disliked the man for how he'd spoken to Brie, and this solidified his opinion.

"He'll be here shortly."

Just then both Mark and Juan walked in. Picking up on the tension, Mark's gaze met Connor's before focusing on Agent Calvin. "I'm Detective Sutton. This is Detective Acosta, and I see you've met Detective Pierce. Special Agent Calvin, I assume."

"Yes." Agent Calvin took Mark's hand. "This is Agent Bara and Agent Miles." The two other agents nodded a curt greeting. Agent Calvin continued, "Do we have any leads yet?"

"We've spoken to Agent Ryan and have some things we're looking into," Mark answered.

"Yes, she mentioned the idea of an internal leak, but it's highly unlikely. Mr. Vale tends to be an exaggerator.

The Sala case ended badly, but it doesn't point to one of our own—"

Connor, Juan, and Mark all shared a look of surprise that Agent Calvin would speak so openly about the leak. "Ms. Ryan thinks that Tory Vale's concerns have merit," Mark said.

"She's too close to the Sala case to be unbiased in her judgment. She's seeing something that's not there. First, she believed there was a leak in the ATF. We spent months looking into that. Now, she's pointing a finger at her own agency."

"Why would she make this up?" Connor asked.

Agent Calvin turned to Connor. "Her informant in the Sala case was killed. She blamed herself, and now she's looking for someone else to blame."

Connor knew all about blame. "So you don't think anything was off with the Sala case? Even the informant's death didn't make you suspicious?"

"Suspicious, yes. But we couldn't find proof. Agent Ryan couldn't let it go. She's a good agent, but she lets herself get too close. In fact, I believe that's why she took a leave of absence. I know her sister died, but she didn't even know her."

"Did you *really* look into the informant's death?" Connor knew even the APD was guilty of treating an informant's death as a statistic.

"Why are we concentrating on that?" Agent Miles broke in. "Do you have anything on Olvera's case besides this conspiracy theory?"

Mark, showing no signs of being annoyed, focused on the light-brown-haired agent. "Someone broke into Agent Olvera's hotel room and assaulted a maid in the process. Tossed the place, as if looking for something."

"You caught them?" Agent Calvin asked.

"No. However, we did get a video of him escaping. We issued a BOLO and are attempting to identify him."

"Did you find anything in the hotel room?" Agent Bara asked.

"Nothing," Mark answered. "But we're still going through everything."

"So you have nothing." Agent Miles's tone hit nerves Connor didn't like hit.

"It's more than we had." Mark's tone deepened.

"If you'll hand us what you've got, we can take over from here," Agent Calvin added.

"That's not going to happen," Connor spoke up.

Mark broke in. "It landed on our doorstep. I understand your stake in this and I think we should be able to work together. As soon as we—"

"You are accusing us of shooting one of our own," Agent Miles said.

Juan jumped in. "We aren't accusing—"

"Then insinuating!" Agent Miles glared at Juan.

Connor noticed that of the three, Miles was the one who protested the most.

"No," Juan added, sarcastically. "We think the person who broke into Olvera's room shot him. We're insinuating one of you hired him."

"This is absurd," Agent Bara said. "We worked with Agent Olvera."

"I understand this is difficult," Mark spoke calmly. "But the sooner you allow us to clear you in our investigation, the sooner we can focus elsewhere."

"What will you need?" Agent Calvin's expression darkened and his words sounded forced, but he appeared willing to concede.

"Access to your finances, phone records, and a copy of the Sala case. And we'll set up interviews with each of you."

"No!" Agent Miles snapped. "I refuse to let you snoop—"

"Let them look. We have nothing to hide," Agent Calvin spoke up.

Agent Miles stormed out of the room, and Agent Calvin stared after him. Miles protested a bit too much.

The senior agent turned to Mark. "Do what you have to do. Set up the interviews. I'll make sure everyone cooperates. But do it fast."

"Can I have a moment in private with you, sir?" Mark looked pointedly at Agent Bara.

Agent Calvin motioned to the door, and Agent Bara left.

Mark looked back at Calvin. "Why would you bring up the possibility of a leak in front of the very agents we'll be investigating?"

The man frowned. "They aren't stupid. When we showed up at the hospital, Agent Ryan had her own people standing guard who barred us from seeing Agent Olvera. The implications of that were pretty clear."

Mark nodded. "I see."

Agent Calvin continued, "Sergeant Brown said we could set up a temporary office in one of the conference rooms. I'll be in there. Meanwhile, I'll take a copy of Agent Olvera's file. After I go over it, we can talk about how to move forward." He left.

Connor waited until the footsteps faded. "What do you think? Is it one of them?"

"It could be. Or it could be random." Mark dropped

into a chair. "Or maybe Agent Olvera had other enemies. You have to admit the whole mole theory sounds... crazy."

"But how many of our cases aren't crazy?" Connor offered.

"I'll admit we don't know Brie Ryan that well," Juan said. "But I trust her more than those guys."

"I agree." Connor looked at the door. "And if she's right... then one of them is guilty."

"Which one?" Mark asked.

Connor tossed out his first thought. "My bet's on Special Agent Calvin."

"Seriously?" Mark asked. "I'm putting ten dollars on Agent Miles."

"That's my second bet." Connor rubbed his hand over his chin. "I know a hit dog always hollers, but Agent Calvin was really upset with Brie. It felt over-the-top."

"Brie? Just Brie?" Mark grinned. "You're with her for a few hours and suddenly you're on a first name basis?"

"Give it a break." Connor frowned.

"Well, I'm waiting to see a few more cards before putting in my bet." Juan pushed a chair under the conference table. "Agent Bara didn't appear too happy about this either." He paused. "Is Brie still here?"

Connor sat on the edge of the table. "She left. She's going to work. Which worries me. If one of those FBI agents is really behind this and they learn she's working at the club, they could rat her out."

Mark rested his elbows on his desk. "One other thing I think we need to worry about. I wasn't able to find Mr. Dunn, the owner of the Mustang. I went to both his home and his work, but no one was home and no one at the job knew where he is. His car has been returned to him, but if he still thinks Brie took it, he might still want his guy to teach her a lesson."

"Crap." Connor stood up. "Text me his information and I'll run him down." He took one step toward the door and turned around. "I really think we need to get someone to go to the strip club to keep an eye on Brie. It shouldn't be one of us. Her boss at the club might recognize us from the Noel case."

Mark stood up. "Yeah, but I don't think Brown will approve a separate detail on Agent Ryan."

"Then we call in a favor. How hard is it to get someone to hang out at a strip club?" Connor asked.

"Not that hard," came a voice from the door. Billy walked in. "What?" he asked, when all three of them looked at each other. "Why do you need someone at a strip club?"

* * *

Brie had lied. She didn't go straight to the hospital. She went to the bridge where Carlos had been found to see if the Willie Nelson look-alike had come back.

The tent was still there. He wasn't. She looked back where Carlos had been found. Had Tomas seen something? A witness to Carlos being pushed out of the car would help put that piece of dog crap behind bars. Hopefully, Willie wasn't drunk or high when it happened.

A cool October gust of wind tossed her hair. Looking up at the darkening sky, it felt like a storm was brewing. The air smelled like rain. Damp. And a little like dead leaves. In the distance, a couple of trees had started to turn gold. Normally, she loved fall, but recently someone had argued the season was nothing but death. The leaves, the grass, it was all dying.

But Carlos couldn't die with them. Pushing away the thought, she recalled how many dinners they'd shared. Movies they'd watched. Jumping from country to country in her younger years, she'd never really had a best friend. Not until she met Carlos. They swapped childhood horrors. His dad never accepting he was gay. Her dad leaving her for his other family.

Her gaze shifted to the dark red stain on the gravel. A stain she knew was Carlos's blood. "I'm gonna catch whoever did this."

She started for her car when she heard something—footsteps, a twig crack. Someone was out there. Breath held, she stared into the thick brush, her gaze shifting from tree to tree.

She pulled out her gun.

"FBI," she called. "Come out!" The wind seemed to carry her words away. "I said, come out! Now!"

Only the rattling of the dry leaves clinging to the trees echoed back.

She started toward the tree line. Only a few feet inside the thicket and it suddenly felt like the dead of night. It took a few seconds for her eyes to adjust and when they did, she saw what looked like a person running behind a tree.

She bolted after the shadowy figure.

# CHAPTER TEN

She lost the figure, but chased the sound of footfalls, dodging trees and jumping over brush. Then suddenly the only steps she heard were her own.

She stopped running. "Come out now!"

Raspy breathing sounds reached her ears. "Don't shoot me," a scratchy male voice said. "I wasn't doing anything wrong."

"Come out where I can see you!" she demanded.

A man rose up from the ground, holding his hands in the air. He had a mop of curly dark hair. His dirty clothes hung loose. He didn't look anything like Willie Nelson.

"Who are you? What are you doing here?" she asked.

"I didn't do anything wrong." His hands remained in the air.

"I asked who you are and what you were doing here." When he didn't speak, she snapped. "Answer me!"

He flinched. "Name's Milton Yates. I was looking for someone."

"Who?"

He hesitated before answering. "Tomas. That's his tent."

"He's not here," she said.

"I know that now."

"Do you know where he could be?"

He stared at her with suspicion. "You ain't gonna shoot me?"

"No." She lowered her gun.

He lowered his arms. "You gonna arrest me?"

"I just want to know where to find Tomas."

"I...don't know. He usually stays here. Sometimes he gets a meal at the shelter on Logan Street but he wasn't there today."

"When's the last time you saw him?"

"Two days ago."

"Were you here yesterday?"

"No. I stay under the bridge off of Main."

She believed him. "Fine. You can go."

She walked up and down the side of the road, hoping to find some evidence, proof. Disappointed and frustrated, she left and drove by the shelter, just in case Tomas was there. He wasn't. She drove by a couple of bridges where some of the homeless hung out. He wasn't there either.

At almost six, feeling as if she was floundering, she headed to the hospital. She longed for some good news and maybe a visit with Eliot. While the man wasn't her father by blood or marriage, he'd been more of one than the two men who'd worn that title.

The rich deep sound of his voice had comforted her through many childhood fears, and even adult ones. Eliot had taught her to be strong and independent, but he'd also been the rock she could always lean on.

She'd been ten when she'd found a framed photograph in Eliot's suitcase after one of their many moves. A family portrait of him with a woman and a girl. She learned the girl was her age—or would have been. Eliot's wife and child had been killed in a car accident a few years before her family had hired him. First, he'd lost his leg working for our country, then he'd lost his family. Life wasn't fair.

The news had devastated her. She'd grieved for what he'd lost but she also felt guilty because she knew if not for their deaths, she wouldn't have had him in her life. It had also explained why in the beginning he'd been standoffish, determined to keep his heart out of the job. Loving someone, when you'd lost so much, was hard. She knew that personally.

But eight-year-old Brie had needed someone desperately, and somehow she'd sensed he needed her, too. He'd caved. He'd cared. He became the source of comfort, hugs, and love to a little girl who felt abandoned by everyone else in her life.

Getting off the elevator, she barely made it up two steps when Eliot spotted her and popped up from his post outside the ICU doors. His first step came with the slight limp of a man wearing a prosthesis. She could remember how shocked she'd been when she'd first seen the artificial leg.

He took a few more steps, then waited for her to come to him. "What happened?"

"Nothing. I just wanted to check in."

"You don't need to check in. You need to rest."

"I have to go to work."

"At the Black Diamond?"

She waited for his disapproval. When she'd told him earlier that she'd been working at the strip club she could have heard an eyelash fall, he'd become so silent. She assured him she was just waitressing, but Eliot had some old-fashioned beliefs. Which explained why she hadn't lost her virginity until college. Try having a six-foot-four ex-Special Forces manny give the respect-her talk with your dates. She'd barely snagged a kiss.

Eliot's frown deepened. "They came after Carlos, they might—"

"I'm not walking away when I'm *this* close to catching my sister's killer." At her words, he gave her a look, but she defiantly glared back at him. "I am," she insisted.

"I know you blame yourself. First for your informant's death and now—"

"You can't stop me from this. Give it up."

"Fine." His voice crackled with frustration. "I'm coming. Sam can—"

"No." Eliot would come unglued if any guy dared to cross the line. And face it, most nights at least one guy put a hand where it didn't belong. She dealt with it. Quite well. No one who tried it once, tried it a second time.

She needed Eliot in her life, but she didn't need him to solve her problems. And he had a bad habit of wanting to do that.

"You promised to stop interfering in my adult decisions, remember?"

"Then make better decisions. If something happens—"

"It won't! Trust me." She looked around. "Where's Tory?"

"In with Carlos." The man continued to frown. "Did you see Agent Calvin?"

"Yeah," Brie answered.

"And?"

"He's pissed that I told the APD about the possible mole. And he's blaming me for Carlos being here." She noted Eliot's scowl. "Everyone seems unhappy with me these days."

"I'm just concerned. If someone from the FBI is protecting the Sala family, they're probably protecting Dillon Armand. And if they discover you're working—"

"If my cover gets blown, I'll quit."

Eliot sighed. "The APD knows all of this, right? Tell me they have your back."

"I don't need anyone."

Wanting a change in the conversation, she told Eliot about the guy with bruises that she let get away. "I should've shot him."

"You're not officially on the job. Shooting someone might have caused some problems."

Her gaze met his. "Yeah, you should know."

A half smile had his white teeth showing.

She put her hand on his chest. "You are so difficult, but I still love you."

"Which is exactly how I feel about you." His smile came wider. He tilted her chin up and looked into her eyes. "You look exhausted."

"I'm okay. Really."

Right then the doors to the ICU opened and visitors walked out. Tory was the last to appear. Everything about him—his gait, his posture, his downcast eyes—spoke of pain.

He must have felt her gaze because he looked up.

"Any change?" She held her breath.

"No." He teared up. "And test results still aren't back. What the hell takes so long?"

"Be patient," she offered through her own forbearing. She took his hand.

"I'm trying." He squeezed, as if her grasp was all the hope he had to hang on to.

Brie remembered what she needed to ask. "We found out that Carlos didn't check in to the hotel until Wednesday. Do you have any idea where he could have gone?"

"No, but he was already upset that he'd told me about the leak. He seldom talked about his work."

She nodded. "Do you have access to his credit cards? The police want to get a list of what cards he has and their numbers in case someone uses them. And could you check if he used any of his cards the last few days? It might tell us where he was."

"Yeah, I pay all our bills. Let me run to my car and get my laptop."

Ten minutes later, Tory had returned and emailed her the list of charges and Carlos's credit card information. He had eaten in Willowcreek, Texas, at a steak house. Was it just a rest stop or did he meet somebody?

With her phone out of battery, she used Tory's phone and sent a message to Connor telling him what they'd found.

After an hour, visitation opened again, so she and Tory went in to see Carlos. Feeling like crying, she slipped her hand into her partner's.

"You need to wake up, buddy." His thumb shifted against her wrist. Gasping, she looked back at Tory. "He moved."

"He did it earlier with me. The nurse said sometimes they have involuntary movements." But Tory still walked over to the bed and stared at Carlos's face.

The lump in her throat grew larger. Tory came and

hugged her, and she heard his breath shudder right along with hers.

A short time later, after more tight hugs and good-byes, she headed home. She needed to get ready for work and give Psycho at least a minute or two of TLC. She'd forgotten about the break-in until she saw her door ajar. It gave her a jolt. Her first thought was to worry if the cat was still locked in the bathroom, as Connor had said. Her second was to wonder if someone could be inside now.

Stopping on the doorstep, she listened. Despite hearing nothing, she still pulled out her Glock from the back of her jeans.

As she inched the door open, she saw the latch had been damaged, preventing the door from shutting. Moving inside with light footsteps, she heard a clattering sound come from down the hall. She stopped. Her hold on the gun tightened.

Then she heard the noise again followed by a meow. The sound had come from her bathroom. Probably just Psycho.

She still did a walk through her apartment to make sure no one was there. Then she grabbed a chair from her table and fit it under the doorknob of her broken door. At least that would make it difficult for someone to get inside. And almost impossible for Psycho to get out. Then she hurried to the bathroom.

Opening the door, she squatted down. "Kitty. Kitty." She'd only had the feline two months. The shelter had set up a temporary adoption center at a strip mall, and just passing time, she had ambled over. A big mistake. She hadn't planned on getting a pet until she saw Psycho. Abandoned and unwanted, he'd looked at her. Sentiments she knew all too well. Both from her father and later even from her mom. They'd warned her the kitten was leery of people. But since she was leery of people, too, she paid the adoption fee and brought him home.

The moment she let him out of the carrier, he'd absconded to her closet. So she'd simply fed him and left the litter box in there as well.

Finally, he'd started crawling into her bed at night. But anytime she moved, he'd dart back. After about a month, he decided he could trust her. She understood, she had trust issues herself. Two weeks ago, when she'd been on the sofa watching television, he'd actually curled up in her lap and purred as she stroked his fur. Brie had almost cried at his tentative trust.

Psycho jumped out of the bathtub and came to her, purring and rubbing against her legs.

"Hey. You okay?"

He lifted up on his hind legs to brush his face against her chin. She considered picking him up and cuddling him, but afraid that might be too much, she just let him rub against her.

She spotted the food and water and the litter box that Connor had left for him. And after the feline had scratched him pretty good, no less. She supposed that said something about the man. He could've just left, and let the cat run away.

He hadn't.

She changed the cat's water and gave him fresh food, then plugged in her phone. She listened to the voice mail from the apartment manager telling her about her apartment being broken in and called her back. Of course, the woman didn't pick up. Brie left a message suggesting they fix the door and saying it would be cheaper to fix it than to have to send a biotech removal crew to come clean up her bloody, murdered body.

Hanging up, she noticed the shoe prints on her comforter, so she stripped the bed and replaced the sheets. Realizing the time, she grabbed the notes she'd kept on the missing women who'd worked at the Black Diamond. She photographed the files and sent them to Detective Acosta. Then after securing her cat in her bedroom, she went to shower.

Her mind still on Acosta, she recalled the day she'd gone to their office and insisted he owed her lunch for the tip she'd given him about his case. In truth, she'd simply been hoping to make a few friends in the department, which she had. She remembered the butterfly feeling she'd gotten when she'd laid eyes on his partner Connor.

Kicking off her shoes, and tugging off her socks, she stepped out of her jeans. When she pulled off her shirt, she caught a whiff of a spicy male scent. Pulling the white fabric up, she buried her nose in it. It smelled . . . good. A little musky, with earthy tones. She recalled catching that scent earlier when he'd stood too close.

Or was it not close enough?

Realizing her thoughts were headed someplace naughty, she tossed the shirt on the counter, started the water, and sat down on the closed toilet lid, waiting for the water to get hot. Sitting there, her bare feet tapping on the cold tile floor, her gaze fell back to the shirt. Picking it up, she took another long deep sniff and let her mind go places it shouldn't.

Only when steam billowed out from the shower curtain did she put his shirt down and crawl into the shower. But she couldn't wash his scent from her mind.

# CHAPTER ELEVEN

Connor had checked both Dunn's office and his home address. The man wasn't at either one. Nor was he picking up his phone. Where the hell was he? Connor left a message telling him he needed to talk to him about his case.

When he hung up, he called Brie, but her phone went straight to voice mail. He left her a message telling her he hadn't gotten in touch with Dunn, so she should be on guard.

Walking back to his car, he realized all he'd eaten all day was a stale donut at the office. Crawling behind the wheel, he headed straight to the closest fast-food joint.

He'd just parked when his phone rang. The aroma of grilled burgers and greasy French fries penetrated his car. His stomach growled as he pulled his cell from his pocket. The anonymous number almost had him letting it go unanswered. Then thinking it might be Dunn, he picked up.

"Detective Pierce."

"You said to call if I saw her." It took a minute to realize it was Brie's landlord.

"Yes, but—"

"Well, I saw her car in the parking lot when I got back from the store, but I had to take another call as soon as I walked in. I'd just hung up when her neighbor phoned to say she'd spotted the same man sneaking into Ms. Colton's place again."

"What? Is Brie still there?"

"Who's Brie?"

"I meant Star." He checked the time. She said she had to be at work at eight. It was still a few minutes before. "Is her car still there?"

"I don't know."

"Do you have a security guard on the premises?"

"No."

"Search for her car right now! If it's there, call 911. I'm on my way."

Connor made the ten-minute drive in six. He was parking when the landlord called to say Brie's car wasn't there. His gut said she'd left before the perp showed up, but what if he'd taken her car, too? He hauled ass to her building. In the glow of a porch light stood the landlord and the neighbor he'd met earlier.

"She's not there," the landlord said. "I checked to be sure she wasn't lying in there hurt. And Mrs. Edwards"— she pointed to the neighbor—"saw the guy leave."

The knot of panic in his belly loosened, and he focused on the neighbor. "Are you sure it was the same guy?"

"Yeah." She appeared nervous and he knew why.

"I thought you said you didn't see the guy who broke in earlier."

She flinched. "I may have seen him briefly. Look, I don't like getting mixed up in stuff."

Connor figured what she really didn't like was cops. "What did he look like and how long was he here?"

"He wasn't here three minutes. And he had red hair. A big guy."

Connor heard a meow. He looked over at Brie's door and saw her cat half-in and half-out the door.

"No." Knowing how sharp the fellow's claws were, he shooed the cat back inside with his foot, then tried to shut the door. It wouldn't shut. The neighbor took that opportunity to run back into her place.

"Do I need to call the police again?" the landlord asked.

"No. But you need to fix her door."

She walked away. Connor saw the cat peer out of the opening again. Great. Now he had to put Psycho back in the bathroom and probably get clawed again.

Careful not to let the cat out, he eased inside. The feline darted under the sofa, staring at him with bright green eyes. He shut the door as far as he could. Right beside the door was a chair. Brie must've used it to keep the door closed.

Turning around, he refocused on the cat. "I'm not the enemy. It's the other guy you should've clawed up." The two of them held a staring contest. "I don't suppose you'd just head on back to the bathroom, would you?"

The cat meowed.

"I didn't think so." He squatted down. "Come here, kitty." Psycho didn't budge. When he tried to reach in, the cat hissed.

Standing up to find a towel to grab the cat, he walked down the hall and stuck his head in the bathroom door.

The smell—her smell—hung thick in the still damp room. The scent, a little like fruity shampoo, filled his senses. Immediately, his mind created a vision of her standing in the shower with droplets of water slipping down soft, touchable, bare skin.

He ran a hand over his face and blew out a mouthful of air. Then he saw his shirt on the countertop. The image of her in the sexy lace bra filled his head.

"Damn," he muttered when a certain southern part hardened.

He grabbed the light blue towel from the rack. It was damp. Her smell wafted up from the thick cotton.

When had a women's scent ever made him hard? Maybe when he hadn't indulged in sex for two months.

Frowning, he stepped out of the bathroom and his gaze shifted to the bedroom. Moving in, his eyes went to the bed, which had new sheets. Then he saw that the dresser drawer was open. Several pairs of panties were strewn on the beige carpet.

Her place had been neat when he'd been here before, so the asswipe who'd broken in must've gone through her things. The need to protect Brie rose up in his chest.

He looked around, wondering if the guy would come back. Would he be waiting for her when she got home?

He pulled out his phone to see if Brie had texted him back. No response, so he sent her another one. He waited for the three dots to appear.

Nothing.

His stomach grumbled. If he could grab the cat and put it back in the bathroom, he could do something about his empty stomach.

He turned to go back to Psycho when his phone rang. Thinking it was Brie, he answered it without checking the number.

"Hello?"

"Detective Pierce?" the deep voice said.

Was this Dunn? "Yes."

"This is Eliot Franklyn."

A vision of the tall, dark, ex-Special-Forces guy filled his mind. "Yes?"

"Brie insisted on going to work, and that I not show up there. I'm concerned. If you're a half-decent cop, you should be concerned as well. Are you doing anything to make sure she's protected?"

"You don't have to worry. We've got someone there."

"Good." The line went silent. He pulled his phone down and stared at it. No "thank you." No "goodbye." Giving thanks wasn't his favorite thing to do either, but his mother had taught him some manners.

He went to shove his phone back into his pocket when the dang thing rang again. This time he checked to see who was calling: Mark.

"Hey," he answered.

"I thought I'd let you know we got someone on this Armand guy. They're headed out to see if he's at his hotel now."

"Good," Connor said. "The asswipe who broke into Brie's place earlier came back. The manager hasn't gotten her door fixed, so he just walked in."

"Shit. Did you catch him?"

"No. He was gone before I got here. I didn't let the landlord call it in either. But I think we might need to have a little chat with the bastard. His interest in Brie might not just be justice for his boss. Looks like he got into her underwear drawer."

"Did Brie know his name?"

"No," Connor said. "And like you, I had no luck finding Dunn. I've left messages, but he hasn't called me back."

"Okay, tomorrow we'll come up with a plan."

"What if he comes back tonight?"

"Warn Brie about it. She should be able to hold her own for one night."

Connor raked a hand over his face. He didn't like that answer.

"Was Brie sure this guy is connected to Dunn?" Mark asked. "I mean, if she's mistaken—"

"She claimed she was sure. But I'll confirm it again."

"Another thing. Juan called me. He got the files from Brie of the other girls who went missing. Since some had also worked the streets, he sent the pictures to the vice unit. One of the cops recognized one. He's pretty sure he arrested her several years back for prostitution. But he said the name Brie had for her didn't ring a bell. He's going to look at old files in the next few days and let Juan know what he finds."

"Good."

"Yeah," Mark said, "but it also leads me to believe that these missing women might not be missing. Just living under fake identities. Not victims of human trafficking. I'm betting management helped them avoid the law by getting fake paperwork."

Connor frowned. "Yeah."

"Oh, I had one of the uniforms walk the route that Brie said the perp probably took when he ran, looking for cameras. He's found two. But most of the businesses were closed, so Billy's going tomorrow. It's a long shot, but who knows."

"Did Agent Calvin get back to you?" Connor asked.

"Yes. He thinks the shooting is related to Brie's sister, not one of their own being behind it. They decided to do their own investigation, beginning with combing through Alma Ronan's file, as if our officers missed something. I asked what they were looking for but he wouldn't say. Of course, they expect us to share anything we learn with them."

"Right." Connor glanced again at Brie's shower, thinking about her in it. "Did we find anything in Olvera's hotel room that helped?"

"No," Mark answered. "Oh, and despite tomorrow being Saturday, Juan and I agreed all three of us should work the case. I'm assuming you're okay with that."

"Yeah."

"Okay. I should go break the news to Annie that I'll be working tomorrow."

No sooner had he pocketed his phone, when Connor heard someone call out, "Hello?" A female someone. Then came a clatter.

He headed to the living room and got there just in time to see the landlord pick up the chair she'd dislodged from the door, and Brie's cat dash outside.

"Shit!"

"Oops," she muttered.

Connor tore past her and couldn't help thinking this gave whole new meaning to "chasing tail."

\* \* \*

"Hello there, Ms. Colton." The tall black bouncer stationed at the door stepped aside for her.

"How you doing tonight, Danny?" she asked. She'd

liked the man the first time she met him. Not because he never hit on her or any of the other girls, but because he reminded her of Eliot. Kind, a little protective, and she'd never heard him curse.

"Fine as frog's hair," he said.

She grinned and walked into the club, which always smelled like beer, hormones, and smoke. While there were NO SMOKING signs posted, the boss never called anyone on it, unless there was a complaint. And it couldn't come from an employee. She'd tried.

As she entered the main section of the club, she remembered to be on the lookout for FBI. She searched for any black suits and her heart jolted when she spotted one. She moved to a partially hidden corner and waited for her eyes to adjust to the obscure club lighting. Pulse fluttering at the base of her neck, she finally got a good look at the man. Not an FBI agent, just a businessman with bad taste in suits.

"Star." Mr. Grimes, a tight frown on his chubby face, waved her over. As she approached the bar, he tossed a cleaning rag behind the counter and walked around.

"My office," he bit out and started toward the back.

Crap. She followed. This had to be about the Mustang.

He barreled through his office door.

"Is something wrong?" she asked, in a calm, oh-so-innocent voice.

"I'd say!" He moved behind his desk, dropping into a chair that screamed for mercy.

He flattened his palms on the desk. "Mr. Dunn believes you took his Mustang."

"Mr. Dunn?" she asked, playing naive.

"Charles Dunn. He's a regular."

"He thinks I took his car?" Her Alabama accent thickened, and she dropped down in the chair. "Why would he think that?"

"Because you waited on him. Because his keys were on his table. Because you left and his car disappeared, but your car was here!"

"A friend picked me up and we went out. I came back and got my car later. I didn't...Wait. Isn't his car like expensive?"

"More than someone like you could afford."

She had to bite her tongue. Little did the idiot know that she'd inherited more money from her stepfather than he'd ever see in his lifetime. "If I stole his car why would I come to work today?"

He paused. "I don't know. You tell me."

"I am telling you. I wouldn't be here. I'd either be halfway across Texas in his schmancy car, or I'd be on a bus with a bundle of cash in my pocket."

"His car was found."

"So they caught the person who took it?"

"No. They found his car. He still thinks you—"

"Just because I waited on him? That's jumping to conclusions, isn't it? He probably dropped his keys on the floor and some customer grabbed them."

"How would they have known what car was his?" Okay, her boss's IQ was showing, not that there was a lot to show.

"They probably pushed the button on the key fob and the car lights came on. But hey, if he thinks I did this, I'll call the police and tell them where I was. They can get witnesses. I'll do that right now." She reached for his desk phone.

He slammed his hand on top of the phone and dragged it toward him. "No. He doesn't want..."

"Want what?" she asked. "I'll work with the police to clear my name. Let me call them."

He seemed to consider what she had said. She held her breath. Losing this job might mean losing Armand, and that wasn't an option.

"Charles doesn't want his...the cops to know that the car was taken from here."

"Well, how else am I going to convince him I didn't take it?"

Mr. Grimes studied her—hard. She could almost see his mind turning—slowly. "I'll talk to him. It does seem unlikely that you'd have come back to work if you were guilty."

"Good." If she hadn't thought the pencil sitting on his desk was sharper than the man sitting behind it, she might have given herself credit for talking her way out of this jam.

"So get to work," he mouthed off. "I don't pay you to do nothing."

She headed for the door.

"One more thing," he said.

She turned. "Yeah."

"A Mr. Armand will be in later. He sat in Candy's section last night. Tall, dark hair, wears expensive suits, has an accent, tips well. He's an investor in the club. He was asking about you."

"Me?" In the beginning she'd worried she might look a little too much like her sister, but then only a few people had said she reminded them of someone. Perhaps Armand paid closer attention to detail. "Why would he ask about me?"

"He likes blondes. So if he sits in your section, make sure he's...well taken care of. Make him happy." Grimes's tone gave her super creepy vibes. Then she remembered delivering some of Candy's drinks last night when the waitress had mysteriously disappeared for about fifteen minutes. Had Candy been told to make Armand happy? Had she been pressured into having sex with him?

She forced herself to smile when what she really wanted to do was go for her boss's double-chinned throat.

A lump of disgust rose in her chest. "You bet." She walked out.

Fury pumped through her veins as she made her way to her locker to store her purse. Little did Mr. Grimes know, Brie would make sure Armand got screwed—just not in the way her boss seemed to be insinuating.

* * *

Ten minutes after clocking in, Brie suddenly felt the hair on the back of her neck prickle as she stood at the bar to collect her first order of drinks. Turning around, she scanned the club. Was it one of her fellow FBI agents? Armand? Or maybe Eliot?

She didn't see any of them.

"Hey." Candy came up and set her tray beside Brie's. She was one of the few waitresses who wasn't trying to move up to dancer, and while Brie had seen her buy some weed, she didn't think Candy did any hard drugs. Her light green eyes met Brie's. "I thought you were getting fired. Mr. Dunn was saying you'd taken his car last night."

"Yeah, he's not very smart."

Candy reached for a few drink napkins and Brie

noticed bruises on both of the waitress's forearms, as if someone had held her down. Bruises weren't uncommon around here, but she'd never noticed them on Candy. An ugly thought hit. Had Armand caused them last night? The earlier fury with her boss and with Armand, came back threefold.

"What happened?" Brie motioned to her coworker's arm.

"Nothing." Candy looked away, but not before Brie noticed a flash of shame in her eyes.

"If someone did that to you, you should report it."

Candy glanced up. "And get fired. As my mom says, 'I get what I deserve for working here.'"

Brie considered her next words carefully. "I'm trying to figure out what kind of a mother would say that to her daughter. The only thing I can come up with is a piss-poor one. It's not true. Seriously, you shouldn't—"

"Shh," Candy said as Mr. Grimes walked up.

Their boss moved behind the bar, then stared at her and Candy. "Go wipe a table down or flirt with the customers instead of standing around yakking."

Candy disappeared. Brie stayed and clenched her fists down at her sides. Grimes moved in close and put his face in front of hers to intimidate her. She didn't budge. "I'm waiting on a drink order."

"Here you go." Brad, the bartender, moved around Grimes and dropped two Jack and Cokes on her tray with a wink. She took off. After delivering the drinks, she started cleaning off a table and felt the hair on the back of her neck start dancing—again.

This time she was sure of it. Someone had her in their crosshairs.

Brie glanced around again, this time catching sight of a guy sitting toward the back of Candy's section, wearing a baseball cap pulled down over his face. He was big and blond.

Connor?

# CHAPTER TWELVE

She took two steps forward, before realizing he didn't have Connor's broad shoulders. But she'd seen him before. Moving to the bar, she picked up a cleaning rag, then headed to the dirty table beside Mr. Ballcap.

Leaning down to give the table a swipe, she glimpsed his face.

*Mother cracker!* It was Officer Johnston. The cop who'd pulled her over in the Mustang.

As if sensing she was onto him, his gaze lifted and he smiled—all smug-like.

Looking to see where Mr. Grimes was, she gave the table another towel swipe and said low enough so only he could hear, "Have you spoken with Connor?"

"Yes." He turned his glass in his hands.

"Why are you here?"

"Enjoying the show," he said.

"Then why are you staring at me?"

"You look like a redhead I met recently."

Her gut knotted. "Look, I'm—"

He held up a hand. "I'm not here to cause a problem."

"Then why are you here?" When he didn't answer, she took a guess. "Connor sent you?"

His silence confirmed it.

"I don't need a babysitter," she muttered. "Someone might recognize you."

"A cop can't come in here?"

She supposed she couldn't argue with that—several cops did—but she didn't like the fact that Connor thought she couldn't handle herself.

Without another word, she headed back to her section.

He continued to watch her as she worked. She continued to try and ignore him and hoped no one else noticed.

While she was cleaning another table, Candy rushed over. "Can you take over my section and tell Grimes I had to go? I'm sick to my stomach. If I don't leave, I'll puke on the customers. Here's everyone's tickets." She handed Brie a stack of checks. "Table five has two beers coming." She turned away quickly.

"Wait," Brie said. "Should you drive yourself?"

"I'll be fine." Candy looked back at the bar, and Brie noticed a man standing there: Armand. And he was watching them. Brie grabbed a napkin and a pen, and wrote down her number. "Here. Call me if you need to talk. You shouldn't let people treat you like that."

Candy took the napkin, stuffed it in her apron, and with tears in her eyes, headed for the door.

Brie's stomach knotted with a sense of injustice. She wanted to confront Armand. Wanted to hurt him. But more than that, she wanted to put him behind bars, to stop him from ever violently touching another woman again. To do that she needed to be patient.

Ten minutes later, Grimes stopped beside her, holding a tray and a cleaning rag. "Where's Candy?"

"She got sick. Nauseous. I told her to leave and I'd cover for her."

"Since when do you have the authority to do that?" he barked.

"Since I saw her almost puke on a customer. I think that's considered bad business and a health code violation."

"Next time, have her come to me."

"Right."

She'd just dropped off another round of drinks to a rowdy group of car salesmen when she saw Armand sit down at her table. Stilling her heart—and her hatred—she set her plan in motion. Get him a drink. Get his fingerprints. Get his ass arrested.

"Beer or whiskey?"

His gaze lingered on the dance floor as Darlene wrapped her leg around the pole. Then he looked over at her. His eyes widened. "You remind me of someone."

Her heart did a tumble. "I get that a lot. What are you drinking?"

"Scotch and water." His accent was thick, but his words clear.

"Got it."

He grabbed her arm, and she caught her breath. His touch sent a wave of nausea to her stomach.

"Where are you from?" he asked.

"Alabama."

"And your name?"

"Star Colton." She fought to keep the wrath from her

tone. Squaring her shoulders, she turned her wrist and he released her.

"You know, sometimes all you Americans look alike."

"Yeah, I've heard that. I'll get you that drink."

Her heart thundered in her chest as she moved away from the table, away from the man who she'd bet had murdered her sister. Her hands shook as she punched in the drink order. The photograph of her sister's bruised and bloody body cuffed to the bed filled her head.

As soon as Brad handed her the glass, she grabbed several drink napkins to wipe away any other prints.

"Dirty?" he asked.

"Just a smudge. I got it."

Her gut clenched as she moved toward Armand, who now slouched in a chair, watching the show. She dropped a drink napkin on the table and then used another one to set the glass down.

"Why aren't you on the stage?" He put his hand on her hip. His touch sent a shot of pain right to the center of her chest.

"I can't dance," she said.

"But if you look half as good as I am imagining you do, then the guys won't care how well you dance. I have some pull with the boss. I could speak to him. Think of how much more money you could make."

"I'm good." Brie ached to grab his hand and break a few of his fingers. Instead, she backed away. "Sorry, too busy to chat."

She watched Armand, and the second he finished his drink, she moved back in. "Another one?"

"Yes. How about you take a little break? We'll go in the back and talk."

"Too busy." She took off, but instead of heading to the kitchen to drop off the dirty glass, she headed to the locker room in the back. Right before she pushed through the door, she looked over her shoulder and saw her boss still helping out at the bar. Her gaze shifted to Armand, who was back to watching the dancer.

Feeling all was clear, she nudged open the door and walked straight to her locker. She pulled out the plastic bag she'd brought with her, put the glass in, closed the top, and put it safely in her purse.

"I got you," she muttered, then pulled her phone out to send Connor a quick message to let him know she had Armand's prints. When she did, she saw her phone was dead. She'd forgotten to plug it back in after sending the file images to Acosta.

Shutting her locker, the clank of metal echoed against the sound of the music playing in the club. Then she heard a voice down the hall.

Crap! Instinct had her pressing her hand on the locker, as if her touch could soften the sound. Then, thinking fast, she reopened the locker and grabbed a tampon out of her purse. Tucking it in her pocket, she closed the door again and headed back down the hall, prepared to run into Grimes.

As she cut the corner, there was no Grimes, but his office door was ajar. Then she heard a voice.

A voice with an accent.

Had Armand followed her? Did he suspect she'd gotten his prints?

Her breath caught, but she assured herself that if he was onto her, he would've confronted her. Easing to the office door, she leaned in to hear the conversation.

"How many do you have?" His words were low, but clear. "That's not enough. I'll get two or three more. Just find a place and wait."

*Two or three more of what?* She eased closer.

"No?" he said. "*Escúchame tu pendeho!*" He slipped into Spanish, which Brie spoke fluently. "Remember who I am!" Pause. "Good." Another pause. "How many are blond?"

She got a sinking feeling in her stomach.

Right then the door leading into the main club swung open. She'd managed to step away from the office door, but she was still close. Too close.

"What are you doing?" Grimes asked.

A very suspicious Armand walked out.

Brie pulled the tampon from her pocket. "Female emergency."

Armand's expression didn't betray if he believed her or not. She started moving, hoping no one grabbed her.

When she pushed through the door, she practically ran right into Officer Johnston.

"Bathrooms back here?" he asked, clearly covering.

"No." She pointed to the other side of the room.

* * *

Exhausted after her shift, Brie got out of her car and headed to her apartment. Her footsteps echoed in the darkness.

Officer Johnston had given her a heads-up that Connor was waiting for her at home, saying the perp who'd broken in earlier had returned.

During her short break at work, she'd borrowed a

charger from one of the other waitresses and checked her messages. She'd had several from Connor, about the break-in, about her scattered panties, about him being at her apartment, and one saying they had a tail on Armand. She also had one from Eliot saying Carlos was the same. Sam was coming to relieve Eliot at midnight.

When she was a few feet from her door, she saw it was actually closed. Had it been fixed? Had Connor left?

She hoped not. She wanted to talk to him about Armand and the conversation she'd overheard, tell him she had the man's prints. And maybe deep down, she even wanted to be reminded that she wasn't doing this all alone.

She turned the knob—it wasn't locked—and pushed the door open. Only the lamp was on, but she could see Connor sitting on her sofa, a piece of pizza held up to his lips.

"Did you get my messages that I was here?" His voice was deep, and while he appeared wide awake, his voice had a sleepy quality to it that reminded her of pillow talk.

"Yeah." Her next intake of air smelled like him, warm and manly, like his shirt. A thrill ran through her body and settled low in her abdomen.

Then the smell of pizza hit. Yeasty, saucy, with a hint of pepperoni. Her stomach growled. When she closed the door, she noticed the old-fashioned slide lock that was attached.

He must have seen where her gaze went. "I got your door to shut, but the lock isn't working. So I put that one on until they can replace it."

"You didn't have to do that."

"I know."

She set her purse on the coffee table and pulled out the plastic bag. "I got his prints."

"Great. No signs of any of your FBI buddies?"

"No."

He nodded and took another bite of pizza. "Want a slice?"

"Thanks. I'm starving." Setting the plastic bag on the side table, she helped herself to a slice.

"I overheard Armand talking on the phone." She told him what she'd heard. Detail by detail.

"At least we have someone following him."

"Where did he go after the club?"

"I was told he went for a drink somewhere else and then drove back to his hotel. Alone."

"Blast it." Glancing down, she sank her teeth into the slice. When she looked back up, her eyes widened. "Crap. What happened?" she spoke around the lump of zesty dough in her mouth as she stared at his bloody T-shirt.

He looked down and put his finger through one of the holes in his shirt. "What can I say? Your cat hasn't warmed up to me yet."

"What?" Then she noticed the scratches on his arms and the side of his neck. As if that wasn't enough, she also noted the knees of his khakis were almost black.

"How...Why would he...?"

"I got here right after the man broke in. Your cat was poking his head out of the door. I came in to put him back in the bathroom, but before I could do that, your landlord came in and Psycho ran out."

"He's gone?" Her chest tightened at the thought of her feline afraid, cold, and hungry.

"No, I found him. Eventually. At least I hope it's him.

If not, you have a cat in your bathroom who looks like your other cat, and who has just as bad of a disposition." He picked up a napkin and wiped his mouth. "It took me three and a half hours, walking around the apartment complex, calling for him. Someone heard me and said they'd spotted a cat in the parking lot. I had to climb under a few cars. One was leaking oil." He reached up and touched the top of his head.

"When I finally grabbed him, he panicked and"—he glanced down at his bloody T-shirt—"this happened."

"I'm sorry."

"Not your fault."

"It's not his either. Because of his past, he's really antisocial."

He almost smiled. "Wow, I'd've never guessed."

"Have you cleaned the scratches?"

"No. I was starving, so I ran out for a pizza and picked up the lock."

She dropped her slice back into the box. "Let me get something to clean them."

Moving down the hall, she opened the bathroom door and knelt down. "Kitty."

She heard a meow and saw the shower curtain shift, but he didn't come out. Moving in slowly, she peered behind the curtain.

Crouched and wide-eyed, he backed up. "It's okay. I know you were scared." She lowered her voice. "And that big guy scared you. Actually, he kind of scares me, too." Though not completely in a bad way. She held her hand out. "Come here, baby. I'm sorry."

The feline slowly eased forward and let her brush her hand over his head. "That's good." She gave him a few more seconds of TLC and then she moved the cat and the litter box, along with his food and water, to the bedroom. Before heading back to Connor, she grabbed a clean washcloth, dampened it, and found some alcohol.

"Please tell me it's your cat," Connor said.

"It is." She turned the overhead light on and dropped down on the sofa beside him. Her leg brushed up against his and she shifted over. An odd thought hit. She'd never had someone sit here with her before. "Pull your T-shirt off."

"You don't have to do this," he offered.

"You didn't have to find my cat. But I'm grateful you did."

Nodding, he popped the last bite of pizza between his lips, sat up, and lifted his shirt off. Brie's mouth went dry when she saw all the warm, bare skin. How long had it been since she'd been this close to an almost-naked man?

If her body's reaction was any indication, it'd been too long. She did the math in her head and realized it had been well over a year. She and the last guy had dated for about two months when it had just fizzled out. Not that there had been that much fizz to start.

She'd been lonely and let it happen. Then hadn't known how to end it.

Connor's spicy scent filled her senses again. And a sweet buzz—with tons of fizz—thickened her breathing and her blood.

Determined to ignore the craving, she leaned in. His chest had four scratches. The one on the left side was the deepest. She touched the damp cloth to the bloody scratch. "He's not a bad cat."

He chuckled. "No, he's a real sweetheart."

She looked up into his smiling eyes and offered him one in return. Their gazes held. "When I got him, the shelter told me they thought he'd been abused."

She continued dabbing his scratch with the damp cloth. "It took him a month before he learned to trust me. Now, he sleeps beside me at night." She shifted to the scratch near Connor's navel, the back of her fingers accidentally brushing across his tight abs.

He drew in a quick slow breath. "He's a lucky cat...to have found you." His words came out low.

"Yeah."

"You're a Good Samaritan all the way around."

"Because I got a rescue cat?"

"And you volunteer at the homeless shelter."

She moved to the scratch over his ribs. "Right."

"How did you get Betty antibiotics?"

She looked up. "There's a free clinic a lot of the women who work at the Black Diamond use. I gave a ride to another waitress who needed stitches after she got hit by her boyfriend. While there, they asked me what I needed, and because I know they seldom do any tests, I described Betty's symptoms. They gave me a prescription."

"See? A Good Samaritan."

"You make that sound like a bad thing." She leaned across him to clean the scratch on his neck. His breath caused a soft tickle on her cheek.

When she cut her eyes to him, he stared at her mouth. Without wanting to, her gaze shifted to his lips.

She pulled back. "Show me your arm." He lifted it up and she ran the cloth over the red line. "Is that all of them?"

"Yeah."

She reached over and grabbed the alcohol and poured some on the cloth. The smell reached her nose. "It's probably going to sting."

"I think I can handle it."

She dabbed the worst of the scratches first. He sucked in air.

Recalling Eliot pouring alcohol on her scraped knees, she leaned down and blew softly on the wound.

"Brie, I think . . ."

She saw the muscles in his abs clench, and only then did she realize how close her head was to the growing bulge in his pants.

# CHAPTER THIRTEEN

She shot up. His green eyes appeared brighter and she knew her face did as well. "I didn't mean...I'm exhausted, I wasn't..." Her embarrassment quickly turned to humor.

She covered her mouth to hold the chuckle in, but failed. "Sorry." Another laugh spilled out.

Suddenly, she wasn't the only one laughing. When they finally stopped, their gazes locked. Humor and then heat danced in his green eyes. He smiled and it reached deep inside her and touched something. She missed this. Being close to someone. Feeling drawn to someone. Laughing with someone.

Not being alone on a sofa.

She handed him the washcloth. "Maybe you should do it."

Disappointment filled his expression. "Yeah." He swiped his scratches then snatched his shirt off the coffee table and slipped it on.

Her mind said he was about to leave. He'd stand up. Pick up his gun. Walk out the door. He'd take that fizzy feeling and be gone. That's what needed to happen.

But she'd be alone again on a piece of furniture meant for two.

"You want something to drink?" *Oh, crap.* She shot up from the couch, questioning her sanity.

He glanced at her. Confused. And damn if he wasn't the only one. She wanted him to stay. She wanted him to go. She wanted...?

"Something to drink would be nice." He leaned back against the cushions. The white T-shirt clung to his chest and drew her attention to his flat stomach.

She went to the kitchen and stuck her head in the fridge. Her face felt hot with the cool air blowing on her.

Why hadn't she let him leave? It was late. He looked exhausted. She was exhausted. This was dangerous. What was she doing?

Until this second, she hadn't realized how empty her life had been. Oh, she'd filled her days working on her sister's case, volunteering a few hours at the shelter. Most of her nights were spent at the Black Diamond. But sometimes being around people didn't make you less lonely.

She stared at the almost empty fridge. "I have one beer we could share," she called out. And that's all they'd share. A little company to chase off the loneliness.

"Okay."

Grabbing the beer and twisting the top, she downed a sip then returned to the living room.

He looked up at her. She looked down at him.

She held out the beer, cold against her palm. He took it. When their hands touched, a spark of something sweet traveled up her arm then slow-walked through the rest of her body. Pressing the bottle to his lips, his eyes stayed locked on hers as he drank. Then he reached into the pizza box and grabbed another slice.

"Sit down and eat," he said.

She lowered herself onto the sofa, leaving a good foot between them. Grabbing her already sampled pizza, she held it to her mouth. "How did you find out the guy broke in?"

"Your neighbor saw him. Are you sure this is connected to Dunn?"

"Positive. I told you I recognized him."

He held up his hand. "Just checking. Tomorrow, I'll find Dunn, even if I have to chase him to hell and back. I'll tell him about the high-end car theft ring in Houston. But...after seeing this perp getting into your...panty drawer, I think that guy might be after more than revenge about the Mustang. We need to do something about him."

"No. If he comes back, I'll deal with him. Speaking of which, you didn't have to send Officer Johnston. I'm capable—"

"I know you're capable. But it's called being careful. It's backup."

"I'm betting if I were a guy, you wouldn't feel the need—"

"I'd still have sent backup." He licked a dab of sauce off his lips.

"How mad was Officer Johnston when you told him you were letting me go?"

"Pissed, but when we explained about your sister, he got it."

Connor took another sip of the beer and his gaze shifted around. "I was looking at your bookshelf. You have several books in Spanish."

"Yeah."

"You can read Spanish?"

"Yeah. Eliot thought I should learn the language in every place we lived."

"How many languages do you speak?"

"Four besides English. Spanish, Mandarin Chinese, Urdu, and Russian."

His eyes rounded. "You're like a genius."

"No. Eliot's just a good teacher."

He continued to stare. "Is your mom still alive?"

"Yeah. She lives in California."

"You close?"

His question didn't completely dart into the no-trespassing zone, so she answered. "We talk every few months. Birthdays and such. I saw her last year at Christmas."

"You're closer to Eliot?" He handed her the beer and picked up another slice of pizza.

She sipped from the bottle. "He raised me."

"And your mom didn't?"

She nipped at her lip. "Her writing career took off. Her first book hit the *New York Times*. She was consumed by it. Eliot just stepped in."

"That sucks."

"It wasn't a big deal." *It wasn't like she abandoned me like my father did.* "She had a demanding career. It would've been the same if she'd been a doctor. After her first book sold, the publisher wanted the next one right away. Strike while the iron's hot."

Her words came out nonchalant, emotionless. While she didn't *really* blame her mom, she knew their distant relationship was a by-product of her career. Brie had always known her place in her mom's life. And it wasn't first.

"What does she write?" he asked.

"Fantasy novels under a pen name, J. C. Marks."

His eyes widened. "That's your mom? I've read a few. You are full of surprises, aren't you?"

"Oh, yeah."

The astonishment in his eyes vanished. "Sorry." The word came out somehow heavier, as if he sensed everything she wasn't saying.

"It's not a big deal." She stared at the pizza and all of a sudden this, whatever "this" was, felt twice as dangerous as before. This wasn't just about a guy on the sofa, this was getting to know that guy. But she didn't want to stop. "Are your parents still alive?"

"No. Well...my dad left when I was eleven." He stared at the pizza he held. "So I don't know if he's dead or alive."

He didn't say, *and I don't care to know*, but she heard it in his tone, saw it in his eyes. Or maybe it was her experience of being abandoned by her own father that had her understanding exactly how he felt.

He continued, "Mom passed away six years ago. Suddenly. A brain aneurysm. While at church, I might add. She was only fifty-four."

"Sorry. Were you close?"

"Mostly. I saw her twice a week. Mowed her lawn, changed lightbulbs, took out the garbage for her. She was a good mom. A good person."

"But?" She was certain she heard a *but*.

He looked like he was about to deny it, then instead said, "You can't compete with God."

"Huh?"

"When my dad left, she found religion. The harder she pushed me to follow that path, the harder I pushed back. Her big dream was for me to become a preacher, marry a God-fearing woman, and give her enough grandkids to fill a whole church pew."

"She had to be proud of you being a cop."

He glanced away. "Not as proud as she'd've been if I'd made a living standing at the pulpit." He turned the bottle in his hands, and his expression said he questioned if he should have kept his mouth shut. She understood that, too. The past could be emotionally cumbersome.

"So you never married?" The question slipped out before she considered the wisdom of asking. Not because she didn't want to know—she longed to unfold the layers of Connor Pierce, discover not only who he was, but why—yet her own marital past was off-limits. Who wanted anyone to know that you'd been completely scammed by someone you loved? That everything she believed about her ex had been a lie. Not that she hadn't made him regret those lies. He and his father got thirty years for it.

"Yeah. I married," he said. "It didn't work out." He held up the beer. "You?"

"Ditto."

"Really? You were married?" Surprise sounded in his voice. "I just assumed..."

What had he assumed? Part of her wanted to know—a part didn't. Needing a conversation U-turn, she said, "You never told me how things went with Agent Calvin."

He studied her, as if he'd seen her no trespassing sign.

"As good as could be expected. He doesn't think there's a mole."

"And I disagree." She glanced away. "What do you and your partners think?" When he didn't answer right away, she went on the defensive. "Then why was Carlos shot?"

"I didn't say we didn't believe it. It's our job to look at all the angles." He seemed to contemplate his next words. "I'll admit Agent Miles protested a bit too much about us looking into his records. And I didn't like how Agent Calvin spoke with you. He seemed almost personally threatened by your accusation."

Brie shook her head. "I don't really think it's Agent Calvin. He's just dedicated to his career and the agency."

"Maybe he was being blackmailed," Connor tossed out.

"I don't think he felt threatened, he was angry. He doesn't like that this makes his office look bad. Has he agreed to work with you guys?"

"He and his men are planning to go over your sister's missing person file. We're supposed to meet daily and compare notes. But we're keeping you and what you're doing out of the conversation." Connor leaned back. "He also brought up your murdered informant from the Sala case. He thinks that you were too close to it. Lost your objectivity. And that's the real reason you took your leave. Not because of your sister."

"Well, he's wrong." She set the crust of her pizza back in the box. "Was I upset about Pablo? Yes. I still am. When he came to me with the gunrunning case, I should've sent someone else in. I knew this was over his skill level. His death is partly on me. And I resented it when Agent Calvin insisted we drop the case, so I secretly kept working it. When he found out, he was pissed."

She leaned back. "But I'm not the one who accused one of our own—Carlos is."

Connor hesitated to answer. "True. But I know guilt can do a real number on you. Sometimes you want to fix the unfixable. You look for answers where there aren't any."

His words seemed to come from personal experience. *What answers was Connor Pierce looking for?* "Maybe, but it's not clouding my judgment. My sister is dead. Pablo is dead. Rosaria Altura may be dead. I know I can't fix that. But I can get them justice. I—"

"Rosaria?"

"Pablo's girlfriend. She'd been living with him when Pablo was murdered. She disappeared."

"Did you look for her?"

"Of course, but nothing turned up. She was from Mexico. Everyone thought she must have gone back home." She leaned back. "And what about the other missing women who worked at the Black Diamond? What if they're in some foreign country chained to a bed like my sister was? What if Armand's here to get more women?"

"Juan's looking into the names you gave him," he said. "If that's what Armand is doing, we'll get him."

They sat there in silence. Looking at each other. Suddenly, it didn't feel awkward. She didn't feel judged. He got it. Like in his office today, she sensed he was on her side. That felt good.

"Do you really remember your sister from when you were younger?"

She nodded. "Our grandmother told us we were second cousins. We bonded. We pretended we were sisters, not knowing we actually were."

"So your grandmother approved of what your dad was doing?"

Brie shrugged. "I don't know. I never saw my grandmother again. Mom was furious with her. I'm told she died shortly after that."

"And you never saw your sister again either?"

"No."

"She never tried to get in touch with you?"

"Only that one time. A few months ago."

"You weren't curious?"

Brie's chest tightened. "Not enough to contact her." Brie wasn't sure why she was telling him this, except...it felt right. "She got *my* father. In my mind, it wasn't my mom he left. It was me. He had chosen Alma over me. I resented her as much as my mom resented her mother."

"Did he stay married to Alma's mother?"

"For nine years."

"You never saw him in all that time?"

"No. When I was ten, my stepdad adopted me. Eliot had my father sign papers to relinquish parental rights. When I got older, I asked Eliot if my dad had resisted at all."

"And?"

She shook her head. "He hadn't."

"Your dad is a real piece of shit." He exhaled. "How involved was he in Alma's life?"

"Don't know. But he said he'd tried to call her for her birthday and when he didn't hear back after a week, he reported her missing."

"How long from the time you knew she was missing until you heard about her body?"

"About a month. I didn't even look that hard. I mean,

I made a report and got a copy of the file, but I told myself she was probably using drugs again."

"And now you blame yourself for it, just like you do with the informant."

"Grief and guilt can fit into the same pocket."

"Yeah." He said it with such certainty that she knew he wasn't talking just about her. Then she remembered him telling her that his partner had been killed. She leaned back on the sofa. And instead of thinking about her own pain she wondered about his.

A thought hit. They weren't sharing just a beer and a sofa, but a part of themselves. He reached for the beer, studied her and took a sip, then offered the beer back.

"No. Finish it." She waited a few seconds. "What happened to your partner? The one you said you lost."

He stared at the beer. "He was shot. Died instantly." He swallowed.

"You were there?"

"Yeah."

"Was the shooter caught?"

He nodded.

She got the distinct feeling he was holding back. But she understood that, too.

He turned the bottle in his hands and focused on it instead of her. "It took two weeks to catch him."

His voice lowered, as if he was divulging a secret. Eager to know it, to know him, she leaned closer. "Is he behind bars?"

He still didn't look at her. "On death row."

"Good."

He took another sip of the beer.

She waited, wanting to reach in and pull out more words, sensing the story wasn't over. "And?"

His green eyes cut toward her. "There were two shooters." His voice became almost monotone.

"One got away?"

"No. I shot him. Watched him die." He gave the bottle another twist. "He was seventeen. Had just started dealing. His sister had diabetes and the family couldn't afford her insulin. And I know this because...they were members of my mother's church. I still get her church newsletter."

He wiped a hand across his face again. "My mom knew the boy. Her church had helped sponsor the family. I even met him once when he was younger. I'd stopped by her house and Mom was watching him and his sister." He swallowed and the tight gulp sounded painful. "After the shooting, I remember thinking I was glad Mom was gone. She'd have been so ashamed."

She put her hand on his arm. She wanted to say, *you can't blame yourself*, but she knew it didn't change anything. "That had to have been hard."

In his eyes, she saw pain. She felt that pain. Knew his pain. Knew what it felt like to blame yourself.

He continued, "Most people say 'It's not your fault,' and honestly, that's what I want to say to you about your informant and your sister, but I'm sure, like me, you've heard it a thousand times. Even when the media crucified me for shooting that kid and my own department didn't defend me, I knew it wasn't my fault. But it didn't change what I felt. Or what I still feel."

She nodded. "I'm hoping it just takes time."

"Yeah." Leaning forward, he put the beer bottle on the

table. "And on that uplifting note, I should go. Let you get some sleep."

Before he rose, she caught his hand. "It's not your fault." She exhaled. "Maybe we just need to hear it over and over again. And maybe it's different when you hear it from someone who understands."

While her words came from the heart, they didn't feel like enough. "And...any guy who would spend three hours hunting for a cat that had already clawed him up is a good soul, right up there with, say...a preacher."

He stared at their joined hands, glanced up, and offered a smile that seemed to say her words mattered. Before she changed her mind, she leaned in and pressed her lips to his.

Bad idea? Probably. But he was hurting. She was hurting.

He cupped the back of her neck and gently pulled her closer. The kiss went from soft to deep. Sweet to sweeter.

He tasted like pizza. Like beer. Like something she'd been hungry for all her life. Unaware of how it happened, she was suddenly on his lap, straddling him.

She needed more. More of him. More of his skin. More of his touch. More.

She tugged his T-shirt up. He lifted his lips from hers and yanked his shirt off. Her gaze lowered and feasted on his ripples of muscle. A light dusting of golden-brown hair fanned across his chest trailing downward past his navel and disappearing into his pants.

He sat there, letting her enjoy the view. Then the view wasn't nearly enough.

She pressed a hand on the center of his chest. The hair

there felt soft. His skin warm. The thump of his heart pulsed against her palm.

Slow seconds passed before he reached for the hem of her shirt.

He held the fabric between his fingers and met her eyes. "This okay?"

The question sobered her for a second. *Was it okay? Was she really doing this?* This could complicate things. But with his body humming below her, and her absorbing every small vibration, she didn't want to stop. Whatever the consequences, she'd take them. "Yeah."

He eased the tank top up. The brush of fabric lifting over her bare stomach sent a thrill whispering through her. Then she got a whiff of cigarette smoke from the club. "I need a shower."

"Want company?"

"It's a small shower."

"Good." His smile was all sin.

"Okay." Envisioning them naked and skin to skin, she felt her lower abdomen tighten with desire. Then, with her still straddling him, he stood from the sofa.

She automatically wrapped her legs around his waist, pressed her forehead against his, and smiling she said, "I can walk."

"But this way I get to put my hands on your ass."

She laughed. He stared at her. "You need to do that more often."

He carried her into the bathroom and slowly let her down. As her pelvis moved over him, she felt the hardness behind his zipper.

She started the shower. When she turned, he pulled her close and kissed her again. His hands slid over bare skin, and she barely felt him unhook her bra. Like a man who had all the time in the world, he eased the straps over her shoulders and down her arms until the lacy fabric cascaded to the floor.

"Wow." His gaze, wide with desire, lingered on her breasts. Reaching up, he brushed his thumbs over her tightening nipples.

His touch sent a thousand sweet nerve endings dancing southbound, and she felt the moisture between her legs.

His hands lowered. He unclasped her shorts, then knelt in front of her, lowered her zipper, and pushed her shorts down until they collected around her ankles. She looked down at him, as he gazed up at her. His eyes were so green, they were startling.

Leaning in, he pressed a soft kiss beside her belly button. The feel of his lips on tender skin brought on a gasp. He slid one hand between her knees and eased it up. She gasped again. When he came to the V of her legs, he slipped one finger under the elastic of her panties. The light friction across her sex had pleasure pulsing between her thighs. His touch moved a little deeper and found a pool of dampness.

"Someone's ready." His voice came out heavy, hoarse, sexy. It washed over her like liquid. Then his finger found her opening and slipped inside her.

Her mind spun. Her knees almost buckled. She caught herself by placing a palm on each of his shoulders.

His finger moved up, down, then pulled out, leaving her feeling empty and desperate. Her panties were whisked down her legs. She stepped out. He rose up and studied her standing naked.

She unbuckled his belt, unbuttoned the clasp on his

pants. He finished the job, pushing the slacks down, underwear included. His hard shaft, freed from the clothes, rose proudly.

Her gaze caught on his sex, pointing upward, thick, long, and hard. She was far from experienced. With only four lovers to her name, she marveled at his size. Her lower body clenched at the thought of him filling her.

The emptiness she felt, the ache between her thighs, doubled. Suddenly embarrassed at her open admiration, she looked up. He studied her face, and her cheeks turned hot.

He smiled. "I think the shower's ready."

She nodded and followed him into a cloud of steam. The stall was small. He pulled her close. His sex, warm and pulsing, pressed against her abdomen.

She sputtered as the water hit her in the face. He adjusted the showerhead.

"Better?" His voice was right at her temple.

"Yes." She put her hands on his waist.

She watched as he found the soap and lathered his hands. His slick palms moved to her shoulders and eased down her body, caressing all the tender spots.

When he was finished, he crouched down in front of her. His day-old stubble pressing against her abdomen as his mouth lowered and his tongue slipped between the folds of her sex.

She let out a sound, half squeal, half moan. Her knees buckled, knocking Connor off his haunches and onto his butt. His fall backward sent her down as well. She'd have landed on top of him if he hadn't caught her and guided her to the small space beside him.

"You okay?" He touched her face.

"That is not meant to be done standing up." She heard her own words and giggled.

His laugh followed and they stayed like that for a long moment, sitting in the shower stall, water cascading on them. He finally stood and offered her a hand.

She took it. After pulling her to her feet, he grabbed the soap and started rubbing his chest.

She took the soap from him. "Let me." She lathered up her palms.

Taking her time, she ran her slick hands over his chest, across his back, down his sides, and ended with one slippery palm on his sex. She couldn't close her fingers around him, but tightening she shifted her hand up and down.

He caught her hand. "Can't take much of that."

He stepped into the spray of water, rinsed off, then took her hand and led her out of the shower.

She grabbed two thick cotton towels. He took one, but instead of drying himself, he dried her. Even as turned on as she was, and as comfortable as she was with her body, she felt self-conscious and got a case of first-time jitters. When he finished, she took the towel and wrapped it around herself as he quickly dried himself.

"Bedroom?" His voice sounded deep with want.

"Yes." Then she realized . . . "No."

"No?" he asked.

"We need protection."

"I got that." He reached for his pants, found his wallet, and pulled out a foiled package.

# CHAPTER FOURTEEN

Something about the way her hand fit in his sent an alarm whispering through Connor. *This could be a mistake.*

But that warning wasn't nearly as loud as his wanting. Not nearly as loud as his heart thundering in his chest.

Getting to her bedroom door, he opened it. Brie's cat, sitting curled up in the center of the bed, hissed. He backed up and let Brie take the lead. When he followed her, the feline bounced up with his back arched, as if prepared to pounce. Connor, having already been used as the feline's scratching post, stepped away from the doorway and cupped his hand over his crotch.

Brie chuckled. The sound rang out like notes of really good music. Connor glanced at her. Wrapped in a towel with humor brightening her eyes, she took his breath away.

"They like to attack anything dangling," he said.

She laughed harder, and that sweet sound was like a favorite song he didn't know he had.

He was so caught up in her, he barely noticed when the cat darted out the door.

Damn, she was beautiful. No, more than beautiful. She was precious. A sudden ache filled his chest.

He glanced at the door. "Alright if I close it?"

"Fine." She pulled the comforter down, tugged the sheet up, and crawled under it. He mourned the sight of her body. Then she reached under the sheet, slipped the towel out, held it up, and dropped it on the floor. While the action hinted at shyness, the slowness with which she pulled the towel out, and the way she held it out there for three seconds before dropping it, was pure seduction.

Consider him seduced.

He set the foil-wrapped condom on the bedside table and slid in beside her.

"You cold?" He rested his hand on her bare hip and moved closer until they were skin to skin.

"A little." The soft, slightly bashful voice brushed across his chest. Was she having second thoughts? "You still okay with this?"

"Yes."

Relief filled him. "Let me see if I can't warm you up." He eased closer and his hard-on pushed against her. The need for release made him even harder. Yet with that yearning came a stronger desire to touch. To taste. To take his sweet time.

He pressed his lips to hers with soft open kisses, while he caressed her breasts. He eased downward and took a tight nipple into his mouth. Wanting to know what she liked, he listened and learned. Focused on her every movement. Every breath. Every little sound spilling from her lips.

While bathing her breasts with his lips and tongue, he slid his hand down between her legs. He eased a finger between her tender folds of skin. Moaning, her hips lifted off the mattress. The slight movement and the moisture between her thighs told him she was ready. He could bury himself in that moist heat.

Instead, he pressed his thumb over the tiny nub while his middle finger dipped in and out of the tight opening. Her sighs grew louder. Then he kissed his way down her abdomen, leaving a trail of moisture.

Under the sheet, he eased her legs apart. Her scent brought more blood pumping to his sex, and his heart boomed in his chest. He kissed her inner thighs. Then he ran his tongue over the cleft of her sex before dipping inside the soft pink skin. Her taste filled his mouth and his hard-on tightened to the point of pain. Her hips came up, then down, then up, meeting his mouth in the age-old movement that drove men wild.

She pressed herself against his mouth, while he suckled, licked, and tasted. He'd barely started when she cried out. Slipping two fingers inside her, he felt her muscles clench in orgasm. Smiling, he moved up, trailing more kisses as he did. When he came out from under the covers, her eyes were closed, her breathing fast.

He pressed his cheek to hers. "You liked that?"

She moaned, then opened her eyes. Her pupils were large, her irises brighter, bluer.

"Yeah." Scooting up, she pushed him back on the mattress, then straddled him.

She eased down his legs, stopping when she got to his knees. Her gaze focused on his throbbing sex saluting the ceiling. Her head lowered and she gazed up. That look, the way her tongue slid across her lips, almost brought him to orgasm.

"No." He caught her and pulled her up.

"But..." She frowned.

He pressed a finger to her mouth. "I'll take a rain check. If your lips touch me, it'll be over, and I want to be inside you."

She swallowed. "Condom. Now." She reached for it on the bedside table.

He laughed. "Why the rush?"

"I'm ready."

"You sure?" he asked, teasing her, loving her eagerness.

She ripped the package open with her teeth.

As she pushed it down, her fist tightened around him. His sex pumped against her soft palm, pulsing with pleasure.

He yanked her hand away, flipped her on her back, and found his place on top of her. Balancing his weight on his forearms, he slid inside her. Slowly. An inch at a time.

Her tight walls surrounded him and had him thinking about baseball, about fishing, about anything to stop him from coming too soon. She wrapped her legs around him. He pushed deeper, the pleasure almost unbearable. Her hips rose up to meet him, her calves tightened around his waist, and the real dance began. In. Out. In. Out. Deep. Then deeper.

Her breathing shortened and a sweet sound left her lips. Only when he felt her orgasm sucking him deeper, milking him, did he let himself go. The intense pleasure brought a growl to his lips. And when he expected it to stop, it didn't. Wave after wave of pleasure spiraled up into his chest, only stopping right before he was certain his heart might explode.

He caught himself before collapsing on top of her. Scooping her in his arms, he rolled to his side, pulling her with him. He kept their bodies joined, wanting every ounce of pleasure this moment offered.

. She eased closer, her soft body melting against him. And he melted with her. He stayed completely still, feeling the air move between his lips, feeling her breathe. She shifted ever so slightly, and pressed her lips to his chest. That soft butterfly kiss passed through skin, through bone, and went straight to his heart.

He pulled her closer. She didn't speak. He couldn't speak. All he could do was feel. And he felt it all. Every nuance of warmth, of tenderness, every inch of her fitting against him. It was several minutes before the pleasure subsided. And when it left, she pressed her lips to his chest again and just like that... nothing felt right. Everything felt wrong.

*Fuck. Shit. Dammit.*

This wasn't supposed to feel this good. He couldn't breathe, and it wasn't the orgasm now.

This wasn't the love-'em-and-leave-'em kind of sex he'd been having since his wife walked away. This was the hold-me, stay-with-me, emotional-attachment kind of sex that he avoided at all cost. He recalled telling her things, things he never talked about. Why?

The answer shot back. *Because I wanted her to tell me her secrets. Because I'm an idiot.*

*Fuck. Shit. Dammit.*

"You okay?" he managed to ask, but he knew it lacked tenderness.

"Yeah," she whispered. He felt her lift her face to look up at him, but he refused to meet her gaze.

"That was amazing." Her words of praise only made it worse. His insides started to shake. The wall he'd built around himself the last three and a half years started to crack.

"I should go. Let you sleep." He pulled away.

"Why don't you stay. It's—"

"No." He bounced off the bed, rushed to the bathroom, tossed the condom in the trash can, then dressed in mere seconds.

Feeling like shit, he started out. When he got to the door and saw the lock, he remembered the panty pervert. "Shit!"

He walked back into the bedroom. She sat up, sheet clutched to her chest, looking precious. Looking perfect. Then he saw the emotion in her eyes.

He'd hurt her. And she'd already been hurting. Hurting because of her partner. Because of her informant. Because of her sister and her piss-poor parents.

He was a real dick.

She tilted her chin up. He got a better look at her face and realized it wasn't just hurt in her blue eyes. The old saying "hell hath no fury like a woman scorned" came to mind.

"You need to lock the door behind me in case that asshole comes back."

"Looks to me like he's already here," she tossed out.

He deserved that, so he didn't argue. "Please lock your door."

"I can take care of myself. It's what I should've done instead of letting you screw me!"

He walked out but stayed there by the door, clenching his fist and calling himself every name in the book. Only when he heard her slide the lock did he leave. And he was only three steps away before he was certain that he was walking away from something he'd miss forever.

* * *

Connor had slept two hours. Not good sleep. He'd woken up every half hour with the weight of remorse sitting on his chest, smothering him. He didn't know what he regretted the most: having sex with her or being such a complete asshole afterward.

Probably being an asshole. But having sex with her was the reason he was an asshole. Oh, hell, he was too tired to even attempt to make sense of this. They'd had sex—not a big deal.

But it *was* a big deal. The whole night had been a big deal. Sitting on that sofa, telling her things he hadn't told...anyone. Why?

He parked at the precinct and walked in. Checking the time, he saw he was about fifteen minutes late.

"Good morning," Mildred said as he approached her desk. He normally liked her cheeriness, but this morning it was too much. He felt hungover in a world where smiles were like noise. In a world where freaking awesome sex turned you into a dick.

"I said 'Good morning!'" Mildred repeated.

He forced himself to mumble something close to hello.

"Whoa," she said when he passed her desk. "You got a message."

Stopping, teeth clenched, he glanced back. "What?"

"Mr. Dunn called looking for you. He said he was on a job, but you could call him."

She held out a sticky note.

He reached for it.

She yanked it back. "What's wrong?"

"Nothing. I gave him my cell number. Why didn't he—"

Shrugging, she eyeballed him, as if trying to get inside his head. "I can usually count on a smile from you."

He forced his lips to spread.

She made a face. "No! Stop. That's pathetic."

He exhaled. "Just give me the number."

"Does this"—she drew a circle in the air, gesturing to his face—"have to do with my crossword buddy?"

"I have a headache."

"I've got aspirin." She reached in her desk drawer.

"I'll be fine."

She shook two pills from a bottle and held them out. "Why do you have a headache?"

He took the pills because arguing with her was like scolding a puppy. "Why are you here? You don't work weekends."

"Mark asked me to comb through some old vice files to look for missing women tied to the murder of Brie's sister. I have five boxes of files heading my way."

"Oh." He held out his hand. "Can I have Dunn's message?"

She handed him the sticky note. "Take the aspirin." She pointed to his hand.

He looked at the paper. It wasn't the same number he'd had for Dunn. He knew because he'd already called it twice this morning. He looked up to offer thanks.

She frowned. "Don't fake-smile like that anymore. You look like you should be doing a constipation commercial."

He laughed. "Why do I like you so much?"

"Seriously, is this about Brie?"

His smile faded as well. "I already said no." He started walking.

"So you don't need me to warn you that..." Her voice trailed off.

He turned around. "Warn me about what?"

"That Brie's in your office, talking to Mark, Juan, and Billy. And she looked about as happy as you do. Did you two have another argument? Please tell me you didn't handcuff her to anything else." The woman's face reddened. "I don't mean...I wasn't implying anything sexual."

Throwing the two aspirin in his mouth, he chewed the bitter pills as he headed to his office.

# CHAPTER FIFTEEN

Connor heard her talking as he moved down the hall. Just the sound of her voice sent elephant-sized regret to weigh down his shoulders. Walking in, his eyes went straight to her. She sat in front of Mark's desk, her back to him. Billy had pulled a chair over and sat beside her. A little too close.

"Hey." Mark spotted Connor. Billy nodded at him as well.

"Hey." Connor went to his desk, busying himself by putting his gun away, so he didn't have to look at her right away. With that task finished, he dropped in his chair. His gaze found her. A huge heavy feeling swelled in his chest.

He expected her to look as miserable as he felt, but no, she looked good. Too good.

He noticed she wore makeup. She'd had a little on last night when she returned from work, but it had mostly worn off. Now, her eyelids had a little sparkle, her cheekbones were more defined, her lashes longer, and her lips—lips he remembered kissing, devouring, tasting—had a glossy sheen.

She wore a gray suit jacket. Under it was a pale blue blouse that matched her eyes. The top two buttons were left open, not exposing any cleavage, but just low enough to make a man's eyes go there and wish. His gaze lowered. The memory of being between her legs hit and sent a wave of lust to his groin.

Was she trying to remind him of what he'd walked away from last night?

Mark cleared his throat. Connor realized she still hadn't cast him a single glance. But everyone else had noticed him eyeballing her.

He swallowed hard. "Did I miss something?"

"No," Mark said. "Brie's filling us in on a phone conversation she overheard Dillon Armand having last night, and she brought in the glass with Armand's fingerprints. I'm going to run them to the lab and then track down how I can compare them with records in Guatemala."

Juan spoke up. "I'm going to try to get phone records from Olvera's office and see if any of those might give us something."

"Have you talked to Agent Calvin about that?" Connor asked, now trying not to look at Brie. "Are they all still coming in today?"

"Yeah. He called." Juan glanced at the computer screen. "And even though he said they'd cooperate, we'll see if he meant it. He also asked if we'd set up the interviews yet."

"Why is he rushing this?" Connor asked.

Mark pushed back from his desk. "Probably just wants them over with. I'll remind him we want to review the Sala files first. I'm going to suggest we look at doing the interviews on Monday or Tuesday. Juan made the request for all three of the agent's bank records yesterday, but since it's the weekend, we don't know if the bank will send them over before Monday."

"What about the restaurant where Agent Olvera ate? Have you checked into that yet?" Connor asked.

"I'm calling today," Juan said. "The bill was sixty-five dollars. I've looked at the menu, and that could cover two meals, or a pricy one with a drink. I won't know until I talk to his waiter."

"Yeah." Connor's gaze shifted back to Brie and his chest tightened. "Dunn called the front desk and asked to speak to me. I'm going to go see him. I think a face-to-face might be more convincing."

Billy's attention went to Brie. "Why don't I go with you to see the homeless guy?"

Connor sat up in his chair. "You found Tomas?" He remembered promising Betty he wouldn't let Brie go alone.

"Not really." She looked at him for one, two seconds, before focusing on Mark as if he'd asked the question. "I ran into someone who knows him, and he said Tomas eats lunch at the Logan shelter."

"I know where that is," Billy spoke up. "That's where Connor and I delivered the toys we collected for the homeless kids last December. I could go with you to the shelter, and afterward you can hit the stores with me to check for security camera footage."

Connor's empty stomach churned the aspirin to dust.

From the way Billy looked at Brie, there was no mistaking the man's interest.

Brie smiled at the guy. Thankfully, he'd seen her real smile and knew this one wasn't even a good forgery. "That's okay. I'm going by the hospital first anyway."

"You sure?" Billy asked. "I don't mind going—"

"Positive." She looked at Mark. "Call me if you learn anything. And I appreciate what you're doing."

"Yeah." Mark cut Connor a quick glance, as if he suspected something was off between the two of them.

She continued, "If I find Tomas and he has any information, I'll bring him in so you can get his statement."

Connor started to speak up about Tomas being dangerous, but that might encourage Billy, so he clamped his mouth shut.

Brie stood. Connor's gaze shifted to her breasts pressing against her shirt. Images of her naked in the shower with water droplets running down her body filled his head.

"What time do you work tonight?" Billy tossed out.

"I'm off until Monday." She turned and left.

Billy stared after her, or rather he stared at her ass. When she was gone, the younger cop looked back, grinning ear to ear. "I shouldn't like her after she busted my balls, but damn, she's hot!" He rubbed his hands together. "You think I stand a chance?"

Mark and Juan looked at Connor.

"What?" Billy asked, now looking at him, too. "Crap. Don't tell me you already called dibs?"

"Stop being an ass," Connor snapped. Reaching into his gun drawer, he grabbed his Glock and hurried after Brie. No way was she going to see Tomas alone.

* * *

Brie was halfway across the parking lot when she heard her name being called.

She looked back, praying it wasn't Connor. Anyone but him. God let her down. Fracking Hades!

Reaching into her purse, searching for her keys, she walked faster. She wasn't above ignoring him, getting into her car, and hightailing it out of there. But that would require finding her dad-burn keys. She hated this purse.

By the time she found them, his steps sounded right behind her. He stopped. She didn't look at him, but a nippy breeze delivered his scent to her. The memory of being surrounded by that warm masculine smell played in her head.

"Gotta go." She hit her clicker to open her locks.

"Can we talk?" He moved a step closer. Her heart skipped a beat.

"There's nothing to say."

"I need to explain."

She looked up, wind whipping her hair in front of her eyes. She pushed it back. "No, you don't. I get it." And she did. Granted, with her lack of experience, she'd never dealt with a commitmentphobe, but she'd heard about them from Carlos. What was the saying, *wham, bam...?*

Meeting his gaze, she realized he looked exhausted. His eyes were bloodshot, and he had frown lines around his eyes and one in the center of his forehead.

"Give me five minutes," he said.

"I told you, I understand. You don't need to explain."

"What do you understand?" He raked a hand through his hair.

"That you're afraid I might think last night meant something. Well, I don't think that. We had sex, Connor. Slot-A-goes-into-slot-B kind of sex. That's it. Frankly, it wasn't even that good."

He stared at her, shook his head, then his eyes narrowed. "Don't—"

"Don't what?" She closed her fist around her key fob until it dug into her palm, setting off the car alarm. It took her three tries to stop it.

"Don't lie."

"Lie?" she seethed. "You mean about it not being that good?"

"Not just—"

"Yeah, I told you it was awesome, but I know how fragile guys' egos are. I'm sure it was just an off night for you."

He frowned. "I'm not talking—"

She rolled her eyes. "Don't tell me you haven't seen *When Harry Met Sally*. Girls know how to fake it. Not that it's a big deal. I'm over it. It's like it never happened."

"Dammit, Brie! It was a mistake. I shouldn't—"

"Wow, you're finally saying something I can agree with. It was a big fracking mistake. So forget about it. I have. In fact, it already feels like a distant bad dream." She reached for the car door.

"Brie." The way he said her name came out a little hurt, a little desperate, a little confused. Mirroring what she felt. He moved in front of her.

"I gotta go," she said.

"I promised Betty that I wouldn't let you go see Tomas alone."

"Hmmm." She tapped her lips with her index finger. "Consider it a lesson. You shouldn't make promises you can't keep."

"Please—"

"Sorry if it bruises your ego, big guy, but I don't need you. I don't need a man to take care of me. I don't need any ho-hum-wham-bam-thank-you-ma'am sex. You got the extra notch on your belt, so drop it. And please," she said, waving him aside. "Get out of my way."

When he didn't move, she darted around him. She opened the door as far as she could with his football-sized, solid, muscled body in the way. Then, heart hurting, feeling like a fool for thinking last night was special, she squeezed into the front seat. Barely settled, she locked her door, started the engine, and peeled off.

Unfortunately, the exit of the parking lot had a red light and a line of cars. As she sat there, the vibration of her idling car made the quivering in her chest more noticeable. She told herself not to do it, swore she wouldn't, but she did it anyway.

Looking up, she found him in her rearview mirror, not much bigger than a speck. A splinter. An irritant she needed to pluck out. He stood in the exact same place, by the empty parking spot, watching her. He looked wounded, rejected, vulnerable.

Had he taken acting and asshole 101 in college? He must have aced every course.

Her eyes stung, but *no way* would she cry. Nope. Why did it even hurt? She barely knew him. Just because they'd shared secrets. Just because his pain had felt so familiar that consoling him had been almost self-healing. Just because last night had been the best sex she'd ever had.

Just because for the first time, in a long time, she hadn't felt lonely.

None of that meant jack shit.

* * *

Connor phoned to see what time lunch was served at the Logan shelter. Then he called Dunn, got his on-the-job address, and informed him he'd be dropping by.

Remembering Brie's panties scattered across her bedroom, he decided to go to the man's office first to see if he could get the name of the redheaded pervert. His gut said something needed to be done about him. He could at least run the guy through the system for priors.

The office was a trailer placed in a half-commercial–half-residential area. A car parked outside told him Dunn had someone manning the office.

He headed to the door where an OPEN sign welcomed him inside. A blond girl, muttering obscenities, cleaned a table littered with coffee cups and fast-food wrappers.

"Can I help you?" She tossed a half-eaten biscuit in the garbage. "Sorry, some men don't know how to clean up after themselves."

"I'm thinking about doing some remodeling and a while back I met a guy who works here. I saw your sign, so I thought I'd pop in and ask about getting an estimate."

"What kind of work are you doing?"

"The kitchen needs everything, cabinets and new flooring."

"Well, Mr. Dunn does plenty of kitchens. He has some pictures of his work if you'd like to see them."

"Sure."

She moved behind the counter and pulled out a binder. He flipped through and pretended to be interested. "Who do I talk to about getting an estimate?" he asked, baiting the hook before fishing for information.

"Leave your number and I'll have Mr. Dunn call you." She pulled out a notepad.

"Why don't you give me his number and I'll call when I'm ready to move forward."

"Just take this." She handed him a business card.

"Thanks." He flipped the edge of his card with his finger. "Does Jimmy still work here? He recommended Mr. Dunn."

"There isn't a—"

"Wait. That wasn't his name. He has red hair?"

"You mean Lawdon." She frowned.

"I don't thin... What's his last name?"

"Davis. He's got red hair, big guy." Saying the name deepened her frown and Connor got a bad feeling.

"That's not him. Maybe this guy quit."

"Hmmmm."

Connor studied her. "I'm glad Lawdon isn't the guy I met."

She looked up. "Huh?"

"You don't seem to like him."

Her eyes widened. "You're very perceptive."

"Yeah." He pushed away from the counter and started out, then stopped and turned around. "I'm probably overstepping here, but if some guy makes you feel uncomfortable, you should report him to your boss. And if he's really crossed a line, you should report him to the police."

"Like my boss would care. I'd lose my job," she said flatly.

Connor lifted a brow. "Doesn't look like such a great job."

She chuckled. "Good point."

When he got to his car, he called Juan.

"What's up?" Juan answered.

"I got the redhead's name. Can you run him? My gut says he's bad news."

"Yeah. What is it?"

"Lawdon Davis." Connor heard Juan typing on the computer.

"Well... your gut's right. He's got a list of priors. Wait. It gets better. He's got a warrant out for... rape and assault."

"I knew it." The thought of that guy getting anywhere close to Brie sent a jolt of protectiveness through Connor. "I'm on my way to see Dunn at his work site. If the guy's there, I'll call you and someone can pick him up."

"Yeah," Juan said. "In fact, it's Detective Quarrels who's listed on the warrant. He's the one who brought over the files that Mildred's going through. We owe him, so this is good."

"Has Mildred found anything?" Connor asked.

"Not yet." Juan paused. "What's up with you and Brie?"

Connor's hold on the phone tightened. "Nothing. Why?"

"Yesterday there was enough sexual tension between you two to blow up Fort Knox. Today you couldn't stop looking at her and she wouldn't look at you. And I was worried you were about to shoot Billy when he mentioned being hot for her."

"I wouldn't shoot Billy." *Punch him maybe.* "I'll let you know if I see Davis." Connor hung up and called Brie to give her the heads-up about Davis. Of course, she didn't pick up.

"Brie," he said at the beep. "I just found out the guy who broke into your apartment has a warrant out for rape. Be careful. And . . . you can't just ignore me. We have to talk."

# CHAPTER SIXTEEN

Yes I can. And no we don't," Brie muttered, listening to Connor's message. She pocketed her phone and looked back at Carlos. "Sorry."

When she got to the hospital, Eliot had just gone to the hotel to sleep. Sam sat guard, and she'd sent Tory out for a walk after he'd broken down when the doctor came by and said there was no change in Carlos's condition.

So when visiting hours opened, she was alone with Carlos. She moved closer and touched the back of his hand. "That was Connor Pierce. He's a real jerk." She filled her cheeks with air then blew it out.

"I slept with him. Yeah, I know. Stupid, right? I guess I've been lonely. But he seemed . . . genuine. We talked. You know when you feel that connection . . . like it might be the start of something? But he turned out to be . . . what was it you used to call the guys who were still orgasming as they were picking up their clothes to leave? An in-and-outer, up-and-downer, or was it a hit-and-goner? I think those three were different, but I can't remember."

Before Carlos met Tory, she and her partner would compare dating nightmares. Wine and whine nights.

She exhaled. "But enough about me. When are you waking up, buddy? I need my best friend." She ran her thumb over the top of his wrist.

"Who did you go see in Willowcreek? Was it about the Sala case? I could really use some help figuring this out."

"He went to see someone in Willowcreek?" The question came from the door and sent Brie spinning around to face Agent Miles.

Why hadn't she shut the door? "What are you doing here?"

"The same as you. I want to catch the person who did this." She could swear she heard a touch of honesty in his words, but she also heard frustration.

Sam, shoulders back in a defensive posture, appeared behind him. "This okay?"

She looked at Agent Miles. Was he stupid enough to try something with her in the room? Her gut said no. Her gut also said this might be a chance to ask him questions.

"Yeah."

Sam backed out. Miles glanced at her. "You really think I could've done this?"

She stiffened her spine. "If it helps, I don't want to believe it."

"I worked with him like you did. I wanted to get to the bottom of the Sala case just as bad as you and Carlos."

"Yeah," she said. "But Carlos found something that convinced him someone from our own agency was involved. And until I know..."

"You won't trust anyone."

"Sorry."

"No, you're not," he snapped. "And while it pisses me off, I get it. But I'm not behind this."

"Did you know Carlos was looking into the case?"

"I knew something was off. He'd been acting strange. He stopped meeting me to play ball."

"Do you think he suspected you?" she asked.

"He treated Bara the same way." His gaze went to Carlos. "Damn." He raked a hand through his hair. "Is he going to make it?"

"Yes!" she said.

He met her eyes, and from his expression she knew he questioned if she believed it herself. "When did he go to Willowcreek?"

She didn't answer.

He exhaled. "Have you looked into his phone records at his office?"

"Why?"

"I just felt like . . . like he was hiding something."

"What?"

"I don't know. But . . . what if it was him, Brie? What if he was the one who leaked the information about the Sala case? He spent a fortune on his wedding and honeymoon. Maybe they offered—"

"Get out!" Brie pointed to the door.

"It's possible."

"I'm sure he shot and assaulted himself as well."

"I'm just saying that he's the one who's been acting suspiciously. Closing the door to his office like—"

"And I'm saying, get out!" She took a step, and he turned around and left.

Brie noticed Carlos's heart monitor beeped faster. Had he heard?

"Sorry," she said. "It'd really help if you'd wake up."

When visiting hours ended, Brie left and headed for the shelter, hoping to find the Willie Nelson look-alike with a bad attitude.

\* \* \*

Connor checked the time when he pulled up to the construction site. No way was he going to be late for lunch at the shelter. But he had half an hour.

The sound of hammering and saws leaked into the car. Getting out, a cold breeze snuck under his blue suit jacket. He walked around, looking for Davis.

He spotted a redheaded guy working on the backside of the foundation. The thought of him rummaging through Brie's panty drawer, coupled with the expression on the blonde back at the office, had Connor wishing he could personally cuff the guy. Another glance around and he spotted an older man, who Connor suspected was Dunn, walking toward him.

"Detective Pierce, I guess?"

"Yeah." Connor held out his hand. Dunn didn't take it.

"I don't know why you think we need to talk. I got the car back. Everything's fine."

"Yeah, but most people like an update on their case. They want the person caught."

"You caught her?" Dunn asked.

*Her?* So Dunn still thought Brie did it. "Not yet. But we're looking at some leads. Did you hear that your car was pulled over by an officer for speeding?" Connor knew he hadn't, because like him, Billy hadn't been able to reach Dunn.

"No. I didn't know. But that pisses me off. You had her and you didn't arrest her?"

"No. The car hadn't been reported stolen yet. But several things point to it being a gang out of Houston. They've been stealing high-end cars like yours. Last week one was taken out of Glencoe." That was misleading, but the truth.

And when he remembered this asshole had sent Lawdon Davis to do God only knew what to Brie, he didn't feel the need to justify it.

Connor paused and decided to get a little bit of justice by making him squirm. "Oh, can you clarify something? We have two reports claiming the car was taken, but they claim it was taken from different locations."

"Yeah, I . . . I was upset when I called the first time and got it wrong. It was at Denny's off Macon Street."

"And that's even stranger. You see we had someone go by there and they hadn't heard about a car being stolen."

"Well, I . . . I hadn't even ordered, and I had a friend with me and I . . . I didn't say anything to the store manager." His tone tightened almost to the squirm level. "My friend drove me to the police station to make the report. But truth is, my wife's got her car back and she's happy."

"Oh, I guess that makes sense. So, it's your wife's car, should I drop by and talk to—"

"No," he practically yelped. "She's out of town now, and since the car's back, you can forget about the whole thing. I work for a living and don't have time to mess with this."

*As if I don't work for a living.* "Oh, well don't worry. It'll only come up if we catch the guy. Then, of course, we'll take his statement. The perp can clarify where the car was stolen from, and where it was left. You know, details. Then you and your wife will need to come to court."

"Fuck it. I got the car back. I don't want to mess with court. Take my name off the report."

*You mean you don't want your wife to know you were hanging out at a strip club where your girlfriend works?*

"We can't do that. You called it in." He hoped the guy lived in fear for at least a couple of months.

Connor left Dunn muttering under his breath, definitely squirming. When he got in his car, he called Juan and told him Lawdon Davis was available for pickup, then he headed off to find Willie.

* * *

A lunch crowd had already started gathering in front of the shelter. Slipping her gun into her shoulder holster, she closed her jacket and got out of the car. The sun was out and the sky blue, but fall brought a nip in the air. She darted across the road, keeping an eye out for a guy who looked like Willie Nelson.

While scanning the various groups standing and sitting on the lawn of the shelter, she continued walking around. A blonde, slumped against the building and gazing down at her tennis shoes, caught Brie's attention. She stopped. Stared.

The woman looked like Candy. Brie stepped closer and the woman looked up—eyes dazed, lids low, as if drunk or drugged. She stared right at Brie. It wasn't her friend.

Exhaling, she remembered Candy's bruises. Was she right that Dillon Armand had caused them? Hate swelled in Brie's chest. She wanted, no, she needed to get the proof to lock his ass up, before he hurt anyone else.

Suddenly, Brie spotted two guys standing at the corner of a building. She recognized the mop of curly hair on the skinnier of the two men. It was Milton, the guy she'd chased into the woods yesterday. Milton lifted his gaze, saw her, and flinched. That's when she realized the guy standing beside him had long salt-and-pepper hair that hung in a ponytail. *Willie freaking Nelson!*

Milton said something to his buddy, and the look-alike country and western singer took off around the corner. Brie started after him, when three people walked right in front of her. "Move!" she yelled. "FBI."

She'd barely made the corner when she heard footsteps pounding the sidewalk beside her. Heart pumping, determination hardening her gut, she glanced to her right. Connor?

"What are you doing here?" She breathed out the words, never slowing down.

"Backup. Is that him?" His voice didn't sound nearly as winded as hers.

"I think so."

He was suddenly ahead of her by five or more feet.

She saw Tomas hauling ass down an alley littered with garbage dumpsters. For an old guy, he moved like the wind.

"Stop! Police," Connor yelled as he gained on the man. Tomas ran hard, his ponytail flopping in the air.

Brie lagged behind about ten feet when Connor reached their mark and grabbed a handful of Tomas's coat. The man tripped, went down hard, and lay in a heap on the ground.

She stopped, caught her breath, and swore to herself she'd get back on a treadmill tomorrow. In the last few months, she'd been way too lax on her exercise regimen.

Connor looked over his shoulder to check on her. That glance back was all it took for Tomas to pop up and start running.

"You might want to catch him again." She couldn't help it if those words came with a smirk.

"Shit!" He bolted. Right before Connor had him, Tomas shot around. From her position, she saw his hand dip under his coat. She saw the sun reflect on something metal.

"Knife!" Brie grabbed her Glock.

Connor stopped on a dime. Tomas swiped the six-inch blade through the air.

Connor leaped back. The blade missed him by less than an inch.

Brie's finger pressed on her trigger. "Drop it, Tomas. Or I will shoot."

Tomas's eyes, gray and wild-looking, shifted to her. He tossed down the knife and it clanked on the gravel at his feet. Connor, looking properly pissed, grabbed the man and pushed him against the back of a brick building.

"Really bad move." Connor's voice rang deep.

"I didn't do it. I swear I didn't do it."

"You pulled a knife on a cop." Connor grabbed hand-cuffs from under his jacket and placed them on the man.

"I didn't...I didn't know you were police. I thought you were with the other guy."

*What other guy?* Brie moved in.

"Don't insult my intelligence." Connor started patting

him down. "I identified myself." Connor stopped searching when he got to the man's pockets. "Do you have anything sharp, or jagged on you?"

When Tomas didn't answer, Connor continued, "Do you have any needles on you, Tomas? If I get stuck—"

"No."

"What other guy?" Brie asked.

Tomas didn't answer.

"What did you mean by 'I didn't do it'!" Brie stepped closer.

Conner turned the guy around. "Answer her!"

"I saw it," Tomas said. "I saw a guy dump a body."

"Where?" Brie asked, certain he was referring to Carlos.

"Under the bridge at Fifth Street," Tomas said.

Connor pulled out a phone and wallet from Tomas's coat pocket. He opened the wallet, then glanced back at Brie. "It's Olvera's." He held out the phone to Tomas. "Whose phone is this?"

"The dead guy's."

"No, he had his phone on him," Connor said.

"Well, he had two phones then," Tomas insisted. "Because I found this one right beside him."

Connor's expression showed confusion. "You sure?"

"Why would I lie?"

Hope sparked inside Brie. "Maybe the phone belonged to the shooter? He could have dropped it?"

\* \* \*

When Connor left the interview room, Mark came walking down the hall. "His name is Tomas Morgan," he told Mark, catching him up on the latest. He mentioned the phone Tomas claimed he found by Olvera, who he assumed was dead.

"But we got Agent Olvera's phone."

"I know. It looks like a burner. A flip phone. Juan's looking at it now."

"Why would he have a burner?" Mark rubbed his chin with his palm.

"We're hoping it might have belonged to the shooter."

"That'd be a nice break."

"I know."

"Did Mr. Morgan admit to seeing the perp?" Mark motioned to the door where he'd left Tomas.

"Yeah, and his description of the man who dumped the body fits the guy at the hotel. I'm trying to get someone to show him the video to confirm it's the same guy."

"You think he's a reliable witness?"

"Right now he's sober, and said he was when he witnessed the body being left as well."

"I guess that's something. But when he walks, we're not likely to see him again."

"Oh, we're keeping him," Conner said. "He came at me with a knife. A big one."

"Crap. You okay?"

"Yeah." Thanks to Brie. If she hadn't seen the knife when she had . . .

"I thought Brie was the one chasing down that lead."

"I met her there."

Mark lifted a brow. "So you're talking again?"

"Yeah." She had spoken about twenty-five words to Connor. He knew because he'd counted. But damn, he wished she'd listen to him. Then again, he didn't have a freaking clue what he wanted to say, except *I'm sorry.*

The only other time he'd had this strong of a reaction to a woman was with Kelly. And he'd married her six weeks after they'd met. He had loved her with everything he had. And it hadn't been enough.

"What happened between you?"

"Nothing," Connor insisted.

Mark studied him. "You slept with her, didn't you?"

"Stop," Connor said.

Mark shook his head. "That wasn't a no. I told you, we need her to cooperate."

Connor frowned. "She's cooperating."

Mark studied him. "For how long?"

"Why are you judging me?" Connor snapped. "You slept with Annie, and she was a witness. And before Annie there was the reporter who was trying to blackmail you. And before that—"

"That's why I can judge you. I know what you're doing."

"What am I doing?" Connor squared his shoulders.

"Before Annie, I only slept with women I deemed safe. Women who I knew never wanted more than a good fuck. And more importantly, women I knew I couldn't even like. God forbid if I accidentally broke that rule, because then all hell would break loose. I think you broke that rule."

Connor frowned. "It's none of—"

"With Sergeant Brown on our asses, we don't need all hell breaking loose right now. Especially with this case." Mark paused. "And personally, I don't like seeing you go through hell. Tell me I'm wrong. Tell me you don't like Brie."

Mark's words were so spot-on, they hit like a steel-toed boot to the gut. He liked Brie too much. He knew it going in, and was going to know it going out. So the sooner he solved the case, the sooner he could move past it.

"It's not going to affect the case. And I'm fine." He changed the subject and asked about the surveillance video they'd found near Carlos's hotel.

"It's fuzzy, but it looks like the guy Brie was chasing. He got into a white Camry. But we couldn't make out the license plate. Billy forwarded it to Juan's email. If Juan can't clean it up, we'll send it off. Which means it could be weeks before we hear back."

Connor rubbed his neck, where he felt the tension building. "He's looking at the phone we brought in now. Any news on the prints Brie got?"

"They ran them. We're waiting for confirmation if they are his or his cousin's."

"From Guatemala?"

"Yeah."

"How long?"

"Who knows."

"Shit."

"It gets worse," Mark said.

"What?"

"Looks like Armand's heading to Houston. Our guy trailed him until Brown called him off. Said we didn't have enough on the guy to follow him out of town."

"What the hell! He's just going to let him go?"

"Chances are he's going to the strip club Brie said he owns there."

"Fucking unbelievable," Connor seethed. "This guy might be the head of a human trafficking ring and they just let him go. Did you tell Brie?"

"Not yet. I heard she's helping Mildred go through the files."

"She's not going to be happy," Connor muttered.

"I called Brown to see if I could change his mind. He said if the FBI wanted this guy, they could put one of their own on him."

Connor exhaled. "I'll tell Brie."

"You sure?"

"Yeah."

Mark studied him. "How much do you like her?"

"Stop." Connor watched Mark walk away, trying not to think about his question. He called to get someone to take Willie Nelson to jail, and was headed up to give Brie the bad news about Armand, when someone said his name.

"Detective Pierce?"

He turned around to see a short stocky man with a receding hairline walking toward him. "I'm Detective Quarrels with vice. Detective Acosta sent me those pictures. Then he called me about Lawdon Davis. I just picked him up on that outstanding warrant."

"You got him?"

"Sure did. I wanted to say thanks. The guy's a real scumbag. Raped and beat up his ex-girlfriend. Slapping the handcuffs on him felt good."

"Glad to help." His protectiveness over Brie spiked again.

"There's one other thing. In addition to the picture looking familiar to one of our guys, one of the names you're looking into—Tammy Alberts—it sounds so familiar to me. I ran it through the system, as I'm sure you guys did, and nothing came up. But it's bugging me. I know that name from somewhere. Last year I helped ICE out on a case. I'm wondering if that's where I heard it. Do you mind if I run it by a buddy there?"

"No. I'd appreciate the help. Call me if you get anything." Connor handed him a card. Heading to the front to tell Brie the bad news, he stopped when he saw her and Mildred laughing. The sight of her caused his chest to tighten but brought a smile to his lips. Yeah, he liked her too much. Way too much.

* * *

"Why not?" Brie fumed at Agent Calvin. When Connor told her the department removed the tail on Armand, she went directly to her boss, who'd taken up residence in one of the conference rooms at the station.

"Because we have no proof that he's behind any crime. We don't even know if he's who Agent Olvera thought he was."

"He was named as being seen roughhousing my sister two days before she was found dead."

"That witness recanted the statement."

"Because he was threatened. He killed my sister and you are going to stand by—"

"We don't know that, Agent Ryan. And right now, I'd rather concentrate on finding out who shot one of my own men than chasing down unverified leads. I'd think you'd want that, too, since you are the reason he's here."

His accusation landed like a sledgehammer right to her heart. She caught her breath. "Fine, I'll tail him myself."

"No, you will not! You are on leave and you'll stay that way until I decide if you are even coming back to the bureau. Do not interfere with this investigation. In fact, I'm thinking it might be best if you leave town."

"I won't leave Carlos." *Or the investigation.*

"You realize how close you are to losing your position at the FBI?"

"I'm good at my job."

"I'm trying to remember that," he said. "It may not be enough."

It took everything Brie had not to reach into her purse, slam her badge on his desk, and tell him what he could do with his job. She couldn't. When she had the proof she needed about the leak, and the proof that Armand was behind her sister's death, she'd need someone to put the cuffs on Armand. And now that he was on the move, she couldn't count on the Anniston PD to do that.

She had to play nice. For now. After this, maybe she wouldn't even want to go back to the FBI.

She stormed out of the room. Connor stood in the hallway. "You okay?" His gentle tone made it worse.

She swallowed to keep from tearing up and walked faster.

He met her pace. "Brie. Talk to me. What did he say?" She kept walking.

"Damn it. Can you put our personal issues aside and deal with the case? We slept together. It was wrong. Then I was a world-class jerk, a dick even, I admit that. You deserve to hate me. I'll take the hate. But we have a case to solve. Work with me to catch who shot Agent Olvera and who killed your sister."

His words slammed into the guilt Agent Calvin had given life to.

Fracking Hades! Connor was right. She stopped. Swallowed her pride. Pushed her hurt aside. She needed his, and his partners', help. "Calvin won't have Armand followed. I threatened to tail him myself and he said I'd be fired."

"Well, Armand knows what you look like, so that wouldn't work. But..."

"What?" she asked.

"I have a friend, a cop, in the Houston area. I can have him go to the strip club and confirm Armand's there."

She nodded. Knowing Armand was there and not getting on a plane headed back to Guatemala would take the edge off her angst. Still, the knot in her throat doubled. "I feel like this case is floundering. We're not getting anywhere."

"That's not true. We've got Tomas. He's a witness. And we've got the phone. You know how investigations go. Not all cases are solved overnight."

Connor's cell rang. He pulled it out and looked at the screen. "It's Juan. Maybe he has something on the phone."

Connor took the call. "Yeah." He smiled at Brie. "Good. We'll be right there."

# CHAPTER SEVENTEEN

W hy would Carlos have a burner phone?" Eliot sipped from his water glass. He'd already eaten his lunch, while she picked at hers.

"I don't know. He must have been worried someone was tracing his phone." After getting all the updates from Juan, she left the precinct, grabbed Eliot, and they went to get some Tex-Mex. Unfortunately, she could barely force any food down.

"Are they sure it was Carlos's?"

"Yeah. He'd called his home number and checked messages." She stabbed a piece of chicken.

"Were there any other calls on it?"

"One to a José Hernandez, but now the phone connected to that number has been shut off. They're trying to find him. But do you know how many José Hernandezes there are? It's like John Doe." She ran her fork through her refried beans.

"Something will come up. You'll get a break."

Damn, she must be pretty pathetic if Eliot was pushing optimism on her. "Agent Miles came to see Carlos earlier."

"Sam told me. Did Miles say anything?"

"He started talking nonsense, saying maybe it was Carlos who was the leak in the Sala case." She looked up. Eliot seemed to chew on that information. "It's not true."

"I don't think it is, but I'm trying to understand what angle Miles had for accusing Carlos."

"To throw suspicion off himself?"

"But wouldn't accusing Carlos just invite further investigation? If he's hiding something, I'd think he'd want to shut down the whole idea of an FBI leak."

"I don't know what to think anymore." She tapped her fork on her plate. "I'm afraid he'll use the fact that Carlos has a burner phone to give credit to his story about Carlos being behind this."

"It's easy to throw out accusations, but they have to be proven. Aren't the detectives looking into Agents Bara and Miles?"

She nodded. "I'm told they are. And I was told Agent Calvin refused to turn over the phone records for Carlos's office. He said there might be confidential informant calls on there, and he won't divulge."

"Then he should redact those he has to, and give them the rest."

"That's what he's doing. But it's just another delay." She exhaled. "I feel like I should be doing something. Not sitting on the sidelines."

"You're assisting the APD. Aren't they keeping you abreast of everything?"

"They are. But they aren't telling me everything," she said.

"What about the charge on Carlos's credit card in Willowcreek?"

"They've spoken with the restaurant. The check was for two people."

"And?"

"And that's all we got. It's another damn delay. The waitress is on vacation. Mexico. She's supposed to be back tomorrow. I'm going to go interview her with one of the detectives."

She stabbed a piece of fajita chicken.

Eliot frowned. "You look exhausted. And playing with your food isn't eating."

"I ate some. And I am tired. Maybe that's why I can't think straight." Or why every few seconds her mind would take her back to last night with Connor. Which made her feel even more guilty. Carlos is on death's door, her sister's killer is still on the loose, and she's fixated on a one-night stand.

"You need to go home and rest."

Her phone rang and she picked it up to check who the caller was, praying it was good news. But when she saw the number, she frowned.

"What?" Eliot asked.

"It's the Black Diamond."

"If Armand isn't there, there's no need for you to go in."

She saw the steely expression in his eyes—parental protection and love. At least for tonight, she agreed with him.

"But I should still answer it." She took the call. "Hello."

"You need to come in," Mr. Grimes said in lieu of hello.

Just the sound of his voice caused what little food she'd eaten to sit heavier in her stomach. "Can't. I'm out of town."

"How far out of town are you? I need you here by eight."

"Can't."

"Look, Candy didn't show up. I need a waitress. So get your ass—"

"I said I can't."

"If you value your job, you'll—"

"Can't." She hung up. No way he'd fire her. He was already down one waitress.

"What?" Eliot asked.

"A waitress didn't show up. I'm pretty sure she was pressured into having sex with Armand two nights ago. And she had bruises that I think he gave her."

Eliot's jaw clenched. "Pressured by who?"

"The boss."

Eliot shook his head. "Have you told your detective this? Why haven't they arrested that piece of scum?"

"It's not illegal. He's careful with his words. He doesn't say it explicitly. Believe me, nothing would make me happier than seeing his butt thrown in jail, but right now nothing would stick. Being a douchebag isn't illegal."

"It should be."

Brie gave up pretending to eat and pushed her lunch away.

The waiter came and removed the plates. When he left, Eliot asked, "How much do you know about your sister's time here?"

"Not much. After one of the dancers said I reminded them of someone who used to work there, I asked about her. They said she was talking about going to school and that she lived with another dancer. I visited the apartment where they lived, but it flooded a month after Alma disappeared, and most everyone had moved out. I found a couple of neighbors, but all they could tell me is that three women and a baby lived there."

"And nothing else from her time at the Black Diamond?"

"No. She only worked there a few months. Her file said she missed work one day, then quit because she had another job. When the cops interviewed her roommate, Linda Kramer, she told the cops Alma had found a new job. But she didn't know where, or even what kind of job it was. Alma's bank records show she deposited her last check from the Black Diamond. After that, there were only cash deposits made into her account."

"Do you think she was doing something illegal?"

"Possibly." Brie had considered it.

"Have you spoken with the roommate?"

Brie turned her glass. "I've tried. She's one of the missing women."

"Missing women?"

She told Eliot about how she'd been searching for ex–Black Diamond employees.

"You told the detectives this?"

"Yeah. I sent them everything I have. They're looking into it. Even going through old files to see if anything matches."

Brie and Eliot went back to the hospital and chatted with Tory and Sam. When visiting hours rolled around, she went in to see Carlos again. And it hurt just as much as it had before. The whiteness of the room, the beeping of the monitor, the sterile smell, it felt like an assault on her senses.

Tory kept saying how his color looked better. Brie didn't see it, but she lied. Because she knew he was grasping at hope.

Before she left the hospital, she got a copy of her

sister's file from Connor on her email, followed by a text. Armand at Houston club.

She typed in the word—Thanks—then almost deleted it. In the end, she sent it. He didn't have to call a friend. He didn't have to save her cat. Then again, he didn't have to be such a dick last night. But for her sister and for Carlos she could do this.

Now if she could just forget how good last night had been. And she wasn't referring to the sex. It was what happened before the sex that left a dent in her heart. The empathy she'd felt for him—empathy about his dad, his mom, his partner, and the young boy he'd killed. It was that need to be understood. To understand someone. To not feel... alone.

Not like love or anything serious. She didn't believe in love at first sight. Lust at first sight, yeah. She saw that played out in the club most nights. But that wasn't what happened with them. Oh, she'd felt attraction, but it was that time on the sofa, sharing, talking, the not-so-alone feeling that had her peeling off her clothes.

* * *

After Brie left, Connor, Juan, and Mark all sat at their desks, reading over files, searching for a lead, a break. The financial records on the three agents had come in. Juan was combing through them, while Connor and Mark were reading over the Sala case.

Come Monday they had to interview the three agents, and they needed to know enough to question them. Know enough to catch anyone in a lie.

But Connor couldn't concentrate. He kept thinking

about Brie. About last night. About how awesome the sex was. About how big a piece of shit he was. Then he kept replaying what Brie had told him about her father, her sister, and her mom. Their childhoods couldn't be more different, yet the emotional damage caused by them felt similar.

It didn't surprise him that the only person Brie was close to was Eliot. At least growing up, he'd had his mom. She might have put God before him, but she'd cared and didn't push raising him onto someone else.

Having been abandoned by his father, Connor knew that pain. It was easy to just slap his old man into the deadbeat-dad, or a sorry-son-of-a-bitch category, but how much more would it have hurt to know his old man had chosen another child over him. That would've taken the pain to a whole new level.

Frustrated with his inability to concentrate, Connor swapped out the Sala file for the Ronan one. He tapped his pencil on his desk and read about Mr. Ronan.

He looked up. "I think we need to talk to Brie's father."

"Why?" Mark looked up from the report.

"Besides me wanting to neuter the bastard?"

"Why do you want to neuter him?" Mark asked.

"You two didn't pick up on the fact that Ronan abandoned Brie as a kid to go live with Alma and her mom, then had the gall to call Brie and ask her to help find the daughter he chose over her? What kind of piece-of-shit person does that?"

"I guess that's pretty low." Mark and Juan shared a look, as if they knew something he didn't.

"What?" Connor asked.

"Nothing," Mark said. "It's just...you seem to be emotionally invested in Brie's issues."

"Not more than any other case."

Juan leaned back in his chair. "Yeah it is. And calling Brie's father out for being a terrible parent isn't going to help this case."

"He lied to the police. This police statement says he hadn't heard from Alma in six months. But Brie told me that he was the one who told her to call Brie. Now, I can't help but wonder if he knows more about Alma's life when she went missing than he's said. And if he knows something, then we need to know it."

"I see your point," Mark said. "Do you have his phone number?"

"I do. But I want to go in person."

Mark lifted his arms over his head and stretched. "Didn't I read he lives in Henderson?"

"Yeah." Connor picked up a pen and rolled it between his palms.

Mark continued to stare. "It's a two-hour drive. You think it merits that?"

"Yeah. I do," Connor said.

"Then call him and set it up," Mark said. "But leave your neutering tools at home."

Connor grabbed his phone and punched in the number. No answer, but his voice mail picked up. "Hi. You reached Mr. Ronan. Looking to sell your house? Want to buy a house? Leave a message and I'll call you back."

"Mr. Ronan, this is Detective Pierce in Anniston. It's about your daughter's case. If you care at all, call me back."

When Connor hung up, he saw Mark and Juan looking at each other again. "What?"

"If you care at all?"

"He's a piece of shit!"

Juan rolled his eyes and leaned back in his chair. "Well, which one of us is going to Willowcreek with Brie tomorrow to talk to the waitress who served Agent Olvera?"

"Billy would love to do it," Mark said smugly.

"Stop!" Connor said.

"Stop what?" Mark feigned innocence.

"I'll go with her," Connor said.

"Without killing each other?" Juan asked.

Connor shot his partners the bird and they all went back to work. At least Connor tried to. His mind kept remembering walking out on Brie.

Five minutes later, Juan blurted out, "Shit!"

"Tell me that's a good 'shit.' As in you've got something."

"It's a suspicious 'shit.'"

"What?" Mark asked.

"Agent Miles made five nine-thousand-nine-hundred-and-ninety-nine-dollar deposits into his account last year. Two were the same month the Sala case went bad. Before that, his account was overdrawn."

"That is suspicious," Connor said. "Isn't ten thousand the number that requires monies be reported to the Treasury Department?"

"Yup," Juan answered.

"Damn," Mark said. "We need to delve deeper into Agent Miles. Look into his family, make sure he doesn't have a rich mama, or hasn't inherited anything lately."

At almost five that afternoon, they hadn't found any departed family members who could have left Agent Miles money, but he did have a rich mama. Unfortunately, Mrs. Miles was on a cruise ship and couldn't be reached. They left a message and emailed her.

"Should we confront Miles?"

"No," Mark said. "Let's wait to talk to his mother. If we accuse him first, he might convince her to lie for him."

"Someone owes me a steak dinner." Mildred stormed into the office.

"You found something?" Mark asked.

"Tell me this doesn't look like the same woman." She put two pictures on Mark's desk.

Mark leaned forward. Connor and Juan jumped up to check themselves.

Connor stared at the images. The same dark brown eye color, the same facial features. "Looks like it to me," Connor said. "Who is this?"

"Linda Kramer. That's the name she went by when the police interviewed her about Brie's missing sister. But this"—she pointed to the mug shot from a file—"claims her name is Regina Berger." Mildred's smile beamed with pride. "I swear, if I keep helping you guys solve your cases, you're going to have to give me a badge."

"Wasn't Kramer the roommate?" Mark asked.

Connor nodded and plopped down on his desk chair to type "Regina Berger" into the database. While it searched, he looked up at Mildred. "If I find her, you can order lobster with that steak."

"Yum. I love lobster. And if I find another one, I expect someone to treat me to a pedicure. I want my toes to look pretty while I'm eating my fancy dinner."

* * *

Connor pulled into the parking lot of a new upscale apartment complex on the swanky side of town, while Juan and Mark went back to studying the Sala case files.

Mildred was searching for restaurants that served steak and lobster and had agreed to take home the rest of the files in hopes of getting pretty toes.

As Connor walked past a new Lexus and an array of other expensive cars in the parking lot, he realized whatever work Regina was doing these days, it paid a lot better than being a detective. Not only were the cars in the lot high-end, but the apartment had to cost upward of two thousand a month.

Definitely a step up, considering Regina Berger had priors that included shoplifting and a three-year-old warrant for a Class B misdemeanor for weed. Which is probably why she'd used an alias while working at the Black Diamond. But thanks to a routine traffic stop three months ago, her car registration had revealed her real name, and she was arrested.

She'd immediately hired a fancy lawyer and got off with a fine and a slap on the wrist.

Connor headed to apartment 106 and rang the bell. He could hear music inside, but no one answered.

A man in his early forties walked up to the apartment next door.

"Excuse me?" Connor asked. "Does Regina Berger live here?"

The man offered a noncommittal shrug. "A woman and her daughter live there."

"Is she in her twenties, brunette?"

"Yeah. The mom's got dark hair and eyes, and as you can hear, she likes her music way too loud."

"Thanks." Connor watched the guy walk into his apartment.

He poked the doorbell again. When that didn't get

him anywhere, he knocked. The loud music stopped. He knocked again.

"Alright already," someone called.

The door opened and the young woman holding a phone to her ear and a wine cooler in her hand was indeed Regina Berger. Granted, the woman wearing a black skirt, red blouse, and a frown, looked a hell of a lot better than either of her mug shots.

Her eyes lifted and her frown turned to a smile.

"Regina Berger?" he asked.

"Just a minute," she said into her phone, "I've got a very hot guy standing at my door." She lowered the phone to her cheek and gave him a slow once-over, then grinned widely. "What can I do for you?"

"I'm Detective Pierce with APD." He pulled back his jacket to show his badge. It never failed. Within two seconds of showing his ID, he always knew how the talk was going to go. From her sudden loss of color, his gut said this one wasn't going to go easy. His gut also said he'd just lost his hot status.

Damn, he hated when that happened.

He continued to stare at her, but over her shoulder he saw a few toy dolls and a baby bottle scattered on the floor.

She hung up the phone. "I took care of that warrant."

"Yes, ma'am, I know. I'm here about another matter. Do you mind if I come in?"

"What matter?" She stayed poised in the doorway.

"A Linda Kramer matter?"

Her olive coloring paled some more.

"Because"—he pulled the mug shot from his front pocket—"she looks a lot like you."

Her mouth thinned. "Look, I've got...I don't have

time for games. If you need to talk to me, you can contact my lawyer."

"Wow. I'm here to ask a few questions and you're wanting a lawyer. That's not a good sign."

"I'm not . . . Fine. Ask your questions and leave."

"Did you ever use that name, Ms. Berger?"

"If there are any warrants under that name, they aren't mine."

"So you admit to using a fake name and Social Security card."

"I'll pay the taxes, if that's what this is about."

"Why did you lie about who you were?"

"Because I had a warrant—which I've since taken care of—and there was a bartender at the Black Diamond who could get you a new ID for three hundred dollars."

"Did you share an apartment with an Alma Ronan?"

Her eyes widened. "I already spoke to the police about her disappearance."

"We have a few more questions."

"Well, I don't have any more answers."

"Can I please come in? We can talk here, or you can come down to the station."

She still hesitated before pushing open the door. "You only have a minute. My baby needs a bottle."

As he walked in, he almost stepped on a stuffed pink dinosaur. As nice as the place was, it could really have used a cleaning. He sat at the dining room table right off the entrance. Trying to focus on her and not on the plate of half-eaten food, which appeared to have been there for a while, he frowned.

"Care to join me?" He waited until she sat down before he spoke again. "Thank you."

She rubbed her palms on her black skirt, as if they were sweating. What did she have to sweat about? Did she know something about Alma Ronan's murder?

He pulled his notebook out of his coat pocket. "How long did you know Alma Ronan?"

"Not long. We worked at the Black Diamond at the same time. We were both having a hard time making ends meet so we moved in together."

"Looks like you're doing okay now."

"Is that a crime?"

Her attitude was beginning to grate on him. "Depends. What kind of work do you do?"

"I work at a maid service."

"You're a maid?"

"I work there. I'm not a maid."

"I see." His gaze went back to the plates on the table.

He looked down at the pad again. "When was the last time you saw Alma?"

"I don't know. Sometime in May. She just disappeared one day."

He met her nervous gaze. "That's odd."

"What's odd?" She rubbed her hands on the black skirt again.

"Back in June, you told the detective that she moved out."

"She did." She fidgeted in her seat. "That's what I mean by disappeared."

Regina Berger sucked at lying. "Have you spoken with her?"

She hesitated. It was a baited question. Would she bite? "Yeah. She called not too long ago."

"When was this?"

"A few weeks ago. I don't remember exactly."

Right then the sound of a child crying came from the back.

"My baby. I need to get her."

He nodded. As soon as she took off down the hall, he phoned his office. Mark answered.

"What's up?"

"The roommate is lying through her teeth. I'm going to bring her in."

"You're kidding me?"

"No. And she has a baby. So I'll need someone there to handle that."

"I'll get someone."

He hung up. The crying continued. Louder. Then louder. One, two, three minutes passed. He stood up. "Regina?" he called out.

She didn't answer.

He walked down the hall. The door at the end was open, but the crying kid appeared to be behind the closed door to his right. He moved to the door at the end and saw there was a back patio and the door was open. "Dammit!" She'd taken off. He started to run after her, but he heard the baby again. He couldn't leave the child.

"Shit!"

# CHAPTER EIGHTEEN

W hat do I do? It keeps crying." Connor gripped the phone, staring at the baby, now red-faced, nose running, sitting up in the crib. He had called in a BOLO for Regina Berger and had Juan and Mark researching what kind of car she drove.

"It? Is it a girl or boy?" Mildred asked, and Connor struggled to hear what she said over the baby's screams.

"I don't know. Can't you come here?" Juan and Mark were supposed to be on the way, but Connor suspected they weren't any more equipped to take care of a baby than he was. When he called the office, he'd discovered Mildred had left the precinct, so he'd called her cell.

"I told you, I'm babysitting for my neighbor. I'm supposed to be there in five minutes. Poor thing, I can hear the screaming. Are you holding it?"

"No."

"Well, pick it up."

"I don't know how!"

"How old is the baby?"

"I don't know."

"Men," she snapped. "How big is he or she?"

"Bigger than a puppy," he answered.

"Is the baby sitting up? Standing up?"

"It was standing, now it's sitting."

"Then you can't break it. Just pick it up."

He walked over to the crib. The baby screamed harder. "It doesn't like me."

"Pick the baby up!"

He put the phone between his shoulder and his ear, and reaching under the child's arms, he picked it up. It squirmed, but he held on tight.

"Okay, I got it. He held the child up a few feet away from his body. "But it's still screaming."

"Does it have a dirty diaper?"

"How can I tell?"

He could swear she laughed. "Smell it. Or stick your finger inside the diaper. The latter one is kind of dangerous."

He lifted the child closer and sniffed. "Oh gawd, it stinks."

She laughed, and this time he heard it clear as day. "Are there any diapers around? A changing table?"

Connor looked around. "I see diapers. I don't know what a changing table is."

"A table with a flat surface where you can lay the baby. But don't let the baby roll off."

"I can't do this," he said.

"Connor, this isn't disarming a bomb. You can do this. I'll walk you through it."

Ten minutes later, he'd managed to change the diaper and was pacing with the baby in his arms. It, or rather she, had curled against his shoulder and was breathing in shaky breaths.

The doorbell rang and he hurried to answer it.

Mark and Juan both stood on the other side of the door.

"Did you find her?" Connor asked.

"No," Juan said, then both of his partners burst out laughing.

"It's not funny."

"I don't know, Mildred called us, and if you could have heard her tell the story it was hilarious," Mark said, laughing so hard he could barely talk. "I heard you gagged changing the diaper."

"Take her." He pulled the child off his chest. The baby screamed.

"No!" Both guys backed up like he'd offered them a poisonous snake.

Connor brought the crying child back to his chest. She buried her face against him, and the crying at least lowered in volume.

"If she were five or older, I could do it," Juan said. "I'm an expert with five-year-olds. But I have no experience with them any younger."

"Don't you have nephews?" Connor asked Mark.

"Yeah, but I never babysat them."

"Did you check and see if Regina had any family?" Connor began bouncing the baby when she started crying harder. He'd found she stopped crying when he did that.

Mark shook his head. "Regina grew up in foster care. But I called CPS. Unfortunately, they probably won't be here for several hours."

"Damn," Connor said. "Mildred said we needed to feed her. I found some formula in the kitchen. But all the bottles are dirty. Can one of you wash a bottle and fill it with formula?"

"I think I can handle that," Mark said.

Connor tried to put the baby back in her bed, but she started screaming again.

An hour later, Connor was holding a fed and sleeping child against his chest when the CPS worker, Mary Stanley, showed up. She was a middle-aged woman who looked crumpled, exhausted, and at wit's end. Connor continued to hold the baby while the woman filled out paperwork.

"Do you know the child's father?"

"No," Connor said. "We came to ask her mom some questions about a case and she fled. We have nothing."

"And the mother has no family?" she asked, as if she hadn't heard what Connor said.

"Our records show she grew up in foster care," Mark answered.

"Great," the woman said and sighed. "First, we take care of them and then their kids."

For some reason that annoyed Connor. It sounded as if she blamed the baby for her mother's abandonment.

"Does the mother work? Who cares for the child during the day?"

"We don't know," Connor answered, this time frustration sounded in his voice. "Like I said, we just came to ask her some questions." Then he remembered. "She said she worked at a maid service?"

The woman made a note of that. "Is the child sick?"

Connor looked at the baby. "I . . . I don't know."

She came over and examined the child quickly. "She doesn't look it."

Connor almost asked where she'd gotten her medical degree, but bit it back.

Then Ms. Stanley haphazardly packed a bag with some diapers, clothes, bottles, baby wipes, and formula.

When she took the baby from Connor's arms, the child screamed.

"Bounce her," Connor said. "She'll stop crying."

The woman frowned. "I got this."

But she didn't. She didn't start bouncing. The child screamed harder and held her hands out to Connor.

Connor's arms suddenly felt empty. "Bounce her," he repeated. The woman frowned at him and started out. He followed her to the door. "Where are you taking her?"

"To a temporary foster home. If you find her mom, call CPS."

Connor wanted to lash out at the woman for her incompetence. Instead, he targeted the real villain. "What kind of mother leaves her child with a stranger?" he spat out the question to Mark and Juan.

"A piss-poor one," Juan said.

"Fuck! I can't believe I let her get away."

"That's not on you. You didn't know she'd run," Juan said.

Connor looked at his partners. "You think the kid is okay?"

Before they could answer, Connor's phone rang. He pulled it out of his pocket.

He looked at Juan. "It's Detective Quarrels from Vice."

* * *

The doorbell woke Brie up from a dead sleep. She jackknifed up, causing Psycho to bolt off the mattress.

She caught her breath and looked at the clock. It was nine p.m.

She'd come home from the hospital around three and started going over her sister's file. When she couldn't keep her eyes open, she'd decided to grab a power nap. So powerful, she'd slept five hours.

Brushing her hair off her face, she scooted off the bed. A knock now sounded at her door.

Remembering her place had been broken into, and the only thing protecting her from an intruder was the old-fashioned slide lock Connor had attached, she grabbed her gun off the bedside table.

Connor had left a message that the perp she'd caught on her nanny cam had been arrested, and Dunn had been given the cover story, but considering she seldom had visitors... better safe than sorry.

She went to the front window and pulled back the curtain. Connor stood perched on her doorstep, looking unhappy. His frown said something bad had happened. Her first thought was Carlos, but surely someone would have called her. Still, she hurried and opened the door.

"What is it?" She stepped back as he walked in.

"Were you asleep?"

"Yeah."

"Sorry."

"What's wrong?"

"We found Regina Berger."

"Who?"

"Linda Kramer. Her real name is Regina Berger. Your sister's roommate."

*Wasn't this good news?* He didn't look happy. "Does she know anything?"

"She's definitely hiding something."

"What's she saying?" She shut the door.

"Nothing now. She got away."

Brie pulled her hair back. "Then how do you know she's hiding something?"

"Because she lied. She said she had spoken to your sister a few weeks ago."

Brie shook her head, still feeling half-asleep. "Wait. You found her and you've already lost her?"

"I know." Frowning, he added, "She said she was going to check on her baby... but then she fled, leaving the baby there, screaming."

His words were running amok in her head. She moved to the sofa and dropped down, her brain trying to play catch-up. "She left her baby?"

"Yeah. What kind of mother does that?" He sat beside her. She almost got up and moved to a chair. "We've got a BOLO out on her. We found out what kind of car she drives. Hopefully, we'll find her. But that's not the only reason I'm here."

"What else?"

"One of the other names you gave us, Tammy Alberts. It was familiar to one of the vice cops. He'd helped out on some cases with ICE last year and he asked if he could run the name by them. He did and found out he was right about the name. On one of their cases, a fake driver's license with that name was found last year at a crime scene right across the Mexican border."

"What kind of crime scene?"

"Six bodies were found in the back of an old delivery truck. All females. They are believed to be victims of human trafficking. The truck had been set on fire, but it appeared the women had died a day or two earlier. Probably from heat exposure."

Brie closed her eyes, then opened them. "So I'm right. That's what happened to my sister. Human trafficking." Brie had believed it from the start, but hearing it brought the hurt to her chest all over again, and not just for her sister, but for the other victims as well.

"It looks like it."

"Do you have the other victims' names? Do any of them link up with the Black Diamond or Dillon Armand?"

"They're looking into it. They couldn't get prints on all of them, and a couple of them still haven't been identified."

"Why didn't the name come up when I searched the database for a Tammy Alberts?"

"ICE used the real names they had on the report. The license was damaged in the fire, all they got was the name on it. They could tell it was a fake, but they weren't even sure which girl's picture was on it."

She shook her head. "And we don't have anyone on Armand. He's in the wind. He could be kidnapping other women right now. He could be halfway to Guatemala."

"ICE has been looking into the human trafficking case. They have agreed to help. We have an agent going to the strip club in Houston where my friend said he spotted him." Connor pulled out his phone. "He should be getting there any time now, and will let us know when he has eyes on Armand."

She swallowed, trying to find relief in what little he offered.

"I also contacted the airlines, and if any changes are made to the ticket Armand flew over here on, we'll be contacted. I want this guy as badly as you do."

Yeah, but wanting something didn't make it happen. If so, Armand would have been behind bars from the instant she'd recognized his name in the Guatemalan police report. And the FBI, her own agency, would have been the ones to investigate it.

"What if he decides to leave the U.S. the same way he got my sister out? There was no record of her leaving."

"I don't think he'd do that unless he believes we're on to him. We're doing everything we can."

She sat there silent, trying to wrap her brain around the new information.

Right then, Psycho came strolling into the room. He moved between the coffee table and sofa, and sniffed Connor's pants leg. It was then Brie remembered what had happened the last time they'd shared the sofa.

Connor didn't move. Neither did her cat. Then the feline jumped up on the sofa between them, almost as if he'd decided Connor wasn't out to hurt him.

Brie's mind went back to the news he'd delivered. "Do you think Berger knows what happened to my sister?" Psycho eased closer and curled up in her lap.

"I think she was lying and ran for a reason."

Before he could say more, Connor's phone rang. When he pulled it out, Psycho watched him—leery—but he didn't jump down.

"It's the ICE agent in Houston." He took the call. Brie held her breath, hoping it was good news.

"You got him?" Connor asked in lieu of hello. His frown told her what she needed to know. "Okay," he said. "Yeah, do that." He hung up.

She fought the wave of disappointment. "He's not there, is he?"

"No."

She shook her head. "How are they proceeding? If they talk to the owner, he could warn Armand we are on to him."

"He's been told to stay completely under the radar. The agent is going to remain at the club to see if Armand returns. Mark and Juan are calling to see if Armand checked into a hotel in the area." He dropped his hand over hers.

The touch sent a spark—part pain, part pleasure—right to her chest. She pulled her hand out from under his. "Thanks for coming here to tell me. But you should go."

For one second, she thought he was going to argue, and a small part of her wanted him to. Instead, he stood up. "I'm going with you to Willowcreek tomorrow to interview the waitress."

The thought of being in the car with him for several hours had her chest tightening. "What time?"

"Nine okay? You want me to pick you up here?" he asked.

"No. At the hospital. I'll be there."

He started for the door then turned. "I called on the way over here and they said Agent Olvera's vitals are doing better."

"Yeah." Was his concern for Carlos supposed to make her feel better? It didn't.

It appeared as if he wanted to say something else, but he finally just walked out.

Her cat meowed. She looked at the feline. "Great. You start trusting him right when I realize I can't."

# CHAPTER NINETEEN

I can't believe we ate it all." Tory stared at the four empty pint-sized cartons of Ben & Jerry's ice cream spread over the table in the ICU waiting room. Unable to sleep, Brie had decided to come to the hospital.

"I can," Eliot said. "I can feel my arteries clogging as I sit here."

"Oh, please," Tory said. "Carlos says ice cream fixes everything."

"I know," Brie said, choking up. "That's why I brought it." She couldn't count how many ice cream runs she and Carlos had made when they lived in the same apartment complex. They'd truly been best friends, turning to each other, because neither of them had anyone else.

As happy as Brie had been when Carlos met Tory, she missed the times they'd shared when they were both single.

Brie hung out at the hospital until eleven, then after

giving out hugs, she headed out. Keys in hand, she'd just walked out of the automatic doors when her phone rang. On the screen, the name DAVID MILES flashed.

Why was he calling her? And this late?

"Yeah?" she answered as she continued walking to her car. Only a few cars filled the lot, but no one seemed to be out. His voice sounded garbled. Then the line went dead. She hugged her leather coat tighter, as the night air brought a chill.

The dark sky above seemed to hang low. One of the lights on a post in the parking lot buzzed, as if about to blow. She kept walking, but her steps suddenly seemed too loud and the night too quiet. The hair on the back of her neck began dancing.

Reaching into her coat, she put her hand on her Glock. Senses heightened, she stopped and did a full circle. Nothing. Nobody.

She started walking again but couldn't shake the feeling of being watched. Clicking her doors open, she slid behind the wheel, locked the car, and sat there, staring out into the night. She checked and rechecked every shadow.

After a few minutes, Miles called her again.

"Hello?"

"Where are you?" he asked.

"Why?" Was he here?

"I need to talk to you."

"What about?" A dark shadow darted between a car and a truck.

"I think I know who Olvera saw in Willowcreek."

"Who?" Brie leaned into the steering wheel, staring toward the truck.

"I don't want to talk about it over the phone."

She pulled her gun from her holster. The cold weight of it against her palm sent a chill through her.

"Brie? Are you listening?"

"Uh-huh."

"I know they're going to blame me. I look guilty, but I didn't do it."

The inside light of the car parked beside the truck came on. A woman appeared, and got inside.

Brie exhaled. "Who's gonna blame you?"

"The detectives."

"Why?" He didn't answer, so she tossed another question out. "Who do you think Carlos met?"

"Not over the phone. I'm at your apartment. I'm coming up."

"I'm not... Wait. How do you know where I live?"

"I followed you earlier."

*Did he also follow me to the Black Diamond?*

"I'm not home. There's a Denny's two blocks from the hospital. On Pebble and Green Street. Meet me there."

Brie hung up and drove straight to Denny's. But she pulled into a spot next door, where she could watch and wait for Miles to arrive. Make sure he came alone.

With her gun still in hand, she waited. Fifteen minutes later, a Toyota pulled into the parking lot. She watched him walk inside.

Did she trust him?

No. But she didn't think he was stupid enough to try something in public. Maybe he wasn't lying. Maybe he did know who Carlos had met. And maybe it behooved her to know why he thought the detectives were going to suspect him.

Pretending she wasn't afraid, she went to meet him.

He sat in a back booth.

She moved in. "How about I take your gun?"

"You think I'd shoot you?" he asked.

"Just do it."

For one second, she thought he was going to argue. Her hold on her piece tightened. "Fine." He handed her his gun. "You want to pat me down to make sure I'm not carrying a second piece?"

She almost said yes, but suddenly she believed him. It hurt to suspect him when less than five months ago she'd been working by his side.

She dropped into the booth, then set both guns beside her on the seat, pulled off her jacket, and covered them up.

"Now. Start talking."

He started to respond just as the waitress walked over. They ordered coffee and when she left, he leaned in. "They contacted my mom, didn't they?"

"They?"

"The detectives."

"Why would they...?"

"They checked my financial records, didn't they? But it's not what they think. I have a problem. A gambling problem. I'd stopped, but this last year...I'm getting help. I haven't gambled in three months. This could cost me my job. But I can prove that's all this is. You're in tight with them. If you—"

"So you lied to get me here? You said you knew who Carlos met with."

"No. I wasn't lying." The conversation halted as the waitress dropped off their coffees.

Once she'd left, Brie asked, "Who did Carlos meet?"

"Are they handing the report over to Agent Calvin?"

"I don't know." But she suspected they would. "Who did Carlos meet?"

"Ask your cop friend to give me a chance to prove what I'm telling you is true, before he takes what he learned to Calvin. He can tell him, just let me get ahead of this first. I'll go to personnel Monday morning. That way, I might salvage my job."

"I'll talk to them, but I can't make any promises. Now tell me who you think Carlos met with."

He nodded. "The day before Olvera came here, he stayed at the office late, I overheard him talking...He said the name Rosaria."

"Rosaria Altura?" Pablo's girlfriend. The one Brie suspected had been killed.

"Yeah. That's why I said he might have been in on this."

"He was trying to find answers. He wasn't...Are you sure you heard right?"

"He called her by her name. And he asked where she'd been all this time."

"Why didn't you tell me this earlier?"

"Maybe I would have if you hadn't told me to get out."

She sat trying to digest the information.

"Look, this afternoon I ran all of her family through the database again. I found out she has a sister who just moved to Texas. She lives right outside of Willowcreek. She recently married a José Hernandez."

*José Hernandez?* The name from Carlos's burner phone.

"I have an address." He pulled a paper from his front pocket and pushed it over.

"Who else knows about this?"

"Knows about what?"

"Do Agents Bara and Calvin know about the call? About you giving me the address?"

"About me coming here and finding the address, no. But I mentioned hearing Carlos talking to Rosaria when we found out he'd been shot. And...if I found this address, either one of them could have as well."

\* \* \*

After Connor left Brie's apartment, he'd gone home and crashed. He'd slept hard for four hours, then had woken up and couldn't go back to sleep. He thought about how Brie looked at him when she insisted he leave. He thought about the other women Brie thought were missing and wondered if they were still alive. He even thought about the baby and wondered if whoever was taking care of her was doing a better job than the CPS worker.

How fucking hard would it have been to bounce her?

Frustrated, he got up, got dressed, and went to the diner. As he walked in, he grabbed a newspaper someone had left on the counter and sat at a table in Flora's section. For some reason, Brie's words filled his head: *grief and guilt can fit into the same pocket.* She was right. He still grieved for his mom, for his partner, and for Flora's son. He grieved for the man he used to be before that god-awful night changed everything. And he felt guilty for it all.

Flora stopped at his table and tapped her pencil on her pad. "You really have no lady friend to keep you company?"

"I'm too big a bastard," he told her, only half-joking.

"All men are bastards, until the right woman changes them."

He smiled. "That seems like a big burden on you women."

"It can be," she said. "Same order?"

"Yup."

"Hey, I need a refill!" a man yelled out from a booth.

Flora flinched and frowned. Connor looked back at the guy as he banged his cup on the table. With him, slumped over, was another man.

Leaning in, Flora whispered, "Of course, some men aren't worth saving." She left, grabbed a coffeepot, and went to refill the drunk's cup.

Connor moved to the other side of the booth, where he could keep an eye on the potential problem.

In a few minutes, Flora set a coffee and some creams in front of him. "You agree?"

"Huh?" he asked.

She pointed to the newspaper. He looked at the article and read the headline. DOES A MARIJUANA CONVICT DESERVE A SECOND CHANCE?

"Oh. I haven't read it."

"Do you believe in second chances?"

He picked up one of the creamers, pulled back the top, emptied it into his coffee, and considered her question. And the irony of the person who was asking.

Without looking at her, he answered, "I think some people deserve a second chance and some don't." Picking up a spoon, he stirred the cream into his cup, watching the dark brew turn lighter. When she didn't leave, he finally looked up. "What do you think?"

"The same. Some do. Some don't. The hard part is knowing which is which."

"Yes," he said. "That's the hard part."

She nodded somberly and left. He stared at the paper without reading it. In a few minutes, a plate of food was set in front of him. "Thank you."

She hesitated, as if wanting to say something. Then she walked away.

He was almost finished eating when the drunk in the other booth yelled out, "You cheated me, bitch. You owe me five dollars!"

Connor set his fork down and watched Flora hesitantly walk over to the man. "No, sir. I gave you the correct change."

"Liar!" He pounded his fist on the booth. "You owe me five bucks."

Flora flinched. "Fine!" She reached into her apron.

Connor stood up. "She said she gave you what you were owed."

"Stay out of it," the bozo said to Connor.

"I'll just give it to him," Flora said, her accent thickening under the stress.

"Who is she to you? The old lady suck your dick or something? If she wants to, she can suck mine instead of giving me five dollars."

Connor leaned down and placed both of his palms on the table. "Apologize."

"Go fuck yourself."

Connor straightened, pulled back his jacket, and showed the guy his badge. "Apologize."

"Just 'cause you're a cop doesn't mean you—"

"I'll just give him the money," Flora said again.

Connor ignored her. "I said apologize."

The man and his friend stood up. Connor moved in. "You aren't leaving until you apologize."

"You can't make me."

"But I can arrest you." He pulled his handcuffs off his belt, and his phone from his pocket.

"For what?" Spittle came out of his mouth. "Not apologizing?"

"For public intoxication." He punched in a number. "This is Detective Pierce. I need a patrol car."

Connor was so focused on the perp in front of him, he didn't see the guy's friend throw a punch.

Then again, Connor wasn't famous for seeing a fight coming. But he was famous for ending them.

# CHAPTER TWENTY

Brie sat in her car, staring at the address scribbled on the piece of paper. Rosaria Altura was alive. Which probably meant she'd been in hiding all this time because she'd seen something or knew something about Pablo's death.

It was about a two-hour drive. She slid her keys into the ignition. Almost started it, then stopped. She hated to admit it, but she was going to need help. Grabbing her phone, she found his number in her contact list and hit call.

It rang once. Twice.

*Hang up. Just hang up.* It was one in the morning. He was probably asleep. Then the line clicked.

She waited to hear his sleepy voice, but instead she heard what sounded like dishes being broken in the background, and a male voice say, "I said stay down!"

"Connor?" Brie asked.

Then came another voice. A female voice. "Hello?" The accent was Spanish.

"Stop resisting!" Connor's voice came across the line again. "Tell them Detective Pierce said to send a car."

"Detective Pierce says to send a car. Watch out!" she screamed.

Brie tried to think. "Where are you?"

"Denice's Diner. 1832 Magnolia Street."

"I'm calling for backup." Brie hung up and dialed 911. Then she started the car.

"Nine one one. What's—"

"Officer in need of backup. Denice's Diner. 1832 Magnolia Street." She hung up and tore out of the parking lot. She was just six or seven minutes away.

With few cars on the road, she drove over the speed limit. When she pulled up at the diner, a patrol car was already there.

She went inside. Connor stood talking to an officer. Two handcuffed men, both who appeared to be under the influence of something, leaned against a wall. One had a busted lip.

Connor looked over at her and his eyes widened in surprise. *You okay?* he mouthed.

She nodded.

He held up a finger, asking for a minute. Before he turned back to the officer, she noticed his swollen eye.

A waitress, a middle-aged Hispanic woman, walked over. "I'm sorry. Just a little problem. You can sit anywhere."

"Thanks, but I'm...here for Detective Pierce."

"Are you the one who called?" the waitress asked.

Brie nodded then pulled out her phone to check the time. Should she just leave?

"Would you like coffee while you wait?"

"No, thank you." She looked back at the handcuffed men. "What happened?"

"They were drunk and saying ugly things. Detective Pierce told them to apologize. One of the men hit him."

"And I'm sure that didn't go over too well." Brie noticed the woman's name tag read FLORA.

"No." Flora gazed at Connor. "He did not like that. Are you his friend?"

"Not really. We're acquaintances."

The waitress kept staring, as if she knew there was more to the answer.

Brie felt compelled to continue. "He's helping me out with something."

"*El que hace zapatos va descalzo,*" Flora muttered and walked away without realizing Brie spoke perfect Spanish.

*He who makes shoes goes barefoot himself.* Because Flora's comment came after Brie's statement about him helping her, she wondered just what kind of help did the waitress think Connor needed.

"Hey." Connor stopped beside her. "Is everything okay?"

"Yeah." Brie pushed away her curiosity over Flora's words. "I got a lead."

"How did...how did you know I was here?"

Brie looked at the waitress. "I called and Flora told me."

"Oh, that was you? I thought it was...I'd just called in and asked for backup but we got disconnected." He pulled his wallet from his back pocket and dropped three twenties on a table. "What lead?"

Brie looked curiously at the huge tip. "I know who Carlos had lunch with in Willowcreek. Rosaria Altura. I'm going there now."

"Rosaria Altura? That's your informant's girlfriend, right?" He slid his wallet back into his pocket.

"Yeah. I found out that her sister just married a José Hernandez. Remember the call—"

"Yeah. How did you get this information?"

"Agent Miles."

His eyes widened. "You were with Agent Miles?"

"He called me. I met with him."

"Alone?"

"I was careful."

"Brie, it looks as if he's the leak in the Sala case. He's probably the one who ordered the hit on Olvera. He could have—"

"After all he told me, I don't think it's him now. And I was careful."

Connor frowned. "You don't know everything. He's had almost fifty thousand dollars deposited into his account."

"I do know. No thanks to you." And this left her wondering what else he'd been hiding. "Look, Miles told me. He's a gambler. He says his up-and-down account is reflective of his winning and losing streaks. But the thing is, he's not the only one who knows about Rosaria. She could be in danger."

He lifted a brow, as if questioning her. "You got her address?"

"Yeah."

"Then let's go."

She watched Connor look back at the waitress. "Take care."

Flora nodded.

Picking up on something odd between Flora and Connor, Brie followed him out. She stopped when she realized he was going to his car. "I can drive. My car's—"

"Let's take mine. In case someone is expecting you to make the trip."

She climbed in. "Have you heard anything from the ICE agent? Did they find Armand?"

"Not yet." He sounded frustrated. "I can't believe you met Miles alone. Did he say anything else?"

"He wants me to ask you to wait to turn over his financial reports until he can talk to personnel on Monday. He wants to go to them himself and see if he can save his job." She looked at him. "Have you already told Agent Calvin?"

"No. We wanted to look into it more first." Connor pulled out of the parking lot. "This could be a setup. Does he know you're heading up there tonight?"

"I didn't tell him my plans." She resented the fact that he'd think she could be so careless.

"But he probably suspects you will."

"This isn't my first rodeo. I'm not—"

Connor held up his hand. "I still think meeting him was too risky. Like going after Tomas alone. It's as if you have something to prove."

"I do. To you and every other man who thinks I can't take care of myself."

"I'm just saying—"

"Yet I'm not the one with a black eye!"

He made a disapproving noise in the back of his throat. "One doesn't have anything to do with the other."

"Right."

They drove in silence for the next several minutes. "I wasn't implying that you couldn't take care—"

"Just drop it."

A few minutes later, he muttered, "I'd rather argue

than get the silent treatment for the two hours it takes to get there."

"Haven't you heard? Silence is golden."

"Not when it's angry silence." He settled back in the seat. "Are you really worried she's in danger?"

"Of course. I wouldn't . . . You think this was just a ploy to spend time with you?"

"A guy could hope." He half-smiled.

"Well, he shouldn't."

He lost his smile. "Sorry. I'm just . . . I'll call the Willowcreek police and see if they'll send a car by there to make sure everything is okay."

"Yeah."

Five minutes later, after explaining twice he didn't have proof there was any imminent threat, he hung up frustrated. "They're doing a drive-by. But you'd think they'd never heard of a safety check."

"Thanks," she said.

"You're welcome."

They fell back into the awkward silence. She remembered her confusing conversation with Flora. "What happened at the diner?"

"Two drunks mouthed off at the waitress." He looked at her.

"You go there a lot?"

"Yeah." His gaze cut back to the road. A little too quickly.

"You live close?"

"No. I like their pancakes." His tone sounded almost defensive. It was clear he didn't want to share. Apparently, whatever alternate paradigm they'd slipped into the other night when they had told each other secrets was a onetime thing. She should be happy.

She wasn't.

"Sorry I asked." She gazed out the window at the world zipping past.

Several minutes later, he said, "That's her."

Unsure what he meant, she asked, "That's who?"

"The waitress. That's the mom of the kid. The one I killed."

Air caught in her chest. "Why would you...?" She shook her head. "That's not good."

He looked back out the windshield. "I wanted to make sure she was okay."

"How long have you been going?"

"A while." He swallowed.

"Has she ever said anything to you? About her son?"

He shook his head. "I'm not even sure...I mean, I know my picture was in the paper. And at times I think..."

"Think what?"

"That she recognizes me."

Brie was sure she did. Then she remembered the tip he left.

"It wasn't your fault." Brie inhaled and felt it—felt his pain right in the center of her chest. "I think...you go there to punish yourself."

He remained silent for several miles. "No. I leave her money. She has a teenage daughter who's diabetic."

"Couldn't you send her money anonymously?"

"I do. The church started a fund for her. But I wanted her to know."

"Know what?"

He took his time answering. "That I can't sleep. That I haven't forgotten. She deserves to know that." He drove white-knuckled for the next five minutes.

He finally spoke again. "I killed him. And I know what it does to a mother to lose a baby."

"He wasn't a baby. He was almost a grown man. Your partner died. You—"

"It wasn't the kid's bullet that killed Don."

"But you didn't know that. He fired at y'all. I'd have done the same thing. Any person carrying a badge would have done the same thing."

"But they didn't. I did."

"Look, I know what it's like to feel guilty. I feel it every day—"

"That's different. You didn't pull the trigger. Your sister got herself in a mess. And every informant knows they run a risk—"

"But my inaction caused it. And it eats at me, but my point is that I don't purposely go out of my way to hurt myself."

"That's not what I'm doing."

"It seems like it to me."

"Well, you're wrong."

She leaned back in the seat and stared holes out the windshield. The sound of the wheels on the road and the low hum of his car's heater were the only noises.

After several minutes, the silence felt heavy. The emotion in her chest felt dense. She imagined what Connor might feel seeing the boy's mother. She recalled that first week after she'd learned her sister was dead, and how she kept picking up the picture of her sister chained to that bed, and staring at it until the pain was too much. Carlos had made her stop.

"You can't tell me that seeing her doesn't hurt, that—"

"Look," he snapped. "You are mad at me, I get it. Leaving your apartment like I did—"

"We're not talking about that."

"Aren't we? Isn't that why you're really upset?"

"No. I'm upset because..." Then she felt the need to be honest. "Can't I be upset about both things!"

He focused back on the road. "I've said I'm sorry."

"No, you haven't."

He cut her a quick look. "Well, I tried to. You wouldn't let me finish."

"It doesn't matter," she said, but it was another lie. "Let's not talk about this anymore."

"It feels like it matters."

"Well, it doesn't."

"You just said you're upset, so it does matter!" He looked at her again. "Next you'll start lying again, saying the sex wasn't good."

Dad-blast him! "It wasn't."

"I was there," he retorted.

She folded her arms over her chest. "Okay, the sex was okay. But—"

"Just okay?" His green eyes twinkled with heat and amusement. "You're still lying."

That just downright annoyed her. What really pissed her off was she suddenly knew he was using this to change the subject away from the waitress. "On a scale of one to ten, you might have gotten a seven. However—"

"Bullshit."

"Maybe an eight. Yet—"

"A ten. Admit it."

She frowned. "Let me finish! The sex might've been good, but for the overall experience, you didn't even score! The only way it could've ended worse was if you'd tossed a couple of hundred bucks on my bedside table."

The playfulness in his green eyes vanished. His hands tightened on the wheel again. He looked back to the road. "I'm sorry."

"Yeah, you've said that. And we have both agreed it was a mistake, and we don't want it to happen again. So—"

"I said it was a mistake." His voice rang sincere. "But I didn't say I didn't want it to happen again. To be honest, I can't stop thinking about it."

"Well, you should stop!" She started tapping her feet on the floorboard. "Since you're being honest, tell me, do you do this with all women? Get your jollies and run?"

He went back to white-knuckling the steering wheel before answering. "Yeah." But there was something about the way he said it.

"You're lying. You don't do this, do you? So why me?"

He swallowed again, she heard the gulp. "You're right. We don't need to talk about this."

"Oh, no! You started it. And I deserve to know. Why did you do it?" She waited one, two, three seconds and then said, "Tell me!"

He exhaled. It sounded loud within the confines of the car. "It happened too fast. I usually make sure my...intentions are clear."

"Your intentions?"

"My lack of intentions. I'm not looking for anything serious."

"And you thought...We had sex. Once. What did you think I expected? For you to get on one knee, sing me a ballad, and swear to love me forever?"

"No!" he said. "But you..."

"I what?"

"Nothing."

"Don't nothing me! Answer the question!"

His jaw tightened. "You...you kissed my chest," he blurted out. Then he flinched at his own words. "I mean—"

"What? Are you like Julia Roberts in *Pretty Woman*? You have some stupid rule of no kissing on the chest? Fracking Hades!"

"There! You see."

"What?"

"You can't even curse. You're like...Mother Teresa! You volunteer at the shelter. You get homeless people antibiotics. You take in feral cats! You're the type of woman a man takes home to his mom. The type who wants that white picket fence, two kids, and promises. I'll bet you even know how many guys you've slept with. And that you cared about every one of them. I don't have a mom. I hate fences. I don't make promises! I lost count of how many women I've been with years ago."

He didn't even stop to breathe, just kept going. "And the bad part is I knew you were this softhearted, sweet, hungry-for-love woman before I slept with you. But I let it happen anyway. I shouldn't have. Then you kissed my chest and I knew you'd have expectations and I knew..."

"Knew what?"

"That I was going to hurt you."

She couldn't believe her ears. Couldn't believe his audacity. "Wow. How do you do it?"

He continued to stare straight ahead. "Do what?"

"How do you manage to coexist with your own ego? It's so huge. Feeding it must cost you a fortune."

He jerked his head around and looked at her. "I don't—"

"You just assume that because I'm a decent person,

I don't curse like a sailor, and haven't played hide the salami with every Tom, Dick, and Roberto that what? I'm going to fall in love with you because we told each other a few secrets. Because you gave me an orgasm? What in the name of all that's holy makes you so special?"

His mouth dropped. She could see him mentally chewing on what she'd said, and to his credit, he looked properly chastised.

She turned, giving him as much of her back as she could, and stared out the passenger window. The anger swelling in her chest made her eyes sting. But what really hurt was that he wasn't wrong.

She was an idiot. A fool. Oh, she could deny it all she wanted, but she had let him hurt her. Just like she'd let her ex ease his way into her heart.

She already cared about Connor. Cared when she was driving to the diner, afraid he'd gotten hurt. Cared that he was punishing himself for something that wasn't his fault.

Thirty minutes passed before he decided to throw out more words. "I didn't mean..."

"Don't." She looked at him. "You'll only make it worse. We had sex. We agreed it was a mistake, and it's not happening again. We have a case to solve. I respect you as a cop. I'm thankful that you're helping me. When this is over, I'll be gone. And there's no reason for us to talk about it anymore."

He inhaled deeply. His nostrils flared. They went back to the silence.

She didn't speak again until she saw a sign announcing they were close to Willowcreek. "Should I put the address into your GPS?"

"Yeah." His voice sounded tight.

She punched in the address on his dashboard. "The Willowcreek police never called about checking on the house. Do you think they did it?"

He frowned. "Probably not. We'll be there in ten minutes."

"Okay." She leaned back against the seat.

"It's four a.m. What's your plan?" he asked. "Knock on the door? Or wait until morning? I mean, we could be wrong and she's not even there."

"I'll knock. Better safe than sorry."

His phone rang. He reached for it in his cup holder. "It's the Willowcreek police." He answered the call. "Detective Pierce." There was a pause, then "What?" Pause. "Shit! Do you have the shooter?"

"Who's shot?" Brie asked, but Connor, glued to the conversation, didn't answer.

# CHAPTER TWENTY-ONE

W e're almost there." Connor hung up and pushed the gas pedal harder.

"What happened?" Brie asked.

He saw the hurt and angst in her expression, most of which he'd put there. "There's been a shooting."

"Rosaria?"

"I don't know. The officer I spoke to wasn't at the scene. When the unit drove by, they heard gunfire. All he knows is that there's one casualty and one being transported to the hospital."

"Fracking Hades!" She slammed her palm against the dash. "I should have driven up here myself. I could have made it here sooner. If she's dead—"

"No, you shouldn't have. And don't assume the worst." He pushed the gas harder and cut the eight minutes in half.

Four police cars, lights blaring, were parked in front of the house. As he pulled up, he looked at Brie warily. "It'd work best if you let me handle this."

"'Cause you think I can't?"

"No. Because..." He hadn't finished his thought, hadn't even turned off the car when Brie bailed out. "Because they don't like FBI," he muttered. But she already knew that, hence the reason her back was already up.

He rushed to where an officer had stopped her at the yellow tape. She'd already flashed her badge. He stopped beside her.

"What happened?" Brie's tone matched her don't-fuck-with-me expression.

"Why is the FBI involved?" the officer asked.

Brie leaned in. "Can you please just tell me what happened!"

"We're still taking statements."

"Then tell me what you know!"

"We're told there was an intruder. The homeowner grabbed a gun and shot the person entering the house. They exchanged gunfire. One person is dead. The other was taken to the hospital."

"Was one of the victims a woman?"

"You don't have the authority to—"

She looked at the man's nametag. "Officer Malory. Is one of the victims Rosaria Altura? Answer me!"

Connor saw the guy flinch. And he didn't blame him. Brie wasn't playing softball. Her emotions hung around her like a cloud, and he felt for her. After what had happened to her informant, protecting this woman was instinctual.

"The deceased, the intruder, and the person shot are both men. There are two female witnesses, but they're being questioned."

Brie's shoulders dropped with relief. "Where are they?"

"I just said. They're being questioned," he repeated, as if suddenly deciding he'd told too much.

"Thank you." Brie stepped over the yellow tape.

"You can't do that." He grabbed her arm.

Brie looked the officer right in the eyes. "Let me go!"

The officer dropped his hand. Brie kept walking.

Frowning, Officer Malory yelled to another officer to stop Brie.

"Hey." Connor pulled his attention back to him. "Is the body of the intruder still here?"

The officer lifted his gaze. "You FBI, too?"

"No, I'm Detective Pierce with the Anniston Police Department." He shifted his coat back to show his badge.

"You're the one who called?" the officer asked.

"Yes." Connor saw Brie talking with a different officer at the door.

"Look," Connor said, "we have information about the case. We need to talk to whoever is in charge."

"That's Detective Samson. He's inside."

"Can you call him and tell him that if he'd like to know what's going on, to step out and talk to Detective Pierce and Agent Ryan."

The officer spoke into his lapel mic. Connor crossed the tape and moved in beside Brie, who was giving hell to the uniform blocking the door.

The front door opened and a man in his late fifties, wearing a rumpled suit and tie, walked out.

He looked at Connor, seeming to purposely ignore Brie. "Detective Pierce?"

"Yes," Connor offered his hand. The detective didn't take it.

"You brought the FBI with you?"

"I'm Agent Ryan." Brie inserted herself into the conversation.

Samson glanced at Brie, then focused back on Connor. "What the fuck is going on? Why bring this little lady?"

"Sir," Brie spoke up.

Samson stared down at Brie. "Missy, you can—"

"My name's Agent Ryan!" Brie's face reddened. "If you'll listen, I'll tell you what the fuck is going on."

Okay, she could obviously lose the *fracking* when she wanted to.

"Rosaria Altura is a witness in an old case. I think I know who is behind the shooting. I'd appreciate it if you'd let me see her right now."

"Sorry. The female subjects in the house are being interviewed. And I'm not—"

Brie's shoulders tightened. "Look, Detective, you don't want to piss me off."

"No, you look, missy. It's four in the goddamned morning. I was supposed to go fishing today. Instead, I got a dead guy with no ID, a case I don't want, and an FBI agent who looks like she should be in high school instead of trying to order me around."

"One more time! My name's Agent Ryan." She gave the man's tie a yank. "And I don't give a flying fuck if you missed out on fishing! I'm—"

Connor shot between her and the detective. "We can stand here and measure each other's dicks, or we can help each other. Agent Ryan and I—"

"I'm not letting you contaminate my scene."

Connor saw Brie take her phone out and start punching in numbers. He caught her arm. "Not yet." Then he yanked his own phone out and focused on the asshole in front of him. "Is this your dead guy?"

Connor found the surveillance image of the man Brie had chased from Olvera's hotel and held it out.

Detective Samson squinted, then his eyes widened. "What's his name?"

"We'll give you everything we've got. But you need to work with us."

The detective frowned. "Let me make a few calls."

As soon as the detective walked back inside, Brie frowned at Connor. "The same guy who shot Carlos tried to kill Rosaria. That's proof it's all connected to the Sala case. And that the leak has to be from the FBI."

Connor nodded. This is what Brie had been trying to prove all along, but confirming it still had to hurt. He knew what it felt like to be betrayed by the people you worked with, people you trusted.

Brie pulled her phone back out and started punching in numbers again.

"What are you doing?"

"Calling Agent Calvin. He can make them turn the scene over to the FBI. Or at least work with us."

"Hang up." When she didn't, he said, "Listen to me!"

She stopped and looked up.

"I know you don't think Agent Calvin is behind this, but you don't have proof of that. At the very least, he's stood in your way of this investigation. Doesn't that make you suspicious? Let's see what we can get from this scene before you call him."

"That's just it. We're not getting shit. Detective Samson isn't going to hand over any evidence to us."

Connor frowned. "I hate to say this, but the biggest problem is you."

"Me?" Her blue eyes shot fire at him.

"Not you personally, but you being with the FBI. Small-town cops and FBI are like cats and dogs. Let me contact my department and see if we can call in a few favors with the Willowcreek PD. All I'm asking for is a little time."

* * *

"It's your guy. But it ain't pretty," Detective Samson led them inside the house as he explained that the homeowner, José Hernandez, shot an intruder, then took a bullet.

Connor's plan of getting his superiors involved had worked. Samson was cooperating.

Still, Brie felt almost disloyal for not calling Agent Calvin. Not so long ago, she'd thought she'd take a bullet for anyone at the agency. She'd considered them like an extended family. Now the only one who mattered to her, the only one she trusted, was Carlos.

"I warned you it wasn't pretty," Sampson repeated as they entered the living room. "Shotgun, close range, to the gut. Most of his intestines are on the wall over there. Good news is, he kept his face, so we can identify him."

Brie forced herself to look at the dead man. The detective was right. He'd kept his face. It was definitely their suspect. The man sprawled out on the living room floor had a hole the size of a football dead center of his torso, and parts of his intestines were hanging out.

"Damn," she heard Connor say.

*Don't puke. Don't puke. Do not puke.* "Do you have his weapon?" Brie forced the words out and looked away.

"It's been bagged," Samson said.

"A forty-five?" Her stomach turned.

"Yup," Samson said.

"We'll need ballistics run on that." Brie turned away from the body. She should be happy the piece of crap was dead, but it left so many unanswered questions.

"How serious is José Hernandez wounded?" She fought her gag reflex.

"Not serious. Flesh wound."

The copper smell of blood, the stench of human waste, filled her nose. She swallowed hard. "You running his prints?"

"They'll do that at the morgue. They'll be taking him in shortly."

"How about his phone?" Connor asked.

"He didn't have one." Samson eyed Connor. "You know I've heard about you and your partners. The Three Musketeers."

"Don't believe everything you hear," Connor said.

"I heard you treat rules like suggestions and have problems with authority."

"And yet I still work with the department," Connor muttered.

Samson laughed. "I also heard you were a damn good cop."

"Can I go in to see Rosaria now?" Brie asked, the need to puke passing.

"Yeah. She's pretty shaken." Detective Samson led Brie and Connor into the back bedroom. "Her sister is on the way to the hospital to be with her husband."

When Rosaria saw Brie, the pretty woman gasped. She stood up, and pain, rage, and a number of other negative emotions filled her expression. Brie hadn't known how Rosaria would react to seeing her, but she wasn't prepared for this.

"You! You killed him!" She charged at Brie. Connor and Detective Samson moved in front of her. Connor caught the woman by her shoulders.

"Let her go," Brie said.

Connor released her. "She's here to help you."

"The way she helped Pablo?" Rosaria asked.

"I didn't kill Pablo, Rosaria." Brie met the woman's eyes, and the guilt and blame she continuously tried to push down came rushing back.

"But it might as well have been you." Rosaria stood, clenching and unclenching her fist. "He trusted you. He said you were his friend!"

"I considered him a friend, too," Brie admitted.

Rosaria looked at Connor. "They're going to end up killing me, aren't they?"

"No," Brie answered. "Look at me. I swear, I'm going to protect you."

Rosaria dropped onto an unmade bed. "Pablo said the FBI would protect him, and it turned out to be one of them who killed him. Then Agent Olvera finds me and promises to protect me if I tell him everything, and this happened. I need to go back to Mexico before anything else happens. I should have never come here."

"Agent Olvera was shot. He's in the hospital in a coma. That's why he wasn't here to protect you. And just so you know, I looked for you. For months I tried to find you. To protect you. But I swear, if you'll help me, I won't let anyone hurt you or anyone else."

Rosaria didn't answer. She looked away from Brie.

"What did you see, Rosaria? What did you tell Agent Olvera? If you don't tell me, they'll get away with it."

"What difference does it make? Pablo's dead."

"I know. But we can make sure the person responsible rots in jail. Please help me catch them."

She looked out the window, tears sliding down her cheeks.

"Talk to me. Please."

Rosaria closed her eyes for a second, then opened them and looked at Brie. "We were at the mall when someone from the FBI called him. He told Pablo he was at our RV, looking for him."

"Who called?"

"I don't know. I could hear it was a man, but that's all I know."

"What else did he say?"

"That Pablo needed to get home. When he hung up, he told me to stay at the mall. I told him if he was worried, he shouldn't go. But he said he trusted the FBI because of you."

A knot formed in Brie's throat. Rosaria swiped a hand over her face to brush off the tears. "He said he'd come back for me. But he didn't. I went home and found him. He was dead." She made a soft moan. "There was so much blood."

Brie knelt down in front of her. "I'm so sorry. I swear, I wasn't behind that."

She met Brie's eyes.

"I left for Mexico."

"Why didn't you come to me?"

"The FBI killed Pablo. I didn't know who I could trust!" She shook her head. "I should've stayed in Mexico.

They shot José, and now they are going to kill my sister and me."

Brie took Rosaria's hands in hers. "I promise you. That's not going to happen."

Rosaria looked up. "I gave him his phone."

"Gave who what phone?"

"Pablo's phone. I gave it to Agent Olvera when we had lunch together. I'd dropped my phone in the pool the day before we went to the mall, and since mine wasn't working, Pablo left his new phone with me and I was supposed to call when I finished shopping."

"No. Pablo's phone was found with his body," Brie said. "I know because I found it."

"That was his old phone. We'd gotten new phones on a family plan. My sister, him, and I. The new phone had the call on there—the one from the FBI. I took it with me, but I was afraid they might trace it, so I removed the battery."

"But how would this agent have gotten Pablo's new number?"

"He must've told someone. He was giving it out so he could shut down the other phone."

Connor looked at Brie. "Who would he have told?"

"He worked closest with me and Agent Bara because we spoke Spanish." Suddenly something occurred to Brie. "The phone must be what our dead guy was looking for in Carlos's hotel room."

* * *

Five minutes later, Brie walked out of the bedroom. Her guilt over Pablo's death rose up in her chest until she couldn't breathe. Connor followed her. Without thinking, she stopped in the middle of the room and looked at the dead man again.

The smell, the blood, all the...her stomach turned.

Connor took her arm and guided her out the front door, past the crowd of officers, all the way across the street to his car.

Cold wind hit her face. She tried swallowing. It didn't help.

He stared at her. "Breathe."

She attempted to pull in air, but right then Rosaria's words echoed in her head and in her heart. *He said you were his friend.*

She bent at the waist and puked. Twice.

When she stood up, Connor held out some napkins. "Here."

She wiped her face. Leaning against the car, she stared into the darkness. It was several minutes before she trusted herself to speak. "Thank you."

"You're welcome."

She met his eyes, but he didn't say a thing. Nothing soft or caring. Not asking her if she was okay. Not even a jab at her for losing it. He just stood there. Solid. Strong. Somehow supportive.

Tears stung her eyes, but she blinked them back. "We have to find Pablo's phone. As long as whoever hired that guy thinks it's out there, he'll keep coming for Rosaria. I have to protect her. I let Pablo down. I won't let her down, too."

"We won't," he said.

Something about the "we" touched her heart.

"I got a text from Juan. He wants to know Pablo's phone number, the new one, and if it's still in service."

"I'll ask her." Brie started back toward the house.

"Wait. You feel like a walk?"

"A walk?"

"I saw a white Camry parked about a block up the street in the driveway of a house with an overgrown lawn that looked empty. Remember the car we saw in the surveillance video?"

She looked back at the house, obviously worried about Rosaria.

"She's got a half-dozen cops around her. She's safe."

"Then let's go for a walk."

"Let me get something first." Connor went to the trunk where he opened a duffel bag.

"What's that?" she asked.

"Evidence bags and gloves. Judges are funny about things like that." He smiled. "I learned that the hard way."

"Such a Boy Scout," she teased.

He pulled out a long metal tool—a slim jim—used to break into cars.

"Okay, so maybe not a Boy Scout."

He smiled—one meant to soothe and chase away the bad memories. And it worked. Their eyes met. Held. How could Connor Pierce be such a stand-up guy one minute and so *not* the next?

Glancing over his shoulder she saw the eastern sky had a golden hue to it. The beginning of a sunrise. "It's almost morning," she muttered and closed her eyes a second.

When she opened them, he'd moved in and shoulder-bumped her. "We're gonna get whoever hired this creep. I promise."

The brief contact sent a spiral of warmth running

through her. For some reason, it was more touching than a hug. "Stop," she said without thinking.

"Stop what?" He shoved the bag back into the trunk.

"Being nice. I don't want to like you that much."

He looked up, a soft smile pulling at his lips. "I feel the same way about you. Fracking sucks."

She hid her smile as they started walking and she tried to decipher what he meant. But when she spotted the car and saw the partial license plate, which did indeed match, her thoughts shifted to the case.

Connor went to work and broke into the car faster than she could've using a key. In minutes, they had a wallet and a phone safely tucked inside separate evidence bags.

He turned the wallet in the bag and opened it, then used his phone's flashlight to read it. "Hello James Norvell. From Louisiana."

"It has to be a fake."

"I know. But it's a starting place. And this may answer a few more questions." He studied the bag with the phone inside. "Do you think it's Pablo's or our shooter's phone?"

"I don't know, but we can't take it," she said. "It's evidence."

"I'm not taking it. Just gonna peek, see if it's password locked." He pushed a few buttons through the plastic. "And if not, I'll forward any calls or texts to Juan. He's good with electronics. Phones, computers. He can..." He smiled. "It's not locked."

"You sure you should do that?" she asked.

He looked up. "Says the FBI agent who stole a car and assaulted an officer."

"It wasn't evidence," she said.

"I once waited three weeks for a small-town police department to get me phone information. I'm not destroying anything. They'll see what I did." He stared at her.

She frowned.

"You want me to stop?" he asked.

She considered it. "No. But you're really going to piss off Detective Sampson."

"That's okay," Connor said, toying with the phone. "He already knows that I'm trouble." Connor continued to push a few buttons through the plastic. "Besides, he likes me better than he does you."

"He just doesn't know you," Brie snapped.

Connor grinned, then refocused on the phone. "Ah, here we go."

"What've you got?" She moved in.

"No calls. But a couple of texts."

"What do they say? Who are they from?"

"All we have is a number, but one of them contains the address here. The next one is...it came in about fifteen minutes ago. Just a question mark. Probably asking if the hit was done."

Connor lowered the bag and let her see for herself.

"Wait?" Brie said. "What time did the text offering the address come in?"

# CHAPTER
# TWENTY-TWO

W hat is she doing here?" Sergeant Brown asked as he entered the Willowcreek precinct and walked past where Brie sat with Rosaria.

"You mean Agent Ryan?" Connor led Brown into a different room where Detective Samson said they could wait.

"What other 'she' could I be referring to?" Brown shut the door with a resounding whack.

Mark had texted Connor a few hours ago and said that he and Sergeant Brown were on their way there. He'd also warned Connor to not piss Brown off. That was easier said than done. Half the time when the sergeant got bent out of shape, Connor wasn't trying. "She gave us this lead."

"That doesn't mean you had to bring her. You say 'Thank you, I'll look into it.'" Brown moved to the table and dropped down in a chair.

"Yeah, I should've thought of that," Connor said, sarcasm thickening his voice.

Brown continued. "She's a liability. She's not even working the case with the FBI."

Connor stepped closer. "Brie's been assisting us in the investigation."

"Brie?" Brown studied Connor. "Oh, hell. You aren't banging her, are you?"

"Slow down," Mark jumped in. "Agent Ryan has been working at the Black Diamond for four months, looking into her sister's abduction and murder."

"And Agent Calvin doesn't know this?" Brown asked Mark.

"Since the leak inside the FBI is tied to the Sala case, and Agent Calvin hasn't been ruled out as a suspect, we didn't feel the need to share that information."

Connor joined Mark at the table and sat across from Brown.

Brown looked puzzled. "I thought you liked Agent Miles for this. Yesterday you said you found something in his financial records."

"We did," Mark said. "But it was Agent Miles who told Agent Ryan about the informant's girlfriend being here. And Miles had an explanation for the deposits. Hopefully, the texts we got will help us find—"

"What texts?" Brown asked.

Connor spoke up, willing to take the hit. "I found the shooter's car. It had his phone and wallet inside. Someone texted the shooter twice: once with the address where Rosaria Altura was living, and a second one, asking for an update."

"You handed it over to the Willowcreek officers, right?"

"Of course. Right after I forwarded the texts to Juan."

"Oh, that's going to make Detective Sampson *real* happy." Brown's frown deepened. "Has Juan gotten anything yet?"

Did that mean Connor wasn't in the doghouse for his indiscretion? "He called right before you guys pulled up. He's put a trace on the number that texted the shooter. And..." Connor decided to throw out the good news. "I think this might help us to quickly eliminate one of the Feds."

"How?" Mark asked.

"Brie realized she'd received a call from Agent Miles at almost the exact time as the text was sent to the shooter. So if the text and call dinged off different towers, we can rule him out. It'd help if we could get the phone to Juan. There might be some deleted texts he could pull up."

"I'll talk to Detective Sampson's captain, but I can't promise they'll share until after they go through it themselves."

Connor leaned back in the chair, feeling justified for sending Juan the information in advance. "We also need to get a protective detail on Rosaria Altura."

Brown let out a big puff of air. "Doesn't she have somewhere she could go?"

"Right," Connor snapped. "We think someone from the FBI put out a hit on her, and as soon as this story breaks, he'll know the hit man failed. And you're just gonna say good luck and send her on her way?"

Brown looked ready to blow when Mark intervened. "Sergeant, Connor's right. We have to protect her. And to Connor's other point, what's the chance of you talking your captain buddy into keeping this story out of the media? Even if we get just a few days to dig into the text messages."

Right then, the door banged open and Detective Sampson walked in. The smile on his face said he had something useful.

"What?" Connor asked.

"We got him. Our shooter's name is Kevin Omen. He's from a small town east of New Orleans. And he's got a rap sheet as long as my arm."

* * *

It was after noon before they headed back to Anniston. The day was gray and wet and looked as tired as she felt. She had to concentrate to keep the phone to her ear.

"How is he?" Brie asked Tory as she watched the wet landscape fly past. The sound of the wipers whooshing across the windshield and the tires sending water splashing to the curb filled the car.

Brie had reservations about leaving Rosaria before the protective detail showed up, but when she learned the story of the shooting was being held from the media, she agreed to ride back with Connor. But before she left, she promised Rosaria she'd see her soon, praying APD would allow her to keep that promise.

"The doctor says the latest CAT scan showed the swelling in his brain has decreased," Tory said. "He almost sounded positive, Brie."

"Great," Brie said. "Is his color still good?" She looked up at the dark gray sky, which felt ominous, as if they were riding right into a storm. She felt it inside, too. Even though she was relieved to know the person who shot

Carlos, and possibly killed Pablo, was dead, the hard part was going to be catching who had hired him. Especially since it had to be someone she had trusted at the FBI—someone she'd trusted with her life.

"Better than ever. He's going to wake up, Brie. I know it now."

"From your mouth to God's ears," Brie said.

Brie's gaze shifted to the splats of rain spidering across the glass. Two Anniston cops would be transporting Rosaria to a safe house soon. Connor, Mark, and their sergeant had pushed to get Rosaria brought to Anniston. They convinced Detective Sampson that the shooting of Agent Olvera took priority.

"I'm about to head back to Carlos's room," Tory said. "Did you want to speak to Eliot?"

"No, I spoke with him earlier." Instead of finishing the sandwich that Connor bought for her, she'd snuck off and called Eliot. In parent-mode, he'd asked if she'd been up all night. She'd assured him she'd go straight home and rest, but her mind was already forming a to-do list.

She wanted to research Kevin Omen. She wanted to help Connor find Regina Berger. She wanted to find Pablo's other phone. Part of her wondered if Omen found the informant's phone when he was in Carlos's hotel room. If so, why was he going after Rosaria? She hadn't seen him. Or was he going after her simply because she could corroborate the FBI involvement?

Hanging up, Brie watched Connor rub the back of his neck. She'd offered to drive, but he'd refused. No doubt he was as exhausted as she was.

He put both hands on the wheel and cut his green eyes to her. "Everything okay?"

"Doctor said the swelling in his brain is down." Her mind went to Pablo's missing phone. "Are you sure they didn't find a phone in Carlos's hotel room?"

"Yeah. Mark oversaw it."

"Omen probably found it at the hotel." Frustration sounded in her voice.

"That's likely. I sent the phone number to Juan, but he says with the battery out, it's practically impossible to trace."

Connor's phone, which he had charging, dinged with a text. After checking the road for traffic, he picked it up and smiled. "That was the ICE agent. When he arrived at the strip club in Houston, Armand wasn't there, but he just showed up."

The tension in her shoulders lessened. "Thank God."

Connor set the phone down. "You know what's been bothering me? You said everyone at the agency knew Olvera was coming here to get Armand's prints. So why wouldn't the mole have informed the Sala family? Why didn't Armand get word of this and leave earlier?"

The question had crossed Brie's mind. "Maybe the agent is no longer helping the Sala family. From the start, I believed Carlos was shot to keep him quiet about the leak. Not about Armand."

Connor ran his hand over the steering wheel. "So maybe the agent didn't help the Sala family out of loyalty or financial gain. Maybe they were blackmailed." He paused for a moment, thinking. "How would you describe Agent Bara?"

Brie bit down on her lip. "A week ago, I'd've said he was a good guy, part of my FBI family. We went for beers. We brought each other coffee—he takes his with three sugars." Her chest tightened. "I'd have taken a bullet for any of them."

"I know." He hesitated. "But what do you know about him?"

She tried to think. "He's divorced. Has a five-year-old boy. He keeps a picture of him on his desk. I hear him talking on the phone to him sometimes." She exhaled. "It's hard to believe that any of them did this."

"Did you know his parents are from Guatemala?"

"Yeah. It came up when we were working the Sala case."

"Do you know if his parents and siblings live in the States?"

"I know some of them do, because he's mentioned seeing them."

"Has he visited Guatemala?"

"Yeah. He's talked about it."

"So maybe he still has family there?"

"You think someone found out we were onto the gunrunning operation and threatened his family if he didn't turn over information?"

"It's possible." His gaze shifted to her.

She closed her eyes, knowing firsthand how a threat like that felt. Her ex-father-in-law had threatened to hurt Eliot if she didn't go back to Todd. So yes, she knew the need to protect those you love was strong. So strong, it led her to the FBI's doorstep and eventually the arrest of her ex-husband and father-in-law.

She got a mental vision of the photograph of Agent Bara's son with a big toothless grin and a cowlick in the same place as his father. Would she have acted differently if the person being threatened had been vulnerable and hadn't been an ex–Special Forces officer?

No, she told herself. Not if it meant she had to take another life.

Connor's phone rang. He started to reach for it when it fell. But he must've answered it because the caller's voice echoed over the speakers. "Detective Pierce." Connor looked down, as if to disconnect it, but before he could, the caller continued, "This is Peter Ronan."

*Peter Ronan?* Air caught in Brie's throat. Why was her father calling Connor?

Hearing the voice sent her back. Back to being young, waiting and wanting to hear that voice. He hadn't been one to dish out a lot of affection, but the times he had, she'd reveled in it. *How's my pumpkin?* The question always came with a kiss on her forehead.

For years, Brie wondered if he also called Alma "pumpkin." Or was that her special nickname?

Pushing the past down, Brie studied Connor, whose expression held a good dose of guilt.

"You left a message," her father said.

"Yes." Connor's attention became equally divided among the phone, the road, and her. "When might be a good day to come up and talk? I have questions about your daughter Alma."

"You probably don't know this, but she's deceased. The FBI looked into it. I'm not sure they found out what happened though."

Brie remembered attending the burial. She'd stood about fifty yards away and watched as they lowered her sister's casket in the ground. She'd been planning to give the bracelet to Alma's mother, but in the end, she couldn't let it go.

"I'm aware of that," Connor said. "But I still need answers."

"I already spoke with the police earlier," her father said. "I'm a busy man, Detective. You can ask me now."

Her father didn't have time to find justice for the daughter he supposedly loved. But why was she surprised? He hadn't even shown up for the funeral.

Connor's hands on the wheel tightened. "No. I think you can make time. I'll drive up to Henderson. When and where is good?"

Her father went silent for several seconds. "Fine. Tuesday at four." He spouted out an address. "Don't be late."

"I'll be there." Connor hung up. "Sorry."

"Why are you talking to him?" A distant cracking of thunder echoed and a bright flash of lightning filled the darkening sky. When he didn't answer immediately, she asked, "You don't think he had something to do with her death, do you?"

"No. But I can't help but wonder if he knew more about what was happening in her life than he let on."

"We know what happened. Dillon Armand happened. This isn't going to help."

"It's an unanswered question and—"

"You're wasting your time." Her voice reverberated over the noise of the outlying storm. "You heard him; he doesn't know anything. He doesn't even care."

"I'm sorry," he repeated, as if he understood her pain. But how could he, when even she didn't understand. Why did this still hurt?

*How's my pumpkin?* Her father's words from long ago had emotion growing hot in her chest.

"Why didn't you tell me you contacted him? Why didn't you tell me about Agent Miles's financial records?

What else have you *not* told me? I come to you when I learn something. But I don't get the same courtesy?"

He glanced at her. "Brie, I'm being as upfront as I can." Honesty, patience, and concern sounded in his words.

Tears stung her eyes. Suddenly, she knew she was taking her anger over her father out on Connor.

"I don't...I'm exhausted. Sorry." It was too much. Carlos still in a coma. Seeing a man with a giant hole in his gut. Knowing someone she had once trusted was responsible for this. Knowing the man responsible for killing her sister was still out there. Knowing her father didn't care enough about his dead daughter to talk to the police. She turned and watched the storm brewing outside her window while feeling one brewing inside her.

*  *  *

Connor pulled into the diner's parking lot at a little past two p.m. and stopped beside Brie's car. The rain was now a lazy drizzle. The gloomy weather had turned day into almost night. Rubbing his eyes, hoping to assuage the brewing headache, he leaned back in the seat. He'd texted Mark earlier that he planned to grab a nap and shower before coming in.

Mark had texted back saying Billy had spent the day looking for Regina Berger but had come up empty. Tomorrow, Connor would get a warrant for the girl's Facebook account. Thinking about Berger got him thinking about her baby girl. The one he'd bounced in his arms. The one abandoned by her own mother.

He could only hope the baby was young enough that

she wouldn't know what her mother had done. That she'd never feel like damaged goods.

Turning his head, he looked at Brie sleeping and remembered the pain he'd seen in her eyes when her father had called. Damn, Connor really disliked that guy.

Halfway here, she'd lowered her seat back and fallen asleep.

At first, she'd given him her back. Then in slumber, she had turned and faced him. Since then, he'd had a devil of a time focusing on the road.

A crazy thought hit. This was what he'd missed the night when he walked out. The chance to watch her sleep.

Every few minutes, she'd wrinkle her nose. A couple strands of blond hair lay against her cheek, her long lashes resting on the tender skin beneath her eyes. Right below her left brow there was a thin scar about an inch long. What had happened? he wondered.

Not driving now, he could study her features even more. Her full lips were bow-shaped on top and enticingly plump on bottom. Occasionally, her tongue would dip out and leave a sheen of moisture.

He remembered those lips on his. Remembered how they tasted. Remembered them pressing against his chest, sending incomprehensible panic spiraling through him. Why had he completely freaked?

Hell, why was he still freaking?

What was it she'd said to him earlier? *I don't want to like you that much.* He knew exactly how she felt.

He recalled the line he'd tossed at her on the ride down, about her kissing his chest and him being afraid he would hurt her.

He hadn't *just* been afraid of hurting her, he'd been

afraid of getting hurt. Of breaking the unforgivable rule of... hell, he didn't even know the rule.

She wrinkled her nose again, looking adorable. Brie Ryan was an enigma. Cute, yet stunningly beautiful. Innocent, yet profoundly sexy. Strong, yet somehow vulnerable. And he wanted to protect her. Protect her from things in her past. From her piece-of-shit father. From the evils in the world. From an FBI agent who she'd seen as family.

Maybe even from himself.

Cumbersome feelings crowded his chest as he continued watching her sleep. Dipping his head down to see her face better, his neck muscles tightened, so he reached down and lowered his seat back, too.

# CHAPTER
# TWENTY-THREE

The ringing of Connor's phone jerked him awake.

Disoriented, he sat up so fast his abdomen hit the steering wheel. Where the hell was he?

Then he saw Brie sit up with the same startling speed. They stared at each other, wide-eyed, dazed, and...when their eyes met, Connor had the craziest thought. He was right where he wanted to be. With her.

He waited for that thought to run all sorts of panic through him, and when it didn't, he let it settle in. *I don't want to like you that much.* But he did.

His phone rang again. He reached for it. It was Mark. Before answering, he spotted the time.

*Shit!* It was after five. He'd slept for three hours. He took the call. "I overslept. Sorry. I'll head that way."

"No," Mark said. "We're calling it a day. I wouldn't have called, but I figured you'd want to know. APD found Olvera's car, parked in front of a restaurant on the south side of town. I was leaving when I got the call. I'm heading there now."

It took Connor a few seconds to follow. He glanced at Brie, who was staring at him. Her hair was a little mussed, her eyes still a little hooded with sleep. The temptation to lean over and kiss her hit him—hard.

"Text me the address. We'll head over."

"We?" Mark asked. "You're still with Brie?"

"Yeah."

"Hmm," Mark said, as if trying to figure out what that might mean. Connor was busy doing the same thing. Then Mark added, "We also got something on the text that went to Kevin Omen's phone."

"What?"

"We can rule out Agent Miles being the bad guy. The phone call to Brie and the text sent to Omen's phone pinged from two different towers on opposite sides of the city."

"So it's either Agent Bara or Agent Calvin." Connor looked at Brie, who appeared to hang on his every word.

"Yup," Mark said. "Juan also put a trace on the number that sent the texts. So far the phone hasn't been turned back on."

Connor glanced at Brie. "Okay, we'll meet you there shortly."

"What?" Brie asked.

"You were right. They were able to rule out Miles. And we found Agent Olvera's car."

"His car?" She sat up a little straighter.

Connor's phone dinged with a text. He looked at the address. "Mark's heading there now. Want to ride with me?"

"Yeah." Blinking, she gazed out the window. "How long did I sleep?"

He started the car. "Four hours."

"Four?"

"You needed it." He pulled out of the parking lot, glancing at her. "I was watching you sleep when—"

"That's creepy," she said.

He smiled. "You're cute when you sleep."

"Still creepy."

He laughed without really knowing why, except...this felt right. Brie Ryan felt right.

She smiled, and warmth filled his chest.

Passing a hand over her eyes, she practically bounced in her chair. "Is it crazy of me to hope we might find Pablo's phone in Carlos's car?"

"Maybe. But crazy likes company. I was thinking the same thing." However, that wasn't the only crazy thing filling his head. He was thinking he wanted more smiles. More time watching her sleep.

And sex. Yeah, he definitely wanted more sex.

He wanted more of Brie Ryan.

Hadn't she told him he was a fool for thinking she expected *love ballads*? What was wrong with letting himself like someone a little? What was wrong with having something real for a while? Real sounded good.

It was a ten-minute ride to Olvera's car. The whole way Connor attempted to define *real*. Spotting the restaurant, he pulled into the parking lot. He hadn't figured out the definition yet, but he decided if it got him more Brie time, then he wanted it. He'd figure out the rest as he went.

Connor got out of his car and looked around for Mark's Mustang. "We must have arrived first," he told Brie.

Connor flashed his badge and introduced himself and Brie to the officer standing beside the car. "Is it locked?"

"No." The officer waved to the car. "The keys appear to be on the seat. I think it was abandoned, hoping someone would steal it. It's a miracle no one did."

Brie walked over to the passenger window, careful not to touch it, and peered inside.

Connor opened his trunk and retrieved two pairs of gloves and handed one to Brie. "Let's see what we've got."

Gloves on, she opened the passenger door and used her phone's flashlight to see inside. Her breath caught. "There's blood."

He leaned in and noticed the car smelled a bit like decomp. The interior was black, but he could see what appeared to be blood splatter.

"I think he was shot here." Her voice trembled. "Look." She pointed to the floorboard, where there was a lug wrench. One end of it was coated in blood.

She rose up and stepped back quickly. Connor touched her shoulder. "You okay?"

"Yeah." It was a lie. Pain brightened her eyes. Seeing your partner's blood wasn't easy. He remembered all too well. The need to protect her filled his chest. She dipped back, as if to continue searching the vehicle.

"Let me do this," he said.

"No," she snapped.

Remembering her stubborn streak, he didn't argue. "The guy who did this got what was coming to him."

"I know." She leaned down.

Connor moved around the Honda, opened the door, and flipped open the console, hoping to see a phone inside. There wasn't one.

He continued to search until a pair of headlights flashed over the car. Connor backed out and saw Mark striding toward them. "Got anything?"

"Looks like this might be the crime scene." Connor's gaze shifted to Brie.

She continued to search, in the glove compartment, under the seats, behind the seats. When she stepped out, she had something in her hand.

"What is it?" Connor asked.

"Just a receipt." Disappointment sounded in her voice. She shined her phone's flashlight on the paper. Her breath caught.

"What?" Connor asked.

"It's a postal receipt." She looked up. "Carlos mailed something from the Willowcreek post office."

Connor moved over and glanced at the receipt. "The phone maybe."

"Where did he mail it to?" Mark asked.

Brie studied the receipt. "To Anniston, Texas." She looked up.

"Does it have the address?" Mark asked.

"Just the zip." She held the light closer to read. "The printing is light. I can't make out the last number."

"Is there a tracking number?" Mark moved in.

"Yet, but it's barely legible." She lifted her eyes, "But the first four digits of the zip are the same as mine. And I haven't checked my mail in days."

\* \* \*

"It has to be the phone." Brie watched Connor drive to her apartment building, wishing he'd go faster. Mark had stayed with Carlos's Honda to secure transport to the police station garage so forensics could comb over it.

"I think so." He looked as if he was about to say something, but his gaze just returned to the windshield.

She leaned back and tried not to think about the blood in Carlos's car.

Inhaling, she refocused on Connor. "What did Mark hand you?"

"The hit man's arrest file."

"And Mark doesn't want me to see it?" She hadn't missed that he'd called Connor over to his car to give it to him.

"He didn't say that." Yet something about Connor's expression said he'd probably said something close to that.

They didn't speak during the remainder of the drive back to her apartment. And it was an odd kind of quiet, too. As soon as he cut the engine, Brie was out of the car, heading to the rows of metal mailboxes along the front of the building.

Brie stopped at the box marked number 110 and dug in her purse for her keys. A few drops of rain hit her face. Connor, carrying more gloves and a plastic evidence bag, stepped beside her. Two light fixtures attached to the overhang spilled out light. Her heart raced with hope that this nightmare was almost over.

Reaching into her deep-as-it-was-wide fake leather bag, she felt around for her keys. "I'm throwing this purse away," she muttered right before she spotted the glint of silver.

She slipped the small key in and turned it as Connor came up behind her. Close. Too close. His scent made her insides flutter, which under the circumstances was a bit disturbing.

She opened the box, praying to see a larger, thicker envelope. She didn't. But she still reached in with gusto, hoping it was buried beneath the circular ads.

Pulling it all out, she quickly started fumbling through it. Electric bills. Plastic surgery flyers. Grocery store ads. A few pieces of mail slipped from her grip and hit the ground at the same time as her hope.

"Fracking Hades!" She looked up at Connor. "It's not here."

"Maybe it just hasn't arrived yet."

"It was mailed on Wednesday. It should be here."

"Weather could have delayed it. We'll check on the tracking number tomorrow."

"It wasn't legible."

"We'll figure it out." He pulled out his phone and began texting. "I'm letting Mark know we didn't find it." He finished and pocketed his cell. "Does Carlos know anyone else in town?"

"If he did, he'd have told me." Then bam. Another possibility came. "What about the hotel? He could have mailed it to himself." She grabbed her phone. "Let me see what the zip code is for the Marriott." She typed it in. "It could be there."

The ride to the hotel took ten minutes. It took five for the front desk clerk to shoot down her hope. Connor left his card and told them he'd check back tomorrow.

"Where else could he have mailed it to?" she asked when they crawled back into his car.

"I don't know. But first thing tomorrow we'll call the post office. And I still say it could just be late."

He pulled into the parking lot of an Italian restaurant. "What are we doing—"

"I'm hungry, and you barely ate your sandwich earlier."

She felt her empty stomach, but she wanted to go to the hospital and then get back to work. "I just want—"

"Brie..."

She turned to him. Their eyes met. Locked. When he didn't say anything, she continued, "I want to look at Kevin Omen's file. I came to you with Rosaria's address. It's because of me that you have that file."

He continued to stare silently at her, then he finally spoke up. "How did you get that scar below your left eyebrow?"

*Why was he asking that?* "Did you hear what I said about the file?"

"Yeah. How did you get the scar?"

"A lowlife weasel hit me. But that—"

"What was his name?" His expression tightened.

"I want to see the file."

"Tell me his name."

"Why?" she asked.

"Because I don't believe in hitting women."

She shook her head, confused. "I broke his nose and he's in a federal prison. You don't need to defend me."

"So you were working a case when it happened?"

"Sort of. Can I look at the file?"

"After we have dinner and you explain 'sort of.'"

"Why should I do that?" she asked.

He shifted in his seat to face her more directly. "Why should you have dinner with me or why should you explain 'sort of'?"

"Both," she said.

"Because"—he hesitated—"because we're both having a hard time not liking each other."

"What does that mean?"

He raked a hand through his hair. "I don't know. I'm trying to figure it out."

"You're not making sense," she bit out.

"None of it makes sense." He reached into the backseat and snagged the file. "Come on." He got out of his car.

She followed him into the restaurant. The smell of garlic, fresh-baked bread, and zesty tomato sauce filled her senses, and her empty stomach grumbled.

She gazed up at him. "I don't understand—"

"Table for two," Connor said to the hostess as he put his hand on Brie's lower back. The touch sent a spark of something sweet running through her. Something sweet that she didn't need right now.

Frowning, she quickened her pace and followed the hostess to a table in the back of the almost empty restaurant.

After handing out menus, the hostess left.

"Their chicken marsala is fabulous."

"Fine. That's what I'll have." She set the menu down. "Can I see the file?"

The waitress came up. Connor focused on her. "We'll take two house salads and two orders of chicken marsala. And could you bring the bread now?" He looked at Brie. "She gets grumpy when she's hungry." He smiled and looked back at the waitress. "I'll take a house beer." His gaze found her again. "Beer?"

"Water." She handed over her menu.

The waitress hadn't gotten one foot away from the table when Connor turned to her. "Give me forty-five minutes. We can eat and talk. Then you can look at the file and we can discuss what the plans are for tomorrow." He put his hand over hers.

She pulled her hand from under his, remembering him saving her from puking all over the crime scene. Remembering the sincere apology she'd gotten when her father called. "No trespassing questions."

"What are trespassing questions?"

"Personal questions."

He rubbed two fingers over his chin. "So the person who gave you the scar was someone close. I thought it was about a case."

"Fine," she muttered. "You tell me all the dirty little secrets about your ex then I'll tell you mine."

His mouth thinned. "It was your ex-husband? That sorry piece of... You put him in jail?"

The waitress appeared with the bread, olive oil dip, and drinks. As if sensing the tension, she dropped everything and left.

Connor tore off a piece of bread, dipped it in the olive oil, then handed it to her. "Try it."

A bit of warm yeasty steam rose from the bread. Her stomach grumbled. She helped herself. The taste of hot sourdough bread, drenched in olive oil with Italian seasoning, danced on her tongue.

He smiled. "Good, isn't it?"

She nodded and considered it a win that he'd dropped the question. He tore off another piece of bread and dipped it into the oil and ate it.

He swallowed and then spoke. "Her name was Kelly. We were married two years. We met at the gym. Got hitched six weeks later. Fast, but it felt right. She was... a good person. The marriage was great. Until it wasn't. She deserved better."

Brie savored more bread. Curiosity pulled the next question from her. "What happened?" When he didn't answer, she tossed out, "You cheated on her?"

"No! That's what you think of me?" His frown deepened.

"I was just guessing. Sorry."

His lips thinned. "She wanted kids. I didn't think I'd be...my father ran off. And when he was there, he wasn't what you'd call a role model." Honesty and hurt filled his voice. "But she wouldn't let it go." His voice lowered.

She leaned in. "You didn't discuss it before you got married?"

"No. It was stupid, I know, but it all happened so fast."

She turned her water glass. "Sometimes people just want different things."

He exhaled. "I gave in. She got pregnant, then lost the baby. Then she got pregnant again. It was a tubal pregnancy. She almost died. They had to operate and afterward said her chances of getting pregnant again were slim. It devastated her. She blamed me...said I didn't even care. But I...they were my babies, too. I cared. I just didn't know how to...I thought she needed me to be normal. She got depressed. She quit working." He ran a hand over his face. "We started counseling. I was determined to fix it. I didn't want to lose her."

"I'm sorry." Brie put her hand over his.

He met her eyes. "Then my partner got killed and I shot...the kid. And I didn't have it in me to keep trying to fix us when I...felt so broken."

She swallowed a knot of emotion. "Maybe she should have been there for you?"

He shook his head. "You don't understand. Losing those babies devastated her." The waitress walked up with two salads. He got quiet and reached for his beer.

Brie picked up her fork and stabbed a piece of lettuce, suddenly angry. Angry that she'd started this conversation. Angry because she cared. Angry because...he was wrong. She shook her head. "Why are we even doing this?"

"Doing what?" he asked.

"Telling each other crap." She didn't need to know more about him. Didn't need to feel...more.

He frowned. "You asked."

"No. That's not..." It was the secret-sharing feeling, the I-care feeling, the we-connect feeling.

She wanted it. She didn't want it. Her gaze shifted to the file. "We met in college. He was charming, caring, but it was all a con. I was stupid. An idiot. Eliot warned me, but I was in love and I thought Eliot was just being his overly protective self."

"What kind of a con?"

"His father was into real estate. He worked with a lot of Russians. Crooked Russians. He married me because his dad thought I'd be an asset to his business. A month after we married, I was working for his father. A few months later, I realized they were laundering money. I went to Todd. He got pissed and punched me. Unfortunately, he forgot that I knew how to punch back."

"Shit!"

"I left and filed for divorce. His dad showed up a week later and threatened me, saying that if I didn't come back something could happen to Eliot. So I went back. After I went to the FBI."

"That's how you started working for them."

She nodded. "I went undercover. I not only got evidence on the money laundering and tax evasion, but his last accountant also had wound up dead under mysterious circumstances. I found emails the man had sent Crumpton senior, telling him he was quitting because he didn't want to be part of anything illegal."

"We're not talking about...Theodore Crumpton."

When she didn't answer, he said, "Fuck. That was a huge case."

She nodded. Silence reigned again, and she felt him staring at the scar under her eyebrow.

"Tell me you really broke his nose."

"I did."

"I'm surprised Eliot didn't kill him."

"He wanted to. In fact, he shot him. Well, nicked him. He took the shot from the rooftop of a nearby building. Then he called him and said he'd aim better next time if he ever hit me again. I think he said something along the lines of 'Even if you kill me. I've got a dozen friends lined up to take over.'"

"Did the bastard ever hit you again?"

"No."

"I'm beginning to warm up to Eliot." Connor turned his beer. "How long before you got the evidence?"

"Six weeks."

"That must have felt like forever."

"It did." But she'd deserved it for being a fool. She pulled the bread over and snatched another piece.

When the silence lingered, she dropped the bread. "So there. My humiliating ex-husband story. You happy now?"

"No. You didn't deserve that." He took another sip of beer. "Am I the first guy you've...seen since then?"

She rolled her eyes. "You might want to button up your collar. Your ego is showing again."

"I didn't mean it like that. I just meant...when shit like that happens it makes one leery."

"Yeah, but no. I've dated a bunch of guys since then." *Two. And had only slept with one.* "Even had a relationship for a few months."

"What happened?"

"It ended." *No sparks. No connection. No I-want-more feeling. Nothing like what she felt right now with this self-proclaimed commitmentphobe.* Yet part of her knew the only reason she stayed in the relationship as long as she had was because she didn't feel that spark. "Is that what's wrong with you? You're leery?"

He frowned, as if he didn't like the question tossed back to him. He passed a hand over his mouth. "Maybe. But I'm realizing that while I can't promise anyone...I can't offer anything like...like forever. But I can offer...right now."

"I'd refrain from using that as a pickup line."

"What do you mean?" he asked.

"Are you kidding? You want to tell a girl 'I don't offer promises, nothing like forever, but hey...how about right now?'" Sarcasm leaked from her voice. "No. Don't ever use that."

He shouldered back in his chair. "You make it sound—"

"Do you even realize what women want..." She stopped talking and held up her hands. "I take it all back. It should work just fine with your type of woman."

His mouth tightened. "What type of woman is that?"

"The kind who date—how did you put it?—a no-intentions man."

"But I just told you... My intentions are for... I mean—"

"Like I said, I'm sure that'd work for what you're looking for." She tore off another piece of bread.

He frowned. "Okay, what do women... No. What do *you* want?"

She shook her head. "This isn't about me. We both admitted it was a mistake."

"What if the mistake was me leaving?"

She swallowed. "No, you were right the first time when you said I was Mother Teresa. And I love fences."

His lips thinned. "You want to know what I think? I think this is you being leery."

*Hell yeah, that was what it was.* She'd loved Todd. Look how that turned out. Connor Pierce, more than any man she'd met in the last five years, had the power to hurt her. "It's me being smart. My life is... it's a fracking mess. I don't want to complicate it with a just-right-now relationship. We can be..." She hesitated. "I want to say friends, but I don't believe people who had sex can really be friends. Until this is over, we can... we can be partners. Good partners. I respect you. I even appreciate you."

"I thought the other part was pretty damn good, too."

"Just because something feels good doesn't mean it's right. Cocaine, BDSM, fried butter, being shot out of a cannon—yeah, people pay to do that—and some people even get a kick out of swimming with sharks. Me? Not so much."

"Here you go." The waitress set two plates of chicken marsala down. She looked at Brie and grinned. "Fried butter is really good. And if you have a safe word..." She gave Connor a sexy look that was clearly an invitation, "Well—"

"I need another beer," Connor snapped.

When she disappeared, Connor looked about as happy as a cat in a rocking chair store with six Dobermans standing guard over the place.

"Can we just eat?" she asked.

"Yeah. Eat."

You'd think with the cloud of tension hanging over her, her appetite would have gone. But the moment Brie tasted the food, the decision was made. If she couldn't have Connor, she could at least have to-die-for Italian food that was probably as bad for her as fried butter.

She almost cleaned her plate. He did more picking than eating.

"Now can I see the file?"

Frowning, he handed it to her. She opened it and started scanning the list of priors.

"Mark said it looks fishy. That many dropped charges usually means one of two things. Either the guy is richer than God and has an exceptional lawyer—this guy's not rich—or the perp is a CI. Mark already has calls out to several New Orleans police departments to determine if Omen was working with a cop. But he asked if you could search for his name in FBI cases that line up with when some of the bigger charges were dropped."

"You think Omen was an FBI informant?"

"Maybe."

Brie tried to think. "I don't have access...Wait. Agent Miles. He's going to be in Baton Rouge, and he might even feel indebted to us."

Connor nodded. "Good idea."

Her phone rang. She pulled it out. Panic shot through her when she saw Tory's name, and just like that she remembered all the blood in Carlos's car.

"Everything okay?" She pressed a hand against her stomach wishing she hadn't eaten so much.

"He woke up, Brie. He opened his eyes and looked right at me."

# CHAPTER
# TWENTY-FOUR

I'm not trying to downplay this good news," the doctor said.

Connor had left cash on the table and driven Brie right to the hospital. Happier than he'd ever seen her, she'd jumped out of the car before he'd even cut off the engine. When he walked toward the family waiting room, he spotted Brie, Tory, Eliot, and his friend Sam all huddled around a doctor.

He moved in, so he was close enough to not miss anything, but not so close as to be intrusive. As the cop on the case, he needed to know Olvera's status, but families had their right to privacy. And after Brie shot down his offer of—as she said—a just-right-now relationship, he felt like an intruder.

He didn't like her description of his offer, although he hadn't been able to argue that it defined almost exactly what he'd put out there. Problem was, he'd screwed up his pitch. He'd made it sound like a passing fling. That's not what he meant, but he couldn't put what he meant to words except he...

He wanted her.

"What I'm saying," the doctor continued, "is that his waking up doesn't mean things are perfect."

"When can we see him?" Brie piped up. "Is he still conscious?"

"He's in what we call a semiconscious state, or some call the very early response stage. He's not following commands completely, but he is responding appropriately to different kinds of stimuli."

"So, how long before you remove the tube and he can talk to us?" Brie asked.

"If he remains alert, we could remove it in the next twenty-four to thirty-six hours. But keep in mind, while this is a step forward, this is also where we'll discover if any long-term issues are present."

"But he recognized me," Tory said.

"Right," the doctor said. "But even if there're no long-term effects, it could still take time before he's functioning normally. And I know you'd like to stay with him, but he needs rest. I'll tell the nurses to come get you if he becomes fully alert."

The doctor walked off. The four of them stood around, holding on to each other and hope. Connor hung back. His phone dinged with a text from Mark. Rosaria had arrived at the hotel where they were housing her.

When he looked up, Brie walked over to him. Their eyes met.

"You don't have to stay," she said.

"Your car's at the diner."

"I can get an Uber."

"Actually, I thought I'd hang around. And I just got a text from Mark: Rosaria's here."

"Can I see her tomorrow? I know she's scared."

"I'll try to make it happen."

She nodded. "I'll call Agent Miles and see if he can dig into the older files. Can you text me the dates that Omen's cases were dropped?"

He nodded. "Yeah."

She looked at Tory, inhaled, then smiled back at Connor. "He's going to be okay. This is the first time..." Her voice shook. "The first time I've really believed it." Her eyes brightened with emotion. Relief.

He pulled her toward him. She came, resting her head on his chest. Her soft weight melted against him. He put one arm around her.

Leaning down, he pressed his chin to the side of her head. Strands of her blond hair caught in his five o'clock shadow. "I'm glad he woke up," he whispered, cherishing that she'd let him this close.

"Me too." She drew away, as if she regretted the bit of trust she'd given. And just like that, he knew he wanted it. He wanted her trust. Wanted her. How could he earn it?

An hour later, while Brie and Tory were in visiting Carlos, Connor sat trying to make sense of the Omen file. Had Omen been an informant?

His phone rang. He recognized the number as Agent Hamilton's with ICE. His contact person for Armand.

*No more bad news*, he thought before he answered. "Detective Pierce."

"It appears our guy is heading back to Anniston."

"You still have eyes on him?"

"Yeah. My guys did some digging on the other victims in the trafficking case."

"And?"

"One of the victims worked for the strip club in Dallas that Armand has ties to. We're really liking this guy for human trafficking. Do you have the prints back yet? I think we have enough to bring him in."

"We're told we'll have them tomorrow. But let's not bring him in until we can keep him. If he leaves the country, we'll lose him for good."

"We can keep him. Misuse of passport is a felony."

"We don't want to get him on just that."

"Yeah, but while he's locked up, we can tie him to the human trafficking case."

He told Hamilton about Regina Berger and his suspicions she knew something.

"Find her," Hamilton said.

"We're working on it," Connor said.

Connor felt someone sit beside him but didn't look over. "Let's get his prints back and regroup."

Connor finished his call before glancing at the man who'd been Brie's savior.

Eliot placed his palms on his knees and leaned forward. "I owe you an apology. I think I read you wrong, Detective Pierce."

"How did you read me?" Connor asked.

"As an asshole."

Connor grinned. "That's okay. I had you pegged as one, too."

Eliot nodded. "Maybe we were both right."

"I have my moments."

Eliot chuckled. "I didn't mean to eavesdrop, but I did. You got information on Dillon Armand?"

Connor didn't see any reason to lie. "It appears he's headed back to Anniston."

Eliot frowned. "Brie's tougher than a lot of men I know. But I like knowing someone has her back."

"I understand." And Connor did.

"You'll have someone at the club."

"Definitely."

He nodded. "Brie said you are leaning toward Bara being behind Olvera's shooting."

"Yeah." Connor sensed Eliot had an opinion. "You know Agents Bara and Calvin?"

"I've met them. Can't say I know them. But something's bothering me."

"What?"

"Why hasn't Agent Calvin put Brie back on active duty? One of his agents is shot and on death's door, and two of his other agents are under suspicion. And he isn't begging Brie to come off leave?"

"Brie believes it's because she told us about the FBI leak."

"Which is more of a reason for him to want to crack this case. She's a damn good agent, and that's not me being biased. Agent Calvin knows this. By not bringing her back in, he's handicapping the case. Why?"

\* \* \*

Connor went back to his apartment, slept for three hours, then woke up thinking about Brie, the case, and his screwups. Her words rolled over him. *The only way it could have ended worse was if you'd tossed a couple of hundred bucks on my bedside table.*

Yeah, he'd screwed the pooch on that one.

Thinking about that fuckup led him to think about his others. He'd told himself that he'd been careful to sleep only with women who knew it wouldn't lead anywhere. But did that make it right?

At three-thirty that morning, Connor grabbed a newspaper from an empty booth, dropped down at his table, and looked over at Flora. Studying him, she grabbed a pot of hot coffee and a cup and headed his way. Her dark eyes, which always seemed to carry pain, met his. What was she thinking? Did she hate him? Did she blame him? Did she know he'd give anything to bring her son back?

She set a coffee cup in front of him, then filled it with steaming hot java. "You really never sleep, do you?"

"Sure I do."

"Hmm." She dropped his creams on the table. "Same order?"

"Yup."

Five minutes later, she placed a small pitcher of syrup on the table and refilled his coffee. Still holding the steaming pot in her hands, she lingered, looking nervous.

He met her dark, haunted eyes. "Everything okay?"

"Yes. I...I went to church yesterday, for the first time in a long time."

He nodded, unsure how to respond.

"The sermon was good."

He pulled his coffee closer but didn't look away, wanting her to know he was listening.

"It was on forgiveness."

He swallowed.

She continued, "The preacher said forgiveness is hard because sometimes the anger is all we can feel. It consumes us. He also said that as hard as it is to forgive others, it is even harder to forgive oneself."

He inhaled. "Yeah, that is hard."

"You should maybe go to church sometimes."

"Maybe," he said.

He watched her leave, trying to decipher what she meant. Had she forgiven him? Was she trying to forgive him? Was she saying he needed to forgive himself?

If he weren't a coward, he'd call her back, ask her outright. Instead, he sat there, replaying her words. He recalled Brie saying he came here to punish himself. Part of him knew it might be true, but right now he also wondered if he didn't come here for forgiveness. Not that he felt forgiven yet. But as Flora implied, forgiving yourself wasn't easy.

*I'd have done the same thing. Any person carrying a badge would have done the same thing.* He heard Brie's reassurance, and yeah, he knew it was true, but it didn't change the fact that he'd killed Flora's son.

The bell over the door rang and he glanced up. His breath caught.

Brie walked straight over to him. She wore jeans that fit her really well, and a pink shirt, with a jean jacket over it. She yanked off the jacket, hung it on the back of the chair, then dropped into the seat across from him. "I thought you might be here."

"Everything okay?" he asked.

"Agent Miles went through the old files. He called me about an hour ago."

"And?"

"Agent Bara worked in the New Orleans FBI office before he moved to Baton Rouge. Miles was able to pull that file."

"Yeah?" Connor asked.

"Kevin Omen, our hit man, was Agent Bara's CI on a case there."

Connor smiled. "Then we've got him."

Brie shook her head. "It could still be considered circumstantial evidence."

"Maybe, but having the connection between them will go a long way."

"Yeah, but it feels...too easy. Why would he pick someone who he knew we could tie him to?"

"He didn't plan on Omen getting caught."

Flora walked up with his order. Eggs, bacon, and hash browns filled one plate, and his pancakes on a smaller plate. She set them down.

Brie smiled. "Hi, Flora."

"Hello. So you don't sleep either?"

"Sure I do," she said.

"He says the same thing." She gave Brie a half smile. He'd never gotten a smile from Flora himself. "You need something to eat or drink?"

"Coffee, please," Brie said.

When she left, Brie unrolled her napkin from her silverware and helped herself to a bite of Connor's eggs.

He watched and smiled. "Have all you want. I'll share." He pushed the plate to the middle of the table.

"Don't you at all see it as too easy?" She grabbed a piece of bacon and took a bite.

He picked up his own fork and helped himself to the

eggs. "Who else would he have gotten to do his dirty work? He knew the guy's record, knew what he was capable of."

She finished off the slice of bacon. "I guess you're right." She reached for the pitcher of syrup and poured a little over one side of his stacked pancakes. Then she grabbed her fork. "Mmm." She licked her lips and pulled the plate closer. "Why is it that other people's food always tastes better than your own?"

He smiled then focused on her doubts about Bara. "Okay, if Agent Bara didn't do this, then it's Agent Calvin. I thought you didn't believe Calvin could do this?"

"I don't. Or maybe I don't want to. Seriously, I don't want to believe either of them would." She cut herself another bite of pancakes and dished it into her mouth. "But wanting and wishing can be a waste of time."

Not so, he thought. He'd practically wished her here and she'd shown up. "We'll bring Agent Bara in for questioning in the morning. This should be enough to get the warrant to search his hotel room. We might find the phone with the text messages to Omen." He glanced up at the clock on the wall. "At six I'll call Mark and see if he thinks we should go for a warrant before talking to Bara." Fork in hand, he leaned back in his chair and watched her eat.

"What?" she asked, looking up at him.

"Nothing. I just…I like seeing you eat my food." He leaned forward and took another bite of his hash browns.

She slid the half-eaten pancakes aside and grabbed a bottle of ketchup. "For the eggs?"

"Only on your half." A grin pulled at his lips, and he

was completely baffled by why he found this so enjoyable. But he did. Then again, maybe it was just having her here.

After dousing half of the eggs, she ate her portion quickly, then grabbed the syrup and emptied the rest of it on the pancakes. She looked up and caught him staring.

"I'll pay for it."

"I'm not complaining."

She stuffed another forkful of pancakes into her mouth, then licked her lips.

He grinned.

Flora appeared and dropped off Brie's coffee and creams.

"Thank you." Brie added cream to her cup. When Flora left, Brie pointed her spoon at him. "It's not your fault. And coming here is still wrong."

He didn't want to talk about that here. "Any news on Carlos?"

She licked a drop of syrup from her bottom lip. "I called before I came here. The nurse said his vitals are great and he opened his eyes a few more times."

"That's good."

"Yeah, it is." She smiled.

Connor sipped his coffee, staring at her over the top. "Do you think Carlos knows who is behind his shooting?"

"Tory said he didn't think Carlos knew who the leak was, but he could have figured it out on his way here." She ate another bite of his pancakes. "What time do you think I can go see Rosaria?"

"I'll check when I get to the office. I'll have to go with you." He probably could have gotten her in to see Rosaria on her own, but he wasn't above using it as an excuse to spend time with her.

She nodded. "I go to work at four. So the earlier the better."

"You may not need to go to the club." He set his coffee down. "If the prints come back like we hope on Dillon Armand, ICE plans on arresting him."

She frowned. "But we need evidence on the human trafficking case. And since he's back here, I might be able to get something we could use. Can't they give me just a few days?"

"ICE thinks they have enough leads to look into while holding him in custody for the false passport. Meanwhile, if I can find Regina Berger tomorrow, she might have something that links him with the trafficking."

Reaching over, he stabbed a forkful of pancakes.

They sat there, eating in silence. Connor pierced the last bite of pancakes, but instead of bringing it to his lips, he held it to hers. She opened her mouth and took the offering. Slowly, he pulled the fork out from between her lips, finding it way sexier than it should be.

Their eyes met and held. A drop of syrup lingered on the corner of her mouth. Leaning over, he caught it with the pad of his finger, then brought it to his lips. As the sweetness touched his tongue, he ached to taste her. His mind took him back to her naked in bed and all the places his mouth had traveled. His jeans suddenly felt tighter.

She glanced away and picked up her coffee cup.

Several seconds passed before she looked up. "Can I be there tomorrow when you interview Bara?"

"I don't know if that's best. He considers you his peer, so he might be less likely to talk."

She frowned but didn't argue. He assumed it was because she knew he was right. Reaching for her purse, she said, "I should go."

"Why? Stay. I like your company, Brie. I like you being here."

"No, I... I'm sorry." She snatched her coat off the chair.

# CHAPTER
# TWENTY-FIVE

His brain sought for something, anything, to say that would change her mind. "You can't eat and run." Connor watched her put her coat on.

She pulled out a twenty from her wallet. "Call me after your interview with Agent Bara." She set the money on the table.

He dropped his hand over hers. "Brie, I don't understand why we can't see where this goes. We could—"

She slipped her hand out from under his. "Talk to you tomorrow."

When she stood to leave, so did he, following her outside. The cold air hit, reminding him he'd left his jacket inside. "You know you never answered my question last night."

She stopped at her car and started digging in her purse for her keys. "What question?"

"What do *you* want?"

She stopped searching and stared into her purse, as if

the answer might be in there, lost with her keys. "I want this case to be over." Lifting her eyes, she continued, "I want who hired Omen to be locked up, and I want Armand behind bars."

"That's not what I mean, and you know it."

"It was a mistake, Connor."

"You really believe that?"

"Yeah, I do."

"Well, I don't. And I know I keep screwing up, saying stupid stuff, but—"

"It's not stupid," she said. "It's the truth. You know what you want. I respect that." She resumed her search and pulled out her wallet and handed it to him. "Hold this."

He took it. She pulled out a handful of other items. "And this." He caught the pack of tissues, a small tube of hand lotion, and two tampons.

"Let me take you out on a real date."

She reached inside her purse again, taking out a few more items. "Can you grab these, too?" She shook the purse again. "Where the hell are my keys?"

Connor juggled the items. "Tell me you didn't wake up thinking about me. Because I woke up thinking about you."

"Finally!" She pulled her keys out and held out her purse for him to return the items in his hands.

He dropped them all into the opened bag. Except one tampon missed and hit the ground at his feet.

She clicked open the locks—the beep piercing the quiet. "You're right. I woke up thinking about you. About all the reasons this"—she waved a hand between them— "would be a stupid idea."

He eased in and dropped his forehead against hers. "Then explain that to me. Because right now it feels like the best plan I've had in years."

She put a hand on his chest, as if to push him away, but she didn't. She left it there. A soft touch that had his heart thumping against his breastbone.

"You're just horny." She cut her big blue eyes up at him. "From feeding me pancakes."

He laughed. "You didn't have to open your mouth."

"I like pancakes, and it was the last bite."

He laughed again. "Okay, but for the record, I'm not horny."

She lifted a questioning brow. Her hand still pressed against his chest felt so damn good. He wanted that touch everywhere.

"Right." Her one word came loaded with skepticism. "You don't want to have sex with me?"

The blood pooling down south answered the question. "Yes, I want to have sex with you, but there's a difference between that and being horny."

"And that sounds like a conversation we don't need to have," she said, but she still didn't pull away.

He dipped his head down just a bit. "Why? Because it'll make you horny?"

"No." She glanced up just a bit, bringing her lips a whisper away from his. "Because..." she didn't finish. He closed that tiny distance. He didn't kiss her, just let his lips touch hers every so lightly. She inhaled and her breath brushed across his lips.

Then she kissed him. He slipped his hand under her jean jacket, around her tiny waist, and pulled her against him.

"No. No. No," she muttered, pulling away. "I'm sorry." She put two fingers over his lips. "Seriously. I don't think this...I have to go."

\* \* \*

Brie went home, watched the ceiling fan whirl, and petted Psycho for an hour. She tried to forget how he'd tasted like bacon and syrup. How just one kiss made her hungry for so much more. More than someone like Connor could offer.

At six a.m., she walked out of the hospital elevator and down the hall. The lights were low. The sound of her shoes on the tile floor echoed too loudly. She stopped at the door of the family waiting room and peered inside. Two people were there, sleeping. One was an older woman whom Brie had seen several times before. Her husband, who'd been in a car accident, was in the room beside Carlos. The other person was Tory. He'd given the woman the recliner and he'd taken the almost cushionless love seat. His feet hung off the end and his head rested at a crooked angle.

For some reason, she was reminded of the moment when Carlos had told her he was going to ask Tory to marry him. Her lack of enthusiasm had pissed Carlos off. "I'm sorry," Brie had apologized later. "I'm just afraid you'll end up getting hurt."

She'd been wrong. She'd never seen Carlos so happy. Tory grounded him. They wanted the same things, they laughed at the same jokes. They finished each other's sentences. They meshed. They completed each other.

A part of her wanted that. A connection. Love. Family.

A sofa buddy. A life mate. Her thoughts shot straight to Connor. He hadn't been wrong when he'd accused her of wanting two kids and a white picket fence. Brie hated being alone. But she knew how easy it was for love to let you down, to make a fool out of you. She'd learned that with Todd and with her mom's marriage to her dad.

So just because someone wanted something didn't mean they had the guts to go after it.

Especially when the person who made you want it, made you ache for it, made you think it was possible, was a proud commitmentphobe who took happily-ever-after off the table.

No doubt about it. Letting herself get closer to Connor Pierce was like... "swimming with the sharks," she whispered.

"Sharks?"

She turned and found Eliot standing behind her. Solid, dependable, and one of the few people in her life who hadn't let her down. "How can you limp"—she lowered her voice—"and still not make a sound?" She moved away from the door.

"Stealth is my middle name," he said, smiling.

She went in for a hug. A tight one.

He put his arms around her, and she soaked up his warmth, his love. This was safe.

"You okay?" he asked.

"Yeah. Just needed a hug." She pulled away and they started walking toward the little alcove right outside the ICU doors where Eliot had set up camp.

He studied her. "What's wrong?"

"If I said 'everything,' would you make me elaborate?"

"Talk to me." He motioned for Brie to sit down.

She dropped down and Eliot took the chair next to her. "Why haven't you ever remarried?"

He studied her. "Why do I get the feeling this is about Connor Pierce?"

"No lectures," she said.

"I wasn't going to lecture you." He hesitated. "I told myself for years it was because I'd never love anyone as much as I loved Janice."

"But?" she asked.

He looked at her. "I think the real truth is I was afraid. Afraid to love someone so much and lose them again."

"But fear's good, right? It keeps us from making the same stupid mistakes."

He nodded. "You're right. Fear does help us avoid the same pitfalls. But it also keeps us from living a full life. I think the trick is figuring out when the risk is worth it."

"How do we do that?"

"I don't know." He smiled. "When I figure it out, I'll tell you."

They grew silent, then Brie offered up her other problem. "Agent Miles got back to me." Eliot had been with her last night when she called him and requested the searches on older cases that Agent Bara had worked.

"This early?"

"He couldn't sleep."

"And?" He motioned for Brie to sit down.

"Omen, the hitman, was Agent Bara's CI."

He must have heard the hurt in her voice; he reached over and squeezed her hand. "I'm sorry."

"I know. No, I don't know. How could he...I liked him. And he's got a kid, and now he's going to be locked up for the rest of his life. Why would he do that?"

"It's hard to understand why people do things."

"And why would he use someone who had a direct connection to him? He had to have known we'd have checked for this."

"He didn't think the guy would get caught. And who else would he have used?"

She frowned. "That's what Connor said, but—"

"You don't think Bara did it?"

"I know it looks like he did. He's got the Guatemala connection. And now we can tie him to the hit man."

"What's his Guatemala connection?"

"His parents are from there."

"Well, the tie to Omen looks bad, but the connection to Guatemala is just bad luck. I mean, you lived in Guatemala for six months. And didn't Agent Calvin's daughter work over there on some mission for the church?"

She turned and stared at Eliot. "I know she did missions for her church, but was it Guatemala?"

"I think so. You should check. I could be wrong, but I think—"

"When was that?" she asked.

"His wife was bragging about her daughter's missionary work at the barbeque. So what was that? Eight months ago?"

"The same time as the Sala case," she muttered aloud.

Brie recalled her earlier conversation with Connor. *You think someone found out we were on to the gunrunning operation and threatened his family if he didn't turn over information?*

*  *  *

"This is a federal agent you're talking about," Judge Bond said, wearing his bathrobe and not looking happy at being woken up before seven in the morning.

"I know that," Connor said. "That's why it's important we get the warrant. He could ditch the evidence if we don't move quickly."

Connor had called Mark and Juan at five-thirty a.m., and they all agreed to go for a warrant. But they needed to get the right judge. The fact that the FBI involvement was based on hearsay didn't help. Hence why Connor came himself. He personally knew Judge Bond, who called him every Christmas and roped him into helping with his and his wife's Toys for Tots program.

The judge let out a big gulp of air. "Are you using our acquaintance to help get this warrant?"

"Yes, sir, I am. But I've known you for eight years, have I ever come to you before?"

"No." The judge sat down at his kitchen table and continued to stare at him. "This could come back and bite you, and more importantly me, in the ass."

Connor inhaled. "I don't think it will."

"Wait. This isn't even a cold case. Why are you working it?"

"Sergeant Brown assigned us to it."

"Seriously? Brown's not what I'd call your biggest fan."

"But he knows we close cases."

"True." He tugged at his robe. "If I do this, you're going to help chair my wife's Toys for Tots campaign. We have a committee meeting next week to start planning. Last year, Glencoe PD donated three times as much as Anniston PD."

"I'd be honored to be on the board."

Five minutes later, Connor walked out with a signed warrant. Mark was waiting in Connor's car.

"Got it." Connor handed him the paper and crawled behind the wheel.

"Okay, let's go visit an agent and search a hotel room."

Connor pulled out of the judge's driveway.

"Hmm." Mark chuckled.

Connor glanced at him. "What?"

"Do you always drive around with a tampon in your cup holder?"

"Brie dropped it," he said in a clipped tone.

Mark grinned then rubbed a hand over his mouth. "How are things going between you two?"

"Don't start." Connor's grip on the steering wheel tightened.

"I'm not. I'm . . . genuinely concerned, and maybe curious. I mean, correct me if I'm wrong, but I think you actually like her. So . . . ?"

Connor shot him a scowl. "So what?"

Mark raised a brow and grinned. "How's it going?"

Connor frowned. "What? Your sex life so boring you want to hear about mine?"

"Whoa. I wasn't . . . My sex life's fantastic. You obviously aren't getting enough, or you wouldn't be in such a piss-poor mood."

"I'm not . . . She doesn't want to see me again. End of story. Let it go."

"Okay." Mark gave him a look, then pulled out his phone. "I'm going to get a nearby unit to meet us at the hotel. We know the man has a gun."

He made the call, and when he hung up, he said, "What do you think about giving Agent Calvin a courtesy call?"

His partner's question was background noise to what Connor had running through his head. *You're right. I woke up thinking about you. About all the reasons why this would be a stupid idea.*

"Stupid." Connor glanced at Mark. "I don't get it."

"You don't think I should call him?" Mark asked.

"The sex was fantastic," Connor said. "And yeah, I screwed up, but I apologized. I told her I said a bunch of stupid stuff and that I wanted to date her. She doesn't even seem mad anymore. And she likes me. She ate my breakfast. Do you eat someone's breakfast if you don't like them?"

Mark shrugged. "I guess not."

"And it wasn't because I fed her that bite of pancake, because I didn't kiss her, she kissed me, then she just cut me off." He slammed the palm of his hand on the steering wheel. "I don't understand."

"Neither do I," Mark said under his breath.

"What?"

Mark rephrased his comment. "I mean, women can be hard to figure out."

"No, shit!" Connor said.

"But I'll tell you this. Most of the time, they're right. They think this shit through."

Connor slammed on his brakes at a light. "You're saying she shouldn't see me?"

"No. I'm saying that she has a reason to think she shouldn't see you. You said you screwed up. Maybe she's still hanging on to that. And if you understand her reasons, then maybe you can convince her that you didn't mean to... to give her that reason. That you deserve a chance."

"How do I do that?"

"Most guys would say flowers or chocolate. But that doesn't work with Annie. I mean, she likes them, but if it's an apology kind of thing, you need something that matters to them. Something small, but grand."

"Small but grand? That doesn't make sense." The light changed and Connor went back to driving.

"I mean...think of something she likes, something that she mentioned or maybe she didn't think you knew about, or that you didn't hear her. And get it for her. I have a things-Annie-likes list on my phone for when I screw up." Mark paused. "Or what's her favorite food?"

"I don't...She likes pancakes."

Mark looked down at the tampon. "You could also do something that guys don't normally do."

"What kind of thing?"

"I went and bought Annie tampons once. You'd have thought I bought her an expensive piece of jewelry. She thought it was a big deal."

"So small but grand and buy tampons," Connor said.

Right then Mark's phone rang. He checked the number. "It's Juan." He answered the call. "You did?" Mark glanced at Connor. "You're kidding me? Shit!"

"What?" Connor asked as he pulled into Bara's hotel parking lot and spotted two black-and-white cars waiting on them.

"Yeah, but hurry." Mark hung up and turned to Connor. "The prints came back. They aren't Dillon Armand's. They are his cousin's, Marcus Armand. He's not using a fake passport. All this time we thought...He's not the guy connected to Brie's sister's murder. She was so certain that—"

"She was certain because he's been saying he's Dillon

Armand. He signed into the hotel here as him. Told everyone he has ties to the clubs."

"Yeah, but impersonating a cousin isn't enough to hold him on. ICE was set to arrest him for using a false passport. They can't do that now."

"Shit," Connor said. "But it doesn't mean he's not connected to Brie's sister's murder. Maybe the witness who said they saw Dillon Armand with Ronan got the two cousins mixed up? They look alike. Or maybe they are both behind it. The whole family is crooked."

"Everything you say is probably true. But it means we have nothing to hold him on. And as for his involvement in Alma's murder, we can't know for sure if he was involved. He's not mentioned in the report, so there's no evidence."

"Then we have to get it," Connor said.

"How?" Mark ran a hand over his face. "At least it looks as though we've got the Olvera case in the bag." He looked out the window at the patrol cars. "Let's see if we can find the phone Bara used to text Omen and bring the agent in to have a chat."

Connor, still spinning from the news about Armand, followed Mark over to the two officers.

Connor spoke up. "We're serving a warrant to search the suspect's hotel room and are going to bring him in for a chat. He's an FBI agent, so he's armed. We don't know how cooperative he's going to be. This may go easy or it may go bad."

"Juan is on his way," Mark said as his phone rang. "Detective Sutton," he answered.

"Yeah." Mark frowned. "How?" Pause. "Thanks for letting us know."

"What?" Connor asked.

"That was Detective Sampson. The story about Rosaria and the shooting got out. It's all over the Internet."

"Shit," Connor said. "If Bara's seen it, he's probably gotten rid of the phone."

A few minutes later, Juan pulled up, and all five of them walked into the hotel.

After getting the room number, and a key from the front desk—just in case Agent Bara had already left— they rode the elevator up in silence. Stepping out on the fifth floor, they were two doors down from his room when Connor's phone rang. He pulled it out and cut it off, but before the screen went dark, he spotted Brie's number.

Connor walked up to the door and knocked. When he didn't hear anything, he knocked again.

Finally, a voice came from behind the door. "Coming."

\* \* \*

Brie left a message on Connor's phone explaining what she'd learned about Agent Calvin's daughter. Then because she wasn't 100 percent sure the girl's mission trip had been to Guatemala, she went home, to search for an old email from Calvin with the information. She couldn't find it.

Suddenly, remembering she'd donated to a GoFundMe page for the mission, she searched for the PayPal receipt. Once she located it, she got the name of the church and checked their Facebook page. She found it. There was a post about the Guatemalan mission. It even included a picture of Calvin's daughter.

"Damn!"

She drew in a deep breath and told herself it didn't mean he was guilty. She still needed something else. Like Pablo's phone. Suddenly, an idea started to form.

She grabbed her keys, went into the kitchen to her junk drawer, and pulled out her old phone. She turned it on to make sure it didn't have any juice, then grabbed a plastic baggie, and took off.

It was ten till eight when she pulled up to the police precinct. Taking a deep breath, she got her story straight in her head.

Walking into the building, she went straight to Mildred's desk.

"Just the person I was hoping to see." The woman pulled her newspaper over. "Nickname of Alabama University. Eleven letters."

"Crimson Tide," Brie said.

"I knew you'd know it."

She forced a smile. "Is Connor in?"

"Not yet. None of them are here. Which is really rather strange."

"What about Agent Calvin?"

"He walked in about five minutes ago. He's set up office in Conference Room A. It's—"

"I know where it is. Thanks."

As she headed that way her chest grew heavier with each step. Was the man who'd brought her into the FBI, the person she'd grown to respect and admire, really behind Pablo's murder and Carlos's attempted murder?

When she got to the door, she reached around and reassured herself by tapping the Glock that was tucked in the back of her jeans. Taking one deep breath, she knocked.

Even if he was guilty, he wouldn't hurt her, she told herself.

* * *

Connor went through the suitcase again as Juan walked back into the hotel room. "No phone in his car."

"It's not here either." Connor slammed the top of the plastic suitcase.

"He could have ditched it when he didn't hear back from Omen," Mark said.

"Yeah," Connor agreed, but he really wanted that phone. Really wanted substantial proof.

Right then Agent Bara stormed into the room, followed by one of the uniformed officers. While Bara had been less than happy when he'd opened the door to their search warrant, he'd handed over his gun.

"What's wrong?" Bara snapped. "Disappointed? I told you I didn't have a second phone."

"Let's go down to the precinct," Connor said.

"What the hell do you think you have on me? Whatever it is, you're fucking up. I didn't leak information on the Sala case and I sure as hell didn't hire anyone to shoot Agent Olvera!"

"And you don't know a Kevin Omen either, do you?" Connor snapped, then studied the guy's expression, hoping to see a flash of guilt. Or maybe a flicker of fear that he was caught.

The man flinched, but Connor couldn't call it guilt or fear. Of course, the guy could just be good at hiding shit. He'd met a lot of skilled liars in his time.

"What does he have to do with this?" Bara asked.

Connor didn't expect Bara to deny knowing Omen, that was too easy to disprove, but the genuine surprise in his voice sent a shot of acid to his stomach. They had the wrong man.

* * *

"Come in," Agent Calvin said from the other side of the door.

Holding the baggie with the phone inside, she opened the door and entered the room. "Hey. I was hoping one of the APD officers was in here."

"No." His gaze lowered to what was in her hand. "Why?"

"I needed to give them something." She lifted the baggie.

"What is it?" he asked. When she didn't answer, he stood up. "Is that Pablo Ybarra's phone?"

And that was exactly why she was here. There was no way he could know about this phone. No way. Unless he'd been the one to call it eight months ago.

Her heart took a nosedive. "Yeah. It came in the mail this morning. I...uh, don't know what's on it. The battery's out."

"Give it to me. I'll have it checked out."

"That's okay. I already told the guys I'd hand it over to them." She didn't even know why she was pushing it, except...

"Just give it to me," Agent Calvin said. "Now, dammit!"

She'd never been afraid of this man. Even now as his six-foot frame came toward her, it wasn't fear bubbling in her gut. It was betrayal, bitterness, and a deep sadness. The kind that robbed you of trust in human kindness.

He tugged the bag from her hand. She lifted her eyes, and before she considered the wisdom of it, the words left her lips. "Did they threaten to kill your daughter? Is that what happened?"

For just a second, she thought she saw shame in his eyes. But then it was gone.

After blinking, he squared his shoulders and said, "They said they'd kill her if I didn't turn over the information. If I didn't take your CI out. They sent me pictures of her in Guatemala. Until you have children you wouldn't understand."

"Then that's what you should tell the cops."

He shook his head. She reached for her gun the same time he did. But she was quicker. "Don't do it."

His hand remained tucked under his coat. "I can't go to prison."

The trigger against the pad of her index finger felt cold. "You had Pablo killed. You ordered a hit on Carlos and on Rosaria. Do you know how hard it is for me to wrap my head around that? I respected you. I trusted you."

"I tried talking Carlos into dropping it. He wouldn't. I didn't want him to die. I tried stopping him."

"And Pablo and Rosaria? They didn't matter?"

"The Sala family insisted Pablo had to die. And Rosaria was the reason Carlos started looking into the case again."

"Drop your hand from your coat."

There was a knock at the door.

"Agent Calvin," Mildred's voice came from behind the door.

Brie's gaze shifted to the door for a fraction of a second. That's all it took for Calvin to grab his gun.

As her eyes cut back, she saw the barrel of the gun being pulled from the lapel of his jacket. Her finger began to depress the trigger—but she hesitated one second too long.

# CHAPTER TWENTY-SIX

I'm sorry." His words had barely reached Brie's ears, when the gun swung up under his chin and exploded. Blood and white matter sprayed all over the ceiling. His body, already lifeless, fell back on the table with a dull thud.

She sank to her knees. A scream lodged in her throat. Air trapped in her lungs. Tears filled her eyes.

She heard the loud crack of the door being swung open and slammed against the wall. Heard voices demanding, ordering. But the words were lost to her, she couldn't look away from Agent Calvin's body splayed out on the table.

Someone knelt beside her. Her gun was pulled from her hand.

More voices surrounded her. "Her gun hasn't been fired. He shot himself." Words echoed all around her.

"Brie." Her name rang out above the noise. Someone

had her hands in theirs. "Come on. I got you." The words murmured in her ear: deep, soft, caring. Her mind and heart rejected the tenderness. She'd just seen a man violently blow his head off.

She studied the person talking. Connor.

"Let's get out of here," he said.

She shot to her feet. When he moved in closer, she waved him off. "Stop!"

He motioned her toward the door. "Come on."

She looked back at Agent Calvin, his eyes still open. The top of his head was gone. She closed her eyes and covered her mouth as a sad sound leaked from her lips.

Connor's arm came around her shoulder. She let him guide her out. He moved her into the hall, where a crowd of police officials gathered.

"Move back," Connor ordered and an opening appeared. He moved her across the hall to another door and gently nudged her inside.

He pulled a chair out and turned it away from the table. "Sit down."

She felt her hands, her knees, her heart trembling. "I'm okay."

"Please sit down."

She dropped into the seat. He pulled another chair over and sat down, facing her.

Meeting his eyes, she said, "He shot himself."

"I know."

He sat there, silent, just looking at her for several minutes. "I saw a phone in the baggie. Is that Pablo's phone? Did it come in the mail?"

"No. It's an old phone of mine. I…I realized he wouldn't know about the phone unless…unless he was

behind everything. So I wanted to see how he'd react."
She had to swallow to keep her voice from shaking. "He
asked if it was Pablo's phone."

"Did he admit to hiring Omen?"

She nodded. "They had his daughter." Calvin would
still be alive if she hadn't gone in there. Guilt started to
build until she remembered Carlos and Pablo. She pushed
it back down, but it didn't stop it from hurting.

"His daughter?" Connor asked.

She took in a deep breath. "I left you a message."

He frowned. "We were bringing in Bara." He reached
for her hands. But she was afraid his touch or any
sort of empathy would bring her to tears. She pulled
them back.

He acknowledged her withdrawal and dropped his
hands in his lap. "Do you need something to drink?"

"No. And please stop."

"Stop what?"

"Coddling me." Her throat tightened.

"I'm not—"

"Can you...I want to be alone. Please! I need a
little time."

He walked out. Brie pulled her knees up to her chest,
hugging her calves. She closed her eyes, but when her mind
replayed the shooting, she forced them back open.

Less than thirty minutes later, the door opened. She
expected it to be Connor. It wasn't.

Eliot walked in. Brie stood up, and he pulled her
against him.

Her throat tightened; her eyes stung. She clung to him
for a few seconds, before drawing back. "I'm okay."

"Are you?"

"Yeah. I just keep thinking about his family." Her chest tightened. "His daughter is going to blame herself."

"He made a lot of mistakes that got him here, Brie. None of this is on you."

"I know." And she did. This wasn't her fault. But fault or not, she felt grief for the man she used to know. "Connor called you?" she asked.

He nodded. "He was worried about you."

"Well, I'm fine now. Someone raised me to be tough."

"Tough maybe, but you're still human."

"Yeah, there is that." She inhaled. "How's Carlos?"

"Really good. He's responding to questions now. Shaking his head yes and no. The doctors are taking out the tube this afternoon."

"Good. I'll go and see him when I'm finished here." She looked back at the door. "I should go. They're going to need a statement from me."

"You need me with you?"

"No. I'll be fine. I promise. You should be sleeping. And tell Sam he doesn't need to stay at the hospital. At least this part of this debacle is over." Brie considered Rosaria—this meant it was over for her, too.

A knock sounded at the door. "Come in," Brie said.

Connor walked in. His gaze went right to her. He had a piece of paper in his hands. "You should see this."

"What is it?"

"A suicide letter. It was on Calvin's laptop. There was a leak to the press about the shooting in Willowcreek. It listed the names of witnesses. Rosaria's name was in it. Calvin must've seen it. It sounded as if he thought Rosaria knew he was the one who had called Pablo. Between believing it was over and the guilt, he had decided to end it."

Brie swore she hadn't felt guilty for pushing Calvin to the brink, but maybe a part of her did, because some heaviness in her chest lightened.

* * *

Connor watched Mark and Brown leave the room, but he stayed seated across from Brie. Considering she'd just witnessed a man kill himself, she came off strong, composed, and professional. Not that he didn't notice the way she closed her fist every few minutes. He recalled all too clearly the days after that dreadful day in the alley. Flashbacks. Don hitting the ground, Don's eyes empty, then the kid: scared and dying, then gone.

She closed her fist again. He felt a tight grip in his chest. Instinct had him wanting to reach for her, hold her, help her, but his gut reminded him she'd already pushed him away.

The interview lasted only twenty minutes. The crime scene told the story. Brie pushed in her chair and met his gaze.

"You called Eliot—"

"It's not because I saw you as weak!" he said quickly. "I know . . . I saw my partner killed. I know he wasn't your partner, but you worked for him for five years. You respected him. At one time he was your hero. You wouldn't let me help, so I called Eliot. You can be pissed—"

"I was going to say thank you." She rested her hand on the table.

Relaxing his defensive posture, he slumped back in his seat. "I'm sorry. I thought . . ."

"I know," she said.

He shifted his hand close to hers. His fingers brushed against the side of her hand. "Are you okay, really?"

"I will be. I probably won't sleep for a few days, but I'll be okay."

He nodded. "If I can do anything. All you need to do is ask."

She pulled her hand away and clenched her fist again. "Is someone contacting Agent Calvin's wife? Should I—"

"No. Sergeant Brown called the FBI. They're sending someone."

She took a deep breath. "Can I go see Rosaria? I'm assuming you'll be cutting the protective detail."

"No one has discussed it yet, but I'm sure we will. Let me clear a few things, and then I'll drive you there."

"You don't have to."

A knock came at the door. Brie flinched.

He frowned at her reaction. "You shouldn't drive, at least for a few hours." He looked at the door. "Come in."

Mildred walked in, tears in her eyes. "I just wanted to give you a hug. When I heard the gun go off, I was so afraid…"

Brie's eyes teared up as she stood and hugged the woman. It lasted several long seconds. Two people drawing strength from one another. So, she'd let Mildred comfort her, but not him. That stung when all he wanted was…Hell, what did he want?

The answer came back. A chance. A chance with Brie Ryan.

When Mildred left, Connor stood up. "You want to hang here? I'll swing by and get you as soon as I can leave."

"Yeah."

He started out.

"Wait," she said.

Connor turned back around.

"Have you gotten the prints back yet?"

His gut tightened. "I was going to tell you later."

"Tell me what?" She studied him. "Why do you look like it's bad news?"

He exhaled. "It's not Dillon Armand. It's his cousin, Marcus. He was using his own passport."

"What?" She dropped back down in a chair. "But he's passing himself off as—"

"I know, but as Mark said, impersonating a cousin isn't enough to hold him on. But I'm confused as to why he'd lie…"

"Access to the girls." Brie nipped at her lip. "By pretending to be part-owner, Grimes worked with him to get him whatever he wanted. Encouraged the employees to…give him favors."

"Yeah, that has to be it. But wouldn't Grimes recognize it wasn't Dillon?"

"I told you, they look alike." Sighing, she looked up, tears in her eyes. "He might not be the one who killed Alma."

"I know."

"Or maybe…Wait. Remember I told you that Dillon wasn't here when she went missing. That's why we couldn't get him, because he wasn't here. But Marcus was. We can prove that now."

"Just being in the country isn't enough, Brie. You know that. And the witness in Guatemala said he had seen Alma with Dillon, not Marcus."

"It's a family business. They might both—"

"We need more."

"So what does that mean for the case?" she snapped.

He saw the desperation in her eyes and would have given anything to assure her that he saw them proceeding as before, but the truth was he didn't know where things stood. "I don't know."

"What do you mean 'I don't know'?"

"I mean, we can't arrest him yet. And I'm not sure ICE will continue helping."

"Maybe we don't have enough for my sister's murder, but we have him for the human trafficking."

"I don't know if we have enough for that either."

"We know two women who worked at the clubs, the one using the fake identity of Tammy Alberts and my sister, are both dead. And we have proof that both were taken outside the country. And you said Regina Berger ran for a reason. You can't just give up."

"I'm not. But right now we have no proof tying Marcus to those girls."

"Then we get the proof. I'll get it."

*How*, Connor thought, but didn't ask. Brie was already taking too much on herself and risking her life. The last thing he wanted was for her to take on more.

* * *

Anger felt good. It helped Brie focus. Or it at least took some of the focus off what she'd seen. Not that she was angry at Connor. She even told him that, but he seemed to be cautiously leery of her. Or maybe just quiet.

They walked into Rosaria's hotel suite.

"She's in the room," the officer said. "I told her you were coming and that she was safe now, but I didn't explain anything."

Rosaria rushed out. "Is it really over?"

Brie nodded. "Yes."

"So you got the agent who ordered Pablo's death? Tell me he will be in prison for the rest of his life."

Brie swallowed. "He committed suicide."

"He's dead?"

"Yeah."

Rosaria put a shaking hand over her lips. "Is it wrong for me to be happy?" Tears filled her eyes.

"No," Brie said, but it hurt. And a part of her wanted to explain to Rosaria that they had threatened Agent Calvin's daughter, to take some of the guilt off the man she'd once known, but to even say it seemed to imply it justified what he'd done. And it didn't. Nothing would.

"Are you sure I'm safe now?"

"Positive."

Brie reached into her purse and pulled out an envelope with a thousand dollars in it. She'd had Connor stop by her bank on the way here. "I want you to take this. It'll help you get back on your feet. I also think you need to contact a lawyer. The FBI should compensate you for what happened. Tell your lawyer if he needs someone to testify, I'll do it."

Rosaria looked at the envelope. "You don't have to give me this."

"Please. It's a gift to Pablo as well."

Rosaria took the envelope. "He was right. You are a good person."

Brie smiled. "I think about him a lot. His infectious grin. His jokes."

Rosaria let out a sound that was half laugh, half cry. "He was so bad at telling them."

"Really bad." Brie laughed and breathed deeply, emotion almost choking her.

"I miss him so much," Rosaria said.

"I know. He was one of a kind."

They hugged. Tight. In the embrace, Brie felt a tiny emotional shift. Maybe now she could let go of the guilt about Pablo. As she pulled back she saw Connor studying her. For one second, she wondered what it would take for him to lose the guilt he carried.

"That went well," Brie said as they left.

"Yeah," Connor said.

Brie and Connor had just settled in his car when her phone rang with an unknown number.

"Hello?" she answered.

"This is Detective Ashmore from the APD. May I ask whom I'm speaking with?"

"What's this about?" Brie glanced at Connor.

"I'm working a missing person case. And this number was found in the victim's things."

"What victim? Who's missing?"

"Candace Brooks."

"Candy's missing?" And just like that, Brie recalled part of the phone conversation she'd heard outside Grimes's office. *How many are blond?*

# CHAPTER TWENTY-SEVEN

It has to be connected," Brie fumed to Connor. "I told you I think he raped her."

"Let's see what the officer knows before jumping to conclusions." Connor drove Brie to Candy's parents' house, where she said she'd meet Ashmore. A gray-haired man in his late fifties met them on the porch. Connor introduced her as an FBI agent. Brie got the feeling Connor and Ashmore knew each other.

"So you think this might be connected to another case?" Ashmore asked.

"It's likely," Connor answer. "What happened?"

"The mother says Candace was going to the store to get a few items on Friday evening and didn't come home."

"And you're just now looking into this?" The anger simmering inside went straight for the detective.

Ashmore frowned. "The mom didn't call the police. She said her daughter works at a strip club, and she expects things like this from her. The reason we're here is because her daughter's car was found abandoned in a grocery store parking lot. Her trunk was open with her groceries still inside, as if she was taken while unloading them. It took two days before the store owner called to report it."

Brie's chest went hot with fury toward the mom.

"We went through Candy's things," the cop continued. "We found a piece of paper with your number scribbled on it."

Brie frowned. "Wait," she said. "Grimes said Candace called in sick on Saturday. He called me into work."

Ashmore appeared puzzled. "I thought you were FBI. You work at the Black Diamond?"

Connor spoke up and gave the man a few details. When the conversation ended, Ashmore agreed to keep looking into the case but let Connor handle the work angle.

"What now?" Brie got back in his car.

"Now I talk to ICE. This might be enough to keep them on the case. Then I'll pay Grimes a visit. After that, I'm searching for Regina Berger."

"What can I do? I don't have to be at the club until four."

"I think you should relax."

"I can't! Candy's been taken."

"Yeah, but we don't have any leads yet."

"At least give me some information on Berger. Addresses of friends and family and the make of her car. If all I do is drive there and check for her vehicle, it'll keep me from . . . reliving today."

Connor relented, and a few minutes later, he pulled into a fast-food drive-thru. He glanced at her. "I'm starving. What do you want?"

"I don't think . . ."

"You need to eat."

She frowned. "You're sounding a lot like Eliot."

"That's not a bad thing. What do you want?" He motioned to the sign.

"A grilled chicken sandwich."

"Fries?"

"No."

"Cookie?" he asked.

"Sure."

"Chocolate chip, oatmeal, or chocolate chocolate chip?"

"Chocolate chocolate chip."

"You like chocolate?" He studied her, as if her answer was important.

"Yeah." She reached into her purse to hand him some cash. When she pulled out her wallet, she also pulled out her sister's bracelet. She held it in her hand, scared that if she couldn't find Candy, she might face the same fate as her sister.

Tears filled her eyes. "We have to find Candy, Connor."

He looked at her. "We will."

* * *

The place looked dingy and smelled like day-old cigarette smoke and stale beer. The last time Connor had come to the club was when they worked the Noel case. Abby Noel had worked in the club before she'd gone missing and was suspected to have been murdered by the same person who'd killed her boyfriend. Connor had come to interview a few of her work associates. Mr. Grimes had been less than thrilled to work with them then, and Connor could only guess the man would feel the same now.

"I can't say I've missed seeing you," Mr. Grimes said.

Connor moved up to the bar where the man stood.

"Ditto," Connor said dryly. After talking to ICE, who

agreed Candace Brooks's apparent abduction was enough reason to stay on the case, Connor had driven straight to the Black Diamond.

"What's it this time?"

"You seem to be famous for missing employees."

He frowned. "Who's missing?"

"Candace Brooks."

To the old man's credit, he appeared shocked. "I . . . don't know anything about it."

"Really? You didn't notice she missed work?"

"Yeah."

"Did she call in sick?"

He hesitated.

"Before you answer, know that I've requested a warrant for your phone records. I'll know if you're lying."

He paled. "She did call in sick."

"What did she say?"

"That she was sick and didn't know when she'd be back in."

"What else?"

His pause told Connor there was more. "And . . ." His frown deepened. "She screamed something and hung up."

"What did she scream?"

"I couldn't make it out."

"What day did she call?"

"Saturday."

"What time?"

"Around two."

"Do you know anyone who might want to harm her? Has anyone taken an interest in her lately?" This was the test.

"No more than usual."

"Who showed an interest in her?" His tone deepened.

The man visually flinched. "No one."

Connor leaned down and got right up in the old fart's face. "My gut says we'll be talking again."

* * *

A red Porsche was parked outside the Black Diamond when Brie pulled up. Her heart lurched. Not from fear, but from fury. Getting this lowlife murderer was gonna feel good. Real good.

She'd been restless and didn't want to keep replaying Calvin's shooting in her head, so she'd left her apartment early. Her search for Berger had been futile. No one had been home at any of the addresses they had for her.

Before going home to get dressed for work, she'd gone to the hospital.

Eliot and Sam were both there. Tory had hugged her extra hard and said he was sorry she'd seen the suicide, but he wasn't sorry Calvin was dead. She told him she understood. And she did. Oddly enough, Brie had started thinking of Calvin as two people. One she had respected, and one who had done horrible things.

The doctors still hadn't removed Carlos's tube. Though she'd been told earlier that he was alert, he slept the entire time Brie was there. But she sat with him until visiting hours were up.

Brie started to reach for her purse when her phone rang. Grabbing it out of the car's console, she checked the number. Connor.

"Tell me you have something."

"We do. We got the phone number Candy used to call Grimes. It's registered to Allen Madden. We also have the cell tower it pinged from, but the phone's turned off now. As soon as we get Madden's address, I'm headed there."

"Good." Brie prayed they found Candy. "Anything on Regina?"

"No, but we're still looking." He paused. "How are you doing?"

Her chest tightened. "Okay."

"You could call in sick."

"No. I'm already at the club. Just pulled up." Her gaze lifted. "The red Porsche is here."

"I know. Billy's already there. So is Agent Hamilton, the ICE agent. I'm texting you his picture, so you'll know who he is."

She frowned. "Make sure they don't blow my cover."

"They won't." He got quiet. "Be careful."

"I always am."

"Call me when you get home," he said.

"It'll be late."

"That's okay."

"Okay." She hung up. Seconds later, her phone dinged with a text. It was the picture of Agent Hamilton with ICE. After studying it, she deleted it. Dropping her phone back in her purse beside her Glock, she slipped on her large hoodie and got out.

Danny, the bouncer, opened the door to the Black Diamond as she walked up. "Doing okay today?"

"I'm here." She forced a smile.

Only a few steps inside, shrouded in darkness, she spotted Marcus Armand at the bar. When he looked over at her, she longed to glance away, afraid he'd see the hatred in her eyes. Instead, she smiled. Smiled for her sister. For Candy. For every woman that man had ever hurt.

\* \* \*

"Does Madden have a record?" Juan asked.

"Petty stuff." Madden's address had come in, and Connor teamed up with Juan in case trouble arose.

He followed his GPS into an older neighborhood that'd seen better days. Most of the properties needed some TLC. But several of the houses had front yards with kids' toys strewn about. Families lived here.

Because the call to the Black Diamond had pinged on the cell tower across town, they didn't think Candy was here. So the plan was simple. Find Madden and get him to talk and pray they could find Candy and the evidence to arrest Marcus Armand.

"How's Brie doing?" Juan asked.

Connor rolled his tense shoulder muscles. "Not good. She respected Calvin."

"That's tough," Juan said.

"Yeah. Hey, do me a favor. Text Billy and ask for an update."

Juan sent a text and soon after his phone dinged.

"What did he say?" Connor gripped the steering wheel tighter. He knew Brie could take care of herself, but it didn't stop him from worrying.

Juan chuckled. "He's said nothing's changed since you asked ten minutes ago. And to stop worrying about your girlfriend. He's not going to steal her from you and he's got her back."

"Asshole," Connor muttered.

"You really like her, don't you? I mean, you got her tampons in your car."

"Mark's got a big mouth! Don't start."

"I'm not. Seriously, I think it's great. But isn't she moving back to Baton Rouge?"

"I don't know." He'd almost asked her earlier, but the timing felt wrong. He figured she'd use that as another reason to keep him at a distance. But Baton Rouge wasn't that far away. In fact, maybe a long-distance relationship would be easier for him. Less scary.

Connor turned onto the road where Allen lived. Another car came from the opposite direction and pulled into a driveway down the street. It was dusk, and visibility was quickly decreasing.

"Is that our address where the Civic just pulled in?" Juan asked.

Connor slowed down. "Shit it is." He passed the house and pulled into the driveway across the street. Both he and Juan turned and watched the guy leave his car and walk toward the porch.

"Is that Madden?" Juan asked.

"I can't tell in this light."

They waited to see if the man knocked or went inside. He didn't knock.

"This is what you call good timing." Juan looked at Connor. "You ready?"

"Does a bear shit in the woods? Damn, I hope that's our guy."

They eased up to the house. Connor looked at Juan. "You knock. I'll go to the back in case he tries to run."

Connor moved to the back corner of the house and waited. Juan's knock sounded. Then Connor heard pounding steps in the house. The back door slammed open and a tall sandy-haired guy bolted out.

Connor took off after him. "Stop! Police!"

He didn't stop. And neither did Connor. He yanked his handcuffs off his belt and tackled the guy. He let out a *whoosh* of disgruntled air.

"Stay down!" Connor fit the handcuffs on the perp's wrists. That's when he noticed the blood on the guy's hands.

"You're police?" the guy asked. "I didn't know you were police."

"Whose blood is that?" With Connor's knees soaking up the mud on the ground, he rolled the guy over. It wasn't Madden. "Who are you? Where did the blood come from?"

"I didn't do it. I swear! I just got here," the perp said.

"Didn't do what?" Connor heard footsteps and looked back as Juan hauled ass around the house, his gun drawn. "I got him."

"I just found her like that!" the cuffed man said.

"Found who like what?" Connor asked.

"The chick."

Connor and Juan met gazes. "What chick?" Connor yanked the man up to his feet.

"I came to check on my brother. He's missed work for a week. I walked in and found that poor girl. When someone knocked, I thought whoever did that had come back." The man bent at the waist and puked.

"Is anyone else in the house?" Connor asked.

The guy rose up and wiped his mouth on his shoulder. "I don't think so."

Connor nudged the guy to move. "How bad is she hurt?" When the perp didn't answer, Connor yanked him closer. "Do I need to call an ambulance?"

The perp blinked. "I think it's too late for that."

# CHAPTER TWENTY-EIGHT

"Watch him," Connor said to Juan. "I'm going in."

"Wait," Juan said, but Connor didn't stop. What if the guy was wrong and Candy was still alive?

Gun out, he nudged open the back door and eased inside. "Police! If anyone is in here, announce yourself. Now!"

Only dead silence greeted him. He moved through the kitchen and stopped at the door to the living room. On the floor was the woman, facedown in a puddle of blood. The dark brown hair told him it wasn't Candy.

He knelt to touch her, hoping she was warm. She wasn't. She'd been dead a while. The smell of decomp hit him hard. He stood, avoiding the blood, and went to check the rest of the house to confirm no one else was there.

It was clear. When he returned to the living room, his gaze shot back to the body. And that's when he recognized her.

"Shit!"

"Police!" Juan's voice rang out behind him.

"It's clear," Connor said.

Juan rushed in, still holding his gun.

"Where's the perp?" Connor asked.

"Cuffed to the porch railing."

Connor's gaze lowered. "She's gone."

"Yeah." Juan made a face and put his hand over his nose.

"Is it Candace Brooks?"

"No, it's Regina Berger."

* * *

Brie went to the bar to get beers for the men at table six. It was ten o'clock. Exhaustion pulled at her mood. She glanced up and saw both Billy and the ICE agent studying her. If they kept that up, someone might notice.

She suddenly felt someone press up against her from behind. Someone sporting a hard-on. And not even an impressive one.

"Hello, beautiful." The accent was Spanish. Her chest clutched. He'd watched her all night but hadn't approached.

She wanted to turn around and knee the sorry excuse for a human being in the balls. But more than that, she wanted to find Candy and put this lowlife, dung-eating scumbag behind bars.

So no ball busting... yet.

She slid out from between him and the bar then turned and faced him.

Armand's eyes held the glassy look of someone who'd had one too many.

"Come with me and chat for a while," he said.

"Can't."

"Don't break my heart. You are the most beautiful girl in the entire club. I want you."

"I have a boyfriend," she said.

He smiled. "I don't mind sharing."

"He does. But I'd like to be friends." The comment sounded naive and stupid, but after the day she'd had, she wasn't at her best.

"Come on." He caught her arm and pulled her toward the back. Brie's mind raced for a plan. One that wouldn't lead to her naked with this man or hurt her chance of saving Candy.

"Leave her be!" The voice rang beside her. She looked at Danny, the bouncer, with his chest puffed out, and fists clutched at his sides.

"Go back to work. I own this place." Armand's eyes glittered with anger.

"But you don't own her," Danny said.

"It's okay, Danny." She yanked free. "We're good." She shot Armand her best smile while seething with fury inside.

He nodded.

Danny moved back to his post.

Armand stared after Danny.

"You really own the club?" She pretended to be impressed to take his mind off the bouncer.

"Yes." He stared at her. "This boyfriend, does he mind you making extra money?"

"Depends on how I earn it."

"I'm having a party on Thursday night. I want someone to serve drinks. To be, what do you call it? Eye candy? I pay big. Five hundred for one night."

Her gut said this was it, her chance to get him, but she couldn't appear too eager. "I work Thursday."

"I'll get Grimes to give you the night off."

"Just serving drinks?" She played hard to get.

"I promise."

And she was sure he never broke a promise. Right. Well, she would definitely be keeping hers: to see this man rot in prison. "Where's the party?"

"I will pick you up."

"You'll be drinking. Give me the address and I'll drive." She reached for the pen on the bar.

"I don't drink much. Do I not look trustworthy?"

Her heart skipped a beat. She cut him another smile. "No, you look dangerous."

He laughed. "We can talk about how you get there later. Deal?"

"Deal." This might be it. Her chance to save Candy. Her chance to prove this piece of crap had a hand in killing her sister.

*  *  *

It was after ten before Connor, Juan, and Mark walked out of the station. The guy they'd caught running from the house hadn't been lying. He was Allen Madden's brother. They also found Allen Madden. In the morgue. His body had floated up in the river.

They didn't know if Madden was behind Regina's death or Candy's kidnapping. Or if it was one or both of Madden's two roommates. Luckily, they'd found their names and mug shots. A couple of night-shift cops were trying to run them down.

Connor had gone straight home to shower. In the three hours it took for the morgue to pick up Berger, the decomp had worsened. Now, with his palms pressed against the shower stall, he let the hot water run. Damn, but he hated death. Especially senseless death. Hated knowing the little girl he'd bounced in his arms a few nights ago would grow up without a mom.

Out of the shower, he went to check in with Billy again. Earlier Connor had been informed that a bouncer had intervened when Marcus Armand had tried to pull Brie into the back.

Holy hell, he didn't want Brie anywhere near that perp. While he doubted Berger had been taken out by Armand, himself, he'd probably given the order. Berger probably got scared the cops were on to her and went to someone for help. They thought she'd end up talking, and had slit her throat.

Billy had agreed to follow Brie back to her apartment when she got off at twelve, but Connor still worried for her safety.

He checked the time: eleven-fifteen. An idea started to form. He hurried, got dressed, and ran out.

* * *

Feeling a bit safer knowing Billy had followed her home, Brie hugged her hoodie closer as she walked to her apartment. The cold air was thick and smelled like rain. Glancing up, she spotted a half-moon, and a few low-hanging clouds that caught the moon's rays—a buttermilk sky, her mom once called it.

She got to her door, thankful that someone had finally

fixed the lock. She let herself in, and Psycho greeted her. Picking him up, she snuggled him close. "Hey, sweetie." Moving into the kitchen she poured food into his bowl. He wiggled free to eat and her mind went back to what she needed to tell Connor.

She pulled out her phone, found his number, and called.

"Hey." He answered on the first ring.

"Tell me you have news," she said.

"I do. Open your door and I'll fill you in."

"My door?"

"Yeah, I'm here."

She exhaled, knowing his presence could be dangerous. She still let him in. He had his arms filled with bags and a frying pan. "What's this?"

"I haven't eaten. You?"

"No, but..." She took the bag he handed her and followed him into the kitchen. "What's your news?"

"You first." He placed the frying pan on her stove. "What did Armand say to you?"

"He asked me to work a private party for him on Thursday. My gut says this'll lead us to Candy."

"My gut says he's planning on grabbing you."

"I know, and we'll let him. You can follow me and save the day. I'm sure you'll like being a hero."

He frowned. "I don't like—"

"We don't have a choice."

His lips thinned in discontent. "You'll have to wear a wire. And—"

"What's your news?" She cut him off.

He looked at the frying pan. "Do you have a spatula? I forgot to bring or borrow one."

*Borrow?* She opened a drawer and pulled one out.

Then she looked inside the bag. "What's this?" She pulled out a plastic container with a white thick substance.

"Pancake batter. I didn't think they'd be good reheated, so I figured we could cook them."

She looked at the container. "You made pancake batter?"

"No. I bought it from the diner."

"They sold..." She shook her head. "Forget that. What's your news? Anything on Candy?"

His expression soured. "No." He turned on one of the burners. "Have you ever cooked pancakes?"

"Yeah."

"Good. I'll need help."

She frowned. "Would you please tell me your news?"

He exhaled and turned off the stove. "We found the address of the person whose phone Candy used to call Grimes."

"Did you find him? Did—"

"No. Well, yeah, but we also found...Regina Berger."

"Wait? You found her at...Does she know anything?"

"She's dead."

Brie's breath caught. She pulled out a chair and dropped down. "Crap."

"I know. We think she probably went to either Allen or his roommates after I'd come to question her. We suspect they're working with Armand. Chances are she was scared and they were nervous she'd talk."

"And the guy the phone belonged to? You found him?"

"At the morgue. His body was found earlier today. But we do have the names of the two people who recently moved in with Allen and we have BOLOs out on them."

"Is this ever going to end?"

"I think we're close."

She shut her eyes. And got hit with the flashback of Calvin shooting himself.

When she opened her eyes, Connor stood in front of her with his hand out. The look in his eyes said he knew exactly what had been going through her mind.

"Come on." He wiggled his fingers.

She glanced up. "What?"

"Let's forget about... Help me cook pancakes."

The look in his eyes told her this was as much for him as it was for her. Considering he'd been the one to find Regina Berger, she understood.

"No feeding me pancakes."

"Got it." He kept his hand extended. His smile was pure sin with sprinkles on top.

"That means no sex."

His smile widened. "Okay, but a woman should reserve the right to change her mind."

"I'm serious."

His smile faded. "I didn't come here for sex, Brie."

Honesty radiated from his voice. "What did you come here for?"

"I'm here because you said you wouldn't sleep. Because I don't think I will either. Because I'm worried about Armand showing up—and I know you can take care of yourself, but it scares me. I'm here because I like pancakes. You like pancakes. Because I really like you."

She slipped her hand in his and he pulled her up. "We're just partners."

"No, we're more than that. Tonight, we're pancake buddies."

She laughed, then looked at the pan. "We'll need a little oil."

"It's in the small container." He pointed to the bag with the spatula.

"The diner gave you oil, too?"

"I tipped the cook fifty bucks."

She grinned. "These are going to be expensive pancakes."

"They'll be worth it." He turned the stove on again. "I have to return the frying pan."

She pulled three sealed containers out of the bag. One had syrup, one had butter, and the small one had oil. Moving to the stove, she poured some of the oil into the pan.

"Is that enough?" he asked.

"Yeah." She picked up the pan and tilted it, this way, then that, so it was evenly coated with oil.

"Look at you. Showing off your moves." He smiled. She smiled back. He draped his arm around her shoulders, his touch soft, warm, and comforting.

She leaned into him just a bit, and it felt like half a hug. Not a sexy type of hug. A healing, I-need-a-friend kind of hug. "I'm sorry you had to find her."

"Me too. But we're not talking about that. We're cooking pancakes."

She nodded. "You know we have to throw the first one out."

"Why?"

"I don't know. Eliot said it never cooks right."

"Well, I'm sure Eliot knows best."

She nodded.

"How's Carlos?" he asked.

"Tory said he's conscious but sleeping most the time. And they removed the tube and he said a few words. I'm going there first thing in the morning."

"Good. We'll need to talk to him."

"I know."

Ten minutes later, they were at her kitchen table, eating and laughing about Connor's impaired flipping abilities. One pancake had landed on the floor and sent Psycho flying from the room.

When they finished eating, they washed the dishes, then Connor said, "Come on. Let's see if we can find something really boring on TV."

"Boring?"

"We might fool ourselves and fall asleep."

She lifted one of the shoulder straps of her tank top up and sniffed cigarette smoke. "I need a shower."

He lifted his brows. "Need someone to wash your back?"

She cut him a stern look, to which he responded without a shred of shame, "Not sex. Just a back wash."

From her bedroom, she snagged a large T-shirt and a baggy pair of sweats. A minute later, she stepped into the hot spray of water, bathing quickly, trying not to remember being in the shower with him before. Trying not to remember his warm soapy body, his kisses, his mouth on...

When she came out, Connor relaxed on her sofa with his arm across the back, his feet perched up on the coffee table. He wore a smile so charming her toes curled.

He gave her a slow once-over. "If you picked that outfit trying not to be sexy, you failed."

"Behave," she insisted.

"I already promised." Laughing, he patted the cushion beside him. She joined him. Not close enough to feel his body heat, but his being there, sharing the sofa with her, filled her with a different kind of heat. When she'd bought the huge piece of furniture, she hadn't considered the size. Hadn't realized how sad sitting on it alone would be. No friends. No family. No romance.

*A woman reserves the right to change her mind.* His words tiptoed across her mind, brushing against her wants and wishes and woes. If they had sex again...leaving would be like stubbing a sore toe.

Connor Pierce had made it clear. He wasn't a hang-around, settle-down kind of guy. As good as this felt, she was just his...pancake buddy.

Grabbing the remote, she said, "I know the perfect show. *Antiques Roadshow*. I save them to help put me to sleep."

The first antique item up for discussion was a chamber pot. They laughed when the woman said she'd thought it was a bowl and had used it to serve soup. After the chamber pot came a painting, then a dog figurine. Brie's eyes got heavy.

When she first let them flutter closed, she was relieved her mind didn't replay the shooting. But was it exhaustion, or Connor's presence, that brought peace of mind?

\* \* \*

Connor woke up with a major hard-on, sharing the sofa with Brie and a feral cat. They'd somehow ended up stretched out beside each other on the oversized sofa.

A sliver of light from the window hit his face, telling him it was later than he thought it was. But because he didn't need to be at work until ten, he didn't jump up. Brie lay on her side, facing him, tucked into the crook of the couch. The cat lay stretched out in the empty space at her feet.

Lifting his head, Connor gave the cat a look to confirm he wasn't about to go on the attack. When the cat just stared, Connor resettled and watched Brie wrinkle her nose. She shifted slightly and it brought her lower body against his, and damn if that didn't feel good. His pelvis wanted to start moving against her in that age-old dance of want and need. What he wouldn't give to kiss her, remove her clothes, and...

Nope. He'd promised.

The cat lifted, stretched, yawned, then jumped down. Brie's eyes opened. She put a hand over her mouth.

"Hi," he said. "How's my pancake buddy this morning?"

She cut her eyes downward, making it apparent that she'd noticed his situation. "You need a cold shower. And I need to brush my teeth."

He sat up, his jeans so tight in the crotch, he gave them a tug.

Brie reached for her phone on the end table. "It's almost eight."

"Wow, we slept five hours," he said. "Do you know how long it's been since I slept five straight hours?" And no dreams.

Her blue eyes, still heavy with sleep, glanced up. "It was the show."

"No. It's your company." He knew Brie Ryan was good for him.

She pushed off the sofa with a quick easy move. "I'm going to brush my teeth."

"Hurry, I gotta pee like a racehorse," he said.

She looked back. "That's crass."

"*That's* crass? You made me watch a show about shit buckets last night."

A sudden laugh left her lips. And damn if he didn't love waking up to that noise. Going to bed with that noise. Sharing a meal with that noise. Yup, good for him.

"Go use the bathroom," she said.

He shot up. "Thanks."

He took care of his bladder, washed his hands, then found her toothpaste and finger-brushed his teeth. When he stepped out, she stood in the hall, looking adorable in the sweatpants and T-shirt. She moved in and grabbed her toothbrush. She didn't shut the door, so he moved behind her and watched her in the mirror. When she started humming the birthday song, he laughed.

"What?" She spoke through a mouthful of minty foam.

"Nothing." He wrapped his arms around her. They stared at each other while she rinsed her mouth. Then turning around, she put her hands on his chest. The soft touch melted his insides and hardened other things.

He wiped a bit of white foam off the corner of her mouth. "I want to kiss you so badly it hurts."

"You probably shouldn't."

"Probably?" He brushed her hair off her cheek. "I like you, Brie. Do you know how long it's been since I . . . liked someone? And it's not just sex. Never mind that it was mind-blowing. I like your company. I like watching you sleep. Watching you brush your teeth. I like how you laugh. I like sharing my food with you. And call me crazy but I think you like me, too."

She blinked. "I do, but this is almost over and it's stupid to start something when it's just going to hurt in the end."

"Baton Rouge isn't that far away."

"I don't think I'm going back to Baton Rouge. Eliot lives in San Francisco. I'm considering going there. And if we...well, it'd just complicate things."

*She was moving to San Francisco?* The thought sank into his chest like a heavy stone. "It already feels complicated. I don't want...I just..." Could he ask her not to go? Did he have that right?

She didn't say anything. And neither did he. She just stared up at him through her lashes.

"Oh, frack!" she said, then her mouth was on his.

It went from a morning kiss to hot damn. Her hands slipped under his shirt and across his bare abdomen. His morning stiffy grew. Pulling back, recalling his promise, he met her eyes, which were wide with want and desire. "You're okay with this?"

For one second, he thought she was going to end it, but then she started pulling off his shirt.

# CHAPTER
# TWENTY-NINE

Brie wanted this. Wanted him. Even if it was just for right now.

Oh, she wasn't lying when she said it was going to hurt later. It was going to hurt like a giant paper cut right across her heart. Like it did when you lost someone you cared about. And she did. She cared about Connor Pierce. It might not be love, but it was a heck of a lot more than like.

But right now...it was going to feel wonderful.

He helped in removing his shirt. Then he removed hers. She unbuttoned the top of his jeans, then ran her hand over the bulge behind his zipper. He pushed his jeans down his legs, and her sweats followed.

"You weren't wearing panties. I wouldn't have slept a wink if I'd known that."

She grinned.

He brushed a finger across her lips. "What do you want?"

"You," she said. *Longer than right now.*

"Bedroom?" he asked.

"Sofa," she said.

"Sofa sex, huh? Did you think about it last night?"

"Maybe," she said.

They moved to the sofa. They kissed. They touched. His mouth grazed over her, leaving a trail of pleasure. He took his time with her. When she tried to speed him up, ready to feel him inside her, he laughed and went back to doing what he was doing to make her lose patience.

"You want me to beg?" she asked, frustrated, a hollow ache pulsing between her legs.

He grabbed his wallet to get a condom. "Do you know how happy you make me?"

"I know how happy you make me." She had to swallow twice to keep the tears from her eyes.

It was no wonder that neither of them lasted more than three minutes. Afterward, she rolled off him and lay on her side. He pulled her against him, but neither of them spoke. She was careful not to touch his chest, but her gut said it didn't matter. There was a tenseness in him.

What was he thinking? Did he long to get up and run again? "You okay?"

"Great," he said. "You?"

"Yeah." She closed her eyes. The silence got thicker than lumpy gravy. "What time do you have to be at work?"

"Ten," he said.

"Maybe you should go shower."

"Yeah." He spoke too fast, as if happy to be free. But then she felt the soft brush of his lips against hers—and all the way to her heart. His eyes met hers and she could swear he wanted to say something, but he didn't. He

simply pulled away and walked out of the living room—
still completely naked.

* * *

Connor shut the bathroom door. It had been wonderful.
Awesome. Better than the first time.

And scarier.

Emotions he didn't know if he was ready to feel
bounced around his chest. Yet he felt them. Every single
one of them.

She was moving to San Francisco. Holy fuck!

Back in the living room, his phone rang and he went
to answer it. Brie must have already gone to her bedroom. He grabbed his cell off the coffee table. He didn't
recognize the number.

"Detective Pierce."

"Yes, this is Mary Stanley with CPS. We met—"

"Yeah, I remember." Had she already heard about the
baby's mother? "I was going to call you today."

"You were?" she asked.

"I suppose you heard."

"Heard what?"

"About Ms. Berger."

"I haven't heard anything. But that's why I'm calling.
We did some research yesterday. We don't think the baby
belongs to Ms. Berger."

"Wait. What?"

"Not according to Ms. Berger's foster mother. She
said she's seen her every three or four months and the
girl's never been pregnant, but one of her roommates
had been."

Connor recalled Berger roomed with two women. One was Alma, Brie's sister. The baby could be Brie's niece. Connor dropped back down on the sofa. "Does she remember the mother's name?"

"No. But she said she was a petite blonde with blue eyes."

Brie, blond and petite, came back into the room. She studied him.

"Look, I'm not at the office yet. I'll call you back." Connor hung up and ran a hand over his face.

"Who was that?" Brie asked, as if sensing it was about her.

"The CPS agent. She was calling about Regina Berger's baby. It wasn't hers."

"Huh?" she asked.

"The baby wasn't Regina's."

"Whose was it?"

When he didn't answer immediately, her eyes widened. "My sister's?"

\* \* \*

"Go on in. All the kids are right there," Melissa, the foster mother, said.

Brie walked into the living room. Connor stayed in the entryway, talking with the foster mom.

There were four children in the room, but Brie zeroed in on the little girl in the walker. She wasn't crying, but she looked like she had been.

The first thing Brie noticed was the baby's large eyes. Light blue with dark rings around the pupils. Just like hers. And her sister's. The baby barely had hair, but what was there was a light blond.

Without warning, the little girl smiled. Her big grin showed two tiny teeth on the bottom.

Brie's breath caught and a rush of emotions did laps around her chest. She'd told herself she could do this and not get ahead of herself; that she would look at the child but wait until the DNA came back before she made conclusions.

Too late. That little girl was her niece. Brie knew it like she knew her own name. Tears filled her eyes at the thought of her sister being kidnapped and worrying about the baby she'd left behind.

Had her father not known Alma had a daughter? What about Alma's mom?

The baby flapped her little arms at her. Brie ached to pick her up, but her hands and heart felt shaky.

Connor and the foster mom walked up beside her. The baby saw Connor and started jumping up and down as she held up her hands. Her little fingers began opening and closing, as if begging to be picked up.

"She wants you to hold her," Brie said.

He didn't move.

"Pick her up," Brie said.

The baby squealed. When Connor still didn't reach for the child, Brie moved in and lifted the little girl into her arms. She was lighter than Brie thought. A tiny palm came against her face, and a lump formed in her throat.

"How old is she?" she asked the foster mom.

"We don't know for sure. The doctor said she thought she was around a year, but she's only got two teeth and is fifteen pounds. She could be younger, or maybe malnutrition slowed down her growth."

"They didn't feed her?" The lump doubled in size.

"She's underweight. However, she seems healthy otherwise. And she's a good baby."

Regret came with Brie's next breath. If she'd called her sister back, maybe the baby wouldn't have lost her mother, she wouldn't have gone hungry.

Ten minutes later, Brie and Connor walked out. She felt Connor's eyes on her.

"Do you think she's your niece?" Connor asked.

"Yes, I do." She inhaled. "Are you still going to see my dad today?"

He nodded.

"Great. I'm coming with you."

"Are you sure that's a good idea?"

"No, but I'm coming."

* * *

"I don't know," Eliot said when Brie told him she was going to see her father. After Connor had taken her home, she'd driven straight to the hospital to visit Carlos before making the trip to Henderson.

Brie bit down on her lip. "I don't want to believe he knew about the baby, but I wouldn't be surprised." Brie looked up at the clock. Five minutes until visiting hours.

"You don't know she's your niece," Eliot said.

"I do. I don't know how, but I know." She swallowed. "She went hungry."

"Scumbags," Eliot spat out, drawing a few stares from the other people in the waiting room. "What do you expect your father to do?" He lowered his voice. "Take the child in?"

"No. He screwed up with both me and my sister. Alma's mother may want her, but...I don't know. I'm sure they'll check that she's decent and capable. And if she isn't, I'll take her. It's the right thing to do."

"Are you ready for that, Brie?"

Tears filled Brie's eyes. "Were you ready for me? I had no one and you were there for me."

"You were the best thing that ever happened to me." He put his arm around her. "And if it goes that way, you know I'll help."

"I expect you to. I'm thinking about moving to San Francisco."

"I'd love that," he said. "I'll support whatever decision you make."

She nodded. "I have an appointment tomorrow to get blood drawn for a DNA test."

Tory, who'd gone to grab something to eat, walked into the room. His expression was complete joy, unlike most of the people there.

"Have you seen him yet?" Tory asked.

"Not yet."

"He's doing so well, Brie. Last night, they let me in a couple of extra times because he asked for me. And when I called to check in a few minutes ago, they said he's awake, and the doctor's moving him out of ICU."

Brie smiled, then had to ask. "Does he remember anything about...what happened?"

Tory nodded. "He didn't say much, but he asked if they'd caught the guy who shot him. I told him that he was gone...dead, but I didn't tell him about Agent Calvin. I'm not sure he can handle it. But he asked about you. I told him you'd been here a lot and would be back again today."

People in the room stood and started heading for the ICU doors.

"It must be time," Brie said.

"You two go in," Eliot said.

When they entered his room, Carlos pushed up. He looked weak, gaunt, and had wires and tubes tangled around him, but his smile was contagious.

She smiled back at him, despite the lump in her throat. "About time you woke up."

"I know." His smile lessened. "What's happened."

Tory spoke up, "We shouldn't worry—"

"Stop." His expression hardened. "Who was behind this, Brie?"

Brie looked at Tory, who shrugged, then she looked back at Carlos. "It was Calvin."

"I didn't want to think that," Carlos said, "but I was afraid."

She gave him the lowdown.

He lay there muttering *shit* and *damn* every few minutes.

When she got to the part about Rosaria, his frown tightened. "Tell me she's okay."

"She is."

"Did you get Pablo's phone?" Carlos asked.

"No."

"I mailed it. I was afraid they were on to me. Rosaria said someone from the FBI called that phone. It was dead, so I couldn't get...any information, but—" His voice seemed to crack.

"She told us. APD is checking with the post office. But Calvin confessed to everything in a note he left."

"He left a note?" He closed his eyes for a second, no doubt feeling everything she did. Anger and yet grief for the man they used to know and respect. "You okay?"

"You know me. I'm resilient."

"Resilient? Yes. Superwoman? No."

"Oh, she had help." Tory chuckled. "A hunky blond. You ought to see the looks they give each other. There's enough sexual tension to blow the hospital off its foundation. If they aren't dirtying up the sheets yet then my name isn't Tory."

Brie shot Tory a stern look, then continued to tell Carlos about her sister's baby and her planned trip to see her dad.

Tory's phone rang. "It's work. I should take this." He gave Carlos's hand a squeeze and walked out.

Carlos leaned back into his pillow, as if already exhausted. "A blond, huh?"

"Your husband exaggerates."

"You didn't deny the . . ."—he paused and swallowed—"dirtying-up-the-sheets comment."

Brie frowned. "It's not serious."

"You've slept with only one guy since your ex. How can it not be serious?"

"He's not . . . the serious type. Especially now," she muttered.

"Now?"

"I might end up with custody of my niece." On the drive back to her place, she and Connor had hardly spoken. Brie's mind had been occupied with thoughts of having to take in the baby and the changes it would bring.

"You don't know for sure she's your niece."

"We might not have had the DNA test yet, but I know. She looks just like my baby pictures and I'll bet her mom's baby pictures."

"Okay, but even if you take her, you can still date."

"He's not the . . . kid type."

"You've talked about kids, and you say it's not serious?"

"It's not like . . . He told me about his breakup with his ex. His not wanting kids was part of their problem."

He sat there, eyes unfocused—the way he always did when digesting information. "Did you tell him about Todd?"

"Yeah. Why?"

"You obviously trust this guy. Why do I get the feeling it's more serious than you want to believe it is?"

"Maybe because you got hit on the head and are imagining things," she snapped.

"I don't think so. But I think it's unfair."

"What's unfair?"

"That I wind up in a coma while you fall for some hot blond without me getting to hear about it." He cleared his throat. "I missed the fun part."

She frowned. "It wasn't all that fun. I thought my best friend was dying. In fact, if you hadn't been in a coma, you'd have kept me from doing this!"

"Are you kidding? You needed to be laid. Besides, I'm too stubborn to die." He chuckled. "Is he good in the sack?"

"I'm not talking about that."

He smirked and shut his eyes.

She sat on the corner of his bed. "I'm really glad you're okay."

He looked up. "Thank you, for everything."

"It's what friends do." She caught his hand and squeezed.

"So how's this party with Armand's cousin going to go down?"

"It's not until Thursday."

Carlos paused, then said, "I don't like it. If this guy—"

"You know I can handle myself."

"Shit happens, Brie. Look at me. I'm worried."

"Well, stop. APD's got this."

She believed it. She did. The bone-cold chill running through her didn't mean anything.

"I'm not crazy about the idea either." The deep, familiar voice echoed behind her. "But I'll do everything in my power to keep her safe."

Brie looked up to see Connor standing at the door. Emotion washed over her. He was right there, yet she was already missing him.

# CHAPTER THIRTY

The ride to Henderson was hard. Brie sat in the passenger seat, worrying about Candy and unsure of what to say to her dad. She didn't know what to say to Connor either.

He'd been quiet. She'd been quiet. The GPS spoke more than they did.

Were they already trying to say goodbye? Why did the right thing have to hurt? Maybe because she'd done wrong by letting anything start between them. Hadn't she known the first night she'd kissed him that it was a mistake?

"Agent Bara dropped by my office before I left the station," Connor said. "He said the FBI has assigned a senior agent to the Baton Rouge office. And he's been asked to return to Louisiana. Supposedly, there's going to be an in-depth look into the whole unit."

Brie closed her eyes. "I owe him an apology. I thought—"

"It was an investigation. You were doing your job."

"No, I was on leave. And even if I weren't—"

"Your partner was shot." Connor's phone dinged with a text. He stopped at a red light and grabbed it from the cup holder to read it.

"What?" she asked when his expression soured.

"Juan's been going through the evidence from Allen Madden's place. There was a computer. On it was evidence that Madden's roommates were trying to sell the baby."

Brie's gut knotted. "Sell her?" Her heart tightened painfully. "I'm so fracking tired of seeing the seedy side of life!"

"That's the hazard of working in law enforcement."

"Yeah." She looked out the window and muttered, "I should've opened a cupcake shop instead of joining the FBI."

"You wanted to open a bakery?"

She glanced at him. "No, I just think it'd be nice to be surrounded by things like cupcakes, icing, and sprinkles. Good things. In a cupcake shop, everything smells sweet and people are happy. Instead, I'm surrounded by hit men, human trafficking, and scum who'd sell a baby."

Connor didn't get a chance to respond as his GPS said they'd arrived. He pulled into the parking lot.

She looked up at the building with a sign that read RONAN REALTOR. Squaring her shoulders, she told herself she was ready to face the music. But who was she kidding? She didn't even know the lyrics.

They both exited the car. When she got to the door, she recalled the last time she'd seen her father. He'd kissed her on her cheek. "*Bye, pumpkin.*"

"You okay?" Connor asked.

"Yeah." *Hell no!*

"Do you want to lead this, or do you want me to?"

She met his gaze and was certain he saw everything she felt.

"We can play it by ear," he said.

She nodded.

He touched her arm. "Last night. Being with you, cooking pancakes, watching boring TV, and waking up with you, that was...It was the good cupcake stuff."

His words eased the ache in her chest. "Yeah." *If only it wasn't ending.*

The door to the office swung open. A man stepped out then stopped abruptly. His hair was light but touched with silver. His eyes were blue, light blue. *"Bye pumpkin."*

His gaze zeroed in on her. "It's been a long time." No shame, no regret, no emotion, sounded in his tone. How could he not feel anything when her chest was a swarm of emotions? Had she never meant anything to him?

"I'm Detective Pierce." Connor's hand rested on Brie's lower back. A touch meant to offer support.

Her father turned back to her. "I wasn't aware you were coming."

A collection of memories played in her mind like an old movie reel—he handing her a souvenir from his latest trip, sitting at the end of the table with a glass of Jack and Coke, walking out the door with his suitcase.

"Sorry to surprise you." She forced herself to speak, not wanting him to know that seeing him hurt her.

"Do you have an office where we can talk?" Connor asked.

Her father frowned but walked back inside. She followed. Head high. Shoulders tight. Remembering what it felt like to have your heart broken by your first hero.

Motioning to the two straight-back seats in front of a

big mahogany desk, he slipped into the larger cushioned chair behind it. She sensed he'd chosen the furniture in the room to make himself feel important—to make anyone on the other side of the desk feel small. It worked. She felt about seven.

How could she have loved this man? Were children just conditioned to adore their parents? To yearn for their love, acceptance?

"So what's so important that it required a face-to-face meeting?"

Connor spoke up. "When was the last time you spoke to your daughter Alma?"

"I don't remember exactly."

"Did you know she had a baby?" Brie blurted out.

Her father's gaze shifted to her.

"Did you?" she asked again. In the corner of her eye, she saw Connor settle back in his chair.

"I offered to help...take care of the problem."

"An abortion? You wanted her to kill your grand-baby?" Suddenly this wasn't about her but about her sister. If Brie was let down by this man, what must her sister have felt?

His expression hardened. "She wasn't ready to be a parent. She was using drugs."

"But she wouldn't do it, would she? She wanted the baby. So she got sober. Did you ever even see your grand-daughter?"

He stiffened his posture. "She came by once."

"Does Alma's mother know about the baby?"

"She told Alma the same thing I did. That she should give it up to someone who could care for it properly."

Connor spoke up, his tone filled with animosity. "Why

didn't you mention the child when you reported your daughter missing?"

"Well, I...For all I knew she'd given it away. She was flighty."

"Who's the child's father?" Brie asked, her heart hurting, realizing that like her sister's parents, she'd let Alma down.

"She never said. I assumed she didn't know."

"What else did you keep from us?" Connor asked.

"Nothing," her father said. "I told the police what I knew. And I don't like being accused of doing something wrong."

Brie slapped her hand on his desk. "The right thing would have been helping when she asked for it."

He pushed away from the desk. "Why is this coming up now? Have you found the child?"

"Yes," Brie said. "No thanks to you."

Her father put up his hands. "Well, I can't take her. I can't deal with a child."

"Don't worry," Brie said. "I wouldn't let you near her. You know, there was a time in my life when I thought Alma was the lucky one. Because you chose her over me. But now I know—I was the lucky one."

Brie stood so fast her chair fell back. She looked at Connor. "He makes me sick. I'll wait outside."

"Don't judge me." Her father jumped up and went around to block the door.

"Get out of my way," Brie said.

He didn't. "I didn't choose to leave you. That was your mother. She told me to leave."

"She said to get out of her way!" Connor's words echoed loudly. Seriously.

When her father didn't heed the warning, Connor picked him up by his shirt and pushed him against the wall. "In my ten-year career as a law enforcement officer, I've met some lowlife fuckers. But you outshine them all."

"Stop!" Brie put a hand on Connor's back. "He's not worth it."

Connor released her father, who slumped against the wall as they left.

Tears clouded her vision when she crawled into the front seat. Connor got in and started his car.

"He's a piece of kangaroo dung." Using her language and smiling.

As much as she knew he was trying to help, she couldn't even smile. Her heart hurt. Her chest hurt. Her head hurt.

"I'm sorry," Connor said, his humor dying a short death.

"Yeah." Eyes on the window, she watched the world go by as he drove back to Anniston. She didn't still love her father. But somehow a little girl inside her still had a broken heart.

\* \* \*

Eliot had called to check on how things went. Just talking to him brought a knot to her throat. She cut him short and said she'd see him in a bit. Thirty minutes later, Connor parked beside her car at the hospital.

Brie turned to him. "Is there anything I can do to help search for Candy? I could—"

"Brown has ten people chasing down every possible lead. And there aren't that many to begin with."

She nodded. "I hate thinking... Can you imagine how scared she is?"

"I know."

Her chest filled with liquid pain. "She's like my sister. She has no one in her corner. No one who cares."

"She has you." He put his hand on her shoulder. His touch sent even more pain across her tender nerves, landing with a thud in her chest.

"You want to come to my place tonight?" he asked. "I'll grill some steaks and we can watch the antique show again."

Brie's head ached and Connor's question made it throb harder. "I don't think that's a good idea."

"Then I'll come back to your place."

She swallowed, her throat raw. "I don't think that's a good idea either."

"Brie, Armand could get to you. We talked about this."

"I'll stay with Eliot or get Eliot to stay at my place."

He drew in a loud breath. "What did I do now?"

"You didn't do anything. But can we stop pretending there's nothing wrong? The longer we let this go on, the harder it'll be to—"

"Even if you move to San Francisco... we could visit. I have tons of vacation time."

"You know it's not just about the move."

A wrinkle appeared between his brows. "No, I don't know. I don't know shit. What's this about?"

"We're on different paths."

"Paths? I don't—"

"You don't want kids, Connor. And I'm about to become a parent."

"Where are you getting...?" He cupped his hands

behind his neck and squeezed. "That's what you got out of our talk? That wasn't the damn point. And I never said—"

"I know that wasn't all you were saying. I know you cared, and your ex blamed you for something that wasn't your fault. But in that information was the fact that you didn't want—"

"No! Damn it. This isn't even about that. This is you being scared. This is you seeing your dad and being afraid of letting anyone close."

She opened her mouth to deny it but couldn't. "Seeing him made me remember what the odds are of someone letting me down. Even someone I believe in."

"And you don't believe in me?" He sounded angry, hurt, desperate.

"From the start, you've made it clear that you don't do long-term. So yes, it's fear. But fear is a tool we use to navigate our lives. It makes us see the risks. And this is too risky."

With nothing left to say, she grabbed her phone, her purse, and her bruised and battered heart and got out of his car.

\* \* \*

"You look like you lost your best friend," Flora said.

The diner was extra quiet tonight. There was only one other customer, a man sitting in the front, reading a book. It wasn't time for the drunks yet.

Connor looked up from the newspaper. Not that he was reading it. It just gave him something to focus on besides the damn hole in his chest. He'd quit trying to sleep around midnight and had driven here.

"Yeah." He didn't elaborate, yet Flora stood there, as if expecting he would. "I'll take the usual."

"So the blonde didn't like your pancake party?"

He hadn't told her who he'd been planning on cooking pancakes for last night, but she'd obviously guessed. "I'll bring the frying pan back tomorrow. Sorry."

She frowned. "No. I'm sorry." She set a cup on the table and filled it with coffee. Then she pulled four creams from her apron and dropped them on the table. "I was hoping she would help you."

"Help me what?"

"Be happier. When she came here and shared your food, you . . . you lost the sadness in your eyes."

That hole in his chest suddenly felt larger. "You think I should be happier? Even when . . . when I'm the reason you're sad?"

She set the coffeepot on the table and dropped into a chair. "At one time, I would have said no. I blamed you. I blamed you so I wouldn't blame myself."

"Yourself?" He didn't understand.

"He was not a bad boy. Moses was trying to help me pay for the insulin for his sister. The month before, he had brought me money, I asked him where he got it from. He told me he was working at a grocery store, but I knew he was lying. I knew he had gotten the money doing something illegal." Tears filled her eyes. "But I took it. If I had refused it, he would have stopped."

Tears slipped down Flora's cheeks, and he forgot his own pain and felt hers. "You were desperate."

"I was wrong. So I blamed you. For a year, I lived off that hate. Then I went to the prison and spoke with Carter, the boy you arrested for killing your partner. I wanted to know that Moses was not part of the shooting. I wanted to find a lawyer and make you go to jail because you had wrongly killed my boy. But Carter told me the truth. That Moses had fired. That he was scared. That he just wanted to get away. That they both just wanted to get away."

"It wasn't your son's bullet that killed my partner," Connor told her.

"I know. But you did not know that in the moment, did you?"

"No." Connor wiped a hand over his face. He hesitated for two painful seconds. "I've wished a thousand times that I'd tried harder to get your son to surrender. I did tell him to throw down the weapon. To come out. But another gun went off, and I didn't know if it was him shooting or the other guy. Had I known he was a kid..."

She nodded. "When you started coming here, I still wanted to hate you. Then I saw your eyes, and I knew you hated yourself. Like I hated myself. And somehow, I knew. I went to the church and demanded to know who gave the money every month to help pay for my daughter's medicine. The pastor didn't want to tell me but I made him. I almost didn't take it anymore. But I couldn't afford not to. And it would have made Moses's death even more senseless. I should have said thank you, but I knew it would require me to admit my own blame. It was easier to stay silent."

"I know."

She nodded. "But I went to the pastor last Sunday. I do not need the money anymore."

"Why? You get a better job?"

"I start work next week at the hospital. Before my

husband left us, I was going to school to be a nurse. I only had one more year. The reason I started working third shift here was so I could finish school. I graduated last month."

"Congratulations."

She nodded. "It is because of your money that I have been able to go to school. Now, I want to pay it back. I have kept a record of all you have given me."

"No. The money is from my mother's life insurance. She would've wanted you to have it."

A few more tears filled her eyes. "She was a good woman. And she raised a good son."

"Thank you."

"If you do not take the money then I will...how do you say? Pay it forward."

He smiled. "Yes."

"Like me, you need to let go of the blame. I am almost there."

He pulled his coffee over. "Yeah."

"So what happened with the blond lady?"

He opened a creamer and added it to his cup. "I think she has things she needs to move past, too."

Flora nodded. "Then maybe you should not give up on her. If we can heal, maybe she can, too. Or maybe you two can help heal each other."

That's what he'd thought, too, but... "She's moving to San Francisco. She doesn't want me in her life."

"Have you told her how you feel?"

"Several times."

"Are you sure? Men sometimes have problems talking about feelings."

"I told her how much I like her. Like being with her. Like hearing her laugh."

She lifted her right brow. "Like? Do you like her, or do you love her?"

He felt gut-punched. Not because of the question, but because of the answer that resonated inside him. Yeah, he'd suspected it. But now, he knew for certain.

"I could be wrong," Flora continued, "but the odds of her changing where she will live because someone *likes* her are small. But for love...a person will do almost anything."

# CHAPTER THIRTY-ONE

He'd even met the baby," Brie told Eliot as she popped a cough drop into her mouth. She was definitely coming down with something. Her throat felt like raw hamburger meat. "But it didn't matter. He said Alma's mother had wanted her to give the baby up, too." She picked up a teddy bear and added it to her cart. Then added three more, remembering the other kids at the foster home.

She'd spent the night at the hotel with Eliot. This morning, after getting blood drawn for the DNA test, she'd decided to go shopping for her niece. Eliot had insisted on coming.

Last night Brie had avoided talking about the meeting with her father. It hurt too much. But he'd brought it up again at the store. It felt safer talking about it in public. She was less likely to break down.

"Isn't that what you expected?" Eliot asked.

Brie stopped pushing the cart. "Maybe, but I thought

him seeing me would...I thought he'd react more. It wouldn't have changed what he did, but I wanted to think he has regrets." She shook her head. "He doesn't. Not about me, Alma, or his granddaughter."

"It's his loss."

"I know." She inhaled deeply, trying to dislodge the lump of hurt in her throat. She stopped at a rack of little-girl dresses and searched for the right size. "Alma's mother said she was too old to raise a kid."

"You called her?" Eliot asked.

She nodded. "I don't get how someone could just not love their own grandbaby."

She coughed again.

"You need to see a doctor. It's probably strep."

"Just a cold," she said with more wishful thinking than belief. She'd had strep more times than she had fingers. Her last doctor said she should consider getting her tonsils out.

Across the aisle, a laughing couple, holding hands, walked up to look at the car seats. The woman looked nine months pregnant. The man, attentive to her every word, was tall and blond and took Brie's heart right to her pancake buddy.

A heaviness filled her chest. Not just because thinking of him made her heart ache, but also because she wanted that. To be a couple. How much easier would becoming a parent be if you had someone? Someone who shared in the decisions, as well as the good times and the bad.

Suddenly, it hit her. She needed a car seat, too. And a crib. And a...There was so much to do. So much to figure out. She had time, she consoled herself. She'd called CPS earlier. They said if the DNA matched it could still take up to a month to complete the paperwork so she could take her niece home.

She looked at Eliot. "I don't even know what Alma named her."

Her phone rang and her heart leaped, thinking it might be Connor. How pathetic was she? She'd told him it was over. But that didn't mean she was ready to let him go. Apparently, he wasn't ready either. He'd texted her several times this morning: Miss you. Didn't sleep. Need u to sleep. We need to talk.

She hadn't answered any of his texts. But that didn't mean she wasn't excited to see them.

She pulled out her phone but didn't recognize the number.

"Who is it?" Eliot asked.

"Don't know." She answered the call. "Hello."

"Hi, sexy."

Her heart took another leap, only this time in repulsion.

"Who is this?" she asked, just to ding his ego.

"Dillon Armand, from the club." He sounded dinged. "My party got moved. It's tonight."

"Tonight?" She swallowed; her throat burned.

"I spoke with Grimes. He is not expecting you tonight. I will pick you up at your apartment at six."

So he knew her address? Connor's fears had been founded. "Just tell me where and when."

"It is hard to find. GPS gets it wrong. Best I pick you up."

"I'm really good with directions. Just give me the address."

He went so silent, she could almost hear him seething on the other end. She felt the fluttering of her pulse at the base of her neck. Had she ruined it? Should she have agreed to let him pick her up?

"Fine." His tone came out curt. "I will text you later."

"Great. See you there."

"Who was that?" Concern echoed in Eliot's voice.

She didn't want to tell him. He'd worry, but she sucked at lying to Eliot.

"Armand."

"I thought that was tomorrow?"

"Now it's tonight." She phoned Connor.

*  *  *

"I'll do it." Connor took the wire from the technician's hands and motioned for Brie to move into another room at the precinct. She followed, wishing the Advil she'd taken would stop her head from pounding. She needed to be at her best.

Brie felt like warmed-over dog poo and was in no mood to play bait or to party. But she *was* in the mood to finally have the person, or persons, responsible for human trafficking behind bars. So she sucked it up and carried on.

Connor had pulled strings to get everyone on board for tonight's operation. ICE and APD were working together. Armand's text came in two hours ago, giving her an address. It was a house in one of the upper-class neighborhoods on an acre lot. They already knew the house was a rental, and had even gotten the floor plan.

For all intents and purposes, it was the kind of place Armand would host a get-together. It was also the perfect place to hold someone against their will. Which is why everyone hoped Candy was there, but if she wasn't and Armand took Brie to another location, they would follow.

Connor already sent a van to case the place. And, in addition to the wire she was about to get, they'd put a trace on her phone and placed a tracker in the toe of her right shoe.

Connor shut the door. His green eyes met hers. "You look nice."

"Thanks." Armand hadn't told her how to dress, so she'd chosen a simple A-line black dress paired with black high-heeled shoes, silver earrings, and a Glock strapped to her thigh.

Connor looked at the wire in his hands. "Your bra is the best place."

"Yeah." She reached back and unzipped her dress.

Pulling the dress off her shoulders, she waited for his touch. Even prepared, she flinched when the back of his fingers brushed the top of her breast. Both from the emotional pain his touch brought with it and because his hands felt like ice. "You're cold."

He touched her brow. "No. You're hot. Do you have a fever?"

"I've got a cold. I just took two Advil." She'd also taken an antibiotic she'd had left over from the last time she'd had strep.

"If you're sick—"

"Stop. I'm doing this."

"We could storm the place."

"He could kill Candy if she's there. And if she's not, we have nothing. Not on my sister's murder, not on human trafficking. I need to get him to incriminate himself. Put the dang wire on me."

"If you push too hard..."

"I know what I'm doing!"

He blew out his cheeks and muttered something under his breath, but started attaching the wire to her bra. "If you need to get out of there, say..."

"Purple. You've told me three times."

He looked into her eyes. "I'll be listening to every word you say."

"I know." And she did. She trusted him with her life. Just not her heart.

Finished with the wire, he moved behind her and zipped her up. He placed his hands on her shoulders. "When this is over, we're talking." His warm breath caressed her ear.

She looked back at him. "We've already said—"

"No. You are going to hear me out! Not now. But when this is over." He moved to stand in front of her. "Promise me if you get the slightest hint things are turning bad, you'll say the word so we can get you out of there."

"I will."

Their faces were so close she could feel his breath. She stood completely still as he drew even closer and kissed her. A soft kiss that felt like promises. Of course, that was just her wishful thinking. Connor Pierce didn't make promises. He'd told her that himself.

\* \* \*

With her head still pounding, Brie pulled up to the house. It wasn't quite dark—a blanket of bright orange color painted the western sky. Parked on the street was a white van with a plumbing logo, and two other cars were parked across the road in a driveway. She spotted two men digging up the neighbor's lawn, looking as if they were working on a broken pipe.

*A bit much*, she thought, but she wasn't running the operation.

Marcus Armand had told her to let him know when she left. She hadn't. Why give him a warning? Grabbing her jacket, she got out of her car. The cold bit into her fevered skin. She slipped on the jacket.

As she stepped onto the sidewalk, she recognized the men digging. Connor and Mark Sutton.

Ignoring them, she climbed the porch and rang the bell.

She heard voices, but no one answered. She waited a few seconds, then knocked.

The door opened. Armand wore a black suit that somehow made him appear even slimier than before. Or maybe that was his smile. Sleazy, snakelike, and just mean.

Her heart hurt wondering if her sister had faced that smile.

"Glad you are here, but I told you to text me."

"Oops."

His smile tightened. "You're a little difficult. But difficult can be fun."

She lifted a brow.

He backed up, and she stepped over the threshold.

Voices sounded deep inside the house.

"How many people are here?" She knew what Connor and the others needed to know.

"Not many."

His hand pressed to her lower back, and it took effort to keep from slamming her knee into his ball sack. She stopped at the end of the hall and counted three guys lounging in the living room. One was dressed in a suit like Armand, and the other two wore jeans. The tall lanky guy with brown hair, wearing a Bob Marley T-shirt, looked familiar.

"So, just four including you?" she said. "And no women? I thought it was a party."

"We have you," Armand said.

"We aren't enough for you?" asked the bearded guy slouched on the sofa.

A cold chill ran through her. "Where's the bar?"

"In the kitchen." Armand motioned toward the right. "I'll take your coat and purse."

She slipped it off, and one of the guys whistled. "Keep going." Dread settled in her gut. She'd been in situations more dangerous than this, but this one was creepier somehow.

She'd feel better if her Glock was in her hand and not strapped to her thigh. She'd feel better if her head wasn't pounding.

As she handed Armand her purse, she forced herself to smile. "Who wants a drink?"

"I'll take a Jack and Coke." The guy wearing a suit spoke up. "Make yourself one, too? It'll loosen you up."

A loud clunk—as if something was knocked over— echoed from down the hall leading to the bedrooms. Armand frowned at the bearded guy.

"What's that noise?" Brie asked, assuming it wouldn't have been picked up by the wire. "Someone else here?" *Was it Candy?*

"My brother." The bearded guy stood. "He drank too much." He started down the hall.

The two other guys sat there leering, as if she was a

gift about to be unwrapped. "One Jack and Coke coming up," Brie said.

"I'll take a beer and a lap dance," said the man wearing the Bob Marley shirt.

"One beer." Brie started toward the kitchen just as Armand's phone rang. She hung back long enough to see him step out the back door. Moving into the kitchen, she looked around and saw three bottles of liquor on one of the counters. Not enough to qualify as a bar.

This was definitely a setup to get her here. But when were they going to make their move?

She grabbed a beer from the fridge and whispered, "Something was knocked over in the bedroom. It could be Candy. Or possibly another man. I'm going to try to investigate."

She stopped speaking when she heard a noise behind her. The Marley-shirt guy in need of a lap dance walked in. He wobbled side to side, as if he'd already over-indulged.

"I thought I'd come get to know you better."

"Great. What's your name?" She set the beer down and grabbed the bottle of whiskey, keeping one eye on him the entire time.

"Todd," he said.

"A shame." She opened the whiskey, poured two fingers worth. "That was my ex's name."

He laughed and moved closer. "How about that lap dance?"

"I'm just here to serve drinks."

"Come on. I've seen you working at the club."

"I serve drinks there, too." She grabbed a Coke from the counter and poured some in with the whiskey.

He leaned against the counter. "What are you wearing under that dress?"

*A Glock 9mm.* "Here's your beer and your friend's drink. I'll be right in." She placed the beer and glass in his hands. "Chop, chop. Go!"

\* \* \*

Connor slung the shovel down. "We need to go in."

"She's got this," Mark said. "Let her see if she can get anything."

"Easy for you to say, that's not Annie in there!" Connor grabbed the shovel back up. From the second he'd watched her walk in, all he could think about was losing her. About some fucking creep hurting her. And listening to the assholes talk to her so disgustingly curdled the cream in his stomach from the coffee he'd drunk earlier.

"She knows what she's doing," Mark said.

Connor gripped his fist. "It's just..."

"Hard, I know." Mark buried the shovel in the dirt.

Connor heard Brie breathe and he pulled in a breath, too.

"Go," Brie's voice echoed in his ear.

Conner measured the distance to the house. How long would it take to get inside? But damn, he wanted her out of there.

\* \* \*

Brie watched as the guy put the beer to his mouth and took a long swig. "I get the first dance." He walked out of the kitchen.

Brie gave the guy a head start, then peered into the living room. When her shoes clicked on the tile, she kicked them off. She knew it was risky, since they had a tracker in them, but she needed to move across the hallway silently. Armand and the two other guys were on the back patio talking. As Lap Dance Dude stumbled to the sofa, his back to her, she hurried across the entryway and down the hall. She opened the first bedroom door and found the room empty. She hurried to the next and eased it open, peering in. There on the bed, tied and gagged, were two women. The one who faced away from her was blond and looked like Candy.

Brie started to move in when she heard the back door shut. Closing the door, she cut into the opened door of the bathroom on the opposite side of the hall.

"Where is she?" Armand's question echoed as she closed the door.

"She was just in the kitchen."

Footsteps echoed.

She flushed the toilet. "We've got two women tied up," she muttered.

The bathroom door swung open. "What are you doing?"

"Duh. It's the bathroom. What are you doing?" She frowned at the glint in his eyes. Her gut said something was about to go down. And before it did, she needed to get him talking. "So, did you know her?"

He studied her. Brie ached to go for her Glock, but she saw he had his gun in his hand. "Know who?"

"My sister, Alma Ronan?"

\* \* \*

Connor froze and listened for the creep's answer. He didn't say anything. Connor cut his eyes to Mark, who had also stopped digging, waiting to hear what came next.

"That's why you look familiar."

"Did you know her?" Brie repeated.

"Yeah, I knew her. I fucked her hard." Marcus's voice came out garbled. "Come on!"

"Did you kill her?" Brie asked. "Or did Dillon?"

"How did you know—"

"Which one of you did it?" Brie's tone went hard, pushy, and Connor feared Marcus would guess she wore a wire.

"My cousin is too high on white powder to do anything right," Marcus answered, proving he was as stupid as he was evil.

"Move in!" Connor looked back at two cars parked down the street. One with two ICE officers and the other car with Billy and Stan, another APD cop.

"She was hardheaded," Marcus said. "Stubborn. Let's see if you can stay alive longer."

"I said move in!" Connor repeated.

Mark held up a hand, as if he wanted Marcus to say more. "Give her a minute."

"No. Now!" Connor yelled. Brie said they had girls tied up. They could get this creep on kidnapping.

"She got to be too much trouble. I had to end her," Marcus said. "And I will end you, too, if you don't . . ."

"We got him now. Move in." Connor heard a clunk from over the wire. Followed by distant voices and then silence. What was going on?

Connor started that way when he heard a loud motorized sound, but not just from over the wire. The garage door from the house was lifting.

Connor grabbed his lapel mic. "A van is pulling out. Stop them!"

"No," the voice of one of the ICE agents answered over the line. "The plan is to follow them. They might have other girls."

Connor didn't give a fuck what the plan was. He needed to know Brie was okay. Why wasn't she talking?

The van pulled out. "Where is she, Juan?" Connor barked out the question to his partner who was in the white van two houses down with another ICE officer monitoring everything.

A black Malibu followed the blue van out of the garage. But the van went one way and the car went the other.

"She's in the blue van." Juan's answer echoed across the line.

"Agent Hamilton, can you and your agent follow the car?" Mark's voice echoed as Connor heard the words in person and through the line.

"Yes," Agent Hamilton answered.

"Connor and I'll take the van," Mark said. "Billy and Stan"—he looked at the other cop—"you follow us in your car in case we get made. Juan, you and the men clear the house." The cars across the street started up.

Connor darted to the unmarked car parked at the curb and got behind the wheel. Mark had barely managed to get in when Connor pulled off. He wasn't losing that van. No way in hell was he losing Brie.

\* \* \*

"Still have her in the van?" Connor questioned not three minutes later.

"Yes," came Juan's answer.

Connor stayed about fifteen yards back from the van with another unmarked car following behind them. Suddenly, the van sped up. Had Connor and Mark been made? Probably, but it didn't matter. Connor slammed his foot on the gas. The van took a sharp turn, too sharp, it hit the curve so hard the front tire exploded, and the van started fishtailing.

"Fuck!" Connor watched, feeling helpless, as the van ran right into a light pole. The sound of crushing metal reverberated around them.

"Get the medics here!" Mark spoke into his mic.

Connor bolted out of his car and pulled out his weapon.

Billy came up beside him. "Driver! Get out of the car!" he yelled.

The passenger door of the van opened, and a bearded guy took off running. "I got him," Mark said.

Connor ran to the van. The unconscious driver lay slumped over the steering wheel, blood running down the side of his face. Billy started pulling him out.

Connor opened the side door, breath held, fearing the worse.

Two women were inside, gagged and bound. A brunette had blood oozing from her head. A blonde lay so still, Connor's gut knotted. "Brie," he called and gently turned her over. It wasn't Brie. He spotted Brie's purse and shoes on the floor.

Connor, running on pure adrenaline, stormed back to the car. "Agent Hamilton, are you still behind the black Malibu?"

"No. They must've spotted us. We lost them!"

"Fuck!" Connor kicked the car tire.

"Has anyone been in the house yet?" Connor yelled.

"Yes," Juan answered. "It's empty."

"Armand's in the car and he has Brie. Find that car, Hamilton! You fucking hear me!"

Right then, a voice came through the earpiece he wore.

"Purple."

# CHAPTER THIRTY-TWO

P urple." Brie felt her body slam against a wall of metal. She went to catch herself but realized her hands and feet were bound. Then she was thrown the other way and this time her head took the blow. The sound of her own skull cracking echoed in her ears. As if her head didn't already hurt enough. The pain brought with it a spinning sensation and then a sense of nothingness.

Jarred awake suddenly, she was unsure how long she'd been unconscious: A minute? An hour? Her mind raced to find reality. She recalled Armand hitting her head with his gun. She attempted to push away the blackness that wanted to suck her back in.

Where was she?

She inhaled. She started to sit up, but her head hit another barrier of metal. Suddenly, she realized the vibrations traveling through her body were from a car's engine. Forcing her eyes open, she cut her eyes left then right. As her mind cleared, she remembered the wire. "I'm in the trunk of a car."

She blinked. What could she say to help them find her?

She clawed at her mind to think, to fight the waves of dizziness. Something hot ran down her face. Blood. She closed her legs and realized her gun was gone. Frack! They must have found it. Had they found the wire, too? No, she didn't think so, for she could feel it in her bra.

The car's brakes squealed and she slammed into the side of the trunk again. Her arm slid across a jagged edge that ripped into her skin.

She pulled at the bonds on her wrists, but they were too strong. Not metal cuffs, but a zip tie. The tie on her feet, however, wasn't as secure. She shifted, using all her strength to try and wriggle her foot loose, not caring when she felt the plastic cut into her ankles. Finally, she slid one foot from the tie. Breathing hard, panic fizzing in her chest, she heard a familiar roar. A train.

"The car just stopped for a train!" The burning from the cut on her arm gave her an idea. She turned until her hands were at the jagged edge that had cut her.

She ran her wrist over it, trying to cut through the plastic tie. The sharp edge ripped into the tender skin of her wrist, but she kept at it. Running the plastic over the edge, again and again and again. Ignoring the pain. Ignoring the fear.

A wave of dizziness hit again. She tasted blood running over her lips. Dizziness overtook her. Concussion? "I think…" Her own voice faded with the incoming blackness. In her mind, she saw her niece. That sweet face. Then Connor. He'd blame himself.

Brie could not die.

\* \* \*

"Where are the trains in this area!" Connor yelled into his mic.

"Already on it!" Juan said.

"They can't be but a few miles out." Connor could hear Juan's fingers hitting the keyboard. His heart hit his ribs at the same frantic pace. His police lights flashed blue from the grille of the unmarked car.

"I know." Juan paused. "There's a train traveling north down 290 right now."

"Every available car hit the railroad crossings," Mark called out into his mic. "It has to be on the south side of the tracks. A black Malibu with…" Mark spouted out the license plate as Connor drove. Darting around cars and forgetting he was mad at God, he prayed. *Let her live.*

Connor heard at least six cars report in that they were on the call. "Find her, dammit!" His chest felt so tight it might crack. Why hadn't he told her he loved her? Why had he let her do this?

"I got the car," Hamilton's voice rang over the line. "Stopped at the crossing on Brighten Lane and 290."

Connor slammed his foot on the gas. He was two minutes away. *Be alive. Be alive.*

"They spotted us. Armand and one other passenger are exiting the car! Running east on 290." Hamilton's voice rang out. "Shots fired. Shots fired." The sounds of gunfire sounded and punctuated the pain Connor felt.

He turned on Brighten Lane, hands white-knuckling the steering wheel, dodging cars, his lungs begging for air, but he needed Brie more than he needed air.

He heard more gunfire, saw men running, then he spotted the black Malibu.

"Both suspects are down." Agent Hamilton's voice rang out and Connor bolted out of the car and ran toward the Malibu. *Please be alive.*

\* \* \*

Loud, sharp, cracking sounds jarred her back to consciousness. Pain. Lots of pain. Lots of noise. Disoriented, she couldn't comprehend it. Then she heard the sound of the trunk opening.

*Fight!*

A bright light blinded her as the trunk lifted. Giving it everything she had, she threw her foot out. Her heel hit flesh. Hard flesh and bone and teeth.

She screamed and struggled to get up, not knowing where she was. Only knowing she was in a fight for her life.

"It's me, Brie. Connor. I got you, babe! I got you."

*Connor?* His strong arms picked her up and pulled her against a wall of muscle.

"Someone give me a knife to cut her ties!" he screamed. "Now! She's bleeding bad. Where's the damn medics?"

The wave of dizziness hit again. This time she didn't fight it. She welcomed it.

She felt safe. Safe in the arms of the man she...loved.

\* \* \*

Connor saw Eliot limping fiercely into the ER. He felt certain Eliot was going to beat him to a pulp. And he'd let him. The last thing Eliot had said to him was, "Don't let anything happen to her."

He'd let Eliot down. Let Brie down.

Eliot stopped and looked down at him. "How is she?"

"The doctor hasn't come out yet. But the medic said it looked as if she was going to be okay."

Eliot plopped down in the chair beside Connor and dropped his face in his hands. After a second, he looked up. "Did you get Armand?"

"Yeah. He and another guy shot at the ICE agents. ICE fired back, Marcus Armand took two bullets. He's in surgery."

"What about the waitress from the club?"

"Got her and another woman. They were banged up in the accident but are okay. My partners are interviewing the other perps now. If there are more women, they'll find out."

Eliot looked at his face. "Who got you?"

"Brie. She was in the trunk of a car. When I opened it, she kicked me. Only half-conscious, but she came out kicking and screaming."

Eliot smiled. "My girl's a fighter."

"I know." Connor decided now was as good a time as ever. "You may hate me, but I'm going to try to steal her from you. I love her."

Eliot's eyes locked on him for one, two, three seconds before answering. "I won't hate you. But if you hurt her, I'll shoot you."

Connor smiled. "I'm okay with that. And I hear you make good on that promise."

\* \* \*

"I need to talk to someone," Brie argued, when the nurse told her she couldn't get out of bed. She'd been patient long enough. She had to know what happened.

"You'll do what the nurse says." Eliot walked into the ER room.

The nurse looked at Eliot. "We're pretty sure she's got a concussion and probably strep throat. She shouldn't be up walking."

"I agree."

"Me too," said another male voice.

Connor stood in the doorway.

"Candy?" Brie asked, holding her breath.

"She's banged up. But she'll be okay."

Brie noticed his face. A swollen nose and lips, and blackened eyes. She almost asked what happened when she got a flash of kicking the person who opened the trunk. "Did I do that?"

"Yeah." Connor grinned.

"I'm sorry." She frowned, then remembered to ask. "Armand?"

"In surgery," Connor answered. "He tried to run, fired at ICE agents, and was shot twice."

Brie dropped back against the bed. "And the other men? We got them, too?"

"Yeah."

The nurse looked at Brie. "The doctor will be in shortly to stitch up your head and arm. And we'll do a strep test on you as well." She looked from Connor to Eliot. "Can you two make her behave?"

"Sure." Connor touched his face. "I'm only a little bit afraid of her."

The nurse laughed.

"I didn't know it was you." Brie frowned when she spotted all the blood on his shirt. "You look worse than me."

The nurse handed Brie a clean cloth. "Hold this to your head. You're bleeding again." The nurse walked out.

Brie pressed the rag to her head. Then she grinned at Connor. "We did it."

"Yeah." He smiled. "We did."

\* \* \*

Brie had begged the doctor to let her go home, but he'd insisted she stay the night. It was after ten before she found herself alone in the hospital room. Connor and Eliot had left two hours ago. But then Tory had wheeled Carlos over, and they'd visited for over an hour.

As she leaned back on the bed, her heart jolted with the memory of being in the trunk. Her phone dinged with a text. Connor's number flashed. Opening it, she laughed. It was a close-up of his face. His eyes had gotten blacker, and at this angle his nose looked huge.

Connor: Handsome, aren't I?

She laughed and texted: Too bad a girl beat you up.

A new message and photograph flashed on the screen: Your cat loves me now.

The photograph was of Connor, on her sofa, with Psycho resting on his chest. Before Connor left, he'd offered to go feed her cat. Again proving he could be a nice guy. A nice guy she was in love with but had to leave.

Her eyes stung. She typed: He just misses me.

Connor: No. He loves me better. He told me.

Brie: Did I say thank you for saving my life?

Connor: I guess you owe me.
Brie: I guess I do.

* * *

"Hi, Casey," Connor said to the little girl crawling toward him. He'd been afraid his black eyes might scare her, but that didn't appear to be the case.

"You know her name?" Melissa, her foster mom, asked.

"Yeah, my partner just called. He found the birth records. Her mom named her Casey Brieanna Ronan." Connor had almost called Brie to tell her the news but decided to see the baby first.

Casey latched on to Connor's pant leg, pulled herself up, and held one arm up to him, as if asking to be picked up. "She's not walking yet?"

"Not yet, but she will be any day now."

He reached down and picked the baby up. She put her hand on his sore nose. "Owie. Owie."

Melissa grinned. "Susie fell earlier and I said she had an owie and we all kissed her knee."

Right then, Casey pressed her lips to his face.

The woman laughed. "And now she's kissing you. She's a smart baby."

"Yeah."

"She knows you, right?" Melissa asked.

"We met once." Connor stared at the child's sweet face.

"Well, you made an impression on her. She's not this affectionate with everyone."

The woman's words had his chest swelling.

"I was just going to give her a bottle. You want to feed her?"

Connor almost said no but remembered feeding her the night he'd found her crying in her crib. "Sure."

"Sit down." The woman gestured to a chair and disappeared into the adjoining kitchen.

Casey settled in his lap and stared at his face.

"Hey there." He smiled. "You do remember me, don't you?"

She grinned, showing her two little teeth peeking out of her bottom gums.

"You think I can do this?"

She touched his nose again. "Owie."

He chuckled. "Yeah, your namesake did that to me. She's a special person. You're a lucky little girl."

Connor pulled out his phone to take a selfie of the two of them.

Melissa walked back in and handed him a bottle. The little girl squealed. She took the bottle from him and rested back on his chest and started drinking. Her big blue eyes stayed on him the whole time.

"Have you taken her in for the DNA test yet?" Connor asked.

"I'm doing it this afternoon." She dropped down on the edge of her sofa.

"Will they still need it, now that we've found the birth record?"

"Good question. I'll call the caseworker before I take her. Ms. Ryan dropped off some clothes for her and some toys for all the kids yesterday, but I wasn't here. Can you tell her I said thank you?"

"Yeah." Connor glanced at the baby. She stopped sucking long enough to smile at him. His heart lurched, and he just knew.

"I can do this." He looked at Melissa. "I can do this."

"Feed her?" she asked.

"No. Love her. Be a father to her."

* * *

The hospital room door swung open, and Brie and Eliot turned at the same time. If home was where the heart was, she felt instantly homesick seeing Connor standing there.

He walked in with a shopping bag, flowers, and a smile. He'd texted her another picture of his face this morning, confessing that he'd stayed at her place last night and even slept in her bed. Then his next picture was of an envelope, with a message that read, Pablo's phone came. I'm handing it over to Juan.

"You look even worse." Eliot laughed. "Are you telling anyone a girl did that?"

"Of course not." The two men laughed. The sound filled her chest with warmth.

"How are you feeling this morning?" Connor moved to the other side of the bed from where Eliot sat.

"Good enough that I'm pissed the doctor hasn't released me yet."

He set the wrapped flowers down on her bedside table. "For you. Not that you needed them." He looked at the other three bouquets. "Who sent you flowers?"

"You think you don't have competition?" Eliot asked.

Brie was shocked at Eliot's words. "Eliot brought those. That bunch is from Tory and Carlos. And that one is from the APD."

"Well, mine are nicer." Connor leaned down and kissed her forehead.

"I'm gonna do a coffee run." Eliot stood. When he got to the door, he looked back. "Watch her. She has a great right hook, too."

Connor laughed.

Brie watched Eliot leave. "You two seem to be getting along."

"I'm a likable guy." He set the store bag down and pulled out his phone. "But if you don't believe me, check this out. Casey loves me as well."

"Casey?"

"Casey Brieanna Ronan. Juan found her birth records."

"What?" Brie asked.

He handed her his phone with a photo of her niece displayed on the screen. Tears filled her eyes. "Alma named her after me?"

"Yeah."

Brie looked at the picture. "You saw her today?"

"Yeah. She touched my face, said 'owie,' and then kissed me."

"She did not." Brie brushed off a tear that accidentally snuck past.

"I swear." He sat on the edge of the bed. "Scoot over."

"I'm contagious."

"I don't care."

He climbed into bed beside her and took his phone. "So here's my case." He swiped his cell's screen.

"What case?"

He showed her his phone. It was the image of him and her cat. "Your cat loves me. And let's not forget he used me for a scratching post, but I forgave him." He swiped the screen again. "Your kid loves me." He pointed to the door. "Your pseudo dad...likes me. I

wouldn't call it love, but you heard him teasing me.
You don't tease people you don't like. And while he did
threaten to shoot me if I ever hurt you, I'm okay with
that."

She shook her head. "What are—?"

He lowered his phone. "All I need is for you to love
me, Brie Ryan. Because...I'm in love with you. And it'd
be nice if you felt the same."

She heard his words but was having a heck of a time
digesting them. "Connor you...you said—"

"I said a lot of stupid shit, Brie."

"But...but you don't want kids and—"

"I never said I didn't want them. I said I was scared.
Scared I'd screw up because my own father had. But
when I held Casey this morning, I knew I could do it. I'm
sure I'll mess up every now and then, but with both of us
trying, it'll work."

"Connor, you..."

He pressed a finger to her lips. "I want to be a part of
yours and Casey's life. I want to be Casey's Eliot. I want
to be your pancake buddy. Your cupcake and sprinkles
when life sucks. And I know this happened fast, but all
I'm asking for—begging for, actually—is a chance. Let
me prove that I deserve you and Casey. And to show you
I'm serious, I brought you this."

He handed her the bag.

Brie swallowed the emotional lump. "What's this?"

He chuckled. "Open it."

She pulled a black purse from the bag. Baffled, she
lifted her gaze.

"It's got a place to put your keys, so you won't lose
them. And a phone compartment."

When she didn't say anything, he suddenly looked insecure. "You complained about your other purse."

"Oh." She opened the purse to check the inside and then looked up, really baffled. "A box of tampons?"

"Yeah. I...I'll buy them for you. It's the same brand and size you dropped in my car. I had to ask a clerk to help me find them. Which was kind of embarrassing, but for you, I'll do it."

She laughed. "I still don't get..."

He frowned. "Mark advised that I needed to do something small but grand. Like buy something you like, you know food and stuff. Show you that I notice things. And he said that when he bought Annie, his wife, a box of tampons, it was a big deal because men didn't like..." He frowned. "It's stupid, huh?"

"No." She had to wipe away another stray tear. "I love my purse and my tampons."

"And there's a chocolate candy bar in there. Because you like chocolate."

"I love it."

"What about me?" he asked.

"What about you?"

"You love the purse and the tampons...?"

"Oh." She grinned. "I love you, Connor Pierce."

He went to kiss her. "I really am contagious."

He put his arm around her, and they sat there silent but happy. "Oh," he said as he pointed to the purse. "There's also a gift card for the diner. For pancakes, because I know you like them."

She grinned. "I do."

He inhaled. "I talked to Flora."

She looked up. "And?"

"It was good." He touched her cheek. "Really good."

She forced herself to ask. "Did Marcus Armand make it?"

"Yeah. We're charging him on three separate kidnapping charges and the murder of your sister. Two of the men working with him are talking. So ICE expects to get the others on human trafficking as well. ICE has contacted the Guatemalan authorities. It's yet to be seen if any arrests there will be made on that end, but they think we have enough to shut them down here."

"Thank you," she said.

"Like you didn't do any of it." He sighed. "Oh, and you were right, the Sala family is behind it. According to one of the men, Marcus has been doing all of Dillon's work for the last year and a half because their brother-in-law, Luis Sala, benched Dillon from the business due to his cocaine habit."

Brie pillowed her head deeper on Connor's chest and breathed in his scent and listened to his heartbeat. He tilted his head down and kissed her forehead. "Say it again."

"Say what again?" she asked coyly.

"Hey, you disfigured me. This nose was perfect before. I think I deserve to hear you say you love me a couple of times."

She grinned. "Your nose is still perfect. But fine. I love you, Connor Pierce."

# EPILOGUE

D"ada. Dada!"

Brie watched Casey flap her arms up and down as Connor picked her up and out of the car seat. It had only been three months but the love between them was palpable. For a man who'd resisted falling in love and having children, he'd taken to fatherhood like a hungry hound to a T-bone.

Last night, when she'd found an engagement ring on top of the pancake he'd made her for dinner, she'd teased him that she was worried he was proposing more to Casey than to her.

He'd responded that his heart was big enough to love them both.

Brie had to admit, she'd never felt more loved. She'd never been this happy.

"I'll get her diaper bag." She pulled it out of the backseat. "Can you come back for the food?"

"Sure." Connor leaned down and kissed her, then Casey leaned in and kissed them both.

"It was so nice of Vicki to throw us a party." They walked up to Juan's porch, and the front door swung open. Vicki, Juan's fiancée, squealed. "Let me see it."

As soon as they got inside, Brie held out her left hand and Vicki eyed the ring. Little did Brie know that when she became part of Connor's world, a bonus would be two great girlfriends. Vicki, and Annie, Mark's fiancée, welcomed her into their pack from the start.

Annie joined them a moment later.

"Let me see," Annie said excitedly. Brie flashed her ring at the kindergarten teacher. Come March, Mark and Annie were taking the leap into marriage. Juan was trying to talk Vicki into making it a double wedding, but Vicki insisted on having their own.

Annie looked up from the engagement ring to Connor. "You sure you didn't have help picking that out?"

"Hey. I'm good at stuff like this."

"Kitty. Kitty," Casey called out when Sweetie, Juan and Vicki's poodle, ran up dancing.

Connor laughed. "No, that's supposed to be a dog, sweetheart."

"She is a dog." Bell, Vicki's six-year-old niece-daughter, ran up to them.

"Nah," Connor said. "That's not a real dog."

"She's a real dog," Bell argued. Then she looked up at Brie. "Can Casey play in my room?"

"Not in your room," Vicki said. "That's the only room I didn't babyproof. Too many puzzle pieces."

"Is Casey my cousin?" Bell asked.

"Not really, but you can call her that," Vicki said.

The doorbell rang and Vicki turned around in the entryway to open the door. "Come in. I'm so glad you could come."

"Look at my two favorite little girls," Mildred said, beaming at Bell and Casey. Bell ran up to Mildred and hugged her around the waist.

"There's wine, sodas, and beer in the kitchen," Vicki said.

Brie took Casey from Connor's arms. "Go get the buns and chips from the car."

He winked at her. "Have I told you how lucky I am that you said yes?"

"Yeah."

Bell looked up at Mildred. "Mommy and me made Connor and Brie congratulation cupcakes. With sprinkles."

"You did?" Brie knelt down. "Thank you."

Bell made a cute face. "I want Casey to be my cousin, because all my other cousins are boys."

"Yeah, and we know girls rule," Brie said while Annie, Mildred, and Vicki all cheered.

"Boys rule, too." Connor walked out to get the food. Everyone else moved into the living room.

"Can I hold her?" Mildred asked.

"You bet." Brie passed Casey to her crossword buddy. They talked almost every morning now as they worked on the puzzle. "Did you finish it this morning?"

"Only got halfway through," Mildred said.

"Look who I found," Connor called out, walking back in.

Brie turned around and squealed. "Eliot?" She ran and hugged him. "What are you doing here?"

"It's your engagement party. I couldn't miss it!"

She looked at Connor. "You knew he was coming and didn't tell me."

"I wanted it to be a surprise."

"Well, I'm surprised."

Eliot smiled at Casey in Mildred's arms. "My goodness, she's already so much bigger."

"Which is why you need to move here," Brie said. She and Connor both had been bugging Eliot to sell his house in San Francisco. He hadn't agreed, but she could tell he was seriously considering it.

When Casey saw Eliot, she started bouncing and calling out, "Pawpaw. Pawpaw." Everyone laughed. No doubt the baby recognized Eliot from their Skyping.

Eliot grinned. "Well, heck. That does it. I'm going to have to move here."

Her "pseudodad," as Connor often called him, moved over toward Mildred. "Can I steal her from you?"

"You bet." Mildred passed Casey over, and the child gave Eliot a big hug.

Right then the front door swung open and Juan's brother, Ricky, and his wife, Christina, and her two boys strode in.

"Looks like a full house," Juan said, walking in with a platter of cooked burgers and hot dogs. Even standing a few feet away, the smell was heavenly. Juan's gaze shifted to his brother's wife. "Tell me you brought the tamales."

"Are you kidding?" Christina said as she held up a big plastic container. "You told me I wasn't invited unless I brought them."

"Not true," Vicki said. "I'm the one who said that. I love your tamales."

Mark came in through the back door with a platter of grilled corn. His gaze shifted to Brie. "Tell me you said yes and we didn't plan this party for no good reason."

Brie held up her hand with the ring.

"Daddy!" Bell called out to Juan. "Connor said that Sweetie wasn't a real dog."

"Well, Connor wouldn't know a real dog if it bit him on his...big toe."

Ricky laughed. "Bell, I was sure you were just about to get another five dollars for your cursing jar. The kid's gonna pay her way through college just from my brother's dirty mouth."

Christina elbowed her husband and handed off her tamales for him to deliver to the kitchen, then came over to see Brie's ring. "It's beautiful," she said, hugging Brie.

The doorbell rang again. "Come in," Vicki called.

Brie went over to Eliot. "Please tell me you were serious about moving here."

Eliot, who was making faces at Casey, smiled down at her. "If you are serious about wanting me here."

"You know I am."

"Can I see the ring?" someone said behind her.

Brie swung around to find Tory and Carlos standing there. She wrapped her arms around Carlos first. "I called you last night and you didn't tell me you two were coming!"

"Connor wanted to surprise you," Tory said, collecting his own hug.

Brie glanced over at Connor, who was on his knees, talking to Bell. He lifted his green eyes and winked at her. Then he mouthed the words *I love you*.

She mouthed them back. And nothing was truer.

The next few hours were filled with good food, laughter, and people who all felt more like family than friends.

Brie went to the kitchen to refill her coffee. She was adding cream to her cup when Connor walked in and wrapped his arms around her. "Having fun?"

She looked at the counter filled with desserts. "All cup-cakes and sprinkles."

There would always be bad stuff in the world, but by surrounding yourself with the people you loved, and laughter, you could make it a good life.

"Yeah," he said. "It's nice, isn't it?"

# About the Author

Christie Craig is the *New York Times* bestselling author of thirty-nine books. She is an Alabama native, a motivational speaker, and a writing teacher, who currently hangs her hat in Texas. When she's not writing romance, she's traveling, sipping wine, or penning bestselling young adult novels as C. C. Hunter.

You can learn more at:
  Christie-Craig.com
  Twitter @Christie_Craig
  Facebook.com/ChristieCraigBooks

## Looking for more romantic suspense?
### Forever delivers with hot, action-packed reads!

**DREAM CHASER**
**by Kristen Ashley**

Ryn Jansen knows she can forget all about her dreams of a simpler life, so long as caring for her niece and nephew requires all her time and money. But when Boone Sadler—the one man she can't stop thinking about—confronts her with evidence that her family's conning her, Ryn is heartbroken. *Again*. Boone is determined to earn Ryn's trust, but to have a future together, *both* will have to open their hearts.

**DREAM MAKER**
**by Kristen Ashley**

Evan "Evie" Gardiner is done being responsible for her family—she's going to pursue her dream of an engineering degree. But when family members land in a deadly scrape, Daniel "Mag" Magnusson insists on offering Evie his protection. Mag knows a thing or two about desperation and disappointment, and he has the skills to guard Evie's life. Yet as they grow closer, he'll need to come face-to-face with his demons in order to protect her heart.

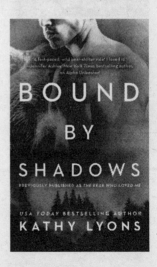

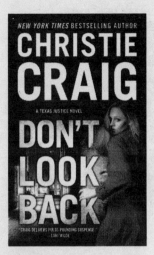

### DON'T LOOK BACK
### by Christie Craig

When FBI agent Brie Ryan's undercover assignment investigating her sister's murder is compromised, she turns to the only man she knows who can help her: Connor Pierce, a too-sexy-for-his-own-good, rule-breaking cop with a knack for solving cold cases. As the investigation—and their attraction—grows more intense, lives are in jeopardy, and Connor finds the most important rule he must break is his own. But can he put his heart on the line?

### NOWHERE TO HIDE
### by Leslie A. Kelly

The last thing LAPD detective Rowan Winchester needs is true-crime novelist Evie Fleming nosing around the most notorious deaths in L.A.—including the ones that haunt his own family. He's torn between wanting the wickedly smart writer out of his city...and just plain wanting her. But when a new killer goes on the prowl, Rowan realizes they must solve this case fast if they want to stay alive.

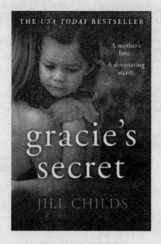

### GRACIE'S SECRET
**by Jill Childs**

Time stops for Jen when her daughter, Gracie, is involved in a terrible car crash. Though the little girl is pronounced dead at the scene, it's a miracle when paramedics manage to resuscitate her. Jen is furious at the driver of the car—her ex-husband's new girlfriend, Ella. But then Gracie begins to tell strange stories about what she heard and saw in the car those moments near death. Something is hidden in Ella's past...but exposing the truth could tear all their lives apart.